STUART DYBEK

Described by the *Atlantic* as 'one of America's
living masters of the short story', Stuart Dybek has
been lauded on all fronts, receiving fellowships
from the National Endowment for the Arts, the
Guggenheim Foundation and the MacArthur
Foundation, as well as a PEN/Malamud Prize,
a Lannan Award, a Whiting Writer's Award and
four O. Henry Prizes. He is the author of five
short-story collections and two volumes of poetry.
His fiction, poetry and non-fiction have appeared
widely in journals such as *Harper's*, *Poetry*, *Tin
House* and the *New Yorker*.

The Start of Something

Something

The Selected Stories of Stuart Dybek

VINTAGE

1 3 5 7 9 10 8 6 4 2

Vintage
20 Vauxhall Bridge Road,
London SW1V 2SA

Vintage is part of the Penguin Random House group of companies
whose addresses can be found at global.penguinrandomhouse.com.

Copyright © Stuart Dybek 2016

The stories in this book have previously appeared in: *Paper Lantern*
copyright © Stuart Dybek 2014, first published by Farrar, Straus and
Giroux; *Ecstatic Cahoots* copyright © Stuart Dybek 2014, first pub-
lished by Farrar, Straus and Giroux; *I Sailed With Magellan* copyright
© Stuart Dybek 2003, first published by Farrar, Straus and Giroux;
The Coast of Chicago copyright © Stuart Dybek 1990, first published
by Alfred A. Knopf; *Childhood and Other Neighborhoods* copyright
© Stuart Dybek 1980, first published by Viking Adult

Stuart Dybek has asserted his right to be identified as
the author of this Work in accordance with the
Copyright, Designs and Patents Act 1988

Quotation from HOWL by Allen Ginsberg. Copyright © Allen
Ginsberg 1956, 1961, used by permission of The Wylie Agency (UK)
Limited. Excerpt from "We Did It" from THE POETRY OF
YEHUDA AMICHAI by Yehuda Amichai, edited by Robert Alter.
Copyright © 2015 by Hana Amichai. Introduction and selection
copyright © 2015 by Robert Alter. Reprinted by permission
of Farrar, Straus and Giroux, LLC.

First published in Vintage in 2017
First published in hardback by Jonathan Cape in 2016

penguin.co.uk/vintage

A CIP catalogue record for this book is available
from the British Library

ISBN 9781784702854

Typeset by Palimpsest Book Production Ltd, Falkirk, Stirlingshire

Printed and bound by Clays Ltd, St Ives plc

Penguin Random House is committed to a sustainable future for
our business, our readers and our planet. This book is made
from Forest Stewardship Council® certified paper.

MIX
Paper from
responsible sources
FSC
www.fsc.org
FSC® C018179

CONTENTS

Paper Lantern

Tosca

Ready!

Aim!

On command the firing squad aims at the man backed against a full-length mirror. The mirror once hung in a bedroom, but now it's cracked and propped against a dumpster in an alley. The condemned man has refused the customary last cigarette but accepted as a hood the black slip that was carelessly tossed over a corner of the mirror's frame. The slip still smells faintly of a familiar fragrance.

Through his rifle sight, each sweating, squinting soldier in the squad can see his own cracked reflection aiming back at him.

Also in the line of fire is a phantasmal reflection of the surprised woman whose slip now serves as a hood (a hood that hides less from the eyes looking out than from those looking in). She's been caught dressing, or undressing, and presses her hands to her breasts in an attempt to conceal her nakedness.

The moment between commands seems suspended to the soldiers and to the hooded man. The soldiers could be compared to sprinters poised straining in the blocks, listening for the starter's gun, though, of course, when the shot is finally fired, it's their fingers on the triggers. The hooded man also listens for the shot even though he knows he'll be dead

3

before he hears it. I've never been conscripted to serve in a firing squad or condemned to stand facing death – at least, not any more than we all are – but in high school I once qualified for the state finals in the high hurdles, and I know that between the 'Aim' command and the shot there's time for a story.

Were this a film, there'd be time for searching close-ups of each soldier's face as he waits for the irreversible order, time for the close-ups to morph into a montage of images flashing back through the lives of the soldiers, scenes with comrades in bars, brothels, et cetera, until one of the squad – a scholarly looking myopic corporal – finds himself a boy again, humming beside a pond, holding, instead of a rifle, a dip net and a Mason jar.

There's a common myth that a drowning man sees his life pass before his eyes. Each soldier taking aim imagines that beneath the hood the condemned man is flashing through his memory. It's a way in which the senses flee the body, a flight into the only dimension where escape is still possible: time. Rather than a lush dissolve into a Proustian madeleine moment, escape is desperate – the plunge through duration in 'An Occurrence at Owl Creek Bridge,' or through a time warp as in 'The Secret Miracle,' Borges's *ficción* in which a playwright in Nazi-occupied Prague faces a firing squad.

In this fiction, set in an anonymous dead-end alley, the reflection of a woman, all the more beautiful for being ghostly, has surfaced from the depths of a bedroom mirror. The soldiers in the firing squad, who can see her, conclude that she is a projection of the hooded man's memory, and that her flickering appearance is a measure of how intensely she is being recalled. Beneath the hood, the man must be recalling a room in summer where her bare body is reflected beside his, her blond-streaked hair cropped short, both of them tan, lean, still young. The mirror is unblemished as if it, too, is young.

'Look,' she whispers, 'us.'

Was it then he told her that their reflection at that moment was what he'd choose to be his last glimpse of life?

Each soldier is asking himself: Given a choice, what would I ask for *my* last glimpse of life to be?

But actually, the hooded man never would have said something so mawkishly melodramatic. As for having the unspoken thought, *Well, so shoot me*, he thinks.

Back from netting tadpoles, the scholarly corporal, sweating behind his rifle again, imagines that rather than recalling random times in bars, brothels, et cetera, the hooded man is revisiting all the rooms in which he undressed the woman in the mirror.

One room faces the L tracks. The yellow windows of a night train stream across the bedroom mirror. After the train is gone, the empty station seems illuminated by the pink-shaded bed lamp left burning as he removes her clothes. Beneath the tracks there's a dark street of jewelry shops, their display windows stripped and grated. Above each shop, behind carbonized panes, the torches of lapidaries working late ignite with the gemstone glows of hydrogen, butane, and acetylene. Her breasts lift as she unclasps a necklace, which spills from her cupped hand into an empty wineglass beside the bed. Pearls, pinkish in the light, brim over like froth. A train is coming from the other direction.

In the attic she calls his tree house, the bed faces the only window, a skylight. The mirror is less a reflection than a view out across whitewashed floorboards to a peeling white chair draped with her clothes and streaked by diffused green light shafting through the leafy canopy. The shade of light changes with the colors of thinning maples. At night, the stars through bare branches make it seem, she says, as if they lie beneath the lens of a great telescope. Naked under a feather tick, they close their eyes on a canopy of constellations light-years away, and open them on a film of first snow. Daylight glints through the tracks of starlings.

In a stone cottage near Lucca, rented from a beekeeper, they hear their first nightingale. They hear it only once, though perhaps it sings while they sleep. At twilight, the rhapsodic push-pull of an accordion floats from the surrounding lemon grove. To follow it seems intrusive, so they never see who's playing, but on a morning hike, they come upon a peeling white chair weathered beneath a lemon tree. When he sits down, she raises her skirt and straddles him. The accordion recital always ends on the same elusive melody. They agree it's from an opera, as they agreed the birdcall had to be a nightingale's, but they can't identify the opera. It's Puccini, he says, which reminds her they have yet to visit Puccini's house in Lucca. Tomorrow, he promises.

Recognize it – the aria playing even now, the clarinet, a nightingale amid twittering sparrows.

Sparrows twitter in the alley from power lines, rain gutters, and the tar-paper garage roofs onto which old ladies in black toss bread crusts, and this entire time the aria has been playing in the background. Not pumped from an accordion, probably it's a classical radio station floating from an open window, or maybe some opera buff – every neighborhood no matter how shabby has one – is playing the same aria over, each time by a different tenor – Pavarotti, Domingo, Caruso – on his antiquated stereo.

The clarinet introduces the aria's melody and the tenor echoes it as if in a duet with the woodwinds. *E lucevan le stelle*, he sings: *And the stars were shining. Ed olezzava la terra: And the scent of earth was fresh . . .*

Stridea l'uscio dell'orto,
e un passo sfiorava la rena.
Entrava ella, fragrante,
mi cadea fra le braccia . . .

The garden gate creaked,
and a step brushed the sand.
She entered, fragrant,
and fell into my arms . . .

Admittedly, 'E lucevan le stelle' is a predictable choice for an execution – so predictable that one might imagine the aria itself is what drew this motley firing squad with their unnecessarily fixed bayonets and uniforms as dusty as the sparrows brawling over bread crusts.

Doesn't the soldiers' appearance, from their unpolished boots to the hair scruffing out from beneath their shakos, verge on the theatrical, as if a costume designer modeled them on Goya's soldiers in *The Disasters of War*? A role in the firing squad doesn't require acting; their costumes act for them. They are anonymous extras, grunts willing to do the dirty work if allowed to be part of the spectacle. Grunts don't sing. In fact, the corporal will be disciplined for his ad-libbed humming by the pond. They march – *trudge* is more accurate – from opera to opera hoping to be rewarded with a chorus, a chance to emote, to leave onstage some lyrical record of their existence beyond the brutal percussion of a final volley. But their role has always been to stand complacently mute. This season alone they've made the rounds from *Carmen* to *Il Trovatore*, and when the classics are exhausted then it's on to something new.

There are always roles for them, and the promise of more to come. In Moscow, a young composer whose grandfather disappeared during Stalin's purges labors over *The Sentence* – an opera he imagines Shostakovich might have written, which opens with Fyodor Dostoyevsky, five days past his twenty-eighth birthday, facing the firing squad of the Tsar. Four thousand three hundred miles away, in Kalamazoo, Michigan, an assistant professor a few years out of Oberlin who has been awarded his first commission, for an opera based on Norman Mailer's *The Executioner's Song*, has just sung 'Froggy Went A-Courtin' to his three-year-old daughter. She's fallen asleep repeating, *Without my uncle Rat's consent, I would not marry the president*, and now the house is quiet, and he softly plinks on her toy piano the motif that will climax in Gary Gilmore's final aria.

And here in the alley, the firing squad fresh from Granada in 1937, where they gunned down Federico García Lorca in Osvaldo Golijov's opera *Ainadamar*, has followed the nightingale call of 'E lucevan le stelle' and stands taking aim at a man hooded in a slip.

If you're not an opera buff, you need to know that 'E lucevan le stelle' is from the third act of *Tosca*. Mario Cavaradossi, a painter and revolutionary, has been tortured by Baron Scarpia, the lecherous, tyrannical chief of Rome's secret police, and waits to be shot at dawn. Cavaradossi's final thoughts are of his beloved Tosca. He bribes the jailer to bring him pen and paper so that he can write her a farewell, and then, overcome by memories, stops writing and sings his beautiful aria, a showstopper that brings audiences to applause and shouts of *Bravo!* before the performance can continue. Besides the sheer beauty of its music, the aria is a quintessential operatic moment, a moment both natural and credible – no small feat for opera – in which a written message cannot adequately convey the emotion and the drama soars to its only possible expression: song.

She entered, fragrant, and fell into my arms, oh! sweet kisses, oh! lingering caresses. Trembling, I unveiled her beauty, the hero sings – in Italian, of course. But in American opera houses subtitles have become accepted. *My dream of love has vanished forever, my time is running out, and even as I die hopelessly, I have never loved life more.*

That final phrase about loving life, *Non ho amato mai tanto la vita*, always reminds me of Ren. He was the first of three friends of mine who have said, over the years, that he was living his life like an opera.

We were both nineteen when we met that day Ren stopped to listen to me playing for pocket change before the Wilson L station, and proposed a trade – his Kawasaki 250 with its rebuilt engine for my Leblanc clarinet. Usually I played at L stops with Archie, a blind accordion player, but it was thundering and Archie hadn't showed. I thought Ren was putting me on. When I asked why he'd trade a motorcycle for a clarinet, he answered: Who loves life more, the guy on the Outer Drive riding without a helmet, squinting into the wind, doing seventy in and out of traffic, or the guy with his eyes closed playing 'Moonglow'?

Depends how you measure loving life, I said.

Against oblivion, Ren said, then laughed as if amused by his own pretension, a reflex of his that would become familiar. A licorice stick travels light, he explained, and he was planning to leave for Italy, where, if Fellini films could be believed, they definitely loved life more. He'd had a flash of inspiration watching me, a vision of himself tooting 'Three Coins in the Fountain' by the Trevi Fountain and hordes of tourists in coin-tossing mode filling his clarinet case with cash. He'd rebuilt the 250cc engine – he could fix anything, he bragged – and even

9

offered a warranty: he'd keep the bike perfectly tuned if I gave him clarinet lessons.

A week later, we were roommates, trading off who got the couch and who got the Murphy bed and sharing the rent on my Rogers Park kitchenette. From the start, his quip about loving life set the tone. The commonplace trivia from our lives became the measure in an existential competition. If I ordered beer and Ren had wine, it was evidence he loved life more. If he played the Stones and I followed with Billie Holiday, it argued my greater love of life.

The university we attended had a center in Rome, and Ren and I planned to room together there in our junior semester abroad. Neither of us had been to Europe. A few weeks before our departure, at a drunken party, Ren introduced me to Iris O'Brien. He introduced her as the Goddess O'Iris, which didn't seem an exaggeration at the time. He assured me there was no 'chemistry' between them. Lack of chemistry wasn't my experience with Iris O'Brien. In a state that even in retrospect still feels more like delirium than like a college crush, I decided to cancel my trip so that once Ren left, Iris could move in. I'd never lived with a girlfriend before.

When I told Ren I wasn't going, he said, I suppose you think that giving up Europe for a woman means you win?

Iris isn't part of the game, I said, and when I failed to laugh at my own phony, offended honor, Ren did so for me – uproariously.

Living with Iris O'Brien lasted almost as long as the Kawasaki continued to run, about a month. Although Ren and I hadn't kept in touch, I figured that if he wouldn't return my clarinet, he'd at least fix the bike once he got back. But when the semester ended, he stayed in Europe.

From a mutual friend who had also gone to Rome, I heard

Ren had dropped out. He spent his time playing my clarinet at fountains across the city, and fell in love, not with a woman, but with opera. That surprised me, as the love of jazz that Ren and I shared seemed, for some reason, to require us to despise opera. With the money he'd made playing arias on the street, he bought a junked Moto Guzzi, rebuilt it, and took off on an odyssey of visiting opera houses across Italy.

That spring I got an airmail letter without a return address. The note scrawled on the back of a postcard of the Trevi Fountain read: *Leaving for Vienna. Ah! Vienna! Non ho amato mai tanto la vita – Never have I loved life more. Living it like an opera – well, an opera buffa – so, tell the Goddess O'Iris, come bless me.*

It was the last I ever heard from him.

I didn't catch the allusion to *Tosca* in Ren's note until years later when I was enrolled in graduate school at NYU. I was seeing a woman named Clair who had ducked out of a downpour into the cab I drove part-time. Nothing serious, we'd agreed, an agreement I kept reminding myself to honor. Clair modeled to pay the bills – underwear her specialty. She'd come to New York from North Dakota in order to break into musical theater and was an ensemble member of Cahoots, a fledgling theater on Bank Street, which billed itself as a fusion between cabaret and performance art. Cahoots was funded in part by an angel, an anonymous financier whom Clair was also sleeping with. Through Clair, I met Emil, the founder and artistic director of Cahoots, and the two of them, flush with complimentary tickets, became my tutors in opera.

Their friendship went back to their student days at Juilliard, where Emil had been regarded as a can't-miss talent until he'd become involved in what Clair called 'Fire Island Coke Chic.'

She'd been Emil's guest at a few of the parties he frequented, including a legendary night when he sang 'Somewhere (There's a Place for Us)' with Leonard Bernstein at the piano. Clair worried that Emil's addiction to male dancers was more self-destructive than the drugs.

Emil worked as a singing waiter at Le Figaro Café, a coffee-house in the Village with marble-top tables and a Medusa-hosed Italian espresso machine that resembled a rocket crossed with a basilica. Each steamed demitasse sounded like a moon launch and the waiters, singing a cappella, were all chronically hoarse. Emil felt even more contempt toward his job than Clair had for modeling. The one night he allowed us to stop in for coffee, Emil sang 'Una furtiva lagrima,' the famous aria from *The Elixir of Love*. His voice issued with an unforgettable purity that seemed at odds with the man mopping sweat, his Italian punctuated by gestures larger than life. The room, even the espresso machine, fell silent.

In the opera, that aria is sung by Nemorino, a peasant who has spent his last cent on an elixir he hopes will make the wealthy woman he loves love him in return. Nemorino sees a tear on her cheek and takes it as a sign that the magic is working. Watching Emil sing his proverbial heart out at a coffeehouse, Clair, too, looked about to cry. He's singing for us, she said. Until that moment, I hadn't recognized the obvious: she'd been in love with Emil since Juilliard – years of loving the impossible.

Emil's voice rose to the climax and Clair mouthed the aria's last line to me in English, *I could die! Yes, I could die of love*, while Emil held the final *amor* on an inexhaustible breath.

The espresso machine all but levitated on a cushion of steam, and patrons sprang to a standing ovation that ended abruptly when Emil, oblivious to the blood drooling onto his white apron from the left nostril of his coke-crusted nose, flipped them off as if conducting music only he could hear.

After Figaro's became the third job Emil lost that year, Clair decided to risk desperate measures. Emil was broke. His doomed flings with danseurs had left him without an apartment of his own. The actors in Cahoots had grown openly critical of his leadership. Refusing to crash with increasingly disillusioned friends, Emil slept at the theater, whose heat was turned off between performances.

He's out of control, we're watching slo-mo suicide, Clair said, enlisting me in a small group of theater people for an intervention. It was an era in New York when the craze for interventions seemed in direct proportion to the sale of coke. Emil regarded interventions as a form of theater below contempt. To avoid his suspicion, Clair planned for it to take place at the private cast party following the opening of the show Emil had worked obsessively over – a takeoff on *The Elixir of Love*.

In the Donizetti opera, Dr Dulcamara, a salesman of quack remedies, arrives in a small Basque town and encounters Nemorino, who requests a potion of the kind that Tristan used to win Isolde. Dulcamara sells him an elixir that's nothing more than wine.

In Emil's script, the town is Winesburg, Ohio, an all-American community of secret lusts and repressed passion. The townsfolk sing of their need for a potion to release them from lives of quiet desperation. Emil played the traveling salesman – not Dr Dulcamara, but Willy Loman. As Willy sings his aria 'Placebo,' sexually explicit ads for merchandise flash across a screen, attracting the townsfolk. They mob Nemorino, and the bottle of bogus elixir is torn from hand to hand. Its mere touch has them writhing lewdly, unbuttoning their clothes, and when the bottle breaks they try to lap elixir from the stage, pleading for more, threatening to hang Willy Loman by his tie if he doesn't deliver.

Willy finds a wine bottle beside a drunk, comatose and sprawled against a dumpster. As scripted, the bottle is half filled with wine, and Emil is only to simulate urinating into it. But that night, onstage, he drained the bottle, unzipped his trousers, and, in view of the audience, pissed.

'Here's your elixir of love!' he shouted, raising the bottle triumphantly as he stepped back into the town square.

The script has the townsfolk passing the elixir, slugging it down, and falling madly, indiscriminately in love. Willy demands to be paid, and they rough him up instead. The play was to end with the battered salesman suffering a heart attack as an orgy swirls around him. In an aria sung with his dying breath, he wonders if he's spent his moneygrubbing life unwittingly pissing away magic.

Script notwithstanding, opening night was pure improv, pure pandemonium. When the actors realized Emil had actually given them piss to drink, the beating they gave him in return wasn't simulated, either. Emil fought back until, struck with the bottle, he spit out pieces of tooth, then leaped from the stage, ran down the center aisle, and out of the theater. The audience thought it was the best part of the show.

The cast party went on backstage without Emil. Stunned and dejected, the actors knew it was the end of Cahoots and on that final evening clung to each other's company. Around midnight, Clair pressed me into a corner to say, You don't belong at this wake. We stood kissing, and then she gently pushed me away and whispered, Go. One word, perfectly timed to say what we had avoided saying aloud, but both knew: whatever was between us had run its course. Instead of goodbye, I said what I'd told her after our first night together and had repeated like an incantation each time since: Thank you.

Emil showed up as I was leaving. He still wore his bloodied salesman's tie. His swollen lip could have used stitches, but he managed to swig from a bottle of vodka.

Drunk on your own piss? asked Glen, who'd played Nemorino and had thrown the first punch onstage.

Shhh, no need for more, Clair said. She took Emil's arm as if to guide him. Sit down with us, she told him. Emil shook off her hand. Judas, he said, and Clair recoiled as if stung.

Keeping a choke hold on the bottle, Emil climbed up on a chair.

I've come to say I'm sorry, he announced, and to resign as your artistic director. I guessed you all might still be hanging around, given that without Cahoots none of you has anywhere else to perform.

Clair, blotting her smeared makeup, began to sob quietly, hopelessly, as a child cries. Emil continued as if, like so much else between them, it were a duet. Sweat streaked his forehead as it did when he sang.

Did you think I didn't know about the pathetic little drama you'd planned for me tonight by way of celebration? he asked. So, yes, I'm sorry, sorry to deprive you of the cheesy thrill of your judgmental psycho-dabbling. But then what better than your dabbling as actors to prepare you to dabble in others' lives? Was it so threatening to encounter someone willing to risk it all, working without a net, living an opera as if it's life, which sometimes – tonight, for instance – apparently means being condemned to live life as if it's a fucking opera?

*

The last friend of mine to say he was living life like an opera was Cole.

He said it during a call to wish me a happy birthday, one of those confiding phone conversations we'd have after being out of touch – not unusual for a friendship that went back decades to when we were in high school. Twenty years earlier, Cole had beat me in the state finals, setting a high school record for the high hurdles. We were workout buddies the summer between high school and college, which was also the summer I worked downtown at a vintage jazz record shop. Cole would stop by to spin records while I closed up. He'd been named for Coleman Hawkins and could play Hawkins's famous tenor solo from 'Body and Soul' note for note on the piano. Cole played the organ each Sunday at the Light of Deliverance, one of the oldest African-American churches on the South Side. His grandfather was the minister. I'd close the record shop and we'd jog through downtown to a park with a track beside the lake, and after running, we'd swim while the lights of the Gold Coast replaced a lingering dusk. His grandfather owned a cabin on Deep Lake in northern Michigan, and Cole invited me up to fish before he left for Temple on a track scholarship. It was the first of our many fishing trips over the years to come.

Cole lived in Detroit now, near the neighborhood of the '67 riots, where he'd helped establish the charter school that he'd written a book about. He'd spent the last four years as a commu- nity organizer and was preparing to run for public office. When he'd married Amina, a Liberian professor who had sought political asylum, 'Body and Soul' was woven into the recitation of their vows. The wedding party wore dashikis, including me, the only white groomsman.

He called on my birthday – our birthdays were days apart – to invite me up to Deep Lake to fish one last time. His grandfather had died years earlier and the family had decided to sell the cabin. When I asked how things were going, Cole paused, then said, I'm living my life like an opera. I knew he was speaking in code, something so uncharacteristic of him that it caught me by surprise. I waited for him to elaborate. Before the silence got embarrassing, he changed the subject.

We'd always fished after Labor Day when the summer people were gone. By then evenings were cool enough for a jacket. The woods ringing the lake were already rusting, the other cottages shuttered, the silence audible. Outboard engines were prohibited on Deep Lake, although the small trolling motor on the minister's old wooden rowboat was legal. Cole fished walleye as his grandfather had taught: at night – some nights under a spangle of Milky Way, on others in the path of the moon, but also on nights so dark that out on the middle of the lake you could lose your sense of direction.

The night was dark like that. There was no dock light to guide us back, but the tubed stereo that had belonged to his grandfather glowed on the screened porch. Cole's grandfather had had theories about fishing and music: one was that walleyes rose to saxophones. His jazz collection was still there, some of the same albums I'd sold in the record shop when I was eighteen. We chose *Ballads* by Ben Webster. The notes slurred across the water as I rowed out to the deep spot in the middle. Cole lowered the anchor, though it couldn't touch bottom. I cracked the seal on a fifth of Jameson and passed it to Cole; tradition demanded that I arrive with a bottle. We'd had a lot of conversations over the years, waiting for the fish to bite.

I been staying at the cabin since we last talked, Cole said.

What's going on? I asked.

Remember I told you I was living life like an opera? You didn't say boo, but I figured you got my meaning, seeing you'd

17

used the phrase yourself. Never know who's listening in. Cole laughed as if kidding, but, given the surveillance on Martin Luther King, Jr, he worried about wiretaps.

Cole, I said, I *never* used that phrase.

Where do you think I got it? he asked.

Not from me.

Maybe you forgot saying it, he said, maybe you finally forgot who you said it about. Anyway, whoever said it, I'm at a fund-raiser in Ann Arbor, everyone dressed so they can wear running shoes except for a woman I can't help noticing. You know me, it's not like I'm looking – just the opposite – there's always someone on the make if you're looking. She's out of *Vogue*. I hate misogynist rap, man, but plead guilty to thinking: rich bitch – which I regret when she comes up with my book and a serious camera that can't hide something vulnerable about her. *Photojournalist*, her card reads, and could she take one of me signing my book, and I say, sure, if she promises not to steal my soul, and she smiles and asks if she can make a donation to the school, and how could she get involved beyond just giving money, and where's my next talk, and do I have time for a drink? Two weeks later at a conference in D.C. she's there with Wizards tickets. And this time I go – we go to the game. In Boston it's the symphony, in Philly I show her places I lived in college and take her to the Clef, where 'Trane played, and in New York we go to the Met. I'd never been to an opera; we go three nights in a row. Was I happy – happiness isn't even the question. Remember running a race – thirteen-point-seven-nine seconds you've lived for, and when the gun finally fires and you're running, you disappear – like playing music those few times when you're more the music than you? She could make that happen again. One night, I'm home working late, Mina's already asleep, and the phone in my office rings. I'd never given her that unlisted home number. You need to help me, she says, and the line goes dead. Phone rings again. Where are you? I ask. Trapped in a car at the edge, she says. Her calls keep getting dropped, her voice is slurred: Come get me before I'm washed away. I keep asking her, Where are you? Finally she says: Jupiter Beach – I drove to see the hurricane. I say, You're a thousand miles away. The phone goes dead, rings, and Mina asks, Who keeps calling this time of night? She's in her nightgown, leaning in the doorway for I don't know how long. Too long for lies. I answer the phone, but no one's there.

She have a husband? Mina asks. You got to call him now.

The business card from Ann Arbor has private numbers she listed on the back, one with a Florida area code. A man answers, gives his name. I say, You don't know me, but I'm calling about an emergency, your wife's in the storm in a car somewhere on Jupiter Beach.

I know you, he says. I know you only too well. Don't worry, she doesn't tell me names, I don't ask, but I know you.

Mina presses speakerphone.

You teach tango or Mandarin or yoga or murderers to write poetry, film the accounts of torture victims, rescue greyhounds. I know the things you do, the righteous things you say, and I know you couldn't take your eyes off her the first time you saw her, and how that made you realize you'd been living a life in which you'd learned to look away. And like a miracle she's looking back, and you wonder what's the scent of a woman like that, and not long after – everything's happening so fast – you ask, What do you want? and she says, To leave the world behind together, and you think beauty like hers must come with the magic to allow what you couldn't ordinarily do, places you couldn't go, a life you'd dreamed when you were young. But now, just as suddenly, she can destroy you by falling from the ledge she's calling from, or falling asleep forever in the hotel room where she's lost count of the pills. She's talking crazy since she's stopped taking the meds you never noticed, and when she said she loved you, that was craziness, too – you're a symptom of her illness. So you called me, not to save her, but yourself, and it's me who knows where she goes when she gets like this, and I'll go, as I do every time, to save her, calm and comfort her, bring her home, because I love her, I was born to, I'll always love her, and you're only a shadow. I've learned to ignore shadows. She made you feel alive; now you're a ghost. Go. Don't call again.

I told you on the phone, Cole said, that I was living my life like an opera, but he's the one who sang the aria.

FIRE!

A borrowed flat above a plumbing store whose back windows look out on a yard of stockpiled toilets filled with unflushed rain. Four a.m., still a little drunk from a wake at an Irish bar, they smell bread baking. Someone's in the room, she whispers. It's only the mirror, he tells her. She strips off her slip, tosses it over the shadowy reflection, and then follows the scent to the open front windows. A ghost, she says as if sighing. Below a vaporous streetlamp, in the doorway of a darkened bakery, a baker in white, hair and skin dusted with flour, leans smoking.

FIRE!

A bedroom lit by fireflies, one phosphorescent above the bed, another blinking in the mirror as if captured in a jar. The window open on the scent of rain-bearded lilacs. When the shards of a wind chime suspended in a corner tingle, it means a bat swoops through the dark. Flick on the bed lamp and the bat will vanish.

FIRE! DAMN YOU! FIRE!

Whom to identify with at this moment – who is more real – Caruso, whose unmistakable, ghostly, 78-rpm voice carries over the ramparts where sparrows twitter, or Mario Cavaradossi?

Or perhaps with an extra in the firing squad, who – once Tosca flings herself from the parapet – will be free to march off for a beer at the bar around the corner, and why not, he was only following the orders barked out by the captain of the guard, who was just doing what the director demanded, who was in turn under the command of Giacomo Puccini.

Or with the hooded man, his mind lit by a firefly as he tries to recall a room he once attempted to memorize when it became increasingly clear to him that he would soon be banished.

FIRE! I AM GIVING YOU A DIRECT ORDER.

How heavy their extended rifles have become. The barrels teeter and dip, and seem to be growing like Pinocchio's nose, although it's common knowledge that rifles don't lie. Still, just to hold one steady and true requires all the strength and concentration a man can summon.

Turn on the bed lamp the better to illuminate the target. On some nights the silk shade suggests the color of lilacs and on others of areolas. See, the bat has vanished, which doesn't mean it wasn't there.

FIRE! OR YOU'LL ALL BE SHOT!

The lamp rests on a nightstand with a single drawer in which she keeps lotions and elixirs and stashes the dreams she records on blue airmail stationery when they wake her in the night – an unbound nocturnal diary. She blushed when she told him the dream in which she made love with the devil. He liked to do what you like to do to me – what *we* like, she said.

In the cracked mirror each member of the squad sees himself aiming at himself. Only a moment has passed since the 'Aim' command, but to the members of the squad it seems they've stood with finger ready on their triggers, peering down their sights, for so long that they've become confused as to who are the originals and who are the reflections. After the ragged discharge, when the smoke has cleared, who will be left standing and who will be shattered into shards?

PLEASE, FIRE!

I can't wait like this any longer.

Non ho amato mai tanto la vita.

Waiting

There is really only one city for everyone just as there is one major love.

—*The Diaries of Dawn Powell: 1931–1965*

I read an essay once – I don't recall who wrote it – about waiting in Hemingway. There's that couple at the station in 'Hills Like White Elephants' waiting for the express from Barcelona, and the little boy with a fever who is waiting to die in 'A Day's Wait.' That situation, waiting to die, is one Hemingway returned to often, as in 'The Snows of Kilimanjaro,' when the man with a gangrened leg is recalling his youth in Paris; nor is he waiting alone – the hyenas and vultures are waiting, too. In other stories, the men *are* alone. Nick Adams waits out the night in 'A Way You'll Never Be.' In 'The Gambler, the Nun, and the Radio,' Mr Frazer listens to a hospital radio that plays only at night – a clever touch – as he waits out the pain of his fractured leg. All these characters have, in one way or another, been wounded.

*

When the phenomenon known as the Men's Movement was in fashion, I was invited to give a poetry reading at a 'gathering.' Chad, the therapist who organized the event, believed that poetry had therapeutic power. We'd met at a literary festival in

Washington, and it was obvious that Chad, who was shopping a book of his poems, also believed in the power of networking. He referred to poetry as the 'Po-Biz.' The term reminds me that, like any troubadour, Orpheus was part hustler, although he couldn't out-hustle Death. I would have passed on the gathering if Chad hadn't also invited a friend whom I didn't get to see often enough, a Vietnamese poet whose family were boat people. After the fact, I learned that my friend accepted the invitation because Chad told him I'd agreed to come.

On the Friday the conference was scheduled to open, with a sweat lodge, I couldn't get myself to go. I slept restlessly and woke early, feeling guilty enough about reneging to make myself get in my car and start driving. The conference was four hours north of where I was living in Michigan. The Vietnamese poet had flown from Philadelphia to Chicago and then on to a commuter airport in Traverse City the day before. It's beautiful country up there. Sand dunes sculpt the edge of the planet's greatest freshwater sea. I had sometimes rented a cottage there on a lake whose name I kept to myself. I've read that Michigan has more coastline than any state but Alaska. I don't know if that calculation includes the coasts of all the weedy lakes and trout streams you can smell hidden in the woods while speeding north on a highway in summer.

By eleven I'd reached the turnoff on Chad's map and continued down a dirt road. It opened from a papery birch forest into a clearing where a rustic compound stood on the shore of a lake glistening with the rings of feeding fish. I parked and walked by deserted cabins to a log lodge beside the dock. The screen door was ajar, and I went in, past a table stacked with books: *Iron John*, *Fire in the Belly*, *The Myth of Male Power*, *Fatherless America*. Copies of my book, *Welfare*, were for sale along with the others and with the three slim volumes by my friend the Vietnamese poet, who was reading to a circle of maybe seventy men. A couple of the men were perched on wheelchairs; the rest sat Indian-style on the plank floor. Each had a drum the size of a toy beside him. My friend was the only one in the circle wearing a shirt.

No one turned when I slipped in; they were absorbed by the poem. My friend had always been a gently charismatic reader, but he was reciting now with an intensity that reflected that of his audience. After each poem there was a collective exhalation, a moment of respectful silence, and then Chad would invite the men to share personal responses. Several of the poems were elegiac portraits of a once-powerful father who had been reduced by immigrant status and the prejudice of his adopted country to an aged, exhausted man on the periphery of all but his family. The men on the floor shared their stories about fathers and Chad would ask my friend to read another poem.

I stood outside the circle, feeling like an unbeliever at a prayer service. I was scheduled to read after lunch and wondered how I would come up with something appropriate. The few vignettes I'd written about my father, also an immigrant, were at best what Chad might term 'conflicted.'

My friend read the title poem of his first book, *Friendly Fire*, an indictment of a criminal American foreign policy simply conveyed in thirty lines about the ghost of his godfather, who had been killed by American fire during the war. When he finished, an older man with a bit of a gut, hirsute, with a silver cast to his ponytail and mustache and a faded SEMPER FI tattoo on his chest, raised his hand and asked, 'Chad, would this be the right time to share my ghost dance?'

'Could we put that on hold for just a moment, Pete Red Crow?' Chad said. He passed out a shopping bag stuffed with so-called scarlet ribbons that looked like tie-dyed rags. 'I want each of you to take as many ribbons as you need and tie them around the places on your body or spirit that have been wounded.' To demonstrate, Chad wrapped a ribbon around what I presumed was a tennis elbow. Men in the circle were winding them around their heads like headbands, around their necks like bandannas, around their chests, their drooping bellies, their legs, ankles, and feet. Later, when I described the scene to a woman I was seeing, she asked, 'Did anyone tie one to his wiener?'

'Maybe symbolically,' I said.

'Where did you tie yours?'

'I didn't take one.'

'Where would you have tied it if you had?'

'That information is to be shared only with the brotherhood.'

The man who wanted to share his ghost dance banded a ribbon around his forehead and knotted one at each wrist, where they hung like streamers. 'Is it a good time yet, Chad?' he asked.

'Thank you for waiting, Pete,' Chad said.

Pete rose, bowed to the circle, raised his scarlet-trailing arms in salute to Chad, to the poet, to the sky above the rafters, and, chanting in a tongue that sounded like Hollywood Indian, he began to gyrate and stamp, twisting while his arms milled and waved and the ribbons swirled as if slashed wrists were spouting loops of arterial light. He stopped abruptly, and without a bow folded back into his seated position, buried his face in his hands, and wept.

'It's all right, Pete Red Crow. That came from a release deep within,' Chad said. His instinct was right: something needed to be said. Hands shot up from men who had more to share. Chad sensed the mood-shift, and thought that it might be wise to calm things down while he still had control of the group. 'It's time to break for lunch,' he said. 'We'll pick up where we left off when we reassemble. But first let us thank our brother Thanh, a true keeper of the poetic flame, who has graced us with the gifts of purifying fire, solace, and wisdom.'

The men heartily applauded, but then a bearded man in a wheelchair festooned with ribbons raised his hand and said, 'Chad, I don't think thanks is enough. We need a raising up.'

Ever since Chad had introduced the ribbons, my friend had watched the proceedings with an increasingly quizzical expression. He'd let the ribbons pass him by and seemed utterly bewildered by the dance and the weeping that followed. I suspected that he'd agreed to the conference with no idea as to what the Men's Movement was about. As the men in the circle began to drum and then rose and pressed in on him, a sudden fear flashed in his eyes and he shouted, 'I have bad knees!' The circle collapsed in on him and he disappeared beneath a scrum of half-naked bodies. I could hear them whispering, 'You are my brother, Thanh . . . you have touched my heart . . . you have touched my soul.' Then, borne by their uplifted hands, he seemed to levitate above us. Around each knee a red ribbon had been tied into a bow.

*

Essays on the conspicuous theme of wounds in Hemingway are common, but so far as I know, there's only that one essay about waiting. And once it is pointed out, you see it everywhere. There's the cynical Italian major of 'In Another Country,' a noted fencer who endures the futile rehabilitation of his mutilated hand. There are stories that are studies in the word *pati*, to suffer – the root in both *patient* and *patience* – like 'A Clean, Well-Lighted Place,' in which an old waiter prays, *Our nada who art in nada, nada be thy name . . .*

Even as a young writer, Hemingway had a knack for portraying old men, not unlike certain actors who make a career of it – Hal Holbrook doing Twain – though I doubt that even Holbrook could play an aging Papa better than Hemingway played himself. It's fitting that *The Old Man and the Sea* got him the Nobel Prize. That book is about waiting, too, but then what fishing story isn't? *Moby-Dick* is waiting sustained over a thrashing sea of pages. That's the problem with the insight about waiting: you have to ask, Why single out Hemingway? Think of waiting as measured by the interminable winters in Chekhov, or by the ticking of clocks in bureaucratic offices at the dead ends of the maze of cobbled streets in Kafka's Prague. Prague, one of those cities that like London is presided over by a clock.

Limiting the catalogue to just a sample of the writers overlapping Hemingway's time, there's Gatsby's green dock light waiting in darkness and Newland Archer in Wharton's *The Age of Innocence*, longing for another woman during twenty-five years of loveless marriage; *Winesburg, Ohio*, a masterpiece about waiting, an entire community stranded in the stasis of secret lives, yearning for something mysterious and unsayable beneath the cover of night; Joyce's *Dubliners*, with its phantasmal patron saint of waiting, the tubercular Michael Furey of 'The Dead'; Katherine Mansfield's heroines waiting for their lives to begin; the passengers on Katherine Anne Porter's *Ship of Fools*, waiting for their baggage-ridden lives to change as they voyage into eternity; Beckett's tramps; Faulkner's devotion to the word *endure* – to suffer patiently, to continue to exist. All these writers, who we think are looking toward us into the present, are actually gazing back.

From that perspective it is as if the forward thrust of narrative, as if the very action of verbs, is illusory, that no matter what the story or how it's told or by whom, the inescapable conclusion is that life – not just life on the page but life at its core – waits. It waits stalled in traffic, doing time at red lights, waits in line for the coffee that signals the beginning of another day, waits for the messages of the day to arrive. Sometimes the wait is imperceptible, but it can also seem interminable – waiting for a phone call from a lover or from the doctor who may pause before delivering what feels more like a sentence than a diagnosis, the kind of call in which the undecided seems suddenly to have been decided long before, as if it's no accident that in the mystical, kabbalistic workings of language, *fate* and *wait* are paired in rhyme.

I don't remember if that essay on waiting mentioned Ketchum, Idaho, on the morning of July 2, 1961. It didn't have to. Whether a public gesture such as Yukio Mishima's seppuku, or a private exit – Virginia Woolf, her pockets filled with stones, sinking into the River Ouse – a writer's suicide becomes the climax of a reality that the reader appends to a lifework of fiction. It has certainly become the final punctuation for Hemingway, an author who traded the typewriter he referred to as his psychoanalyst for a shotgun. Playing analyst, literary critics wrote that his suicide had been lying in wait since 1928 when Hemingway's father, Clarence, a doctor, shot himself at the family home in Oak Park, Illinois, with a Civil War pistol passed down from his father.

In 'Indian Camp,' an early story, the father, a doctor, while on a fishing trip to Michigan, performs a C-section with a jackknife and tapered gut leaders on an Indian woman who has been in labor for two days. The story is set not all that far from where I rented that cottage up in Michigan, although any trace of Native Americans, Ojibwa probably, is gone. The Indian woman's husband can't endure the suffering and cuts his own throat. Afterward, Nick, the boy who has witnessed both the birth and the suicide, asks his father, 'Is dying hard, Daddy?'

'No, I think it's pretty easy, Nick. It all depends.'

The story ends: *In the early morning on the lake sitting in the stern of the boat with his father rowing, he felt quite sure he would never die.*

*

The woman, Liesel – she went by Lise – who wanted to know where on my body I would choose a wound to bind, despised Hemingway. She despised the popular legends about him and the values they represented, despised bullfights and braggarts who spent their considerable disposable income on shooting animals in Africa, despised what she called the Arrested He-Man School of American Fiction. When I suggested that Hemingway deserved his unfashionable reputation, but still, he had written some genuinely original stories that continued to influence writers even if they didn't acknowledge it, Lise told me she preferred stories that reached for a transformative epiphany to those that settled for irony. I don't know how much of Hemingway's work she'd actually read. She revered Dawn Powell, a writer who like Lise had fled a small town in central Ohio for the city. I recall a conversation we had that prompted me to say that Hemingway had referred to Powell as his favorite living writer, and there was another time, on the night we met, when I quoted a Hemingway phrase about how grappa took the enamel off your teeth and left it on the roof of your mouth, and she laughed. Otherwise Hemingway wasn't a writer we discussed much, let alone argued about. I wasn't going to defend a guy rich enough for safari vacations beating his chest for shooting the last of the lions.

Lise took her literature seriously, although she'd probably say not seriously enough. She was a self-described ABD – All But Dissertation – initials she likened to those indicating a disease, or a social stigma like a welfare mother on ADC. She was kidding, but before I caught myself, the comparison between an ADC mother and an ABD from the University of Chicago reminded me of the lack of proportion in those few poems by Sylvia Plath that used Holocaust imagery to convey the pain of a young woman from Smith.

'Actually, ABD *is* a minor epidemic at the U of C,' Lise said. 'There should be a graveyard in old Stagg Stadium, not under the stands where the atom bomb was hatched, but right out on the playing field where Jay Berwanger dodged tackles, little crosses marking all the dissertations that suffered and died there.'

Her unfinished dissertation was titled *One City, One Love: Endless Becoming in the Work of Dawn Powell*. Its three-hundred-plus pages awaited completion behind a closed door in a sewing room she called Limbo in the apartment she rented over a dry cleaner in Hyde Park. To pay the rent, Lise augmented a small trust fund by teaching freshman comp at a couple of community colleges in the Chicago area. One was near Arlington, and sometimes, when I'd drive in from Michigan to see her, we'd meet at the Thoroughbred track there. Our first time at the races we won big – for us, anyway – $687 on a horse we couldn't not bet on named Epiphany. The following night at a French restaurant overlooking an illuminated Lake Shore Drive, we blew our winnings on a four-course meal washed down with a magnum of a champagne from a village fittingly called Bouzy. After the waiter had ceremoniously buried the empty bottle neck-down in the ice bucket, Lise said, 'You have to promise we'll run away to Bouzy together.' She pronounced it *boozy*.

'Tonight?' I asked, checking my watch.

'Tonight's too late, Jack. It's already tomorrow in France,' she said, and then, leaning in to be kissed, knocked over the flute with the last of her wine.

Lise was a self-described 'promiscuous kisser,' though that didn't keep her from regarding a kiss as deeply intimate – especially, she added, if it's my tits being kissed. After a few drinks, she had a way of releasing from a kiss with her mouth still open, shaped as if the kiss continued, a facial expression that her good looks allowed her to get away with, as they allowed her to get away with sounding a little breathless on the subject of sex. The restaurant was closing, the chefs, sans toques, leaned in the doorway of the kitchen, drinking red wine and watching what Lise called our PDAs. We joked that night about calling it quits as high rollers while we were ahead, but over the racing season we returned to the track in Arlington hoping for another score. This time we'd invest in tickets to Bouzy.

We'd been drinking the night we first met, too, though it was pitchers of Rolling Rock, not champagne. I'd driven into Chicago for a reading and book signing by a friend who'd been a teacher of mine when I was in a graduate program in American studies there. After his reading, a small group, Lise among them, adjourned to a Hyde Park neighborhood pub. I'd noticed her in the audience at the bookstore. It was bitterly cold, and I'd taken a chance driving in but thought I could make it back to Michigan before the predicted lake-effect snow. She was wearing a furry Russian hat à la *Doctor Zhivago* that accentuated her cheekbones and the green of her eyes. There should be a word for a flair for looking stylish in hats. For Lise that included baseball caps, bathing caps, rain hoods, bicycle helmets, headbands, and probably tiaras and babushkas – anything that swept her hair up and bared her delicate face. Tendrils of auburn hair kept straggling out from under the fur hat and she'd tuck them back with the unconscious self-consciousness of a girl tugging up her swimsuit.

Later, when we'd tell each other the story of how we met, the word we'd use was *effortless*. We found ourselves seated directly across the table from each other in the pub and discussing our mutual friend's new book. Then, looking for things in common, we went on to talking about books that had changed us, movies that had swept us away, music we loved, food, travel, all the while refilling each other's beer steins, until inevitably we reached the subject of our personal lives.

Lise brought it up in the spirit of recounting what changed her, what had swept her away. I hadn't drunk anywhere near enough to tell her about the ill-advised relationship I'd had after I'd quit my job as a city caseworker, with a woman named Felice, who had once been on my caseload. She'd managed to get off welfare by working as a cocktail waitress in a mob bar. Her dream was to go to law school. At the time we met, her daughter, Starla, was in remission from leukemia. When the disease returned, Felice turned to drugs. We'd go together to the children's wing of County Hospital to read to Starla. She loved stories about cats, especially a series about Jenny Linsky, a black cat who wore a red scarf. I bought Starla a red scarf she took to wearing, which was as close as we could get to bringing her the cat that Felice was determined to sneak into the hospital. Starla's death after months of wasting away left Felice inconsolable. It wasn't numbness or escape she was after; she wanted to hurt herself, and I couldn't find a way to help her. Talking about her like that sounded wrong, though – psychologized, abstracted, factual, but also censored, sanitized, and less than honest. I didn't know how to tell what had happened, even to myself, and felt too guilty to try. After Felice disappeared, I had lucked into a teaching job in Michigan on the strength of my

PAPER LANTERN

newly published first book. A few threatening letters from Felice were forwarded to me – letters threatening herself. They arrived with a Chicago postmark but no return address. I never knew where she was living or with whom, and felt braced for worse to come. That night in the pub with Lise, back in the city from which I felt exiled, was the first time in a long while that it seemed natural to share a drink with a woman. When Lise asked me directly, I simply told her I wasn't seeing anyone.

Lise said that she was involved, off and on, with an older man who was a collector.

'A what?' I asked.

She laughed. 'Whenever I say what Rey does, people do a double take.'

'Tax collector? Butterfly collector? Juice loan collector?'

'An everything and anything collector. He's got a great eye! That's the name of his business: Great Eye Enterprises. He has this talent for stuff. This stein – he could give you a disquisition on beer steins that would make you have to have a set of them. It's sexy. He's sexy. It's partly smell – I don't think anything indicates sexual attraction more than smell. It's the sense most directly linked with memory. With Rey it was love at first sniff. The first time I met him, I literally started to tremble and had to hide in the Ladies'. Even when we're apart I keep one of his undershirts in my closet for a fix.'

'So, is this an off or an on cycle?'

'Sort of in between. He's starting a business in Denver. We talk on the phone at least twice a day. There's so much history between us, and we deserve to be together, but I don't know. I need my doctorate, and though he gets me, he doesn't get that. He's a salesman, not a scholar. He made a half a million dollars last year and wants to support me, but he's getting tired of waiting. He says he needs a woman in his bed every night, which sounds hot, but he's major needy, and in the culture he was raised in I'm not sure "in his bed" doesn't extend to "in the kitchen."'

'So, how long have you two been involved?'

'Seven years.'

The people we'd come in with were bundling up to head out into a blizzard that had howled in ahead of schedule. We hugged our mutual friend goodbye, and it was only Lise and me left at the table when the waitress announced last call. We moved to the bar, looking for something to cap off the evening and clean away the aftertaste of beer. I suggested grappa. 'Perfect,' Lise said. But the bar didn't stock it.

'How about a couple shots of Drano instead?' the bartender offered.

Lise said she had a bottle at her place that she'd brought back from Rome, a trip she'd taken with Buck, a paintings conservator, during an off phase with the collector. She'd bought the grappa because it was flavored with rose petals; it took pounds of petals, thousands of roses, to make a single bottle. In Italy, the relationship with Buck had seemed a romantic adventure, but once back in the States she began to suspect that Buck, despite the macho way he dressed – the Wolverine boots and his prized Stetson Gun Club hat that he had worn during their trip to Europe – was gay and didn't know it. She returned to her ne plus ultra – Rey.

'Once someone has taken you across a line into the best sex of your life, you can't go back. It's not easy for other men to turn my head from Rey,' she said. I didn't ask what she meant by 'across a line,' and I wondered how many other times Rey had been there to collect her yet again.

The sleety horizontal snow had plastered my wipers to the windshield. Given the alcohol, the hour, and the weather, Lise suggested that rather than find a hotel, let alone trying to drive back to Michigan, I sleep on her couch.

The couch was more about decor than comfort, a quality shared by most of her furnishings. Stuff – chiming clocks, threadbare tapestries, knickknacks, ornate mirrors, and murky oil paintings – crowded her small apartment. The room looked as if it might have a musty resale shop smell. I supposed it was decorated in Great Eye. There was a sense of recycled pasts that brought her phrase 'so much history between us' to mind.

'Like it?' she asked.

'Very quaint.'

'Please, the operative term is *whimsical*. I meant the grappa.'

'The operative term is *thank you, I never tasted anything like it.*'

'So what do you collect?' she asked.

'What do I collect?'

'Everyone collects something,' she said. 'First editions, baseball cards, saltshakers . . .'

'Frankly, since moving to Michigan, I've been trying to get rid of shit.'

I interpreted the alarmed look she gave me to mean that we were on a subject sacred to her, beyond anything in common between us.

She unrolled an unzipped sleeping bag over the brocade cushions and fluffed a pillow faintly scented by her shampoo against the single fin of the couch. 'At least you've dared to remove your shoes, or do you always sleep fully dressed?'

'I forgot to pack my footy pajamas.'

'Will you be warm enough without them?'

'If my feet get cold I might need the loan of that fur hat.'

'It's been a lovely evening. Thank you. Sweet dreams, Jack,' she said, and tucked the flap of the sleeping bag over me.

'No peck good night?'

Amused, she leaned toward me, chastely kissed my forehead, and let me draw her in. Her mouth tasted of rose petals and white lightning. She pulled away, and went about the apartment switching off lights, then, silhouetted against the street glow of the windows, stood as if she might be listening for something. Neither of us spoke – a silence made palpable by ticking gusts of sleet. She was shivering when finally she returned to the couch and slid in beside me under the sleeping bag.

From that first night, I always preferred that room in the dark. The windows above Dorchester, steamy with radiator heat, appeared tinted by the northern lights – an aura reflected from the blinking neon hangers in the dry cleaner's shop window below. The storm faded to a tape hiss in the background of her breathing as we kissed and she lay back with her mouth open, waiting for another kiss.

'I think we can dispense with the pretense of you sleeping in your clothes,' she said.

'In my wildest imaginings I couldn't have anticipated this. Not to be forward, but besides no jammies, I don't have protection.'

'Me neither,' she said. 'Just so you know, I've never done a one-nighter.'

'I've been tested since the last time I was with someone.'

'You're safe with me,' she said, and though I hadn't the slightest idea on what that assurance rested, I couldn't at that moment summon the nerve to ask.

The following evening, when I phoned from Michigan, more than a hundred miles away, I said, 'That thing about you never having done a one-nighter, how about keeping your record intact?'

'You'd do that for the sake of my record? I'm glad to hear it because I spent the day thinking about you. Not to be forward, but when are you back in town?'

'How's this weekend?'

'Not good, I'm sorry,' she said, without explanation. 'The weekend after?'

'I'm in New York then, doing a program at the Donnell Library.'

'I love New York. I could meet you there.'

All it took were those intervening two weeks of waiting for our initial effortlessness to turn into anxiety about seeing her again. I didn't know what I might be getting into, but I knew already that despite the lightness of that first night together, her effect on me was powerful.

I arrived in New York on a Thursday and stayed at a friend's unoccupied pied-à-terre, a fifth-floor walkup on Waverly Place, around the corner from the Village Vanguard, where Sonny Rollins was playing. On Friday night, after a dinner with my library hosts during which I tried to conceal my distraction, I went alone to the late set at a jammed Vanguard and stood by the bar letting the waves of tenor sax wash over me. It was a practice run of sorts: I imagined Lise beside me.

'Still remember me?' she had asked when I'd phoned her on landing at LaGuardia.

'Everything about you but your face,' I'd said. 'Still coming?'

'I can hardly wait. Maybe you're suffering from prosopagnosia?'

'Is there an over-the-counter remedy?'

'For lack of facial recognition? Not to be forward, but a direct application of moist heat is rumored to be efficacious. And, Jack, don't be duped by an imposter.'

I could recall her green eyes beneath the brooding brow of a Russian hat, her amber tendrils of hair, the shape and shade of her lips, but not her face, as if that single snowy night we'd spent together had left me dazed.

In the crowd at the Vanguard, I felt as if I were waiting for a stranger, a stranger scheduled to arrive the next morning in a cab from LaGuardia and ring the buzzer. Having already undone the intricate battery of locks peculiar to New York, I'd race down the five flights to where she'd be waiting in the cold with her overnight bag. We'd kiss hello, and then climb back upstairs together. Just like that she entered my life.

*

That winter and spring, I gave readings at a literary festival in D.C. and at universities in Chapel Hill, Berkeley, and Miami, from the book of prose poems and vignettes I'd written while working for the Cook County Department of Public Aid. The book began three years earlier as a record of the stories I'd hear from welfare *recipients*, as they were officially called, which I'd write down at the end of the workday as I rode the L from Bronzeville back to my apartment on the North Side. Working on it had seemed effortless. I'd be lost in a trance of writing on the train, and sometimes my stop would go by before I noticed. It was shortly after meeting Felice that I realized I had the rough draft of a book I had never planned to write. If I cut back expenses, I had enough money saved to get by for five months or so, and I quit my casework job to finish a book that still seemed more like an accident than a gift.

There's a tradition of books that have managed to survive their working titles: *Something That Happened* became *Of Mice and Men*, *The Inside of His Head* became *Death of a Salesman*, *Trinalchio in West Egg* became *The Great Gatsby*. My book was in that company thanks only to its inept working title, *Farewell to Welfare*. I had intended to dedicate it to Felice and Starla, but after Starla's death, the book was published without a dedi-cation. It was my first and, I now thought, possibly my only book, one from which I felt increasingly dissociated. Back when I'd started on it, I had felt there was so much that needed to be recorded in the plain language that people spoke on the street, a language real and by nature subversive, in opposition to the sanitized bureaucratic jargon of the case reports I had to file. But since Starla's death, I hadn't written a word.

At each university that spring, once free of obligation, I'd wait for Lise to arrive. The anticipation was a kind of foreplay. She'd fly in and we'd spend my honorarium on a weekend in a hotel as if we'd won at the track and the college towns were our Bouzy. In North Carolina it was the Grove Park Inn in the mountains near Asheville, where Scott Fitzgerald stayed when he'd visit Zelda. In D.C. we slept on a rickety antique bed at a place that referred to itself as an inn where, Lise agreed, the operative word was indeed *quaint*. At Berkeley we drove down the coast to the Vision Perch, a bed-and-breakfast in Big Sur.

The school that invited me to Miami had a deal with the Fontainebleau for housing guests. Late in the evening after my reading, I called Lise from the hotel. When she asked about the room, I told her I was stretched out on a bed surrounded by floor-to-ceiling marbled mirrors, and was at risk of being inhab-ited by a spirit who called himself the Angel Frankie.

'Well, then, should you come down with another attack of prosopagnosia before I get there tomorrow, I'll expect a spirited rendition of "Strangers in the Night,"' she said. 'Maybe I'll show up with something to share in return.'

'I'm not kidding about the bed being surrounded by mirrors.'

'I'm not kidding, either, Jack,' she said.

While I waited for her, I had a Friday to swim in the ocean. The weather when I'd left Michigan was spring in name only.

In Miami, the summery light seemed tangible enough to blow about like the rattling palm fronds. I woke too early for breakfast. The surf was audible from the boardwalk and the all-but-deserted beach was open despite the wind. I ignored the single red flag that warned of rip currents, since I planned to swim parallel to the shore once I was beyond the breakers.

I wasn't prepared for how quickly it swept me out. I remembered reading that even strong swimmers, exhausted by fighting a rip, drowned, but that if you resisted the panicky urge to swim against the pull, sooner or later the current released you. This one showed no intention of letting me go. I rode it, testing constantly whether I could swim back toward shore, and feeling flooded by mortality, as if the real danger of drowning were from the undertow within. I had no proverbial flashbacks of scenes from my life, only an eerily calm recognition of the obliteration that lurked at the center of each moment – moments I'd taken for granted. That awareness – however fleeting – was a reminder of the privilege of each breath. Lise would be arriving later that day and I desperately wanted to live, if only to learn what would become of us.

I waded ashore shaky from exertion and far down the beach from where I'd spread my towel. I lay on the warm sand, catching my breath beneath gulls yipping as they Holy Ghosted against the wind. I was ravenously hungry but couldn't move. A squadron of pelicans crash-landed where fish must have been schooling beyond the breakers. On Central time, Lise would be up early, grading papers, still hours from leaving for O'Hare. I couldn't imagine Felice, not without wondering if she was still alive. Those trips to County Hospital with her to visit Starla seemed farther and farther away, a distance Felice could never allow herself to accept. She had written the previous November that she could no longer bear seeing me because I'd once made

41

it seem as if the impossible were possible for her, and she hoped for my sake that, should there be a next time, I'd be better at recognizing the difference between the two, as it was cruel and dangerous not to. She had tucked the letter in a perfumed black nylon stocking and folded it into a paperback copy of *The Great Gatsby* – one of the many books I'd given her. That was her last letter to me.

Lise arrived that evening with her satchel of freshman themes and new strappy green heels. We went to Little Havana for dinner and drank too many mojitos as if, beyond our usual shared celebration, we each had some private cause for getting drunk. It seemed hilarious when I forgot where I'd parked the nondescript rental car; neither of us was sober enough to drive anyway. We caught a cab to the hotel and walked out along the beach to clear our heads. A massive cruise ship sketched in electricity passed slowly beneath a low-slung moon. Lise, her dress hiked for wading in the surf, lost a shoe. I was sure the rip had carried it off and tried drunkenly to describe how, when I'd been swept out that morning, I had wanted to live to see her again. She pressed a finger to my lips. 'Baby,' she said, 'you had a revelation. I had one, too.' She told me she'd been waiting for the right time to tell me that a week earlier, while Rey was on a buying trip, they'd decided during a long-distance call to end it.

'Stunned silence?' she asked.

'You caught me by surprise. I hope I didn't pressure you.'

'Not to be forward, but that's not quite the desired response.'

I woke to dazzling brightness. Lise had drawn the drapes on the morning. She was naked, her small, up-tilted breasts momentarily striped with the shadows of the slats of the blinds she was hoisting. The mirrored walls threw back a likeness of sea and sky, and the room filled with the expanse of the horizon. Our reflections appeared superimposed on light and water.

'Look at them, still young,' Lise said. 'Don't forget their faces.'

*

By early summer I had lucked into the place up north on a spring-fed lake small enough to swim across, and clean enough for loons. The cottage connected to a dock perched at water's edge in a sunlit clearing at the end of a two-track gravel road that crossed a culvert for a trout stream before emerging from the ferny woods.

The sink pumped silver-tasting well water. The shower was a head outside; there was no stall. And no Internet – there wasn't even a phone; cell reception was spotty. A chipped white enamel table; wooden folding chairs with green canvas seats; a blue corduroy couch; a bed whose wire headboard twined like the morning-glory vines that laced the porch screens; a pine writing desk supporting an Underwood typewriter, which seemed as archaic as the kerosene lamp that drew luna moths to the porch. Some nights we'd unroll sleeping bags there on the porch and fall asleep to the lap of water.

The college that hired me expected publication. I had applied for a few positions abroad in case my appointment wasn't renewed, including a Fulbright to Trinidad, but that was before meeting Lise. In graduate school, I'd published some freelance features, the best of them about a Michigan vintner determined to make champagne. The winter day I visited his winery, our interview was punctuated by the sound of bottles dangerously exploding in the cellar – as they continued to explode for months to come. I thought now of trying a feature again that I might sell to a magazine like *Michigan Out-of-Doors*, anything just to reconnect with language and get myself writing. I needed a subject that wasn't a city. Weren't there subjects enough for books on one small Michigan lake? – fish, frogs, ferns, wildflowers, mushrooms, the sandhill cranes that announced themselves on arriving punctually each noon, the resident loons? How many lakes were named for loons? I thought of writing about how lakes came to be named. There had to be stories behind the names. The article could open with a list that read like a line in a poem: Loon, Crystal, Mud, Bullfrog, Rainy, Devils, Little Panache, Souvenir, Gogebic (an Indian name meaning 'where rising trout make small rings'). Or I could write about what had become of the Native Americans who had lived here when Hemingway was a boy, or about the environmental changes to the rivers since he had fished them. He'd fished the nearby Black River, but his famous story 'Big Two-Hearted River' is set in the Upper Peninsula, and actually it was the Fox, not the Two-Hearted, that he'd fished there. The story wouldn't have been the same had he called it 'Fox River.'

I'd packed a beer box of books for the cottage, including Dawn Powell's collected stories and her novel *A Time to Be Born*. After supper, Lise would read aloud from Powell's diaries. They were set in the New York City of the 1930s, but even to the trill of night noise from the woods around us, the words sounded as if composed fresh that morning. I'd packed Hemingway's collected stories, too, which I hadn't read since school, in case I needed to refer to them for a feature. The rest were books on ferns, mushrooms, wildflowers, birds, Native American tribes. A subject search revealed a surplus of magazine articles on Hemingway in Michigan, so I went with loons. Their presence on a lake is an indicator of its health. I could taste the clarity of our lake water in the pike I hooked at dusk, fishing from my kayak at the edge of an acre of lily pads, and in the hand-sized bluegills I caught at the end of the dock when they fed at sunrise. I'd fry them with bacon for a breakfast of eggs, potatoes, and ice-cold Heineken that Lise and I would have at the picnic table beside the scorched, lopsided fieldstone grill after our swim across the lake.

We swam early each morning in the company of loons, through smoldering mist that hid the shore. Invisible in mist, the loons glided near, their manic bolts of laughter reverberating through a veiled forest. By the time we were swimming back to our dock, the mist had burned off. The only other cottage on the shore was shuttered, and Lise swam naked. She taught summer school during midweek and would drive up from Hyde Park for long weekends. I'd already be missing her when I watched the dust hanging behind her retreating blue Honda. On the day she was due back, I'd work at the picnic table, listening through birdsong and the thrum of insects and frogs for tires on gravel.

When she didn't arrive at the start of the Labor Day weekend, I figured she was held up in holiday traffic. We had gone without seeing each other for two weeks while she finished grading at the end of the summer semester. That morning, I'd caught three brook trout in the stream that ran through the culvert, I'd bought homegrown tomatoes, sweet corn, and giant sunflowers from a roadside stand, and I'd started a low fire on the grill so the coals would be ready when she arrived. By the time the third round of coals had burned to ash I was afraid she'd had car trouble on the road or worse. Twice I drove the nine miles to a gas station where there was a pay phone, but got only her voice message. By midnight, I couldn't stand the wait and decided to drive the three and a half hours back to my place to retrieve any message she might have left. I worried we'd pass each other in the dark, that she'd get to an empty cottage. I'd left a note and the key beneath the step where she'd know to look, and watched the headlights coming toward me, wondering if they were hers.

There was no message waiting. I almost set out for her apartment in Hyde Park to make sure she was all right. What stopped me was an inescapable flashback to another panicky drive to Chicago when, shortly after moving to Michigan, I had found a letter from Felice forwarded to my campus mail – a suicide note postmarked from Chicago a week earlier. I had been kayaking on a river that morning, and without stopping to cancel classes or to remove the kayak from the rack on my car, I found myself speeding down I-94 as if, despite the postmark, I could get there in time to stop her. I drove through sun showers; an incongruous rainbow, washed out beside the glistening, flame-wicked September trees, spanned the interstate. I went instinctively to Felice's old Bronzeville neighborhood and parked by Banks, a soul-food place we'd frequented, across from the DuSable Hotel, now boarded up for demolition. I checked the restaurant's huge windows as if she might be gazing out drinking a beer, and then walked for blocks, stopping to knock frantically on the doors of welfare recipients whose caseworker I'd once been, reappearing now as a crazed white guy with no business except to ask if they knew where Felice might be. No one did. When I returned to my car, I found all seventeen feet of my white fiberglass kayak spray-painted with initialed hearts, obscenities, and gang graffiti. I drove to the cocktail lounge where Felice had worked as a waitress in net stockings before they'd fired her and she'd had to go back on welfare. Finally, I contacted a friend at the police department. We checked the morgue and hospitals without finding a match. The next day, when I returned to Michigan, another letter was waiting that said she was sorry she'd sent me the suicide note but she couldn't think of anyone else to tell, and she was also sorry she hadn't been able to go through with it.

Lise finally called around nine in the morning. I'd barely slept. I'd played our last conversations over in my mind for some hint of what might have happened. I kept returning to her mention – only a vague one, but it made her voice change – of how, after seven years, breaking up with Rey on the telephone didn't seem right; she needed to see him again, she said, to tie up loose ends and finish things properly. I didn't know what 'loose ends' she was referring to and I didn't ask because by then I knew her well enough to expect her to be evasive. Despite her initial frankness, once we started going together she'd begun to censor her history with Rey. There'd been in her voice the same uncharacteristically deferential tone I had noticed when she'd told me that it was hard for other men to turn her head.

She'd been away, she told me, and had only just received my messages. There'd been a last-minute change in her plans. She wasn't thinking clearly, she was sorry, she hadn't meant to make me worry.

'Want to tell me what's going on?'

'What do you think is going on? You never ask directly, Jack,' she said.

'I'm asking now.'

'I was pregnant.'

'You *were* pregnant? What does that mean? Why wouldn't you tell me?'

'Maybe it caught me by surprise. Maybe I hoped not to pressure you. You can understand not wanting to pressure someone, can't you?'

'No,' I said, 'I don't understand. Are you all right? Let's start with that.'

'Why not with surprise? Why aren't you surprised? When Rey and I began sleeping together I was on the pill, but I went through a time when I had to get off, and he didn't like using protection, so we went without it for years, and since he has a son by another woman I assumed it was me who couldn't conceive. Obviously I was wrong.'

'That's not what I'm asking. I'm down to the simple, basic questions.'

'You mean, like, Will you stay in Michigan or keep running if you get the chance to hide out on an island somewhere, an ocean away?'

'You know that's not fair. How about more like, Does he think the child was his? Or was it his?'

She said nothing.

'Look,' I said, 'I'm going to hang up now and drive to your place so we can talk.'

'Don't, please, Jack, I won't be here later.'

'Where will you be?'

'Basic questions don't necessarily make things simple,' she said, ignoring my question. 'What if I said I didn't tell you because one morning I watched you from the dock fishing for dinner and suddenly wondered who is that out there on this little hidden lake in his kayak tagged like a viaduct wall in the inner city? What is he doing here, so out of place, trying so hard to fit into a new life he's making up as he goes? And I went inside and opened your book and sat reading it as if for the first time on the bed – all mussed from our lovemaking – and the words were so sad and angry, more than I'd realized, more than the writer realized, and I wept, not just for the words themselves. I was thinking that ever since that first trip together in New York, I've been trying to fit in, too.'

'Fit in? Into what? Like we haven't been making it up together as we went along? Lise, what are you trying to do?'

'To give you an answer. Remember that first night in the snowstorm, you came over for a grappa I brought back from Italy?'

'Flavored with rose petals. I remember that night in exact detail. I've remembered it countless times. What does it have to do with now?'

'Just listen, okay? I told you I went with Buck to Italy. Buck always bought art on his trips to Europe, mostly legit, though some he smuggled back into the States. After Rome, we went to a private auction in Amsterdam because he knew I loved Dutch painters – I'd collect them if I could – and among all the paintings and etchings there was this drawing of a hand and its shadow, unsigned, that I couldn't stop looking at. It was as if I'd seen it before. Each time I changed the angle I looked from, the hand changed. At first it was as if it might be from a body that had suffered or was suffering, and then from a body asleep – a hand in a dream – or a hand still stinging that had just delivered a blow or left its handprint on a woman's bottom – it was almost as if I'd felt it. Or a hand waiting to hold an unseen pen, waiting to write a secret message that could change a life, a message I knew was coming before it was written. Buck said it probably was a study for a painting, that its realism suggested the Dutch Caravaggisti – the painters influenced by Caravaggio, who in turn influenced Rembrandt and Vermeer. I asked if it could possibly be Rembrandt, and he said more likely it was someone like Hendrick ter Brugghen. You had to have a dealer's card if you wanted to bid, so Buck did it for me. I paid six hundred euros – more than I could afford, but I had to have it. Buck said I needed to get an expert appraisal. If it turned out to be someone like ter Brugghen it would be worth money. "And if it's Rembrandt?" I asked him. He just smiled, then kissed me, and that night we – well, let's just say we got intimate in Amsterdam in a way we hadn't before. But when I came home, I never had it appraised, because if it was really worth something, I knew that in all fairness Buck and I were partners, like sharing a winning lotto number, like you and me at the track, and it wasn't until I faced up to that partnership that I had to admit it didn't feel right, not for the long term. Do you understand what I'm trying to say?'

'I never noticed that drawing.'

'It's over my desk, in Limbo.'

*

There's that couple at the station waiting for the express from Barcelona. One can guess that the woman is going off alone to have an abortion, but we know little beyond that about either of them. It's hot. The woman wants to try an Anis del Toro, so they order two with water. She says it tastes like licorice. 'Everything tastes of licorice. Especially all the things you've waited so long for.'

'Oh, cut it out,' the man says.

That green light at the end of Daisy Buchanan's dock is the color of hope. At the start of the novel, it seems that hope and waiting might be the same shade. Jay Gatsby, Newland Archer, all those nocturnal citizens of Winesburg, Ohio, hope, dream, yearn, and wait. They wait for love, which is, as such stories go, indistinguishable from waiting for life. Even the sickly Michael Furey in 'The Dead,' singing in the chill rain, who dies for love, is waiting for life. His ghost still waits. Waiting is what ghosts do. If, in such stories, the wait ends in disillusionment, then at least that defines what it means to have lived. Then there are writers like Beckett or Kafka, for whom the disillusionment is

so profound that it transcends the theme of love. The disillusionment isn't merely with mankind but with God, the kind of
disillusionment that is by definition beyond understanding. *Our
nada who art in nada, nada be thy name . . .*

In Kafka's *The Trial* – where a man, all but anonymous, waits
to be judged for an undisclosed crime – the situation is not
unlike the wait in Hemingway's 'The Killers,' a story that was
often anthologized before Hemingway fell out of fashion – as
if fashion could erase the influence of a style that rearranged
the molecular structure of American letters.

'The Killers' is supposedly an inspiration for Edward Hopper's
iconic *Nighthawks*, which hangs in the Art Institute of Chicago.
There are so many reproductions of it that when you finally
see the original, at 331/8 by 60 inches it seems more modest
than one might have expected. Although it's a nocturne, it is
paradoxically as much about light as any of the Impressionist
paintings a few galleries away. The diner illuminates a dark city
corner with a stark light it doesn't seem capable of throwing
on its own. There's a counterman and three customers – a man
and a woman, who might be lovers, and a thickset man off by
himself, who could be a hit man. He could be Death. They sit
as if waiting, not for something to begin, but to end.

In 'The Killers,' two hoods from Chicago, sawed-off shotguns
under their black overcoats, wait in a diner for the Swede. The
clock in the diner runs twenty minutes fast, a clever detail like
that hospital radio that plays only at night. The streetlight
flickers on outside the diner's window. The killers order bacon-
and-egg sandwiches to eat while they wait, but the Swede
doesn't show. He's back at his rooming house, on his bed, face
to the wall, when Nick Adams, who works at the diner, goes
to warn him. The warning has no effect; the Swede knows his
situation is hopeless.

'I can't stand to think about him waiting in the room, and knowing he's going to get it. It's too damn awful,' Nick tells his coworker, George, back at the diner.

'Well,' George says, 'you better not think about it.'

I put off going back up north to the cottage until the landlord there – a kindly man who'd told me, when I'd first stopped to buy raw honey from him, that he read Yeats to his bees – asked me to retrieve my things, as he needed to close the place for winter. So on a Saturday in October I drove through the last of the color change, an achingly beautiful time in Michigan, tinged as it is with the knowledge that it will be a long, hard season before the leaves reappear. I packed my kayak and my fishing gear, a duffel bag of clothes, the unfinished piece on loons, and a few of the books from the beer box – the field guides, mostly, which I thought I might want to page through again someday.

The Caller

Let us love, since our heart is made for nothing else.
—Saint Thérèse of Lisieux, *The Story of a Soul*

The phone is ringing in the crummy downstairs flat where Rafael lives, ringing and ringing, but Rafael isn't home. It rang this morning at five and on and off all day through the hot afternoon. Now it's after midnight, still sweltering as if the satin nickel moon is throwing heat, and this time the ringing doesn't sound as if it's going to stop. Someone really wants to talk to Rafael, someone who obviously hasn't heard he's disappeared.

That's the word on the street: Rafael's gone – as thoroughly as people disappeared in Argentina, removed as efficiently as if he's been ethnically cleansed, or maybe one of the death squads from Central America went out of their way one night to stop by the southwest side of Chicago and pay Rafael a visit.

He's joined the disappeared, but in the barrio incongruously called Pilsen, a hood famed for its graffiti art, there won't be mothers with the mournful Madonna look, bringing down the government by holding blowups of Rafael's picture – the self-portrait with respirator and nighthawk wings – pasted to placards that read MISSING. At St Paul's on Hoyne Avenue, or St Procopius on Alport, or St Ann's on Leavitt, where Rafael was baptized, there won't be radical padres risking martyrdom by protesting from their pulpits that Rafael must not be forgotten.

A stooped, veiled figure lights a candle for a soul. It's Sister Two Teresas, who chose her name in honor of both the Little Flower of Lisieux and Saint Teresa of Ávila. Her life has been lived by the words of Saint Teresa of Ávila: *Accustom yourself continually to make many acts of love, for they enkindle and melt the soul.* She once oversaw the altar boys when St Ann's still had a grade school and now, in her dotage, arranges the altar flowers. She can't remember yesterday, and yet recalls how twenty-three years ago Lance Corporal Milo Porter, the most devout boy she'd ever coached, stood in his dress blues as if they were a surplice, cradling the son he'd named after an angel, while Father Stanislaus dribbled the water of eternal life over the wailing infant's head. And she remembers how two years later when Lance Corporal Porter, missing in action, couldn't attend his own requiem mass, she wept and prayed: *Oh, how everything that is suffered with love is healed again.*

In the years after the requiem, first Rafael's mother deserted – paid off by the alderman whose bastard she was carrying, or so the rumor went – then one by one the extended family scattered into oblivion, until only Rafael was left in the care of Tia Marijane, his 'beatnik aunt,' an exotic dancer half blinded by lasers, who spent her days painting watercolors of the cosmos and her nights praying the rosary to the opera station. Rafael liked to say he was raised by the spray-painted streets of Pilsen in the way that kids in fairy tales are raised by wolves. And now he's MIA like the father he never knew. Those superpatriots Sly Stallone and Chuck Norris won't be dispatched to liberate him. He'll be lucky to make the Eleventh District's list of missing persons. It runs in the family to disappear.

The vigil candle at St Ann's will melt into smoke, though at this moment, after midnight, its tiny flame has the locked church to itself and in the darkness emits a numinous green light that has the stained-glass windows facing the L tracks on Leavitt glowing from the inside out. If a soul flitted mothlike, lost in a once-familiar neighborhood, the light might attract it. An empty L, lit by a similar glow, rattles by like massive links on the chain of a ghost. Blocks away the ring of a phone echoes in a musty airshaft, and all along the street graffitied pay phones, most of them out of order and all of them obsolete and scheduled to be torn out, begin ringing. And then the steeple bells of three churches toll.

When a phone rings long enough it acquires a voice of its own. You hear it despite the pillow squashed over your ears or the boom box turned up until the guy next door starts hammering the wall. With your eyes closed each ring is a spray of color – karma-violet, clandestine-red, revolving-dome light blue – the auras of a voice that's as beyond words as the night cries of urban animals – nighthawks wheeling above mercury-vapor lights, chained watchdogs that won't stop barking, a rat tossing in the trap that's managed only to break its back.

Come on, man, fucking pick up.

The call seemed merely impatient at first, like Rafael's gangbanger homey Milton who suspects that Rafael is skimming on their petty dope deals. They'd agreed on 50/50, Rafael supplying the supposedly aphrodisiac, hallucinogenic gummies called liana smuggled from a research study at the U of C, and Milton doing the pushing. *I'd rather huff fumes like a punk than drop that shit, man,* Milton said after he tried liana. *Crazy fucking colors, closing your eyes just makes it worse, jungle cats jumping out of doorways,* ese, *you call that a love potion?* He thought he'd mess with Rafael's head in return by leaving a warning that the Devil's Disciples were looking to express their displeasure with the recent apparitions of bare-assed girlfriends – phantom reflections on the cracked windshields of junkers and the soaped plate glass of deserted storefronts – that Rafael, masked like a surgeon, had spray-painted along Eighteenth, a street otherwise made sacred by its murals of the Virgin of Guadalupe. *Yo, van Gogh of the Krylon can, when you gonna get that piece-of-shit answering machine fixed? I got a message might save your sorry ass. Why you can't paint nothing but chicas? Do you always have to paint with your dick?*

By late afternoon desperation has crept into the jangle of the Good Humor Man's bells and into the gut of the plain-looking woman who's been feeding a pay phone that rings and rings, then chucks back her loose change as if ejecting a cartridge. Cindy, the 'older woman' – she's thirty-two – who cleans condos on the Gold Coast, is calling from the Blue Island Laundromat, where, between the boil of washing machines and cyclone of dryers, it's hot enough to faint. Rafael has immortalized the cracked walls in his flat with a portrait of her dressed in glass platform heels and a transparent gown that makes the wall phosphorescent in the dark as if painted with a spray distilled from a hatch of fireflies. Actually, it's Cindy's body showing through the gown that's luminous.

Where'd you come up with that beautiful gown for me, babe?

It's a web, he told her, spider silk stronger than steel. Once, I found a field of it.

He'd been tripping one Friday night, on his way to Motown in a hot-wired Buick to see the murals Diego Rivera had painted for Henry Ford. Radio playing whatever was hymning in the

CD changer, and not a coin in his pocket, Rafael blew through tollgates and kept going until lost somewhere in Michigan, the Buick rolled to a stop, out of gas along a deserted road. Rafael stood wasted, knee-deep in mist, taking a leak, and suddenly, like a lens focusing, he could see how every weed and wildflower beyond the barbed-wire fence was connected as far as the horizon. Dawn shimmered through dew-beaded webs as if a goddess had tossed her gown over the gone-to-seed field. The spiders must have spun a new gown each night. He imagined all the silk that had been spun since the origin of spiders, unspooling into a single thread with the tensile strength to connect the cosmos. The murals in Motown could wait; he needed to hitch back to Pilsen while that thread still connected his mind.

If she could just talk to Rafael, Cindy would stop touching her tongue to her front teeth. She's calling to tell him that her hotheaded, jealous old man, Darrell, is on to them. Jade, the stepdaughter who never accepted her, snitched to Darrell that when she got home early from school because of cramps, she caught Cindy passed out, and Rafael, high in the shower, flashed his thing before slamming the door. Cindy wants to say she knows that flashing part's a lie, right? Ever since Cindy dropped some weight and started to fix herself up and feel alive again, Jade's been competing with her. Her stepdaughter's got a dirty mouth and each morning is a battle to keep her from going to school dressed like a slut. Darrell called them both whores, smacked them around, and punched Cindy in the stomach so she still can't breathe. So Jade has run away from home and Cindy's calling from the *lavanderia* on Blue Island because she's got nowhere else to go. Her front teeth are chipped and her lip split where it collided with his wedding band. She hasn't worked up the courage to look in the mirror, and oh, babe, Darrell slammed the clip into his army .45 and is looking for you.

And if it's not Cindy then maybe it's that walking hunger strike Brianna, calling because someone's spreading evil rumors, saying that she caught needle disease, and she hopes it hasn't soured their relationship because it isn't true. Okay, there was that one time he told her she owed him a twenty for the Zithromax he had to take, and maybe she *has* been looking a little faded lately, sleeping all day, but that's because she's been depressed that things between them haven't been going well, and when he disappears as if he never wants to talk to her again it makes her terminally anxious. She wonders if he isn't answering because he knows it's her calling. Sometimes she's convinced that Rafael's got telepathy, a way of getting inside your mind that feels intimate until he uses your own thoughts against you. *Oh, baby, don't make me keep calling and calling when all I need to ask is a single question: Am I still the little* maja *posing on your bedroom wall, Sleeping Beauty drifting on the crystal ship of your mattress down the wavy, black river of her unloosed hair? I been growing it out for you. It grows twice as fast when I'm asleep.*

There's a lull after supper when what's left of the day filters through the dusty blinds. Each slat is a ray – runway-blue, mescalito-violet, replicant-red. Above a horizon of tracks where L trains hurtle past looking as if they've been tagged while moving, the sky reverberates around a sinking fireball. The phone can no longer hide its utter lack of control. It repeats itself, a soprano practicing scales, in the airshaft, rousting pigeons, like the voice of that biker, face half hidden by the visor on the black helmet, who cruised the hood photographing murals. Stomper boots, black leather jeans, jacket scarred by zippers, KA-BAR knife slung from a tread belt – the full macho, but he didn't move like a guy. Then, on a night of record-breaking heat, the biker rumbles up wearing a tank top that reads SERA OUTLAW and shows off her underarm hair and nipples punctuating white cotton as she bumps the red Custom Harley with its vanity plate over the curb and parks it on the sidewalk. Her arms look pumped. A chartreuse luna moth has alighted on one shoulder blade. On the other, there's a symbol that could be a ram's horns or a rune from an ancient alphabet, welted up raw so that you wonder if she hit high C when she was branded. She pays the kids hanging out in front a buck each to watch her bike. Until then, she was the *he* they'd nicknamed Mr *Mariposa*. Seeing her in the tank top, with her green moth tat, she's rechristened Madame Moth.

Not like she cares. She saunters to the corner, buys a snow cone from the old vendor who doesn't scoop crushed ice, but shaves it off a block kept cold beneath a canvas as it was done in the country where he was a child. Yellowjackets swarm his bottles of tropical flavors. Madame Moth orders electric-blue syrup that tastes like no flavor in nature. Beneath the black visor, her lips at the melting edge of the paper cone turn frostbite-blue. Not pausing to drop her change into the sombrero of the blind accordion man pumping conjunto, she strolls back as if the only reason she's come to the barrio is for a snow cone and, without raising the visor, vanishes through the doorway and up the stairs into the building's ripe, unlit corridors.

It's not long – time enough to finish the cone, maybe for a toke or two, or to snort a line or huff fumes or chew one of those spooky gummies Rafael deals – before the airshaft echoes a chant that has renounced words, but not meaning. The city is full of people who can't understand one another's language but get the meaning – like listening to opera when all you have to go on is the pure emotion of the voice. Her voice sounds naked, and though the kids outside mock it, they know they're listening to a sin.

If in the stifling heat Rafael put on his respirator and painted only her streak of voice, he wouldn't have to worry about finding the space on his walls to fit in a life-sized portrait of Sera Outlaw from the burbs, slumming on a pricey Harley, in her defiantly arrested *Wild One* getup. The portraits of the women from the hood who have staked out a place on the walls feel it's already overcrowded. They don't need Sera Outsider playing let's pretend. Maybe there's a patch of peeling plaster beneath the sink in the cramped john with its roaches and running toilet where Rafael could squeeze in a still life: the black helmet draped with a Victoria's Secret cinnabar thong, weighting down the tank top, leather trou, knife, belt, stompers, piled on the buckled linoleum.

The women see themselves reflected on Madame Moth's visor. They can't see her face. They wonder how they look to her, if she's able to see beyond her own reflection. The women's eyes don't blink, never close, don't sleep – even Sleeping Beauty's eyes are painted open. Night is when they're most awake. They watch over the dreaming artist tossing on a sweat-stained mattress surrounded by melted candle stubs. Their lips are parted as if they're about to moan, pray, or whisper a lullaby, but he's left them mute, a limitation they were unaware of until now as they silently listen to the yearning voice amplified by the airshaft. To paint her voice, Rafael would need to feather the spray into the icy impression of her lips; he'd need a hue that matched the unnatural taste of the blue nectar that's soaked into the tongue she licks along his body.

Sera Outlaw has her own ideas of what he'll paint. She's discussed the fantasies that haunt her at obsessive length with her shrink, Dr Fallon, for whom talk is decidedly *not* cheap. 'You need to work through them. Life is risk: experiment,' he's counseled her. 'When you'll instinctively recognize the right one, it will shake you to the core.' If her fantasies could be perfectly realized outside the secret cell of her mind, then perhaps she could separate from them.

Pose me as a queen blindfolded at the wild border of a realm I once ruled, bind me to a signpost to be abused by passing wanderers who care only for their own pleasure; paint me as the desecrated, living statue of a goddess, a deity from a shattered urn in a temple defiled by barbarians – brutish-looking men have always turned me on. Paint me as Saint Teresa in Ecstasy, or as Joan of Arc, stripped of armor and, threatened with punishment, flaring colors as if the mattress she's staked to is a stained-glass window in the cathedral at Rouen.

'Where?'

'France.'

'There's not enough wall space. I'll have to make up a big canvas.'

'No, I want it to be a mural locked away in this room. I'll need a key to visit it. You can whitewash the walls, paint over the others. You did them free, right? I'll pay.'

The voiceless women on the walls have begun to scream.

'It'll be your first commission. Paint the walls the white of a bride's veil. Obliterate the skanks, then call me. It'll be a new start for both of us. I'll be your masterpiece.'

*

She returns during Fiesta del Sol, a time in August when Pilsen is baubled in lights. Blue Island Avenue closes from Eighteenth to Twenty-first Streets – three congested blocks of carnival rides whirling to mechanical mariachi music. A Ferris wheel, tall enough to reflect its luster along a shadowy church spire, rotates hypnotically. A ring has been erected in which masked *luchadores* wrestle in the way that life and death are locked in daily combat. There are galleries for games of chance, booths where fortunes are told, concession stands, and food stalls. A spicy haze from grilling chorizos smolders in the beam of an enormous searchlight battered by moths. For five tickets you can pan the beam along the undercarriage of clouds or off the skyline of downtown. When firecrackers start popping like a drive-by, no one dives for cover.

Blocks away, inside St Ann's, a vigil candle strobes as it sputters in melted wax and the bullet-pocked stained-glass windows flicker.

Stumbling back to his flat, buzzed on a cocktail of liana and mescal, Rafael notices the red Harley parked on the sidewalk. He looks up and down the empty street. Everyone not asleep, including the snow-cone vendor and the accordion man, must be at the fiesta. Rafael climbs the dark stairs yodeling out *gritos* in a soulful *yi-yi-yi!* Ordinarily, he's quiet, tight-lipped. Perhaps he has confused his flirting with a fortune-teller for feeling intimations of the future. When the fortune-teller asked to read his palm, Rafael told her he was sorry, but he didn't have the five tickets that seeing the future cost. She caught his wrist and pulled him close. 'For you, a free sample,' she said. Smiling at his handsome face, she turned his palm over and traced its lines, before jerking her finger back as if she'd been shocked. Or as if she had seen too many cheesy movies where a phony gypsy fakes the same theatrical response – which is what Rafael told her.

'If you don't believe in telling the future, do you believe in telling the past? The past is just as secret and mysterious,' she said. 'But I can read what's hidden in your eyes.'

'I'm listening,' he said.

'You are hiding twelve tickets. If your first fortune didn't please you, you'd of had enough tickets left to buy a completely new one. Only a fool thinks he can deceive a Roma.'

Rafael laughed, reached in his pocket, and dropped a handful of tickets on the counter before her.

'Too late,' she told him. 'Once you miss your chance you can give all you got, but won't catch fate's attention again.'

'I guess it's good night, then,' he said.

'Don't go without this,' she said, and handed him the key to his flat. 'You just tried to give it away along with your tickets. You're drunk, angel.'

'So are you,' he said, and leaned into the booth to kiss her.

'I told you, it's too late,' she said. 'Even a kiss that will be my first thought in the morning won't matter.'

In the dark hallway, at the door of his flat, Rafael searches his jeans for the key. He knows the fortune-teller returned it. He can summon the cinnamon taste of her mouth. She must have been eating churros. The key is in his shirt pocket where he never puts it.

'Somebody had a fun fiesta,' Sera Outlaw says. 'How come you didn't invite me? We could've held hands on the Ferris wheel. I've been waiting for you to call, I can't say patiently. Any idea what that feels like – waiting when you really want something, when you can't stop thinking about it, and the more you obsess, the more you need it?'

He unlocks the door and she follows him into the dark flat and strikes a match to light the twist of a joint. The eyes on the walls reflect the flame of the match. Cindy's transparent gown glimmers. 'They're still all here,' she says. 'Did you even get the fucking whitewash?'

'Been busy.' He accepts the joint, sucks the smoke, and holds it in.

'Don't turn on the light,' she says. 'Creeps me out when roaches run for cover.' She strikes matches until all the candle stubs ringed around the mattress are flickering.

Down the street, L trains traveling from opposite directions, jammed with fiesta revelers, arrive with a simultaneous screech at the muraled Leavitt station. The station's stairs and their risers are a mosaic waterfall. After the trains racket off, regular street noise passes for quiet.

'Your bitches don't like me,' she says, 'and I don't appreciate the way they're glaring at my tits. You're their master, make them disappear.'

'I'm no one's master – including my own.'

'Don't get vanilla on me, Rafael. How old are you? Twenty-one? I told you I'll pay. What's holding things up? You fall in love with your own creations, your own fantasies? They demand allegiance, don't they? Hard to let go. It's lonely without them adoring you, waiting when you come home at night. Look at the cummy stains on this mattress!'

She inhales as if sighing and lazily passes him the joint, and then, before he can react, draws her knife and flings it into Sleeping Beauty.

'Whoa!' he says, exhaling smoke.

'No scream? Blood should be gushing down the wall, puddling the floor. You got to get your red paint out if you want to see that. So, okay, no more passivity, we're going to have a little private fiesta of wall-cleaning.'

She springs up, yanks the knife from Sleeping Beauty's heart, and jams it into the painting's face, then wheels into a practiced kickboxing move, and the heel of her stomper boot caves in one of Sleeping Beauty's plaster breasts. She's balletic in her fury. Rafael finishes the joint, while watching from the mattress what looks like a cardio routine run amok. She jabs, whirls, slashes, kicks, and plunges the knife, working herself into a breathless tantrum of destruction. Good thing whoever lives next door is probably at the fiesta.

On Blue Island, the Ferris wheel is stuck. Couples lean over the sides of their gondolas shouting, 'Yo, get us down!' A carny worker shouts up, 'Remain seated, please! Do not try climbing out!' 'Yo, we going to have to fucking spend the night up here or what?' 'No need to panic. The fire department is on the way!' It's a still, sultry night, and the gondola at the very top – nearly the height of the steeple – has started to stir in the rhythmic way that lovers can get a parked car rocking. It catches the attention of a few people in the crowd. They're pointing up.

Tonight, Sera Outlaw is a warrior – Joan of Arc, stripped of armor and waiting to suffer further indignities. Twisted coat hangers secure her ankles and bind her arms over her head. On the mattress beside her, Rafael sits baking one end of a straightened wire hanger over a candle. Along with the scent of weed and melted wax, and the musty updraft of the airshaft, the flat has acquired an acrid, metallic smell.

'What do you think you're doing with that?' she asks. 'Get your paints.'

'Too bad I'm out of marshmallows.'

'That's a guy crack. I took you for someone who could get into the drama. You think the saints didn't know submission's how you get the attention we crave from God?'

'I'm setting the mood,' he says. 'You told me when they threatened her, she like got off in Technicolor.'

'I don't play with fire – at least not that way.'

'Somebody did,' he says, and gently lowers his lips to the brand on her shoulder.

'That was an initiation. I'm an Aries. Untie me, I mean fucking now.'

Instead, he blindfolds her with her white tank top. He fastens his mouth over hers, and then touches the tip of the clothes hanger to the luna moth. It's not the end that he's heated, but she screams with a force that makes him swallow as if she's filled his mouth with electric-blue syrup. Her teeth clench on his lower lip and he hollers back.

On Blue Island, a kid who's spent his last five tickets on the searchlight instead of buying a taco has trained the beacon on the gondola at the top of the stalled Ferris wheel. The dazzling beam doesn't inhibit the couple who's up there. They've ducked down and must be lying together flat on the bench seat, and can't be seen from the ground. Still, the spotlight has made them stars – daring acrobats without a net, determined to put on a show. The gondola rocks recklessly, desperately, as their grand performance builds to a climax against the night sky. The crowd below cheers, even as sirens wail and the fire trucks run red lights down Eighteenth toward the fiesta. The firemen will be here any moment with their axes, bullhorns, and ladders. No one in the crowd is leaving until a ladder rises as it would to a blazing tenement window and, to riotous applause, the couple climb out and begin their descent back to the ordinary world.

Rafael presses her white tank top to his bloody mouth. 'I was just messing with you,' he says. 'You bit through my lip, you goddamn flake. Look what you did to my walls.'

'Untie me, you crazy dick. Do you know who you're fucking with? I'm like totally connected. You have any idea who my uncle is?'

'You're the one came to me to get painted. You don't have to pay. I work better free.'

He slips on his respirator, conscious of his swollen lip, and, careful of her bound legs kicking at his balls, fits her visored helmet over her coral Mohawk while she spits nonstop curses. He starts with her bare feet: sprays them alchemy-gold. The black stompers standing beside the mattress get a coat of rubber-ducky yellow. Candy-cane stripes twirl up her legs and polka dots float from navel to the Cousteau-blue ruff inspired by her tongue. On the back of her helmet he paints a cherry-red honker and a white-lipped, watermelon-slice smile from which a blue tongue sticks out at the world. When she's on the bike, a clown will appear to be looking backward. Raphael takes the precaution of dislodging the knife from where she's rammed it into one of Cindy's eyes after the spiderweb gown resisted her attempts to hack it to shreds.

'Even though you're about as convincing a badass as Michael Jackson, something tells me it would be a mistake to return your blade just now,' he says. 'Sorry I don't have something to swap for it like a rubber horn to honk on your Harley.'

'I'll be back for it with a nine-mil to honk up your ass, and not by myself, either. You just used up all your lives in one fucking evening.'

On Blue Island, the aerial ladder truck has successfully completed its rescue of all the couples on the Ferris wheel. By the time the ladder cranked to the top of the wheel, the highest gondola was hanging motionless, becalmed on the still night air. The crowd stared up, waiting for the disheveled, daredevil lovers to emerge. They would become fiesta legends, a Romeo and Juliet crisscrossed by beacons, their suspended, pearlescent boat sailing past the suffering Christs on all the steeples in the city, afloat on dark matter with novas exploding like flak, and the infinite blackness decaled with skyrockets and gold-glitter comets. Actually, when a fireman reached their gondola, they were gone. Where, who can say? Maybe the rocking gondola had been an optical illusion – a gentle sway in an indiscernible breeze – as seen from below. A few measly skyrockets pop and parachute down on Pilsen, a signal that the fiesta is over for tonight. Bulbs blink off in the shuttered stalls. With the mechanical mariachi music silenced, it's possible to hear the accordion. The snow-cone vendor pushes his cart along Eighteenth dragging a trail of melted ice.

Alchemy-gold footprints trail down the stairs and out the doorway. Her motorcycle is parked illegally on the sidewalk where she left it. Some joker returning from the fiesta in a party mood has tied a pink heart-shaped balloon to its handlebars. The streets resound with the pipes-and-tambourine laughter of blitzed revelers heading toward the L station. The searchlight, shooting from Blue Island, sweeps along the apartment buildings. A painted woman sits on her motorcycle, staring up as the beam crosses Rafael's dark third-story window. He stands half naked, looking out, the bluish beam smoldering with the smoke of his cigarette, each slat in the blinds a slash along his body.

'You motherfucker,' she yells at the window, in a voice nothing like that soprano in the airshaft, 'I'm coming back packing, when you least expect it. You're going to beg. You're already a dead man, asshole.' She revs her bike as if the snarling engine knows words she can't find and guns along the sidewalk, sending revelers jumping out of the way and shouting at the goofy face looking back at them, '*Pendeja loca!*'

The whine of the engine grows increasingly distant but refuses to disappear, as if someone were riding in furious, self-destructive circles at the edge of consciousness, a 500cc Buell Blast boring into sleep, invading dreams, and morphing into the ringing of a phone.

Squash a sweaty pillow over your ears, but the reverberations continue. The call is no longer pleading. When it's hopeless to plead, there's rage. When it was hopeless to rage, Rafael stood staring at the mattress he no longer could lie on. The silhouette of her body was visible, shaped by the pointillist spray around it, like the impression of a body chalked on a sidewalk by police. He lugged the mattress to the bathtub, squirted it with lighter fluid, watched the flames ignite and wither. When the bathroom filled with smoke, he turned on the water taps, and sat beside the airshaft window.

He wasn't going to sleep anyway, so why not stuff some clothes in the backpack with his paints and, from the can of bandages, take the skinny tube of dope-deal dollars and, checking that the street is empty, walk off? The extension lamp of a mechanic working on the Ferris wheel to the wheeze of an accordion illuminates the street behind. The street ahead is unlit as if there were a power outage. It must be that the strobing vigil light in St Ann's has guttered out. Still, within the darkened sanctuary, the resident saints and angels continue their supplications. *One must not think that a person who is suffering is not praying. Oh, how everything that is suffered with love is healed again.*

Wait alone on the L platform for an empty night train, the kind of train that clatters through sleep, a train boarded by nightmares and dreams masked like *luchadores*, indistinguishable from one another in their babushkas, fedoras, respirators, and dark glasses. When it reaches the end of the line it won't stop. It goes by I'm Sorry Street, by Forgive Me Avenue, by Fucked Up Again Boulevard. By the time it passes What Have I Done, it's traveling too fast. Maybe this once it will hurtle by fate and you'll be free. And then what? Rafael might have boarded that train, if he could have thought of where to get off.

Listen, the telephone, driven mad with rejection, doesn't even want to be answered any longer. It is like an alarm that, rather than a warning, wishes to be the thing it's warning against – a break-in or a fire burning out of control. The caller's ring is like an ambulance siren that wants to be the accident itself – a head-on collision or a hit-and-run, a mugging, a drive-by.

The women on the wall with their hacked faces and staved-in bodies hear it ring but don't answer. Maybe they are calling themselves. Cindy locked for the night in the laundromat, too weak with internal bleeding to speak, or her lost daughter, Jade, calling Rafael's number in the hope that her stepmother might answer, or Brianna, OD'd on pills, calling to say *adiós* through the plastic bag she's pulled over her head, or Rafael's old *tia*, who holds the receiver to the radio so for once in his life he can hear Pavarotti hit that high C in *Turandot*, or his mother calling to say that his half brother, Gabriel, was stillborn, or his father calling from Hanoi; nuns, priests, teachers, cops, parole officers, social workers, the Devil's Disciples, Darrell, all in a snaky line waiting before a gutted pay phone for their turn.

Now that it's gone on long enough to assume a life of its own, the call never wants to stop. It's too late for talk now anyway, and if someone, anyone, answered, suddenly picked up the receiver and said hello, there'd be no answer in return.

'Hello? Hello . . . who is this? Who the fuck are you? What

fucking business do you have calling and calling at this hour? Don't you get it: nobody's fucking home.'

Not even the breath of an obscene breather. Only silence.

'After all that fucking ringing, say something . . . anything . . . please, talk to me.'

Paper Lantern

We were working late on the time machine in the little make-shift lab upstairs. The moon was stuck like the whorl of a frozen fingerprint to the skylight. In the back alley, the breaths left behind by yowling toms converged into a fog slinking out along the streets. Try as we might, our measurements were repeatedly off. In one direction, we'd reached the border at which clair-voyants stand gazing into the future, and in the other we'd gone backward to the zone where the present turns ghostly with memory and yet resists quite becoming the past. We'd been advancing and retreating by smaller and smaller degrees until it had come to seem as if we were measuring the immeasurable. Of course, what we really needed was some new vocabulary of measurement. It was time for a break.

Down the broken escalator, out the blue-lit lobby past the shuttered newsstand, through the frosty fog, hungry as strays we walk, still wearing our lab coats, to the Chinese restaurant around the corner.

It's a restaurant that used to be a Chinese laundry. When customers would come for their freshly laundered bundles, the cooking – wafting from the owner's back kitchen through the warm haze of laundry steam – smelled so good that the customers began asking if they could buy something to eat as well. And so the restaurant was born. It was a carryout place at

73

first, but they've since wedged in a few tables. None of us can read Chinese, so we can't be sure, but since the proprietors never bothered to change the sign, presumably the Chinese characters still say it's a Chinese laundry. Anyway, that's how the people in the neighborhood refer to it – the Chinese Laundry, as in, 'Man, I had a sublime meal at the Chinese Laundry last night.' Although they haven't changed the sign, the proprietors have added a large red-ribbed paper lantern – their only nod to decor – that spreads its opaque glow across the steamy window.

We sit at one of the five Formica tables – our favorite, beside the window – and the waitress immediately brings the menu and tea. Really, in a way, this is the best part: the ruddy glow of the paper lantern like heat on our faces, the tiny enameled teacups warming our hands, the hot tea scalding our hunger, and the surprising, welcoming heft of the menu, hand-printed in Chinese characters, with what must be very approximate explanations in English of some of the dishes, also hand-printed, in the black ink of calligraphers. Each time we come here the menu has grown longer. Once a dish has been offered, it is never deleted, and now the menu is pages and pages long, so long that we'll never read through it all, never live long enough, perhaps, to sample all the food in just this one tucked-away neighborhood Chinese restaurant. The pages are unnumbered, and we can never remember where we left off reading the last time we were here. Was it the chrysanthemum pot, served traditionally in autumn when the flowers are in full bloom, or the almond jelly with lichees and loquats?

'A poet wrote this menu,' Tinker says between sips of tea.

'Yes, but if there's a poet in the house, then why doesn't this place have a real name – something like the Red Lantern – instead of merely being called the Chinese Laundry by default?'

the Professor replies, wiping the steam from his glasses with a paper napkin from the dispenser on the table.

'I sort of like the Chinese Laundry, myself. It's got a solid, working-class ring. Red Lantern is a cliché – precious chinoiserie,' Tinker argues.

They never agree.

'Say, you two, I thought we were here to devour aesthetics, not debate them.'

Here, there's nothing of heaven or earth that can't be consumed, nothing they haven't found a way to turn into a delicacy: pine-nut porridge, cassia-blossom buns, fish-fragrance-sauced pigeon, swallow's-nest soup (a soup indigenous to the shore of the South China Sea; nests of predigested seaweed from the beaks of swifts, the gelatinous material hardened to form a small, translucent cup). Sea-urchin roe, pickled jellyfish, tripe with ginger and peppercorns, five-fragrance grouper cheeks, cloud ears, spun-sugar apple, ginkgo nuts and golden needles (which are the buds of lilies), purple seaweed, bitter melon . . .

Nothing of heaven and earth that cannot be combined, transmuted; no borders, in a wok, that can't be crossed. It's instructive. One can't help nourishing the imagination as well as the body.

We order, knowing we won't finish all they'll bring, and that no matter how carefully we ponder our choices we'll be served instead whatever the cook has made today.

After supper, sharing segments of a blood orange and sipping tea, we ceremoniously crack open our fortune cookies and read aloud our fortunes as if consulting the *I Ching*.

'*Sorrow is born of excessive joy.*'

'Try another.'

'*Poverty is the common fate of scholars.*'

'Does that sound like a fortune to you?' Tinker asks.

'I certainly hope not,' the Professor says.

'*When a finger points to the moon, the imbecile looks at the finger.*'

'What kind of fortunes are these? These aren't fortune cookies, these are proverb cookies,' Tinker says.

'*In the Year of the Rat you will be lucky in love.*'

'Now, that's more like it.'

'What year is this?'

'The Year of the Dragon, according to the place mat.'

'*Fuel alone will not light a fire.*'

'Say, did anyone turn off the Bunsen burner when we left?' The mention of the lab makes us signal for the check. It's time we headed back. A new theory was brewing there when we left, and now, our enthusiasm rekindled, we return in the snow – it has begun to snow – through thick, crumbling flakes mixed with wafting cinders that would pass for snowflakes except for the way the wind is fanning their edges to sparks. A night of white flakes and streaming orange cinders, strange and beautiful, until we turn the corner and stare up at our laboratory.

Flames occupy the top floor of the building. Smoke billows out of the skylight, from which the sooty moon has retreated. On the floor below, through radiant, buckling windows, we can see the mannequins from the dressmaker's showroom. Naked, wigs on fire, they appear to gyrate lewdly before they topple. On the next floor down, in the instrument-repair shop, accordions wheeze in the smoke, violins seethe like green kindling, and the saxophones dissolve into a lava of molten brass cascading over a window ledge. While on the ground floor, in the display window, the animals in the taxidermist's shop have begun to hiss and snap as if fire had returned them to life in the wild.

We stare helplessly, still clutching the carryout containers of the food we were unable to finish from the blissfully innocent meal we sat sharing while our apparatus, our theories, our formulas, and years of research – all that people refer to as their 'work' – were bursting into flame. Along empty, echoing streets, sirens are screaming like victims.

Already a crowd has gathered.

'Look at that seedy old mother go up,' a white kid in dread-locks says to his girlfriend, who looks like a runaway waif. She answers, 'Cool!'

And I remember how, in what now seems another life, I watched fires as a kid – sometimes fires that a gang of us, calling ourselves the Matchheads, had set.

I remember how, later, in another time, if not another life, I once snapped a photograph of a woman I was with as she watched a fire blaze out of control along a river in Chicago. She was still married then. Her husband, whom I'd never met, was in a veterans' hospital – clinically depressed after the war in Vietnam. At least, that's what she told me about him. Thinking back, I sometimes wonder if she even had a husband. She had come to Chicago with me for a fling – her word. I thought at the time that we were just 'fooling around' – also her words, words we both used in place of others like 'fucking' or 'making love' or 'adultery.' It was more comfortable, and safer, for me to think of things between us as fooling around, but when I offhandedly mentioned that to her she became furious, and instead of fooling around we spent our weekend in Chicago arguing, and ended up having a terrible time. It was a Sunday afternoon in early autumn, probably in the Year of the Rat, and we were sullenly driving out of the city. Along the north branch of the river, a factory was burning. I pulled over and parked, dug a camera out of my duffel, and we walked to a bridge to watch the fire.

But it's not the fire itself that I remember, even though the blaze ultimately spread across the city sky like a dusk that rose from the earth rather than descended. The fire, as I recall it, is merely a backdrop compressed within the boundaries of the photograph I took of her. She has just looked away from the blaze, toward the camera. Her elbows lean against the peeling gray railing of the bridge. She's wearing the black silk blouse that she bought at a secondhand shop on Clark Street the day before. Looking for clothes from the past in secondhand stores was an obsession of hers – 'going junking,' she called it. A silver Navajo bracelet has slid up her arm over a black silk sleeve. How thin her wrists appear. There's a ring whose gem I know is a moonstone on the index finger of her left hand, and a tarnished silver band around her thumb. She was left-handed, and it pleased her that I was, too, as if we both belonged to the same minority group. Her long hair is a shade of auburn all the more intense for the angle of late afternoon sunlight. She doesn't look sullen or angry so much as fierce. Although later, studying her face in the photo, I'll come to see that beneath her expression there's a look less recognizable and more desperate: not loneliness, exactly, but *aloneness* – a look I'd seen cross her face more than once but wouldn't have thought to identify if the photo hadn't caught it. Behind her, ominous gray smoke plumes out of a sprawling old brick factory with the soon-to-be-scorched white lettering of GUTTMAN & CO. TANNERS visible along the side of the building.

Driving back to Iowa in the dark, I'll think that she's asleep, as exhausted as I am from our strained weekend; then she'll break the miles of silence between us to tell me that, disappointing though it was, the trip was worth it if only for the two of us on the bridge, watching the fire together. She loved being part of the excitement, she'll say, loved the spontaneous way we swerved over and parked in order to take advantage of the spectacle – a conflagration the length of a city block, reflected over the greasy water, and a red fireboat, neat as a toy, sirening up the river, spouting white geysers while the flames roared back.

Interstate 80 shoots before us in the length of our racing headlight beams. We're on a stretch between towns, surrounded by flat black fields, and the candlepower of the occasional distant farmhouse is insufficient to illuminate the enormous horizon lurking in the dark like the drop-off at the edge of the planet. In the speeding car, her voice sounds disembodied, the voice of a shadow, barely above a whisper, yet it's clear, as if the cover of night and the hypnotic momentum of the road have freed her to reveal secrets. There seemed to be so many secrets about her.

She tells me that as the number of strangers attracted by the fire swelled into a crowd she could feel a secret current connecting the two of us, like the current that passed between us in bed the first time we made love, when we came at the same moment as if taken by surprise. It happened only that once.

'Do you remember how, after that, I cried?' she asks.

'Yes.'

'You were trying to console me. I know you thought I was feeling terribly guilty, but I was crying because the way we fit together seemed suddenly so familiar, as if there were some old bond between us. I felt flooded with relief, as if I'd been missing you for a long time without quite realizing it, as if you'd returned to me after I thought I'd never see you again. I didn't say any of that, because it sounds like some kind of channeling crap. Anyway, today the same feeling came over me on the bridge, and I was afraid I might start crying again, except this time what would be making me cry was the thought that if we *were* lovers from past lives who had waited lifetimes for the present to bring us back together, then how sad it was to waste the present the way we did this weekend.'

I keep my eyes on the road, not daring to glance at her, or even to answer, for fear of interrupting the intimate, almost compulsive way she seems to be speaking.

'I had this sudden awareness,' she continues, 'of how the moments of our lives go out of existence before we're conscious of having lived them. It's only a relatively few moments that we get to keep and carry with us for the rest of our lives. Those moments *are* our lives. Or maybe it's more like those moments are the dots and what we call our lives are the lines we draw between them, connecting them into imaginary pictures of ourselves. You know? Like those mythical pictures of constellations traced between stars. I remember how, as a kid, I actually expected to be able to look up and see Pegasus spread out against the night, and when I couldn't it seemed like a trick had been played on me, like a fraud. I thought, *Hey, if this is all there is to it, then I could reconnect the stars in any shape I wanted. I could create the Ken and Barbie constellations* . . . I'm rambling . . .'

'I'm following you, go on.'

She moves closer to me.

'I realized we can never predict when those few, special moments will occur,' she says. 'How, if we hadn't met, I wouldn't be standing on a bridge watching a fire, and how there are certain people, not that many, who enter one's life with the power to make those moments happen. Maybe that's what falling in love means – the power to create for each other the moments by which we define ourselves. And there you were, right on cue, taking my picture. I had an impulse to open my blouse, to take off my clothes and pose naked for you. I wanted you. I wanted – not to "fool around." I wanted to fuck you like there's no tomorrow against the railing of the bridge. I've been thinking about that ever since, this whole drive back.'

I turn to look at her, but she says, 'No . . . don't look . . . Keep driving . . . Shhh, don't talk . . . I'm sealing your lips.'

I can hear the rustle beside me as she raises her skirt, and a faint smack of moistness, and then, kneeling on the seat, she extends her hand and outlines my lips with her slick fingertips.

I can smell her scent; the car seems filled with it. I can feel the heat of her body radiating beside me, before she slides back along the seat until she's braced against the car door. I can hear each slight adjustment of her body, the rustle of fabric against her skin, the elastic sound of her panties rolled past her hips, the faintly wet, possibly imaginary tick her fingertips are making. 'Oh, baby,' she sighs. I've slowed down to fifty-five, and as semis pull into the passing lane and rumble by us, their headlights sweep through the car and I catch glimpses of her as if she'd been imprinted by lightning on my peripheral vision – disheveled, her skirt hiked over her slender legs, the fingers of her left hand disappearing into the V of her rolled-down underpants.

'You can watch, if you promise to keep one eye on the road,' she says, and turns on the radio as if flicking on a night-light that coats her bare legs with its viridescence.

What was playing? The volume was so low I barely heard. A violin from some improperly tuned-in university station, fading in and out until it disappeared into static – banished, perhaps, to those phantom frequencies where Bix Beiderbecke still blew on his cornet. We were almost to Davenport, on the river, the town where Beiderbecke was born, and one station or another there always seemed to be playing his music, as if the syncopated licks of Roaring Twenties jazz, which had burned Bix up so quickly, still resonated over the prairie like his ghost.

'You can't cross I-80 between Iowa and Illinois without going through the Beiderbecke Belt,' I had told her when we picked up a station broadcasting a Bix tribute on our way into Chicago. She had never heard of Bix until then and wasn't paying him much attention until the DJ quoted a remark by Eddie Condon, an old Chicago guitarist, that 'Bix's sound came out like a girl saying yes.' That was only three days ago, and now we are returning, somehow changed from that couple who set out for a fling.

We cross the Beiderbecke Belt back into Iowa, and as we drive past the Davenport exits the nearly deserted highway is illumin-ated like an empty ballpark by the bluish overhead lights. Her eyes closed with concentration, she hardly notices as a semi, outlined in red clearance lights, almost sideswipes us. The car shudders in the backdraft as the truck pulls away, its horn bellowing.

'One eye on the road,' she cautions.

'That wasn't my fault.'

We watch its taillights disappear, and then we're alone in the highway dark again, traveling along my favorite stretch, where, in the summer, the fields are planted with sunflowers as well as corn, and you have to be on the alert for pheasants bolting across the road.

'Baby, take it out,' she whispers.

The desire to touch her is growing unbearable, and yet I don't want to stop – don't want the drive to end.

'I'm waiting for you,' she says. 'I'm right on the edge just waiting for you.'

We're barely doing forty when we pass what looks like the same semi, trimmed in red clearance lights, parked along the shoulder. I'm watching her while trying to keep an eye on the road, so I don't notice the truck pulling back onto the highway behind us or its headlights in the rearview mirror, gaining on us fast, until its high beams flash on, streaming through the car with a near-blinding intensity. I steady the wheel, waiting for the whump of the trailer's vacuum as it hurtles by, but the truck stays right on our rear bumper, its enormous radiator grille looming through the rear window, and its headlights reflecting off our mirrors and windshield with a glare that makes us squint. Caught in the high beams, her hair flares like a halo about to burst into flame. She's brushed her skirt down over her legs and looks a little wild.

'What's his problem? Is he stoned on uppers or something?' she shouts over the rumble of his engine, and then he hits his horn, obliterating her voice with a diesel blast.

I stomp on the gas. We're in the right lane, and, since he refuses to pass, I signal and pull into the outside lane to let him go by, but he merely switches lanes, too, hanging on our tail the entire time. The speedometer jitters over ninety, but he stays right behind us, his high beams pinning us like spotlights, his horn bellowing.

'Is he crazy?' she shouts.

I know what's happening. After he came close to sideswiping us outside Davenport, he must have gone on driving down the empty highway with the image of her illuminated by those bluish lights preying on his mind. Maybe he's divorced and lonely, maybe his wife is cheating on him – something's gone terribly wrong for him, and, whatever it is, seeing her exposed like that has revealed his own life as a sorry thing, and that realization has turned to meanness and anger.

There's an exit a mile off, and he sees it, too, and swings his rig back to the inside lane to try and cut me off, but with the pedal to the floor I beat him to the right-hand lane, and I keep it floored, although I know I can't manage a turnoff at this speed. He knows that, too, and stays close behind, ignoring my right-turn signal, laying on his horn as if to warn me not to try slowing down for this exit, that there's no way of stopping sixty thousand pounds of tractor-trailer doing over ninety.

But just before we hit the exit I swerve back into the outside lane, and for a moment he pulls even with us, staying on the inside as we race past the exit so as to keep it blocked. That's when I yell to her, 'Hang on!' and pump the brakes, and we screech along the outside lane, fishtailing and burning rubber, while the truck goes barreling by, its air brakes whooshing. The car skids onto the gravel shoulder, kicking up a cloud of dust, smoky in the headlights, but it's never really out of control, and by the time the semi lurches to a stop, I have the car in reverse, veering back to the exit, hoping no one else is speeding toward us down I-80.

It's the Plainview exit, and I gun into a turn, north onto an empty two-lane, racing toward someplace named Long Grove. I keep checking the mirror for his headlights, but the highway behind us stays dark, and finally she says, 'Baby, slow down.'

The radio is still playing static, and I turn it off.

'Christ!' she says. 'At first I thought he was just your everyday flaming asshole, but he was a genuine psychopath.'

'A real lunatic, all right,' I agree.

'You think he was just waiting there for us in his truck?' she asks. 'That's so spooky, especially when you think he's still out there driving west. It makes you wonder how many other guys are out there, driving with their heads full of craziness and rage.'

It's a vision of the road at night that I can almost see: men, not necessarily vicious – some just numb or desperately lonely – driving to the whining companionship of country music, their headlights too scattered and isolated for anyone to realize that they're all part of a convoy. We're a part of it, too.

'I was thinking, *Oh, no, I can't die now, like this*,' she says. 'It would be too sexually frustrating – like death was the ultimate tease.'

'You know what I was afraid of,' I tell her. 'Dying with my trousers open.'

She laughs and continues laughing until there's a hysterical edge to it.

'I think that truck driver was jealous of you. He knows you're a lucky guy tonight,' she gasps, winded, and kicks off her sandal in order to slide a bare foot along my leg. 'Here we are together, still alive.'

I bring her foot to my mouth and kiss it, clasping her leg where it's thinnest, as if my hand were an ankle bracelet, then slide my hand beneath her skirt, along her thigh to the edge of her panties, a crease of surprising heat, from which my finger comes away slick.

'I told you,' she moans. 'A lucky guy.'

I turn onto the next country road. It's unmarked, not that it matters. I know that out here, sooner or later, it will cross a gravel road, and when it does I turn onto the gravel, and after a while turn again at the intersection of a dirt road that winds into fields of an increasingly deeper darkness, fragrant with the rich Iowa earth and resonating with insect choirs amassed for one last Sanctus. I'm not even sure what direction we're traveling in any longer, let alone where we're going, but when my high beams catch a big turtle crossing the road I feel we've arrived. The car rolls to a stop on a narrow plank bridge spanning a culvert. The bridge – not much longer than our car – is veiled on either side by overhanging trees, cotton-woods, probably, and flanked by cattails as high as the drying stalks of corn in the acres we've been passing. The turtle, his snapper's jaw unmistakable in the lights, looks mossy and ancient, and we watch him complete his trek across the road and disappear into the reeds before I flick off the headlights. Sitting silently in the dark, we listen to the crinkle of the cooling engine, and to the peepers we've disturbed starting up again from beneath the bridge. When we quietly step out of the car, we can hear frogs plopping into the water. 'Look at the stars,' she whispers.

'If Pegasus was up there,' I say, 'you'd see him from here.'

'Do you have any idea where we are?' she asks.

'Nope. Totally lost. We can find our way back when it's light.'

'The backseat of a car at night, on a country road – adultery has a disconcerting way of turning adults back into teenagers.'

We make love, then manage to doze off for a while in the backseat, wrapped together in a checkered tablecloth we'd used once on a picnic, which I still had folded in the trunk.

In the pale early light I shoot the rest of the film on the roll: a close-up of her, framed in part by the line of the checkered tablecloth, which she's wearing like a shawl around her bare shoulders, and another, closer still, of her face framed by her

86

tangled auburn hair, and out the open window behind her, velvety cattails blurred in the shallow depth of field. A picture of her posing naked outside the car in sunlight that streams through countless rents in the veil of the cottonwoods. A picture of her kneeling on the muddy planks of the little bridge, her hazel eyes glancing up at the camera, her mouth, still a yard from my body, already shaped as if I've stepped to her across that distance.

What's missing is the shot I never snapped – the one the trucker tried to steal, which drove him over whatever edge he was balanced on, and which, perhaps, still has him riding highways, searching each passing car from the perch of his cab for that glimpse he won't get again – her hair disheveled, her body braced against the car door, eyes squeezed closed, lips twisted, skirt hiked up, pelvis rising to her hand.

Years after, she called me out of nowhere. 'Do you still have those photos of me?' she asked.

'No,' I told her, 'I burned them.'

'Good,' she said, sounding pleased – not relieved so much as flattered – 'I just suddenly wondered.' Then she hung up.

But I lied. I'd kept them all these years, along with a few letters – part of a bundle of personal papers in a manila envelope that I moved with me from place to place. I had them hidden away in the back of a file cabinet in the laboratory, although certainly they had no business being there. Now what I'd told her was true: they were fueling the flames.

Outlined in firelight, the kid in dreadlocks kisses the waif. His hand glides over the back of her fringed jacket of dirty white buckskin and settles on the torn seat of her faded jeans. She stands on tiptoe on the tops of his gym shoes and hooks her fingers through the empty belt loops of his jeans so that their crotches are aligned. When he boosts her closer and grinds against her she says, 'Wow!' and giggles. 'I felt it move.'

'Fires get me horny,' he says.

The roof around the skylight implodes, sending a funnel of sparks into the whirl of snow, and the crowd *ahs* collectively as the beakers in the laboratory pop and flare.

Gapers have continued to arrive down side streets, appearing out of the snowfall as if drawn by a great bonfire signaling some secret rite: gangbangers in their jackets engraved with symbols, gorgeous transvestites from Wharf Street, stevedores, and young sailors, their fresh tattoos contracting in the cold. The homeless, layered in overcoats, burlap tied around their feet, have abandoned their burning ash cans in order to gather here, just as the shivering, scantily clad hookers have abandoned their neon corners; as the Guatemalan dishwashers have abandoned their scalding suds; as a baker, his face and hair the ghostly white of flour, has abandoned his oven.

Open hydrants gush into the gutters; the street is seamed with deflated hoses, but the firemen stand as if paired off with the hookers – as if for a moment they've become voyeurs like everyone else, transfixed as the brick walls of our lab blaze suddenly lucent, suspended on a cushion of smoke, and the red-hot skeleton of the time machine begins to radiate from the inside out. A rosy light plays off the upturned faces of the crowd like the glow of an enormous red lantern – a paper lantern that once seemed fragile, almost delicate, but now obliterates the very time and space it once illuminated. A paper lantern raging out of control with nothing but itself left to consume.

'*Brrrr.*' The Professor shivers, wiping his fogged glasses as if to clear away the opaque gleam reflecting off their lenses.

'Goddamn cold, all right,' Tinker mutters, stamping his feet. For once they agree.

The wind gusts, fanning the bitter chill of night even as it fans the flames, and instinctively we all edge closer to the fire.

Ecstatic Cahoots

The Start of Something

Subway grates, steaming tamale carts, charcoal braziers roasting chestnuts, the breaths of the pedestrians outpacing stalled traffic, the chimneys Gil can't see from the window of the airline bus – all plume in the frigid air. It's cold enough for Gil to wear, for the first and only time, the salt-and-pepper woolen trousers he bought at an estate sale last summer. He'd stopped on a whim when he saw the sale sign, an excuse to tour a mansion that looked as if it once could have belonged to *The Great Gatsby*'s Tom Buchanan before he'd moved from Chicago's North Shore to Long Island 'in a fashion,' Fitzgerald wrote, 'that rather took your breath away . . . he'd brought down a string of polo ponies from Lake Forest.' Perhaps the deceased had left only debts, for the heirs, haughty with grief, were selling off the furnishings. Those there to buy spoke in subdued voices as if to seem less like scavengers. Gil browsed the sunlit rooms with no intention of buying anything, then in an upstairs bedroom he found an open cedar wardrobe filled with old, handsomely made men's clothes. He selected the trousers and held them up before a walnut-framed full-length mirror, and told himself he might wear them for cross-country skiing even though he hadn't skied in years. Later, when he tried them on at home, they fit as though they'd been made for him, causing Gil to wonder who the man who'd worn them had been. In one of the pockets there was an Italian coin dated 1921, and Gil thought it might be worth something to a collector. He kept it in a cuff-link box with spare buttons, a St Christopher medal, a class ring, and cuff links he never wore. Even after he'd had the trousers dry-cleaned they smelled faintly of cedar.

The airline bus has nearly reached downtown when the woman in the seat across the aisle leans toward Gil and asks, 'Are those lined?'

'Pardon?' he says.

'Are those lined? They're beautiful but they look itchy.' Wings of dark glossy hair and a darker fur collar frame her narrow face. Her smile appears too broad for her, but attractive all the same.

'Partially,' he says.

'Knee-length?'

'Not quite. Actually, they are a little itchy, but they're warm.'

'They look right out of the Jazz Age. They've got that drape. I love anything from the twenties – music, furniture, the writers.'

'Some of my favorite writers, all right,' Gil says.

'They still read so alive! Like that newly liberated, modern world was just yesterday.'

It sounds like she's speaking in quotes and Gil smiles as if to agree. Her hairstyle and the coat she's bundled in both suggest another time. The coat has a certain Goodwill-rack look that exempts a woman from the stigma of wearing fur. Gil has no idea what kind of fur it is. It matches the luster of her hair. He has the vague feeling they've met before, which makes talking to her effortless, but Gil doesn't say so for fear it would sound like a line. She'd know a man would remember meeting someone who looked like her.

'Where'd you find them?' she asks.

'At a kind of glorified garage sale.'

'I didn't think they were new. When designers try to bring back a style they never quite get it right.'

'They're the real deal all right, complete with little buttons for suspenders. I probably should be wearing suspenders.'

'Not even half lined, though, huh? Bet it feels good to get them off.' She smiles again as if surprised by what she has just said.

'You sure have an eye for clothes,' Gil says.

'Don't I, though?'

Outside, snow settles on Chicago like a veil, as if it is the same veil of snow that was floating to earth earlier in the day when he boarded the plane in Minneapolis, returning from his father's funeral. The airline bus has stalled again in traffic. She's turned away, staring out the window. He doesn't know her name, has yet to ask where she's traveling from, if she lives in the city or is only visiting, let alone the facts of her personal life, but all the questions are already in motion between them.

Why not end here, without answers?

Aren't there chance meetings in every life that don't play out, stories that seem meant to remain ghostly, as faint and fleeting as the reflection of a face on the window of a bus? Beyond her face, snow swirls through steam from exhausts and manholes. Why not for this one time let beginning suffice, rather than insist on what's to come: the trip they'll take, before they know enough about each other, to Italy; those scenes in her apartment when she'll model her finds from vintage stores, fashions from the past he'll strip from her present body? Her name is Bea. She'll say they were fated to meet. They'll play at being reincarnated lovers from the First World War. Sometimes he's a soldier who died in the trenches, sometimes a young trumpet player poisoned by bathtub gin. Scene added to scene, fabrication to fabrication, until a year has passed and for a last time he visits her apartment in the Art Deco building on Dearborn with its curved, glowing glass brick windows. There's an out-of-place store on the ground floor that sells trophies – an inordinate number of them for bowling. Its burglar alarm, prone to going off after hours, as if the defeated have come by night to steal the prizes they can never win, is clanging again. She's been doing coke and tells him that in a dream she realized she's been left with two choices, one of which is to kill him. She laughs too gaily when she says it and he doesn't ask what the other choice is. She's mentioned that she's been 'in touch' with her ex-boyfriend – a man who over nine years, with time-outs for affairs, has come and gone at will in her life, a relationship it took her a while to reveal fully because, she explained, she didn't want to give the impression she has a taste for 'damaged men.' If she's implying it's a relationship that redefines her, she has a point.

'Does he know about me?' Gil asked.

'I'd *never* tell him you exist,' she said, her eyes suddenly anxious and her voice dropping to a whisper as if an omnipotent master might overhear.

'In touch' means Gil has noticed bruises when he hikes her skirt to kiss the curve of her bottom. She'll have asked for them, he knows, she'll have begged, 'Leave your mark.' The boyfriend is an importer, she says. He's a connected guy whose family owns a chain of pizza parlors. He carries a gun, which she says makes her feel safe, though what she really means is that she finds it thrilling, and when she disappears into her bedroom Gil isn't sure whether she'll emerge armed or wearing a chemise from the thirties that she's found at some flea market. No matter how often he strips the past from her body, she finds a way to wear it again. His impulse is to let himself out, but he doesn't want her – and for that matter, doesn't want himself – to be

96

left with a final image of him running for his life. An escape might make it seem as if the choice in her dream were justified. He doesn't want to admit she's made him afraid, and so he sits and waits for her to reappear.

The heirs were selling off the furnishings. Gil browsed the sunlit rooms with no intention of buying anything, but in an upstairs bedroom he found an open wardrobe smelling of cedar. He held the trousers up before a full-length mirror that like everything else in the house wore a price, everything except the clothes – for those he'd have to bargain. His reflection, gazing back, fogged behind layers of dust, appeared ghostly. The trousers looked as if with a little tailoring they'd fit, and maybe he could wear them for cross-country skiing. How could he have known then that he was only at the start of something?

Córdoba

While we were kissing, the leather-bound *Obras completas* opened to a photo of Federico García Lorca with a mole prominent beside a sideburn of his slicked-back hair, slid from her lap to the jade silk couch, and hit the Chinese carpet with a muffled thud.

While we were kissing, the winter wind known locally as the Hawk soared off the lake on vast wings of snow.

While we were kissing, verbs went uncommitted to memory.

Her tongue rolled *r*'s against mine, but couldn't save me from failing Spanish. We were kissing, but her beloved Federico, to whom she'd introduced me on the night we'd first met, was not forgotten. *Verde que te quiero verde. Green I want you green. Verde viento, verdes ramas. Green wind, green branches.* Hissing radiator heat. Our breaths elemental, beyond translation like the shrill of the Hawk outside her sweated, third-story windows. *Córdoba. Lejana y sola*, she translated between kisses, *Córdoba. Far away and alone.* With our heads full of poetry, the drunken, murderous Guardias Civiles were all but knocking at the door.

> *Aunque sepa los caminos*
> *yo nunca llegaré a Córdoba.*
> *Though I know the roads*
> *I will never reach Córdoba.*

Shaking off cold, her stepfather, Ray Ramirez, came home from his late shift as manager of the Hotel Lincoln. He didn't disturb us other than to announce from the front hall: 'Hana, tell David, it's a blizzard out there! He better go while there's still buses!'

'It's a blizzard out there,' Hana told me.

It was then we noticed the white roses in a green vase that her mother, who resembled Lana Turner, and who didn't much like me, must have set there while we were kissing. We hadn't been aware of her bringing them in. Hana and I looked at each other: she was still flushed, our clothes were disheveled. We hadn't merely been kissing. She shrugged and buttoned her blouse. *Verte desnuda es comprender el ansia de la lluvia. To see you naked is to comprehend the desire of rain.* I picked her volume of Lorca from the floor and set it beside the vase of flowers, and slipped back into the loafers I'd removed to curl up on the jade couch.

'I better go.'

'It's really snowing. God! Listen to that wind! Do you have a hat? Gloves? All you have is that jacket.'

'I'll be fine.'

'Please, at least take this scarf. For me. So I won't worry.'

'It smells like you.'

'It smells like Anias.'

At the door we kissed goodbye as if I were leaving on a journey.

'Are you sure you're going to be all right?'

Hana followed me into the hallway. We stopped on each stair down to the second-floor landing to kiss goodbye. She snuggled into my leather jacket. The light on the second-floor landing was out.

'Good luck on your Spanish test. Phone me, so I know you

got home safe, I'll be awake thinking of you,' she called down to me.

'*Though I know the roads I will never reach Córdoba.*'

'Just so you reach Rogers Park.'

I stepped from her doorway onto Buena. It pleased me – amazed me, actually – that Hana should live on the only street in Chicago, at least the only street I knew of, with a Spanish name. Her apartment building was three doors from Marine Drive. That fall, when we first began seeing each other, I would take the time to walk up Marine Drive on my way home. I'd discovered a viaduct tunnel unmarked by graffiti that led to a flagstone grotto surrounding a concrete drinking fountain with four spouts. Its icy water tasted faintly metallic, of rust or moonlight, and at night the burble of the fountain transformed the place into a Zen garden. Beyond the grotto and a park, the headlights on Lake Shore Drive festooned the autumn trees. For a moment, I thought of going to hear the fountain purling under the snow, but the Hawk raked my face and the frosted trees quavered. *Green branches, green wind.* I raised the collar of my jacket and wrapped her green chenille scarf around my throat. Even in the numbing wind I could smell perfume.

By the time I slogged the four blocks to Broadway, it wasn't Lorca but a line by Emily Dickinson that expressed the night: *zero at the bone.* No matter which direction I turned, the swirling wind was in my face. My loafers felt packed with snow. Broadway was deserted. I cowered in the dark doorway of a dry cleaner's, peeking out now and again and stamping my feet. The snow-plastered bus stop sign hummed in the gusts, but there wasn't a bus visible in either direction. A cab went by and, though I wasn't sure I could make the fare, I tried to flag it down. It didn't stop. The snow had drifted deep enough so that the cabbie wouldn't risk losing momentum. Finally, to warm up, I crossed the street to a corner bar called the Buena Chimes. Its blue neon sign looked so faint I doubted the place was open. If it was, I expected it to be empty, which I hoped would allow the bartender to take pity on me. I was twenty, a year shy of legal drinking age.

The cramped, low-lit space was packed, or so it first appeared. Though only three men sat at the bar, they were so massive they seemed to fill the room. Their conversation stopped when I came in. I'd heard the rumor that players for the Chicago Bears sometimes drank there but hadn't believed it, probably because I'd heard it from Hana's stepfather, Ray, who'd also told me that as a cliff diver in Acapulco he once collided with a tiger shark, whose body now hung in the lobby of the Grand Mayan Hotel. With all of Rush Street waiting to toast them, why would Bears drink at a dump like the Buena Chimes?

I undid the green scarf that I'd tied around my head babushka-style, and edged onto a stool by the door – as respectful a distance as possible from their disrupted conversation, but it wasn't far enough.

'Sorry, kid, private party,' the bartender said.

'Any idea if the buses are running?' I asked.

'We're closed.' He seemed morose. So did the Bears at the bar, who sat in silence as if what they had to say was too confidential to be uttered in the presence of a stranger. The team was having a losing season.

'Buy the kid a shot,' one of the Bears said.

'Whatever you say, Jimbo,' the bartender replied. He set a shot glass before me and, staring into my face rather than at the glass, filled it perfectly to the brim. Each man has his own way to show he's nobody's fool, and pouring shots without looking at the glass was the bartender's: he knew I was underage.

'Hit me, too, Sambo,' Jimbo said, and when the bartender filled his glass, the tackle or linebacker or whatever Jimbo was raised the teeny shot glass in my direction. 'This'll warm you up. Don't say I never bought you nothing,' he said, and we threw back our whiskeys.

'Much thanks,' I said.

'Now get your puny ass out of here,' Jimbo told me.

Back outside, I hooded my head in the green scarf and watched a snowplow with whirling emergency lights scuff by and disappear up Broadway. Waiting was futile. I decided to walk to the L station on Wilson. Rather than wade the drifted sidewalks, I followed the ruts the snowplow left in the street. I trudged head down, not bothering to check for traffic until I heard a horn behind me. Headlights burrowed through the blizzard. The beams appeared to be shooting confetti. The car – a Lincoln, maybe – sported an enormous, toothy grille. Whatever its make, the style was what in my old neighborhood was called a pimp-mobile. I stepped from the ruts to give it room to pass. It slowed to a stop. A steamed window slid down.

'Need a ride, hombre?'

I got in, my lips too frozen for more than a 'thanks.' The rear wheels spun. I sat shivering, afraid I'd have to leave the blast of the heater in order to push that big-ass boat out of the snow.

'You can do it, baby,' the driver said as if urging a burro. I was tempted to caution that giving it gas would only dig us in deeper, but knew to keep such opinions to myself. 'Come on, baby!' He ripped the floor shift into reverse, slammed it back into drive, back into reverse, and into drive again. 'Go, go, you got it,' and as if it were listening, the car rocked forward, grabbed, and kept rolling.

'Thought for a second we were stuck,' I said.

'No way, my friend, and hey, you're here to push, but not to worry, there's no stopping Lino tonight.'

I unwound the scarf from my head and massaged my frozen nose and ears.

'Yo, man, you wearing perfume?' he asked.

'It's the scarf,' I said.

'You in that scarf, man! When I saw you in the street, I thought some poor broad was out alone, you know? I told myself, Lino, the world is full of babes tonight. Where you headed, my friend?'

'Rogers Park,' I said. 'Just off Sheridan.' I couldn't stop shivering.

'Man, you'd a had a tough time getting there. Whole city's shut down. What you doing out so late? Getting a little, dare I ask?' He smiled conspiratorially. His upturned mustache attached to his prominent nose moved independently of his smile.

'Drinking. With the Bears,' I said.

'You mean like the football Bears?'

'Yeah, Jimbo and the guys.'

'Over at the Buena Chimes, man?'

'How'd you know?'

'Everybody knows they drink there. You got the shakes, man? Lino got the cure – pop the glove compartment.'

I pressed the button and the glove compartment flopped open. An initialed silver flask rested on a ratty-looking street map. Beneath the map I could see the waffled gray handle of a small-caliber gun. I closed the glove compartment, and we passed the flask between us in silence.

'What are we drinking?' I asked. It had an oily licorice taste with the kick of grain alcohol – not what I expected.

'We're drinking to a night that's going to be a goddamn legend, hombre. The kind of night that changes your life.' He took a swig for emphasis, then passed the flask to me. 'To our lucky night – hey, I'm spreading the luck around, right? – your luck I picked you up, mine cause I got picked up.'

'Huh?' I wasn't sure I liked the sound of that, and held off on taking my swig.

'Check this out.' He fished into his shirt pocket, handed me a folded scrap of paper, and flicked on the overhead interior light.

The paper unfolded into a lipsticked impression of a kiss, a phone number inscribed in what looked like eyebrow pencil, and the words, *Call me tonight. Tonight* underlined.

'You ever seen a woman so hot you didn't want to stare but couldn't take your eyes off her? I don't mean some bimbo at a singles bar. I'm in the Seasons and I see this almost-blond in a tight green dress. She's drinking with this guy and don't look happy. He leans over and whispers something in her ear, and whatever he said, it's like, you know, an eye-roller. She turns away from him and as she's rolling her eyes to no one in particular she catches me staring. She got these beautiful eyes. And I roll my eyes, too, and just for a sec she smiles, then goes back to her drink. Doesn't look at me again, but five minutes later she gets up to go to the ladies', and when she does I see that green dress has a plunging back. Sexiest dress I ever seen. She walks right by my table, and on her way back she drops the note.'

He reached for the flask, took a hit, and flicked out the interior light. Blowing snow reflected opaque in the headlights; it was hard to see ahead. He flicked the headlights off, too. 'Better without them,' he said. 'Ain't no oncoming traffic to worry about.'

We'd driven blocks, passed the L station on Wilson, and the little Asia Town on Argyle, ignored all the traffic signals on Broadway to keep our momentum, and hadn't seen another car. We were approaching Sheridan Road. I was finally warmed up, though my feet were still numb. He took another swallow – he was drinking two to my one – and passed the flask. It was noticeably lighter.

'You believe in love at first sight, man? Romantic crap, right? An excuse some people need to get laid. I'm thirty-four years old and that's what I always thought, but now I don't know. Or it's more like I *do* know. I know what's going to happen like it already happened. This snowstorm, the whole city shut down, you know, like destiny, man, destiny in a green dress.'

'*Verde que te quiero verde*,' I said.

'Say what?'

'Lines from a poem.'

'My mind keeps going over how she rolled her eyes.' He rolled his droopy eyes to demonstrate. 'And suddenly across the room we're staring at each other like strangers in the night, you know, that old Sinatra song, and from that moment it's like *do be do be do . . .*'

I'd wondered why he stopped to give me a ride – out of kindness or because he'd mistaken me for a woman alone, or to have someone along who could push, in case we got stuck. I recalled a Chekhov story from a Lit class called 'Grief,' about a horse-cab driver who on a freezing Moscow night tries to tell his story to every passenger he picks up, but rather than listen, each person tells him his own story instead. Finally, near dawn, as he unharnesses his pony, the cabdriver tells the story he's been trying all night to tell – that his little daughter has just died – to his pony. Lino was driving with a story to tell, not about grief or love or even male vanity. It was about luck, and he needed someone to hear it.

'What you going to do?' I asked him.

'What am I going to do? I'm going to call her! She's hot, man. She's waiting. She wants me. It's a sin if a woman wants you and you don't go. You ever had anything like this happen to you? What would you do?'

'Probably worry about what to say for openers.'

'You could recite a poem. I got the perfect line, man. I'm going to ask her: What did that guy whisper to make you roll your eyes? See, that's what I meant about destiny. I already know what to say.'

'You know her answer?'

'Man, that's the fun part. I know she'll answer, but not what. I know we'll kiss, but not how she kisses, I know she'll give me some tit right off, but not what kind of nipples she has – some guys are tit-men, I'm a nipple-man – or what perfume she wears, or what her name is. I know she's probably home by now waiting for the call, but I won't know till she picks up that phone what her voice sounds like. Just one little scrap of paper, and a lifetime history of questions. You can't really tell nothing from her handwriting. Let me see that.'

'I gave it back to you,' I said.

'No, man, you didn't give it back.'

'Yes, I did. I handed it back when you turned the overhead light out, right before you flicked the headlights out. I handed it back to you blocks ago.'

'You didn't, man, you never gave it to me.'

'Check your pockets.'

He checked his shirt pocket and the pockets of his topcoat.

'I wouldn't have put it in my topcoat, man, you still got it. Empty your jacket pockets, *cabrón*.'

I did as he asked. There wasn't anything but white petals from one of the roses Hana must have slipped in a pocket. She did things like that.

'What you trying to pull, my friend? This is how you repay me for saving your ass from the cold? If you think that babe is going to be a slut for any jerk who calls her up you're crazy. You ain't ready for a woman like that.'

'I didn't take it, man.'

He braked hard and the car swerved and came to a stop in the middle of the street. He flicked the overhead light on. 'Get up, *cabrón*, maybe you're sitting on it.' I rose in my seat and so did he. It wasn't on the seats. 'Check the floor.' We looked on the smeary floor mats and felt under the seats. 'Check the bottom of your shoes.'

'It's got to be here,' I said.

'I'm going to ask you polite one more time, you going to give me that phone number?'

'I gave it to you. Why would I take it? I got my own girl. She insisted I wear her scarf.'

'I thought you said you were drinking with the Bears. More bullshit, huh? Listen carefully, *cabrón*. Last fucking time – a simple yes or no.'

His droopy brown eyes stared hard into my face. I said nothing. He unscrewed the flask and drained it. 'Excuse me, man, I want to put this back.' He reached past me, popped the glove compartment, and I was out of the car, running up Sheridan in the headlights he flicked on, bounding drifts, zigzagging along the sidewalk, hoping I'd be a harder target to hit. I could hear the tires whining behind me. He'd probably tried to give it gas and run me down and now the car was stuck. I could hear it grinding from a block away, and stopped to look back. He was trying to rock it from reverse back to drive, but just digging it in deeper. I actually thought of going back and saying, *Look, man, you were kind enough to give me a ride, would I have come back to push you out if I'd stolen your phone number?* It was a nice thought, but one that could get me killed. Instead, feeling light on my frozen feet despite the drifted sidewalks, I jogged four more blocks up Sheridan Road, checking at each corner to make sure he wasn't following me. The snow fell more slowly and the wind had let up some, but I could barely see his headlights five blocks back in the haze of snow when I turned onto my street.

In my studio apartment, I kicked off my loafers, stripped off my frozen socks, and, not bothering to remove my jacket, I sat in the dark on my one stuffed chair, clutching my soles in my palms and watching the snow gently float in the aura of the streetlight visible from my third-story window. The surge of lightness I'd felt running down Sheridan had left me shaky. *Zero at the bone.* Finally, I felt recovered enough to switch on the lamp and slip off my jacket. I'd promised to call Hana. She'd be asleep with the phone under the pillow beside her, so that its ring wouldn't wake anyone else. What time is it? she'd ask in a groggy voice, and I'd say getting on to one, and she'd say she worried about me getting home, and I'd tell her Córdoba was easy next to tonight. I'd thank her for the loan of her scarf. I'd have frozen without it.

It wasn't until I unwound it from around my neck that I noticed the scrap of paper caught in the chenille. I unfolded the note and there was the kiss and the phone number in eyebrow pencil.

I sat in the stuffed chair, my feet wedged under the cushion, dialed, and when the phone began to ring, I flicked the lamp off again and watched the snow. It rang several times, which didn't surprise me; I didn't expect anyone to answer. The surprise came as I was about to hang up, when someone lifted the receiver, but said nothing as if waiting for me to speak.

'I hope it's not too late to call?' I said.

'That all depends,' a woman's voice answered.

'On what?'

'On who you are and what you have in mind. Coming over?'

'I can't tonight. The city's shut down. My car's stuck in a snowdrift.'

'Then why did you bother to call?'

'I wanted to hear your voice. To see if you're real?'

'That's a strange thing to say. Are you real?'

'No,' I said, 'actually, I'm not.'

'At least you know that,' she said, 'which puts you ahead of the game. Most unreal men – which is the vast majority – don't know they aren't, and those few that do usually can't bear to admit it. So there's still a chance that hopefully some night years to come, you'll have a different answer. Good luck with that.' The phone clicked.

I listened to it buzz before hanging up. If I rang again, I knew she wouldn't answer. I sat with the soles of my feet in my hands, rubbing the warmth back into them, waiting to call Hana, thinking of all the years to come, still young enough to wonder who I'd be.

Ravenswood

The Nun rides the streetcar named Asylum to the end of the Asylum Lake line. There's no lake there, never was, but at least the buckled acres of parking lot becalmed before the abandoned shopping mall reflect the gliding shadows of circling gulls.

'End of the line, Sister,' announces the Conductor; his name tag reads *Martin*. Conductor Martin rises from his seat in order to crank another name, the return destination, onto the front of the streetcar.

'I'm not in the habit of doing this,' the Nun says from behind him. The Conductor hears the clack of the rosary beads girdled about her waist, and a rustle crackling with static electricity as she discards her woolly black robes, and as he turns still holding the crank, she knocks him silly with a blow from her missal.

When he regains consciousness the Conductor finds himself hanging from a hand strap toward the rear of the streetcar. The rosary binds his wrists. He's dressed – draped would be more accurate – in the Nun's black robes; her sensible shoes, untied, pinch his feet. At least she has pinned the *Martin* name tag from what was his conductor's uniform onto what is now his habit.

At the front of the streetcar, cranking a new destination, the Nun wears his uniform and conductor's hat. The blue jacket is too long for her arms; her breasts strain against the brass buttons. A shock of red hair tilts the hat at a rakish angle.

'When I was a child, I thought nuns must be bald,' Martin recalls, and speaks the thought aloud in hopes of making conversation. 'How wrong I was,' he adds in what he hopes is an ingratiating tone.

She looks so jaunty as she thumbs tokens from his coin changer in the sunlight streaming through the front windows that he can't be angry with her. Gulls caw and yipe excitedly as if out on Asylum Lake the smelt are rising. Sparrows gang on a single tree and make it twitter. He suddenly realizes that yes, it's peaceful, even beautiful here at the end of the line to be a conductor stacking tokens in the sunlight. She reminds him so much of himself that he wants to emulate her. From his new perspective of dangling like a sausage, a rush of the pathetic emotion that a victim sometimes feels toward an oppressor overwhelms him: the illusion that such brutal attention is misguided love. He finds it poignantly flattering that this strange, undoubtedly fervent, religious woman has been driven to take such risks and employ such desperate measures to subdue him. What made her snap? he wonders. How often must she have sat unnoticed yearning for his attention? How many times at vespers did his name obliterate in her heart the name of the Lord?

'*Te amo, te amo,*' he calls out to the Nun. It's as close as he can come to speaking Latin, a dead language that he hopes will sound sacred to her.

A miscalculation, for the Nun evidences little, if any, feeling for either dead languages or the Conductor – make that the ex-Conductor. Apparently, she has not confused him with the streetcar any more than a hijacker confuses the pilot with the airplane. Apparently, it is the streetcar itself she desires, that incredible conveyance with blue voltage sparking at the junctures of overhead cable, a vehicle part city, part dream.

Ding, ding. A blue spark crackles, electricity enough to depopulate Death Row jolts the rear wheels, and the streetcar embarks toward the destination she has chosen.

Swaying from the hand strap with his bound hands clasped as if in prayer, Sister Mary Martin can make out the lettering the Nun has cranked at the front of the streetcar, although, as it appears backward, he must decipher it letter by letter. D-O-O-W-S-N-E-V-A-R. Doowsnevar. R-A-V-E-N-S-W-O-O-D. That was never on his route! He's never heard of such a street or neighborhood before.

But then, he can't help wondering if he's experiencing partial amnesia from that concussion with the missal. The blocks the streetcar rattles down look only vaguely familiar, but perhaps that's because he's been displaced from his customary perspective gazing down rails of narrow-gauge track from the front of the car. Careening from the hand strap as the streetcar races between corner stops, he thinks the ride seems more herky-jerky than he remembers.

'Move to the rear!' the Nun yells over the hiss of pneumatic doors opening and slamming shut on the surprised faces of commuters who have not been given the chance to board.

In the rear, the ex-Conductor twirls from the hand strap, abstractly fingering his beads, feeling disoriented, forgotten, suffering like a martyr on the verge of a mystical experience.

'Je t'aime, je t'aime,' he whines.

No answer. Clearly, the Nun couldn't care less about Romance languages. Through the rear window, among the crowd of commuters that wildly pursue the streetcar, futilely grasping for the grillwork on the rear platform, he can see vaguely familiar faces. Isn't that flushed gentleman furiously waving a transfer in his fist as if bidding farewell Mr Hedmund, his old English teacher who used to warn him,

'Martin, you're a dreamer and when dreamers wake, sometimes they find themselves digging ditches or punching transfers on streetcars'? And that gimpy black man trying to hook the grille of the streetcar with his cane, isn't that Coach Bender, complete with his old football knee, who used to warn him, 'If you don't open your eyes and smell the coffee, Marty-boy, you're going to blindside yourself.' And that heavyset bleached blond who's just tripped over her purse and is now being trampled by the others running down the curving streetcar track – take away twenty years and forty pounds and she might have been the woman who used to sign her letters to him *the Girl of Your Dreams*, a name she later shortened to *GOYD*.

He can't recall GOYD's real name anymore, but the mere thought of her now in the context of his current situation leaves him no choice but to reevaluate his relationship with the Nun. Tears, unsuccessfully searching for tracks on his face, roll helter-skelter down his cheeks as he realizes that now, when he has finally discovered that love is surrender, he's been wasting his time trying to surrender to the wrong person. It's not the Nun herself but her example that he should identify with. She's obviously a woman with the courage of her convictions, unafraid of commitment no matter the sacrifice it entails, someone willing to discipline her life around a vow. Had he committed himself to the streetcar when he was its conductor, perhaps it would have remained faithful to him and never seduced the Nun. His sins all become achingly clear – his insensitivity, his blindness (those letters the Girl of Your Dreams would write to him came, after a while, to be addressed to *Dear Mr Oblivious* – later abbreviated to *Dear Mr O*, as if she were writing love letters to a cipher), and the worst sin of all, lack of passion: he'd taken being a conductor for granted, treated it as merely a job, an identity he stripped off with the uniform, when, dear God!, it was his life.

Dear Mr O strikes his head despairingly against the chrome handrail. Advertisements to which he's long been oblivious swim before his eyes. So these are the daydreams of silkier hair and ageless complexions upon which the hordes filing past him each day dwelled as they embarked on their journey together. He remembers all those days, weeks, years that he and the streetcar, now improbably named Ravenswood, have shared, intimately connected no matter how much traffic or how large the crowd. While commuters sat gabbing, or lost in newspapers, or gazing blankly out the window, Martin had registered, just below the threshold of consciousness, each nick in the track, hitch in the cable, surge of current, subtle whir, and shifting of gears. Oh, for those luminous hours between morning and evening rush, merrily clanging along on schedule down sunny streets.

He becomes bitter, glares at the Nun bouncing and chuckling on *his* air cushion seat, and wishes he could beat her knuckles bloody with a ruler, could make her stand in a corner with aching arms outstretched balancing a Bible on each palm, could deprive her of recess and banish her to the wardrobe closet.

But the Nun, now no longer a nun but a conductor in her own right, seems oblivious to all but the streetcar. Throttle open, bell clanging, and a fine sweat gathered like a mustache along her upper lip, suddenly boisterous as a gondolier, she breaks into song, its melody a cross between 'funiculi funicula' and a hymn, its lyrics a psalm.

> *Although the Lord be high above*
> *He doth recall the lowly*
> *And deep within thy secret heart*
> *The Lord shall surely know thee*

Her flashing teeth bite into the apple from the Conductor's lunch bag. Each crunch of the apple seems transmitted to the streetcar as if spikes of electricity were driving it forward in a more and more abandoned way, and Martin remembers drives down a country two-lane in his old Camaro with the Girl of His Dreams beside him, unzipping his trousers, urging him, *Faster, faster*, as if the way she touched him were actually propelling the car. If a motorcycle cop had been pursuing them then the way cops are pursuing the streetcar now, it would have looked to him as if the female passenger suddenly vanished, and though Martin was gripping the wheel and it was his foot on the gas, the Camaro was responding to what her tongue was doing.

> *I love you with mine own true heart*
> *Before the world I'll praise thee*
> *Your love was there before the stars*
> *And mercy doth amaze me*

With an enormous jolt, haloed in blue lightning, the streetcar leaps the track, and as it hurtles airborne Martin glances out the back window to see if he might catch one last glimpse of that woman who'd reminded him of GOYD. Instead, he sees the motorcycle cops pitching headfirst over their handlebars and the crowd pulling up in a way that's almost ceremonious, like a procession of mourners who have allowed the hearse to escape, as the streetcar plunges through a canopy of trees.

Ex-Conductor Martin, who was once so aware of any imperfection in the smooth steel rails, now feels the streetcar grinding savagely over earth, kicking up dust, crashing through bush. He feels his connection with the machine of whose identity he was once a part, slipping away, its familiar track a fading memory.

He thinks of all the streets they've been down together, streets with their misleading, disappointing names: Blue Island – just an asphalt aisle through bankrupt factories; Sunset – a street perennially in the shadow of tenements; Tree Haven – an artery of concrete paved in broken glass. Why don't those streets bear the names that tell their stories? Grand View with its pawnshops, bars, and crack houses should be called Dead End. When was the last time the stains on treeless Mulberry actually came from ripened berries? Better to call it Blood Street. And that noble-sounding intersection of Lincoln and State deserves to be Hooker and John. But Ravenswood is Ravenswood.

The doors whoosh open long enough for the commuters of the woods to file on. Their somber dress makes Martin grateful for the first time that he is wearing the black robes of the Nun. The shadows of their cloaks darken shafts of sun. The Nun who has become the Conductor continues her hymn:

> *How precious are thy thoughts to me*
> *How great thy loving kindness*
> *How blind the man who cannot see*
> *That God will ease his blindness*

But the commuters of Doowsnevar can only croak in a split tongue that must be older than any dead language.

A blur of vegetation streams by, limbs whapping the windows; humidity beads into sweat on Martin's shaved head and streams down his wimple. He joins with his fellow commuters in croaking a hymn he didn't know he knew, like when he was a child and prayed in Latin, never really understanding the words or what it was for which he prayed.

Fiction

Through a rift in the mist, a moon the shade of water-stained silk. A night to begin, to begin again. Someone whistling a tune impossible to find on a piano, an elusive melody that resides, perhaps, in the spaces between the keys where there once seemed to be only silence. He wants to tell her a story without telling a story. One in which the silence between words is necessary in order to make audible the faint whistle of her breath as he enters her.

Or rather than a sound, or even the absence of sound, the story might at first be no more than a scent: a measure of the time spent folded in a cedar drawer that's detectable on a silk camisole. For illumination, other than the moonlight (now momentarily clouded), it's lit by the flicker of an almond candle against a bureau mirror that imprisons light as a jewel does a flame.

The amber pendant she wears tonight, for instance, a gem he's begun to suspect has not yet fossilized into form. It's still flowing, imperceptibly, like a bead of clover honey between the cleft of her breasts. Each night it changes shape – one night an ellipse, on another a tear, or a globe, lunette or gibbous, as if it moved through phases like an amber moon. Each morning it has captured something new – moss, lichen, pine needles. On one morning he notices a wasp, no doubt extinct, from the time before the invention of language, preserved in such perfect detail that it looks dangerous, still able to sting. On another morning the faint hum of a trapped bee, and on another, a glint of prehistoric sun along a captured mayfly's wings. Where she grazes down his body and her honey-colored hair and the dangling pendant brush across his skin, he can feel the warmth of sunlight trapped in amber. Or is that simply body heat?

The story could have begun with the faint hum of a bee. Is something so arbitrary as a beginning even required? He wants to tell her a story without a beginning, a story that goes through phases like a moon, the telling of which requires the proper spacing of a night sky between each phase.

Imagine the words strung out across the darkness, and the silent spaces between them as the emptiness that binds a snow-fall together, or turns a hundred starlings rising from a wire into a single flock, or countless stars into a constellation. A story of stars, or starlings. A story of falling snow. Of words swept up and bound like whirling leaves. Or, after the leaves have settled, a story of mist.

What chance did words have beside the distraction of her body? He wanted to go where language couldn't take him, wanted to listen to her breath break speechless from its cage of parentheses, to travel wordlessly across her skin like that flush that would spread between her nape and breasts. What was that stretch of body called? He wanted a narrative that led to all the places where her body was still undiscovered, unclaimed, unnamed.

Fiction – 'the lie through which we tell the truth,' as Camus famously said – was at once too paradoxical and yet not mysterious enough. A simpler kind of lie was needed, one that didn't turn back upon itself and violate the very meaning of lying. A lie without dénouement, epiphany, or escape into revelation, a lie that remained elusive. The only lie he needed was the one that would permit them to keep on going as they had.

It wasn't the shock of recognition, but the shock of what had become unrecognizable that he now listened for. It wasn't a suspension of disbelief, but a suspension of common sense that loving her required.

Might unconnected details be enough, arranged and rearranged in any order? A scent of cedar released by body heat from a water-stained camisole. The grain of the hair she'd shaved from her underarms, detectable against his lips. The fading mark of a pendant impressed on her skin by the weight of his body. (If not a resinous trail left by a bead of amber along her breasts, then it's her sweat that's honey.) Another night upon which this might end – might end again, for good this time: someone out on the misty street, whistling a melody impossible to recreate . . .

I wanted to tell you a story without telling the story.

I Sailed With Magellan

Live from Dreamsville

Their voices floated across the musty mud smell of the gangway into our room. Mick and I sat at the edges of our beds and listened, laughing until we were afraid we might be heard, then burying our faces in our pillows to muffle the laughter. Next door, Jano was drunk and cursing. His gravelly voice slurred from some cavity deep within the dilapidated frame house.

'Hurry up the goddamn food,' he kept repeating, and every time he said it, Kashka would fire back, 'Don't get a hard-on.'

'Hurry up the goddamn food.'

'Don't get a hard-on!'

We got a whiff of food frying in the smoky crackle of lard.

'Phewee!' Mick whispered. 'It smells like they're cooking a rat.'

We both dove for our pillows, choking with laughter. I buried my face until it got sweaty and I could smell the feather ticking. Mick was still laughing; it sounded as if he was being strangled.

'Cool it,' I said, 'or Sir'll hear us.'

'Don't get a hard-on,' Mick said.

We pushed our faces against the screen, trying to peer into Kashka's house. Her window was a little below ours and off to the right so that we couldn't see much beyond the torn bedspread half draped across it. Even where we could see, the windowpane was the color of soot. A bare light bulb gleamed through blackened glass. There were crickets in the gangway among the ragweed, trilling louder than the distant sirens rushing to some calamity.

Mick climbed onto the inside windowsill, squatting to get a better look. We were sleeping in our underwear because it was hot, though despite the heat we both resolutely wore homemade nightcaps cut from one of Mom's old nylons. They fit tightly over our heads to hold our Brylcreemed d.a.'s in place. I reached up and pinched his ass.

'*Ow!*' he yelled, and banged his head on the sash.

'Shut up, you want Sir to hear? Get down, ya lubber.'

'Where's the goddamn food?' Jano demanded, his voice getting louder, moving toward us.

'Don't get a hard-on.'

'How can I without you?'

We tried very hard to stifle our laughter because we wanted to hear what would happen next.

'Don't tear my goddamn dress . . . for crissakes take it easy, Janush.' Kashka's rough voice sounded different than I'd ever heard it when she called him Janush. We heard a heavy thunk and then a clank like a pot falling from a table.

'You're hurtin my titties.' She moaned. 'Suck 'em, don't bite 'em, Janush.'

Then, except for an occasional groan, they got quiet, and we lay straining to hear, the word *titties* still hanging in the gangway like an echo that refused to fade. I'd always figured women, even Kashka, referred to them as their *bosom* or *breasts*, words more dignified than *titties*. Titties were for girls, something blossoming, maybe the size of tangerines. Kashka was built like a squat sumo wrestler. She had the heaviest upper arms I'd ever seen, rolls of flab wider than most people's thighs, folding

126

like sleeves over her elbows. She didn't have titties, she had watermelons, and Jano, missing half his teeth, was sucking them. I listened for the slurping but heard nothing. I wondered what Mick was making of it all. I wasn't sure how much he really understood about sex yet. The creaking of their house became audible, as if a galleon was anchored beside our window, and the moans resumed, louder and more frequent, though no sexier than those that came from behind the frosted glass of Dr Garcia's office, sounds we always regretted over-hearing as we waited our turns in the dental chair. Then, mercifully, they fell silent.

'What do you think they're doing?' Mick asked.

I thought of different possibilities but said nothing.

'Hey,' he asked, 'you going to sleep?'

I lay listening to him tossing in his bed, flapping his sheets.

'I know you're up, ya swab. You're just fakin',' he said.

My eyes were closed, though he couldn't see me in the dark.

'If you're sleeping, then you won't hear me calling you Toes. I won't lose any points. Ha ha, Toes! Hey, Toes? Toesush?'

I totaled up his lost points, grinning in the dark. Minus five for each time he called me Toes. Those were the rules according to the Point System. Mick wasn't old enough yet to go alone to the movie theater on Marshall Boulevard, and if he wanted to tag along with me on Saturdays, he had to lose less than a hundred points during the week. He could gain points for doing things for me, too, like folding my papers before I delivered them. Or some-times he'd get something on me and blackmail me for points not to tell Sir. He'd just lost fifteen and was already 120 in the hole.

'Hey, Toes, you eat boogers.'

Invasion of the Body Snatchers was coming this weekend, and Mick really wanted to see that.

I heard him getting out of bed, and I tensed, keeping my eyes closed and trying not to break up. I could feel him standing over me.

'Hey, Toesush,' he whispered.

I heard him rubbing his fingers together near my face, beneath my nose. He was chuckling maniacally. 'I guess you really are sleeping,' he said, then got back in bed.

We lay there completely quiet for a while.

'I'm sure glad you're sleeping, because you know what I did? I cleaned my kregs and sprinkled the toe-jam on your face.'

My not saying anything was really driving him nuts. He shut up for a long time after that. When I figured he was about to drop off to sleep, I started to snore.

'Shut up! I know you're fakin.'

I mumbled in my sleep and snored louder, and he bounced up again and gave my bed a shake. I rolled over with a groan as if in the middle of a dream. He gave me a jab in the back, then threw himself into bed.

He was turned toward the wall, convinced against his best judgment that I really was asleep, and trying now to sleep himself. Except for the *ding* of a freight train blocks away and a single cricket still trilling in the gangway, it was very quiet.

'You just lost a hundred points, matey,' I said.

He kind of flinched, then pretended *he* was sleeping.

'You might as well forget about that movie. I bet it's really gonna be great, too. The coming attractions were fantastic. Oh well, I guess you didn't want to see it anyway. That's why you're not saying anything. At least you ain't gonna beg. Which is smart because there's no way I'm changing my mind. Not after having toe-jam sprinkled in my face. And getting socked in the back. That was a test. Now I know what kind of stuff goes on when I really am sleeping. Well, okay, good night, I'm going to Dreamsville.'

I tucked the sheet over my head and curled up in the middle of the mattress. Both of us knew he no longer believed in Dreamsville, but neither of us was about to admit it. A year ago he'd still been convinced I had a secret trapdoor in my bed that led to a clubhouse full of sodas, malts, popcorn, candy, a place where the stray dogs and cats in the neighborhood gathered at night. In Dreamsville, animals could talk. Sometimes celebrities like Bugs Bunny would drop in.

Mick would hear fragments of our merrymaking, muffled as if the trapdoor had been left ajar: my voice saying, 'Hi, Whiskers. Hi, Topsy. Oh, hi there, Mousie Brown, you here tonight?'

Whiskers was our cat, supposedly out for the night. Topsy was Kashka's ginger-colored watchdog. He was supposed to guard the chickens she kept illegally, but he'd let me sneak over her fence, and while he wagged his tail, I'd untie the clothesline noosed around his neck and boost his back end over the fence into the alley. Whenever we managed an escape, he'd spend the rest of the day following Mick and me around the streets until Kashka or one of her demented wino friends caught him again. Though Kashka had never caught me in the act, she knew I was the one springing Topsy, and hated me for it, not that I cared. Mick and I loved Topsy and had planned to steal him for good when we got old enough not to need Sir's permission to keep him, but a couple of weeks ago I'd sprung him and the dogcatchers caught him. Kashka had just replaced him with a black puppy.

Mousie Brown was the name of Mick's favorite stuffed animal, one he slept with until a night when, sick with flu, he puked all over it. When Moms tried to clean it, the fur washed off, leaving behind a raggedy, bald lump that reeked of vomit, so she threw it out on the sly.

They'd all bark and meow hello, and Mousie Brown might squeak, 'Have a Dad's Old Fashioned Root Beer, Perry.'

It was during the winter, back before there was a Point System, that Mick still believed in Dreamsville. I'd made it up as a joke, one I didn't expect he'd take seriously, but he must have wanted to believe, and once he did, he wanted to go to Dreamsville, too. In winter, I slept beneath a *piersyna* – a big old feather tick our grandmother had brought from Poland – and once I disappeared beneath it into Dreamsville, Mick would get out of bed and try to lift the *piersyna* up to get at the trapdoor. I'd lie tucked into a ball, holding the *piersyna* to me, with him on top tugging at it, punching me through the goose feathers, getting worked up so loud sometimes that Sir would hear the noise and charge in swinging a belt or a shoe or whatever was handy, an attack he called a 'roop in the dupe.' Seeing the covers ripped and me getting my *dupa* beat tended to weaken Mick's belief in Dreamsville. Though for a while I was able to convince him that, in order to preserve the secret, I'd come up through the trapdoor just before Sir whisked off the covers. Since Mick was getting rooped, too, he couldn't really be sure. Then one night, instead of first yelling down the hall that we better get to sleep, Sir snuck up on us and suddenly stepped into the room, flicking on the light and stripping the *piersyna* off me where I lay bunched up in the middle of the mattress.

'What the hell do you guys yak about so much in here anyway?' he asked.

As usual we both pretended to be groggy, as if he'd just awakened us from a sound sleep.

'You're the older guy, Perry,' he said to me. 'You should be setting him a good example instead of this fooling around every night. You know he's like a monkey – copies whatever you do. Then in the morning your mother's gotta fight with you guys to get up for school and she's nervous the rest of the day.'

I lay there hoping he'd control his temper, feeling naked in the light, and diminished, like the room made suddenly tiny without its darkness. Finally, he switched the light back off and left. I guess when he was angry enough to come in swinging, he didn't like the light on any more than I did.

A few nights after that I decided that I'd finish off Dreamsville before Mick did. He'd already stopped begging me to take him there. I was under the *piersyna* talking in my pirate accent to the animal crew: 'Whiskers, pass the peanuts, matey, and squirt a ducat of catsup on these fries. Yum, tasty! Purr, purr. Squeak, squeak. Hey, Mousie Brown, hoist that case of cold pop off the poop deck, yo-ho-ho, pass that cotton candy, please. Pass the popcorn, pass the pop, pass the poop, me hardies.'

We both exploded into laughter. When the laughter would let up, one of us would say, 'Pass the poop, me hardies.' Mick laughed so hard he had to go to the bathroom, but I convinced him it would be a mistake to let them know he was still awake and talked him into pissing out the window.

It was cold and raining. We quietly slid up the window, then the storm window. The radiator was in front of the window, and Mick had to slide over it in order to sit on the sill. I held on to him so he wouldn't fall.

'I'm getting soaked,' he complained, and I started laughing hysterically again. 'What's so funny?'

'You must be totally crazy hanging out a window and pissing.'

'Okay, get me in,' he demanded.

'Oh-oh, you know what?'

'What?'

'I bet Kashka's looking out her window and saw what you just did.'

'Get me in, get me in!' He was getting frantic, struggling for leverage.

'She's probably coming around the back way to grab your legs and pull you outside.'

'Come on, quit fooling around, get me in.' He sounded ready to cry, so I let him in.

'My pajamas are all wet. Now I can't sleep.' He was wearing his flannel pirate pajamas.

'Let that be a lesson to never piss out a window.'

Even though Mick no longer believed in Dreamsville, it still got to him when I'd disappear under the sheet, like now, describing scenes from *Invasion of the Body Snatchers* as if I had my own private screening room down there.

'The pods are coming! Aaayyiiii! Everyone's a pod! This is the scariest movie I ever saw.'

'If you were up, why didn't you say so? I was just seeing if you were fakin'.'

'Almost too horrible to look at!'

'I didn't really mean it.'

'Hold it. Stop the movie a second. I think I hear something. What? Did you wake up?'

'I didn't mean it.'

'Didn't mean what?'

'Whatever I lost points for.'

'Like what?'

'Calling you Toes.'

'Okay, even though I ought to take extra off for *ush*ing me, you can have the fifteen points back. Anything else?'

'Like sprinkling toe-jam in your face.'

'Jesus Christ! You might as well forget apologizing for that.'

'I swear I didn't really do it.'

'Don't lie. I felt it. I smelled it.'

'Honest to God! I didn't do it! I was just rubbing my fingers together making the noise.'

'His fingers sure smell a lot like his kregs, ladies and gentlemen.' *Kregs* was a name Mick had coined for the spaces between toes.

'I did it just like you did the peanut butter.'

'Just because I'm laughing don't mean I believe you,' I said, breaking up just thinking about it. A few days earlier, while Mick was reading a *Mad* comic, I'd snuck up on him with a glob of peanut butter on a sheet of toilet paper, smeared it on his arm, and told him it was shit. At first he didn't believe me, so I told him to smell it. He did and started screaming, 'You really did it! You're crazy! I'm telling Moms!' I tackled him before he could get away and began trying to smear the glob off his arm into his mouth. He was fighting back hard, yelling I'd gone completely crazy, wrenching his face away, spitting it out every time I got it near his lips. I thought once he tasted it he'd see the joke, but I had a hard time getting him to believe that it was only peanut butter.

'You only gave me seventy-five points for not telling about that, so it's not fair I lose a hundred for this.'

'All right, you want to get a hundred points back?'

'How?'

'Stick your head out the window and tell Kashka you love her.'

'Go to hell! I wouldn't do that for a million stinking points.'

'I'll give you fifty if you just admit it to the ladies and gentlemen.'

'Admit what?'

'The truth, just say it out loud: Ladies and gentlemen, I admit it, I love Kashka.'

'No, it's not fair.'

'Okay, ladies and gentlemen, he had his chance. He didn't want to see the movie anyway.'

I disappeared under the sheet again and began to snore. Suddenly, I felt him land on top of me. He'd jumped from his bed onto mine and was trying to strangle me through the sheets while kneeing me in the back.

'Hey, take it easy,' I said, 'or Captain Roopus will hear.' But he wouldn't stop. 'This is gonna cost your scurvy ass another hundred points.'

That made him punch all the harder. He tried to gouge my eyes through the sheet. 'I don't care what you do,' he said.

'Sir's gonna hear.'

'I don't care.'

I squirmed loose, grabbed my pillow, and smashed it in his face, sending his head thudding off the wall.

'They'll hear that for sure. Better get in your own bed.'

Mick was half crying. 'I don't care. I'll tell them everything. I'll tell about the Point System. I'll tell I saw you playing with matches.'

He tried to break away toward the bedroom door. I grabbed him by his undershirt and tried to wrestle him down, but it tore away.

'I'm gonna tell you ripped my T-shirt.'

'No tell, no tell, Mickush,' I pleaded.

'Don't *ush* me.'

He managed to open the door and slip out with me still pulling on his arm. 'No tell, no tell,' I kept whispering. It was too late to force him back. We were halfway down the dark hallway. The fluorescent light in the kitchen was still on and lit up the end of the hall. Their voices carried to us. Mick stopped.

They were arguing. We could hear them very clearly. Moms was already at that point when her hands shook; we could hear the tremors in her voice. When what she called her 'nerves' got bad enough, her lower jaw would tremble, too, as if she was on the verge of a fit. She would continue trying to talk even though she could no longer control her voice, and it sounded as if she was gagging on words stuck in the back of her throat. Her attacks of nerves had begun a couple years earlier. Usually, they'd come on at night. I'd wake to her walking the apartment in the dark, talking to herself, praying, crying. Sometimes, thinking us asleep, she'd enter our room and sit shaking at the foot of my bed. Once, Mick woke, heard her crying, and began crying, too, so now when the attacks came she'd lock herself in the bathroom and turn on the water taps.

'You gotta get ahold of yourself before you're in the same boat as your brother, Lefty,' Sir was saying. 'I'm gonna call that phony-baloney doctor and tell him I'm taking those da-damn pills he's giving you to the police.'

There was a crash like a dish breaking. 'I-yi-yi c-c-can't stand it,' Moms gagged out.

'He's turning you into an addict,' Sir said. 'You take the pills and act like a zombie, and without them you fall apart.'

'Y-y-you ever t-t-try li-li-living without any sympathy? I-yi-yi can't stand it.' Something else broke.

'Go on, act like a da-damn nut and break it all so I can work harder to support us.'

'I'll give you all the points back. I'll take you to the movie,' I whispered. 'Come on back to bed.'

Mick followed me, both of us creeping back to the room. I closed the door, and it was dark again. We climbed into our beds and lay there not saying anything.

*

I was nearly asleep when the whining started from across the gangway. At first it was just there, a night sound like the crickets, sirens, and freights, but it grew louder and sharper and I realized I was feverish with sweat and sat up.

'It must be their new dog,' Mick said.

'Jesus, what's the matter with him? I never heard a dog sound like that.'

We tried to look through the screen again, but all we saw was the bulb behind the bedspread. Then we heard Kashka's voice.

'Janush, stop beating on him.'

The whining went on.

'That sonofabitch, that dirty bastard. He's torturing that puppy in there.' I threw myself back in bed and started punching the pillow until the whining stopped. In the quiet I could feel my lungs heaving and realized I'd been holding my breath. Then the whining started again.

'Why's he doing it?' Mick asked.

'I'll get him for this, the sonofabitch. I'll steal that dog and burn their goddamn house down. I'm not kidding. I'll wait till the bastard's passed out drunk and get him with a brick. I'm going to call the Humane Society tomorrow.'

'For shitsake, Jano, stop beating the goddamn dog,' Kashka yelled. She sounded more irritated by the noise than anything else.

'You said you wanted him mean, not like the other one, didn't you?' Jano answered. 'This is when you gotta get them if you want 'em mean.'

He kept at it as if proving his point. There was an even worse sound, like a choking squeal, and I could imagine Jano holding the dog up by the clothesline they kept tied around his neck while his hind legs danced off the floor.

'Shut up!' Jano shouted, and it was abruptly silent.

'Maybe he killed him,' Mick whispered.

I pulled the nylon stocking from my head and peeled my undershirt off and put it on the radiator. It was soaked through with sweat. I lay back down and waited, my insides braced for the whining to start again. It was quiet, but I couldn't relax.

'Want to have a Radio Show?'

'Okay, you start,' Mick said.

'Hello again out there, ladies and gentlemen, this is your friendly announcer, Dudley Toes, coming to you live from Dreamsville in the heart of Little Village over station KRAP, brought to you by Kashka Marishka's dee-licious melt-in-your-fat-mouth Frozen Rat DeLuxe Dinners!'

'And Jano's Hard-on Pickles. The only pickles especially made for shoving up your nose.'

'Thank you, Mick the Schmuck, and now, ladies and gentlemen, let's get the show on the road with the thing you've all been waiting for. Hey, ladies and gentlemen! Wake the hell up! I said the thing you've all been waiting for!'

Applause, cheers, boos from Mick's bed.

'And here it is! The Great Singing Competition between the world's two greatest singers – Tex Robe and Boston Blackhead!'

'I'm Tex Robe,' Mick said. 'I made it up.'

'But you made it up for me. And I made Boston Blackhead up for you. There's no reneging on Blackhead, old buckaroo. Now shut up till it's your turn, or you're disqualified. Right, ladies and gentlemen?'

'Right, right, right,' the ladies and gentlemen answered from the sides of their mouths.

'And here he is, ladies and gentlemen, Tex Robe singing the great new hit "Saxophone Boogie"!'

Saxophone Boogie, yeah yeah,
Saxophone Boogie, yeah yeah,
Saxophone Boogie, yeah yeah,
Oh man, that music's cool!
You hear the saxophone
When you're sittin there at home,
Hear that saxophone
And know you're not alone,
Hear the saxophone
When you're sittin there in school,
Oh man, that music's cool.
Saxophone Boogie, yeah yeah . . .

'Let's hear it for Tex Robe, ladies and gentlemen!'
Thunderous applause.

Then it was Boston Blackhead's turn. The ladies and gentlemen cheered again. Some booed and hissed. Boston Blackhead began to sing in a quavery, haunting voice, the voice of a ghost, of an ancient mariner.

'Oh no, ladies and gentlemen, not that, any song but that,' the master of ceremonies implored, but it was too late. There was no stopping the song, the same song that Mick had been singing on and off over the past months, ever since I'd brought a book on explorers home from the library, and, adrift on our beds in the expanse of darkness, we circumnavigated the world. Instead of returning the book on time, I'd hid it along with a flashlight behind the radiator, and after the house was quiet I'd read in a whisper about the five ships and 277 men who'd set sail, about the Patagonian Giants with their strange words – *ghialeme* for fire, *settere* for stars, *chene* for hand, *gechare* for scratch – words we began to use, as in 'I hear you gecharing your balls, matey.' They passed the Cape of Desire, the Cape of Eleven Thousand Virgins, the Land of fire – *ghialeme* – under the Southern Cross, past the Unfortunate Isles, the Robber Islands. There were doldrums, ship-wrecks, mutinies, demasting storms. 'My men die fast, but we approach the East Indies at fair speed . . . I know a ship can sail around the world. But God help us in our suffering.' Their ankles swelled enormously, their teeth dropped out, the flesh of penguins stunk in the hold, they soaked the leather wrappings from the masts in seawater for days, ate sawdust and wood chips. Three years, forty thousand miles, only eighteen men returned.

> *I sailed with Magellan, ooo-ooo-ooo*
> *Oh, oh, oh,*
> *I sailed with Magellan . . .*

Each time Mick sang it, the song got weirder, rambling without any one melody, its scale sounding foreign like a Muslim prayer, Mick never pausing, even if I laughed, he'd just keep singsonging on into a kind of trance . . . I sailed with Magellan, oh, oh, oh . . . boiled our shoes . . . ate our sails . . . without teeth . . . chewed our ship down to the nails . . . I sailed with Magellan, ooo-ooo-ooo

> *Oh, oh, oh . . .*

It kept getting softer and softer until finally he faded out. I could hear his breathing heavy and rhythmic and knew he was sleeping. The light across the gangway went out, leaving the room a shade darker. After a while, when the dog felt it was safe to softly whimper, I knew Kashka and Jano were sleeping, too.

Breasts

Sundays have always been depressing enough without having to do a job. Besides, he's hungover, so fuck Sunday. Taking somebody out on Sunday is probably bad luck.

And Monday: no wheels. He's got an appointment with the Indian at the Marvel station on Western. That man's a pro – can listen to an engine idle and tell you the wear on the belts, can hear stuff already going bad that won't break for months. The Indian is the only one he lets touch the Bluebird, his powder-blue, 312 Y-block, Twin Holley, four-barrel T-bird.

Tuesday, it's between Sovereign and hauling more than a month's laundry to the Chink's. Not to mention another hang-over. He strips the sheets, balls them into the pillowcases, stuffs in the towels. He's tired of their stink, his stink, of dirty clothes all over the floor, all over the apartment. He's been wearing the same underwear how long? He strips naked and stares at himself in the bedroom mirror. His reflection looks smudged, and he wipes the mirror with a sock, then drops to the carpet to do a hundred pushups – that always sharpens the focus.

He manages only seventy, and then, chest pounding hard enough to remind him that his father's heart gave out at age forty-five, lights a cigarette. He slaps on some Old Spice, slips back into his trousers and shirt without bothering to check the mirror, stuffs another pillowcase with dirty clothes, and since he's cleaning, starts on the heaps of dishes unwashed for weeks. Then, wham, it hits him like a revelation: who needs all this shit? Into trash bags go not only pizza cardboards and Chinese food cartons but bottles, cans, cereal boxes, plates, bowls, glasses, dirty pots. The silverware can stay. Next, it's the refrigerator's turn: sour milk, moldy cheese, rancid butter, all the scummy, half-empty bottles of mustard, mayo, pickles, jam, until the fridge is completely empty except for its cruddy shelves.

He removes the shelves.

Now he's got room for the giant mortadella that Sal brought from Italy. Sal came back from his trip bearing gifts and saying '*Allora!*' whatever that means. The mortadella is scarred with wounds from another souvenir Sallie brought him, a stiletto. He's wanted an authentic stiletto for his knife collection, and this one is a piece of work, a slender pearl handle contoured to slide the thumb directly to the switch, and the most powerful spring he's ever seen on a knife. When the six-inch blade darted out, the knife actually recoiled in his hand. It felt as if the blade could shoot through Sheetrock, let alone flesh. He tested it on the mortadella, a thick sausage more muscular than Charles F-ing Atlas. He wondered if the knife could penetrate the rind, and was amazed when the thrust of the spring buried the blade to the hilt. It was a test he found himself repeating, and the mortadella, now propped in the empty refrigerator, looks as if it's seen gladiatorial combat, like Julius F-ing Caesar after Brutus got done with him.

Whitey calls. 'Joey, you take care of business?'

'Still in the planning stage.'

'Well, the decision's been made, you know? Let's not be inde-cisive on this.'

'No problem, Whitey.'

Taking care of business. Last Saturday night at Fabio's what

Whitey said was 'Blow the little skimming fuck's balls off and leave him for the birds.'

'Not like there's vultures circling the neighborhood,' he told Whitey, and Whitey said, 'Joey, it was a manner of fucken speaking.'

Okay, *allora!* motherfucker, no more procrastination. He can haul out the garbage, drop his laundry at the Chink's, *and* take care of Johnny Sovereign. Let's get this fucking thing over with even though he hasn't made a plan yet and that's not like him. Things are chancy enough without leaving them to chance. The man who's prepared, who knows exactly what he's going to do, always has the advantage. What seems inevitable as fate to such a man, to others seems like a surprise. Problems invariably arise, and he wants to be able to anticipate them, like the Indian who can listen to an engine and hear what will go bad. He wants to see the scars that appear before the wounds that caused them.

With a cotton swab he oils the .22, then sets the Hoppe oil on a glass ashtray on his dresser beside the Old Spice so it doesn't leave a ring, and tests the firing mechanism. He fills the clip with hollow-point shells and slides it into the Astra Cub, a Spanish-made Saturday-night special that fits into the pocket of his sport coat. The sport coat is a two-button, powder-blue splash – same shade as the Bluebird. He'd conceal the stiletto in his sock, but he's stuffed all his socks into the dirty laundry, which forces him to dig inside the pillowcases until he comes up with a black-and-pink argyle with a good elastic grip to it. He can't find the match, so he puts the argyle on his right foot and a green Gold Toe on the left – nobody's going to be checking his fucking socks – then slides the stiletto along his ankle.

From his bedroom closet he drags out the locked accordion case that belonged to his grandfather. There's a lacquered red accordion inside that came from Lucca, where Puccini lived. In a cache Joe made by carefully detaching the bellows from the keyboard is an emergency roll of bills – seven Gs – and uppers, downers, Demerol, codeine, a pharmacopoeia he calls his pain-killers. In a way, they're for emergencies, too. Inside the accordion case there's also a sawed-off shotgun, a Walther PPK like the one James Bond uses, except this one is stolen and has the serial number filed off, and a Luger stamped with a swastika, supposedly taken off a dead German officer, which his father kept unloaded and locked away. After his father's death, Joe found ammo for it at a gun show. There's a rubber-banded cigarillo box with photos of girlfriends baring their breasts, breasts of all sizes, shapes, and shades of skin, a collection that currently features Whitey's girlfriend, Gloria Candido, and her silver-dollar nipples. She told Joe the size of her nipples prevented her from wearing a bikini. It's a photo that could get Joe clipped, but he's gambling that Gloria Candido is clever enough to play Whitey. Whitey's getting old, otherwise a punk-ass like Johnny Sovereign wouldn't be robbing him blind.

Capri St Clair is in the cigarillo box, too, not that she belongs with the others. Her letters he keeps in his bureau drawer. She was shy about her breasts because the left was wine-stained. No matter that they were beautiful. To her, it was the single flaw that gives a person something to hide. Joe understood that, though he didn't understand her. There's always some vulnerability that a personality is reorganized to protect, a secret that can make a person unpredictable, devious, mysterious. Capri was all those, and still he misses her, misses her in a way that threatens to become his own secret weakness. Her very unpredictability is what he misses. Often enough it seemed like spontaneity. He doesn't have a photo of her breasts, but one surprising afternoon he shot a roll of her blond muff. He'd been kidding her about being a bottle blond, and with uncharacteristic swagger she hiked her skirt, thumbed down her panties, and said, 'Next time you want to know is it real or is it Clairol, ask them to show you this.' She'd been sitting on his windowsill, drinking a Heineken, and when she stood the sun streamed across her body, light adhering not just to her bush but to the golden down on her stomach and thighs, each hair a prism, and a crazy inspiration possessed him with the force of desire, so strong he almost told her. He wanted to wake to that sight, to start his day to it, to restart his life to it, and maybe end his life to it, too. The breasts could stay stashed in the cigarillo box, but he wanted a blowup on his bedroom wall of her hands, the right lifting her bunched skirt and the left thumbing down her turquoise panties. He took the roll of film to Walgreens to be developed, and when he picked it up, photos were missing. He could tell from the weight of the envelope, but went down the Tooth Care aisle to open it and be sure. He returned to the photo counter and asked the pimply kid with 'Stevorino' on his name tag who'd waited on him, 'You opened these, didn't you? You got something that belongs to me.'

'No way,' the kid said, his acne blazing up.

'Zit-head, I should smash your face in now, but I don't want pus on my shirt. It's a nice shirt, right? So, see this?' Joe opened his hand, and a black switchblade the width of a garter snake flicked out a silver fang. 'I'm going to count to five, and if I don't have the pictures by then, I'm going to cut off Stevo's dickorino right here to break him of the habit of yanking it over another man's intimate moments.'

'Okay,' the kid said, 'I'm sorry.' He reached into the pocket of his Walgreens smock and slid the pictures over, facedown.

'How many of my boob shots have you been snitching, Stevorino? What is it? You think of me as the Abominable

Titman, the fucken Hugh Hefner of St Michael's parish? See me coming with a roll of Kodak and you get an instant woodie?'

'No, sir,' the kid said.

Joe went outside and sat in his idling car, studying the photos, thinking of Capri, of the intensity of being alone with her, of her endless inventions and surprises, but then he thought of her deceptions, their arguments, and of her talk of leaving for L.A. It was there, in the car with her photos on the dashboard, that he let her go, accepted, as he hadn't until that moment, that she had to want to stay or it wasn't worth it. He didn't let thinking of her distract him from his plan of action, which required watching the Walgreens exit. A plan was the distinction between a man with a purpose and some joker sitting in a car, working himself into a helpless rage. Two hours passed before the kid came out. He was unlocking his bicycle when he saw Joe Ditto.

'Mister, I said I was sorry,' the kid pleaded.

'Stevo, when they ask how it happened say you fell off your bike,' Joe said, and with an economically short blur of a kick, a move practiced in steel-toed factory shoes on a heavy bag, and on buckets and wooden planks, hundreds, maybe thousands of times until it was automatic, took out the kid's knee.

Joe never did get around to making that blowup of Capri. He hasn't heard from her in months, which is unlike her, but he knows she'll get in touch, there's too much left unfinished between them for her not to, and, until she's back, he doesn't need her muff on the wall.

Tuesday afternoon at the Zip Inn is a blue clothespin day. That's the color that Roman Ziprinski, owner and one-armed bartender, selects from the plastic clothespins clamped to the wire of Christmas lights that hangs year-round above the cash register.

With the blue clothespin, Zip fastens the empty right sleeve of his white shirt that he's folded as neatly as one folds a flag.

It's an afternoon when the place is empty. Just Zip and, on the TV above the bar, Jack Brickhouse, the play-by-play announcer for the Cubs. The Cubbies are losing again, this time to the Pirates. It's between innings, and Brickhouse says, It's a good time for a Hamm's, the official beer of the Chicago Cubs.

'Official,' Zip says to Brickhouse, 'that's pretty impressive, Jack.'

To the tom-tom of a tribal drum, the Hamm's theme song plays: '*From the land of sky-blue waters,*' and Zip hums along, '*from the land of pines, lofty balsam, comes the beer refreshing, Hamm's the beer refreshing . . .*'

Hamm's is brewed in Wisconsin. Zip has a place there, way up on Lac Courte Oreilles in the Chain of Lakes region famous for muskies. It's a little fisherman's cottage no one knows he has, where he goes to get away from the city. A land of sky-blue waters is what Zip dreamed about during the war. Daydreamed, that is. If Zip could have controlled his night dreams, those would have been of sky-blue water, too, instead of the nightmares and insomnia that began after he was wounded and continued for years. Sometimes, like last night, Zip still wakes in a sweat as sticky as blood, with the stench of burning flesh lingering in his nostrils, to the tremors of a fist hammering a chest – a medic's desperate attempt to jump-start a dead body. No matter how often that dream recurs, Zip continues to feel shocked when in the dark he realizes the chest is his, and the fist pounding it is attached to his missing right arm.

When he joined the marines out of high school, his grandmother gave him a rosary blessed in Rome to wear like a charm around his neck and made him promise to pray. But Zip's true prayer was one that led him into the refuge of a deep northern

147

forest, a place he'd actually been only once, as a child, on a fishing trip with his father. He summoned that place from his heart before landings and on each new day of battle and on patrol as, sick with dysentery, he slogged through what felt like poisonous heat with seventy pounds of flamethrower on his back. He'd escape the stench of shit and the hundreds of rotting corpses that the rocky coral terrain of Peleliu made impossible to bury, into a vision of cool freshwater and blue-green shade scented with pine. When I make it through this, that's where I'm going, he vowed to himself.

Sky-blue water was the dream he fought for, his private American Dream. And so is the Zip Inn, his tavern in the old neighborhood. He's his own boss here. Zip uncaps a Hamm's. It's on the house. The icy bottle sweats in his left hand. He raises it to his lips, and it suds down his throat: he came back missing an arm, but hell, his buddy Domino, like a lot of guys, didn't come back at all.

He can't control his night dreams, but during the day, Zip makes it a practice not to think about the war. Today, he wishes for a customer to come in and give him something else to think about. Where's Teo, that odd Mexican guy who stops by in the afternoon and sits with a beer, humming to himself and writing on napkins? The pounding in his temples has Zip worrying about his blood pressure. He has the urge to take a dump but knows his bowels are faking it. The symptoms of stress bring back Peleliu – the way his bowels cramped as the amtrac slammed toward the beach. They lost a third of the platoon on a beachhead called Rocky Point to a butchering mortar barrage that splintered the coral rock into razors of shrapnel. Zip stands wondering, how does a man in a place so far from home summon up whatever one wants to call it – courage, duty, controlled insanity – in the face of that kind of carnage, and then say nothing when two goombahs from across Western Avenue come into *his* place, the Zip Inn, and tell him it would be good business to rent a new jukebox from them? Instead of throwing those parasites out, he said nothing. Nothing.

Only a two-hundred-dollar initial installation fee, they told him.

The two of them smelling of aftershave: a fat guy, Sal, the talker, and Joe – he'd heard of Joe – a psycho for sure with a Tony Curtis haircut and three-day growth of beard, wearing a sharkskin suit and factory steel-toes. The two hoods together like a pilot fish and a shark.

'Then every month only fifty for service,' fat Sal said, 'and that includes keeping up with all the new hits. And we service the locked coin box so you won't have to bother. Oh yeah, and to make sure nobody tries to mess with the machine, we guarantee its protection – only twenty-five a month for that – and believe me when we say protection we mean protection. Nobody will fuck with your jukebox. Or your bar.'

'So you're saying I pay you seventy-five a month for something I pay fifteen for now. I mean the jukebox don't net me more than a few bucks,' Zip told them. 'It's for the enjoyment of my customers. You're asking me to lose money on this.'

'You ain't getting protection for no fifteen bucks,' Sal tells him.

'Protection from what?' Zip asked.

The hoods looked at each other and smiled. '*Allora.*' Sal shrugged to Joe, then told Zip, 'A nice little set up like you got should be protected.'

'I got Allstate,' Zip said.

'See, that kind of insurance pays *after* something happens, a break-in, vandalism, theft, a fire. The kind we're talking here guarantees nothing like that is going to happen in the first place.

All the other taverns in the neighborhood are getting it too. You don't want to be the odd man out.'

'A two-hundred-dollar installation fee?' Zip asked.

'That covers it.'

'Some weeks I don't clear more than that.'

'Come on, man, you should make that in a night. Start charging for the eggs,' Sal said, helping himself to one. 'And what's with only six bits for a shot and a beer? What kinda businessman are you? Maybe you'd like us to set up a card game in the back room for you on Fridays. And put in a pinball machine. We're getting those in the bars around here, too.'

'Installation was fifty for the box I got. Service is fifteen a month.'

Joe, the guy in the sharkskin suit, rose from his barstool and walked over to the jukebox. He read some of the selections aloud: 'Harbor Lights,' 'Blue Moon,' the 'Too Fat Polka,' 'Cucurrucucu Paloma,' 'Sing, Sing, Sing.'

'These songs are moldy, man,' Joe said. 'Where's Sinatra, where's Elvis the Pelvis? Your current jukebox dealer's a loser. They're gonna be out of business in a year. Their machines ain't dependable. Sallie, got a coin?'

'Here, on me,' Zip said, reaching into the till.

'No, no, Sallie's got it.'

'Yeah, I got it,' Sal said, flipping a coin to Joe.

'Requests, Mr Zip?' Joe asked.

'I hear it anytime I want.'

'So, what's your favorite song?'

'Play, "Sing, Sing, Sing,"' Sal said, yolk spitting from his mouth. 'Did you know Benny Goodman's a yid from Lawndale? Lived on Francisco before the *tutsones* moved in.'

Joe dropped in the coin and punched some buttons. Zip could hear from the dull *clunk* that the coin was a slug.

'Goddamn thing ate my quarter!' Joe exclaimed. 'I fucken hate when machines snitch from me. Newspaper boxes are the worst. Selling papers used to be a job for blind guys and crips. No offense, Mr Zip, I'm just saying a paper stand was decent work for these people, and then they put in newspaper boxes. I'm trying to buy a *Trib* the other day and the box eats my quarter. Know what I did to that newspaper box?'

'Here,' Zip said. 'Here's a refund.'

'But, see, Mr Zip, it's bad business to be covering for these lousy fucking jukes. You know if you whack them just right it's like hitting the jackpot.' Joe kicked the jukebox knee-high and its lights blinked out. From the crunch, Zip knew he'd kicked in the speaker. 'No jackpot? Well, guess it ain't my lucky day.' Joe laughed. 'So, listen, Mr Zip, we got a deal to shake hands on?' Joe extended his hand. Then, eyeing Zip's clothespinned sleeve, Joe withdrew his right hand and extended his left.

'Let me think it over,' Zip said. He didn't offer his hand. He wasn't trying to make a statement. It was the only hand he had.

'No problem,' Joe said. 'No pressure. Give it some careful thought. I'll come by next week, maybe Friday, and you can give me your answer.' He pulled out a roll of bills, snapped off a twenty, and set it on the mess of eggshells Sal had left on the bar. 'For the egg.'

Big shots leaving a tip stolen from the pocket of some workingman. After they walked out of his bar, Zip snapped open his lighter and watched the burning twenty turn the eggshells sooty. In the war, he'd operated an M2 flamethrower. They must have figured a kid his size could heft it, lug the napalm-filled jugs, and brace against the backward thrust of the jetting flame. Its range was only thirty yards, so Zip had to get in close to the mouths of caves and pillboxes that honeycombed the ridges where the Japs were dug in ready to fight to the death. He had to get close enough to smell the bodies burning. A flamethrower operator was an easy target and always worked with a buddy, whose job it was to cover him. Zip's buddy on Pelelui was Dominic Morales, from L.A. They called him Domino. During a tropical downpour on a ridge named Half Moon Hill, Domino was killed by the same mortar blast that took off Zip's right arm. They were both nineteen years old, and all these years later that astonishes Zip more than it ever did at the time. Nineteen, the same age as kids in the neighborhood shooting each other over who's wearing what gang colors in some crazy, private war. He thought he'd paid his price and was beyond all that, but now Zip stands behind the bar waiting for the days to tick down to Friday, when Joe Ditto comes back. Zip could call the cops, but he can't prove anything, and besides, hoods wouldn't be canvasing taverns if the cops weren't on the take. Calling the cops would be stupid. What if he simply closed down the bar, packed his Ford, drove north into the mist of sky-blue waters?

Zip recalls putt-putting out just after dawn in his aluminum boat into a mist that hadn't burned off the water yet. The lake looked like a setting for an Arthurian legend, the shore nearly invisible. Zip felt invisible. He'd packed a cane pole, a couple brews in a cooler of ice, and a cottage-cheese container of night crawlers he'd dug the night before. He was going bluegill fishing. Fresh from the icy water of Lac Courte Oreilles they were delicious. Even in the mist, he located his secret spot and quietly slid in the cement anchor. But when he opened the container of night crawlers, he found cottage cheese. If he went all the way back for his bait, he'd lose the first light and the best fishing of the day. Defeated, he raised anchor, and the boat drifted into acres of lily pads, nosing sluggish bullfrogs into the water. Zip noticed tiny green frogs camouflaged on the broad leaves, waiting for the sun to warm them into life. He caught a few and put them in the ice cooler. He'd seen bluegills come into mere inches of water alongshore for frogs. Once they were paralyzed by cold, Zip had no trouble baiting a frog on a hook one-handed. Returned to water, the frog would revive. Zip swung his pole out, and his bobber settled on the smoldering water. He watched for the dip of the bobber, the signal to set the hook, while the mist thinned. Zip was wondering where the bluegills were when the bobber vanished. He'd never seen one disappear underwater. Before he could puzzle out what happened, the water churned and the pole nearly jerked from his hand. The bamboo bent double, and he locked it between his thighs and hung on. The fish leaped, and if Zip hadn't known it was a muskie, he might have thought it was an alligator. It wagged in mid-air and appeared to take the measure of Zip, then belly-flopped back into the lake and torpedoed beneath the boat. Zip braced, tried horsing it out, and the pole snapped, knocking him off balance onto his butt, crushing the Styrofoam cooler, but he still clung to the broken pole. The fish leaped again beside the boat, swashing in water. It seemed to levitate above Zip – he smelled its weediness – and when it splashed down, the broken pole tore from his hand and snagged on the gunwale. He lunged for it, almost capsizing the boat, then watched the stub of bamboo, tangled in line and bobber, shoot away as if caught in an undertow. It was too big a fish for a cane pole. Too big a fish for a one-armed man.

Zip drains the last of his Hamm's, sets the bottle on the bar, and stares at his left hand, the hand Joe Ditto wanted to shake. Blood pulses in his temples and a current of pain traces his right arm, and the thought occurs to Zip that if he ever has a heart attack, he'll sense it first in his phantom arm.

*

Whitey calls in the middle of a dream:

Little Julio is supposed to be in his room practicing, but he's playing his flute in the bedroom doorway. Julio's mother, Gloria Candido, is wearing a pink see-through nightie, and Joe can't believe she lets Little Julio see her like that because Little Julio is not *that* little and he's just caught Joe circumnavigating Gloria's nipples with his tongue and Little Julio wants some, too. 'He's playing his nursing song,' Gloria says. The flute amplifies the kid's breath until it's as piercing as an alarm. To shut him up, Joe gropes for the phone.

'Joe,' Whitey says. 'What's going on?'

Drugged on dream, Joe wakes to his racing heart. 'What?' he says, even though he hates guys who say *what?* or *huh?* It's a response that reveals weakness.

'Whatayou mean what? What the fuck? You know *what*. What's with you?'

What day is this? Joe wants to ask, but he knows that's the wrong thing to say, so he says, 'I had a weird night.'

'Joe, are you fucken on drugs?'

'No,' Joe says. He's coming out of his fog, and it occurs to him that Whitey can't possibly be calling about Gloria Candido. A confrontation on the phone is not how Whitey would handle something like that. Whitey wouldn't let on he knew.

'Well, what's the problem then?' Whitey demands.

It's Johnny Sovereign that Whitey is calling about, and as soon as Joe realizes that, his heart stops racing. 'Ran into a minor complication. I went to see him yesterday and—'

'*Maron!*' Whitey yells. 'Joe, we're on the fucking phone here. I don't care what the dipshit excuses are, just fucking get it done.'

'Hey, Whitey, suck this,' Joe says and puts the receiver to his crotch. 'Who the fuck do you think you're yelling at, you vain

old sack of shit with your wrinkled *minchia?* Your girlfriend's
slutting around behind your back making a fucking *cornuto* of
you. You don't like it I'll cut you, I'll bleed you like a stuck pig.'

Joe says all that to the dial tone. Telling off the dial tone
doesn't leave him feeling better, just the opposite, and he makes
a rule on the spot: never again talk to dial tones after someone's
hung up on you. It's like talking to mirrors. Mirrors have been
making him nervous lately. There's a dress draped over his
bedroom mirror, and Joe gets out of bed and looks through
his apartment for the woman to go with it. That would be
April. She's nowhere to be found, and for a moment Joe
wonders if she's taken his clothes and left him her dress. But
his clothes are piled on the chair beside the bed where he
stripped them off – shoes, trousers with keys and wallet, sport
coat with the .22 weighting one pocket. He's naked except for
his mismatched socks. The stiletto is still sheathed in the black-
and-pink argyle.

Yesterday was supposed to have been a clean-up day. His plan
was to pitch the trash, drop his laundry at the Chink's, and
then stop by Johnny Sovereign's house on Twenty-fifth Street.
The plan depended on Sovereign not being home, so Joe called
from a pay phone, and Sovereign's good-looking young wife
answered and said Johnny would be back around four. Okay,
things were falling into place. Joe would wait in the gangway
behind Sovereign's house for him to come home, and suggest
they go for a drink in order to discuss Johnny setting up
gambling nights in the back rooms of some of the local taverns.
Once Joe got Sovereign alone in the car, well, he'd improvise
from there.

So around three in the afternoon, Joe parked beside the
rundown one-car garage behind Sovereign's house. The busted
garage door gaped open, and he saw that Sovereign's Pontiac

Bonneville was gone. Bonnevilles with their 347-cubic-inch engines that could do zero to sixty in 8.1 seconds were the current bad-ass cars – in Little Village, they called them Panchos. Sovereign's splurging on that car was what made Whitey suspect he was skimming on the numbers. New wheels and already leaking oil, Joe thought, as he looked at the fresh spots on the warped, birdshit-crusted floorboards of the garage. If Sovereign wasn't careless and all for show, he'd have taken that Pancho to the Indian.

Johnny Sovereign's back fence was warped, too, and over-grown with morning glories. His wife must have planted them. She'd made an impression on Joe the one time he'd been inside their house. Johnny had invited him, and they'd gone the back way, the entrance Joe figures it was Johnny's habit to use. Johnny didn't bother to announce their arrival, and they caught his wife – Vi, that was her name – vacuuming in her slip. When she saw Joe standing there, a blush heated her bare shoulders before she ran into the bedroom. She was wearing a pale yellow slip. Joe had never seen a slip like that before. He would have liked to slide its thin straps down her skinny arms to see if her blush mottled her breasts the way some women flush when they come. Sovereign's Pontiac was yellow, too, but canary yellow, and Joe wondered if there was some connection between Vi's slip and the car.

He sat in the Bluebird and lit a cigarette, then unscrewed the top from a pinch bottle of Scotch and washed down a couple of painkillers. Sparrows twittered on the wires and pigeons did owl imitations inside Sovereign's shitty garage. The alley was empty except for a humped, hooded figure of a woman slowly approaching in his rearview mirror – a bag lady in a black winter coat and babushka, stopping to inspect each garbage can. Except for the stink of trash, Joe didn't mind waiting. He needed time to think through his next moves. From where he'd parked, he could watch the gangway and intercept Sovereign before he entered the house. He'd ask Sovereign to have a drink, and Sovereign would want to know where. 'Somewhere private,' Joe would tell him. And then – wham – it came to Joe, as it always did, how he'd work it. He'd tell Sovereign, 'Let's take *your* wheels. I want to ride in a new yellow Bonneville.' He'd bring the bottle of Scotch, a friendly touch, and suggest they kill it on the deserted side street where the dragsters raced, a place where Sovereign could show him what the Pancho could do. He couldn't think of a way to get the shotgun into Sovereign's car, so he'd have to forget about that. Joe was scolding himself for not thinking all this through earlier when a woman's voice startled him.

'Hi, Joe, got an extra smoke?'

'What are you doing here?' Joe asked.

'Trying to bum a Pall Mall off an old lover,' April said. 'You still smoke Pall Malls, don'tcha?'

Her hair was bleached corn-silk blond and she wore a dress the shade of morning glories. Joe wondered how she'd come down the alley without his seeing her. The scooped neckline exposed enough cleavage so that he could see a wing tip from the blue seagull tattooed on her left breast. She looked more beautiful than he'd remembered.

'I thought you went to Vegas,' he said. 'I heard you got married to some dealer at Caesar's.' He didn't add that he'd also heard she'd OD'd.

'Married? *Me?*' She showed him her left hand: nails silvery pink, a cat's-eye on her index finger going from gray to green the way her eyes did. Joe leaned to kiss the pale band of flesh where a wedding ring would have been, but he paused when sunlight hit her hand in a way that made it momentarily appear freckled and old with dirty, broken nails. She lifted her hand the rest of the way and sighed when it met his lips.

'You used to do that thing with my hand that would drive me crazy,' April said.

'Hey, we were kids,' Joe said.

He worked back then for a towing service Whitey ran, and he'd met April when he went to tow her Chevy from a private lot off Rush Street. He'd traded not towing her car for a date. She was a senior at Our Lady of Lourdes High, still a virgin, and on their first date she informed him that she was sorry, but she didn't put out. That was the phrase she used. Joe had laughed and told her, 'Sweetheart, it's not like I even asked you. And anyway, there's other things than *putting out*.' 'Such as?' April asked, and from that single question, Joe knew he had her. It was nothing about him in particular, she was just ready. 'Imagine the knuckles on your fingers are knees and the knuckles on your hands are breasts,' Joe had told her, extending her index and middle fingers into a V and outlining an imaginary torso with his finger. 'Okay, I see. So?' she asked. 'So this,' he whispered and kissed the insides of her fingers, then licked their webbing. She watched him as if amused, then closed her eyes. Even after she was putting out three times a day, nothing got her more excited than when he kissed her hand. 'Lover,' she'd once told him, 'that goes right to my pussy.'

'Aren't you going to ask me if I'm still using?' April asked. 'I'm clean. And I been thinking about you ever since I've been back in the neighborhood. I'm staying with my sister, Renee. Remember her? She had a crush on you, too. I dreamed last night I'd find you here, and when I woke I thought, Forget it, you can't trust dreams, but then I thought, What the hell, all that will happen is I'll feel foolish.'

'You dreamed of meeting me *here*?'

'Amazing, huh? Like that commercial, you know? "I dreamed I met my old boyfriend in an alley, wearing my Maidenform bra." Nice ride,' she said, gliding her fingertips along the Bluebird as if stroking a cat. She came around to the passenger side, climbed in, leaned back into the leather seat, and sighed. 'Just you, me, and a thousand morning glories.'

Joe flicked away his cigarette and kissed her.

'You taste like Scotch,' she said.

He reached for the pinch bottle and she took a sip and kissed him, letting the hot liquor trickle from her mouth into his.

'What are *you* doing here?' she asked.

'That information wasn't in your dream?'

'In my dream you were a lonely void waiting for your soul mate.' April took another sip of Scotch and swallowed it this time. 'Maybe we should have a private homecoming party,' she said.

He remembers driving with April down the alleys back to his place, stopping on the way at Bruno's for a fifth of Bacardi and a cold six-pack of tonic water, and later, covering his kitchen table with Reynolds Wrap and laying out lines of coke. He remembers the plink of blood on foil when her nose began to bleed, and April calling from the bathroom, 'Joe, where's all the towels?'

'Forgot to pick them up at the Chink's.'

'No towels, no sheets. Are you sure you live here? What's in the fridge? Anything at all? I dread to look.'

They lay kissing on the bare mattress while darkness edged up his bedroom walls. How still the city sounded. Between shrieks of nighthawks, an accordion faintly wheezed from some open window. Joe's bedroom window was open, too, and the breeze that tingled the blinds seemed blued with the glow of the new arc lights the city had erected. Before the mirror, April, streaked by the same glow, undid her ponytail.

Mimicked by a reflection deep in the dark glass, she slipped her dress over her head. No Maidenform bra, she was naked. He came up behind her and bit her shoulders. He could see what appeared to be disembodied blue hands – his hands – cupping her luminous breasts. Otherwise he was a shadow. His thumb traced the tiny seagull flying across her breast. In the mirror it looked graceless, like an insignia a gang punk might have India-inked on his forearm. Her reflection appeared suddenly to surge to the surface of the glass, and he saw that the mirror was blemished with hairline fractures superimposed on her face like wrinkles. She flipped the dress she was still holding over the mirror as if to snuff a chemical reaction. It snuffed the residual light, and in the darkness he could feel something flying wildly around the room, and they lost their balance, banged off a wall, and fell to the bed. She took his cock, fit it in, then brought her hand, smelling of herself to his lips.

Joe remembers all that, but none of it – the booze, the coke, the Demerol, the waking up repeatedly in the dark already fucking – explains how it can be afternoon, or what her morning-glory dress is doing left behind. He yanks the dress off the mirror and is surprised to find a crack zigzagging down the center. Maybe it was the mirror they'd staggered into. He staggers into the kitchen and washes down a couple of painkillers with what's left in a bottle of flat tonic water, then palms Old Spice onto his face and under his arms, tugs on his clothes, and dials Sovereign's number. He knows it's not a good idea to be calling from his place, but that can't be helped. When Vi answers on the third ring, he asks, 'Johnny there?'

'He'll be home around four,' she says. 'Can I tell him who's calling?'

Joe hangs up.

From the closet, he digs out a gym bag stuffed with dirty gym gear and canvas gloves for hitting the heavy bag. He lifts the mirror from the bedroom wall, bundles it up in the dress, totes it into the alley, and sets it beside the garbage cans, then throws the gym bag into the Bluebird. Joe drives down the alleys, formulating a plan for how to get the shotgun into Sovereign's car. Off Twenty-fifth, he scatters a cloud of pigeons and nearly sideswipes a blind old bag lady in a babushka and dark glasses who's feeding them. When he pulls up behind Sovereign's, Joe can smell the baking motor oil spotting the floorboards of the empty garage. Demerol tends to heighten his sense of smell. Wind rustling down the alley leaves an after-taste of rotten food and the mildewed junk people throw away. He makes sure the alley is empty, then slips the sawed-off shotgun from under the seat and buries it in the gym bag, beneath his workout gear. The Scotch bottle rests on top, and when he zips up the bag, the ghost of old gym sweat transforms into a familiar fragrance.

Marisol stands in the alley as if she's emerged from the morning glories. She has a white flower in her auburn hair. Her perfume obliterates the scent of pigeons, garbage, and motor oil he's come to associate with Johnny Sovereign. She's dressed in white cotton X-rayed by sunlight: a shirt opened a button beyond modest, tied in a knot above her exposed navel, and white torea-dor pants. The laces of the wedged shoes he used to call her goddess sandals snake around her ankles. Her oversize shades seem necessary to shield her from her own brightness.

'See you're still driving the B-bird,' she says, sauntering to the car. 'That's cute how you name your cars. Kind of boyish of you, Joe, though when you first told me your car had a name, know what? I thought, Oh no, don't let this be one of those pathetic wankers who names his penis, too. Hey, I like the color coordination with the sport coat. That splash pattern is perfect for eating spaghetti with tomato sauce. Recognize this shirt? It's yours. Want it back?'

She still speaks in the fake accent that when they first met had Joe believing she was from London. He's not sure he's ever heard her real voice, if she has one. He'd heard she broke her Audrey Hepburn neck in Europe when she blew off the back of some Romeo's BSA on the autobahn. Who starts these rumors about dead babes? Maybe Sal told him; Sal's a know-it-all with a rep for spreading bullshit. Well, fucking *allora*, Sallie, if a very much alive Marisol, trailing perfume, doesn't get into the Bluebird, help herself to a smoke from the pack on the dash, and ask, 'Know where a girl can get a drink around here?'

Joe unzips the gym bag, hands her the bottle of Scotch, and she asks as if she already knows, 'What else you got in that bag, Joe?'

'Whataya mean, what else? Gym stuff.'

'Whew! Smells like your athletic supporter's got balls of *scomorza*,' Marisol says. 'But what do I know about the secret lives of jockstraps.'

Joe looks at her and laughs. She always could break him up, and not many beautiful women dare to be clowns. Capri was funny like that, too, and no matter who he's with he misses her. Where's Capri now, with who, and are they laughing? Marisol laughs, then quenches her laughter with a belt of Scotch and turns to be kissed, and Joe kisses her, expecting the fire of alcohol to flow from her mouth into his, but it's just her tongue sweeping his.

'What?' Marisol says.

'I thought you were going to share.'

'Dahlink,' she says in her Zsa Zsa accent, 'you don't remember I'm a swallower?'

Joe remembers. Remembers a blow job doing eighty down the Outer Drive on the first night he met her at the Surf, a bar on Rush where she worked as a cocktail waitress; remembers the improv theater he'd go see her in at a crummy little beatnik space in Old Town where sometimes there were more people onstage than in the audience; just say something obscene about Ike or Nixon or McCarthy and you'd get a laugh – shit, he laughed, too. He remembers the weekend right after he got the Bluebird when they dropped its top and drove the dune highway along the coast of Indiana to Whitey's so-called chalet on the lake, water indigo to the horizon, and night lit by the foundries in Gary.

'So, luvvy, is here where we're spending our precious time?' Marisol asked, turning on the radio.

Joe shifted through the gears as if the alleys were the Indianapolis Speedway and pulled up to Bruno's. He left Marisol in his idling car, singing along with Madame Butterfly on the opera station, while he ran in for a fifth of Rémy, her drink of choice, then brought her back to his place.

'Where's all the sheets and towels?' she asked. 'Joe, how the bloody hell can you live like this?'

'They're at the Chink's. I been meaning to get them, but I been busy.'

'You better watch it before you turn into an eccentric old bachelor, luv. I think maybe you're missing a woman's touch.'

That was all she had to say, *touch*, and they were on the bare mattress.

Her blouse, an old white shirt of his, came undone, and he pressed his face to her breasts, anointed with layers of scent, lavender, jasmine, areolas daubed with oil of bergamot, nipples tipped with a tincture of roses. He recalled the single time she'd invited him to her place on Sedgwick and how, in her bedroom, a dressing table cluttered with vials and stoppered bottles smelled like a garden and looked like the laboratory of a witch. *Touch*, she said, and he straddled her rib cage, thrusting slicked with a bouquet of sweat, spit, and sperm between perfumed breasts she mounded together with her hands. *A woman's touch*.

When he woke with Marisol beside him it was night and his room musky with her body – low tide beneath the roses. An accordion was playing. It sounded close, as if someone in the alley below was squeezing out a tune from long ago. 'Hear that?' he asked, not sure she was awake.

'They're loud enough to wake the dead,' Marisol said. 'When I was little I used to think they were bats and their squawks were the sonar they flew by.'

'I didn't mean the nighthawks,' Joe said. 'Those new mercury vapor lights bring the bugs and the bugs bring the birds. Supposed to cut down muggings. Or at least line the pockets of a few contractors. I had to buy fucking venetian blinds to sleep.'

'You need earplugs, too,' Marisol said. She rose from the dark bed and crossed through the streaky bluish beams, then raised the blinds. The glare bestowed on her bare body the luster of a statue. 'Liking the view in the vapor lights?' she asked. 'Ever think of a window as an erogenous zone?'

'Always the exhibitionist,' Joe said. 'But why not? You're beautiful as a statue.'

'Statues are by nature exhibitionists, even when they've lost their arms or boobs or penises. Where's your mirror? I want to watch statues doing it in mercury vapor.'

'No mirror.'

'You don't have a mirror? Don't tell me – it's at the Chink's.'

'It's in the alley.'

'That's a novel place to keep it. I may be an exhibitionist but I'm not going to screw in the alley.'

'It's broken.'

'Seven years' bad luck, Joe. Poor unlucky bloke doesn't get to watch the statues with their shameless minds.'

'*Allora!*' Joe said. 'It's not that broke.'

He went down the back stairs into the alley. The mirror was still where he'd set it beside a trash can. April's morning-glory dress was gone; some size-six bag lady must have had a lucky day. The mirror no longer appeared to be cracked, as if it had healed itself. It reflected an arc light. Nighthawks screeched. No one was playing an accordion in the alley, not that Joe thought there would be, but he could still hear it, a song he'd heard as a child, something about blackbirds doing the tango that his grandpa played on Sundays when he'd accompany scratchy 78s on his red accordion. Joe listened, trying to identify the open window from which the song wafted. Every window was dark. The music was coming from *his* window. He saw the flare of a lighter, and a silhouette with its head at an awkward angle, gazing silently down at him.

Marisol was still at the window, smoking a reefer, her back to him, when he returned to the room. 'You didn't get mugged. See, those new streetlights must be doing their job,' she said.

He propped the mirror against the wall.

'I'll share,' she said, and exhaled smoke into his mouth. He felt her breath smoldering along the corridors of his mind. She handed him the reefer, and the crackle of paper as he inhaled echoed off the ceiling. 'That paper's soaked in hash oil,' she said. The accordion pumped louder, as if it tangoed in the next room. Lyrics surfaced in his mind and dissolved back into melody. '*E nell'oscurita ognuno vuol godere* . . . in the darkness everyone wants pleasure.' When he opened his eyes, he could see in the dark. '*L'amor non sa tacere* . . . love can't keep silent . . .' She was in his arms, and he smoothed his hands over her shoulders, down her spine, over her hips, lingering on and parting the cheeks of her sculpted ass.

'Have any oil?' she whispered.

'What kind of oil?'

'Like you don't want me that way. Almond oil, baby oil, bath oil, Oil of Olay, Vaseline if that's all you got.'

'Hoppe's Number 9,' he said.

'That's a new one on me.'

He gestured with the reefer to the bottle in the ashtray next to the Old Spice on the bureau top. She picked it up and sniffed. By the lighter's flame, she read the label aloud: '"Do not swallow. Solvent frees gun bores of corrosive primer fouling and residue. Preserves accuracy." Jesus, Joe! Don't you have some good, old-fashioned olive oil? What-a kinda Day-Glo are you?'

'Maybe in the kitchen,' Joe said.

Brandishing the lighter like a torch, she went to the kitchen. Joe waited on the bed, listening to the accordion playing with the mesmerizing intensity that marijuana imparts to music . . . 'Love can't keep silent and this is its song . . . *la canzon di mille capinere* . . . the song of a thousand blackbirds . . .' when Marisol screamed. 'God, what am I stepping in? What's leaking out of your fridge, Joe? You have a body in there?'

Wounded wing, how strange to fall from blue. Like a fish that suddenly forgets the way to swim. When men fly, they know, by instinct, they defy. But to a bird, as to a god, nothing's more natural than sky . . .

Needing somewhere to think about the words forming to a nonstop percussion in his mind, not to mention needing a cold brew, Teo gimps out of daylight into the Zip Inn. A slab of sunshine extends from the doorway. Beyond it, the dimness of the narrow, shotgun barroom makes the flowing blue water of the illuminated Hamm's beer sign on the back wall look like a mirage. The TV screen flickers with white static that reflects off the photos of the local softball teams that decorate the walls. Teo doesn't remove his dark glasses. Zip, the folded right sleeve of his white shirt fastened with a yellow clothespin, stands behind the bar before a bottle of whiskey and raises a shot glass.

'*Qué pasa, amigo!*' Zip says, a little loudly given there's just the two of them.

'*Nada, hombre.*' Teo is surprised to see him drinking alone in the afternoon, an occupational hazard of bartending to which Zip has always seemed immune.

'Knee acting up? Have one with me,' Zip says, filling a second shot glass.

'What's the occasion?' Teo hooks his cane on the lip of the bar, carefully sets the bowling bag he's carrying onto a stool, and eases onto the stool beside it.

'Today is Thursday,' Zip says, 'and if you ask me, and I know nobody did, Thursday's a reason for celebrating.'

'To Thursday,' Teo says. '*Salud!*'

'*Na zdrowie,*' Zip answers. He draws a couple of beer chasers.

'Let me get the beers,' Teo says, laying some bills on the bar. Zip ignores his money. After a meditative swallow, Teo asks, 'TV broke?'

'No game today,' Zip says. 'Giants are in tomorrow. You work Goldblatt's?'

'No, Leader Store,' Teo says. He pushes a dollar at Zip. 'At least let me buy a bag of pretzels.'

'I heard Leader's is going under. Any shoplifters even there to pinch?' Zip asks, ringing up the pretzels.

'A kid in Pets trying to steal one of those hand-painted turtles. A pink polka-dotted turtle.'

'Give him the full nelson?' Zip asks.

'Only the half nelson. He was just a grade-schooler.'

'I think the dress disguise actually reduces your effectiveness, my friend. I mean, if there was a problem in my tavern, you know, say, theoretically speaking, somebody pocketing eggs—'

'The eggs are free,' Teo says.

'Then pretzels. Say I got a problem with some pretzel sneak-thief, so I hire you and you're sitting here, supposedly undercover, in a polka-dot dress wearing a wig and dark glasses and a cane and maybe smoking a cigar. I mean, you wouldn't be fooling nobody. It might be a deterrent, but not a disguise. You might as well be sitting there in your secret wrestler's getup. Whatever the hell it is.'

'Amigo, you really want to see the wrestler's outfit?'

'Why not?' Zip says. 'Liven things up. This place could use a little muscle.'

'You'd be disappointed. And, by the way, it was the turtle with the polka dots, not the dress.'

Lately, Teo has been stopping at the Zip Inn on weekday afternoons when the bar is mostly empty. Zip seems to know when Teo is in a mood to sit scribbling or simply to sink into his own thoughts, and he leaves him alone then, but other times they swap stories. Zip has told Teo hilarious tales of the world-record muskies he's lost, and Teo, trying to make his story funny, too, told Zip how his knee was injured when he was thrown from the ring onto the pavement during an outdoor wrestling match.

'You mean like those masked wrestlers when they set up a ring on Nineteenth Street for Cinco de Mayo?' Zip had asked. 'What are they called?'

'*Luchadores*,' Teo had told him.

'So, you're a . . . *luchador* . . . with a secret masked identity?' Zip had sounded genuinely curious.

'Not anymore,' Teo had answered.

Now, from the bowling bag, Teo pulls the hem of the dress he dons occasionally as part of his store security job. It's the dress they gave him when he began working for Goldblatt's – blue paisley, not polka dots – and, contrary to Zip's wisecracks, Teo has caught so many shoplifters that he's begun moonlighting at Leader Store on his days off.

'Yeah, this one is more you,' Zip says, fingering the fabric, then asks, 'What the hell else you got in there?'

Teo lifts out the pigeon.

This morning, he tells Zip, on his way to work he found the pigeon, a blue checker cock – *Columba affinis* – dragging its wounded wing down an alley, and took it with him to Leader's, where he kept it in an empty parrot cage in Pets and fed it water and the hemp seed he carries with him as a treat for his own birds. Teo thinks of it as the Spanish pigeon. He doesn't mention the message, in Spanish, that he found tied to its unbanded leg.

'So it ain't one of your birds?' Zip asks.

'No.' Teo shakes his head. He's told Zip how he keeps a *palomar*, a pigeon loft, on the roof of the three-story building on Blue Island Avenue where he rents a room, but he hasn't told Zip about the messages arriving there. Teo hasn't told anyone but the sax player, and he's gone missing. Over the last month, Teo's pigeons have been coming home with scraps of paper fastened with red twine to their banded legs. The first message arrived on a misty day, attached to the leg of one of his bronzed archangels. It wasn't Teo who first noticed it but the sax player, Lefty Antic, who practiced his saxophone on the roof. Teo untied the message, and he and Lefty read the smeared ink: 'Marlin.'

'Mean anything to you?' Lefty Antic had asked.

'Just a big fish, man,' Teo had told him.

'Maybe it's his name, Marlin the Pigeon,' Lefty Antic said.

'No,' Teo said. 'They don't tell us their names.'

The next morning, slipped under his door, Teo found 250 dollars in crisp bills rubber-banded in a folded page from a Sportsman's Park harness-racing form with 'Merlin' circled in the fourth race and a note that read, 'Thanks for the tip. Lefty.'

Teo saved the winnings and the message in a White Owl cigar box. A few days later, out of a drizzle, a second, barely legible message arrived fastened to one of his racing homers. As far as Teo could tell, it read: 'Tibet.' He took the message and half his winnings and knocked on Lefty Antic's door. There was no answer, and Teo had turned to go when the door opened, emitting the smell of marijuana. The sax player looked hungover, unshaven, eyes bloodshot, and Teo was sorry he'd disturbed him, but Lefty Antic insisted he come in. Together they studied the harness races in the newspaper and found a seven-to-one shot named Tidbit in the fifth race. There was also a buggy driver, J. Tippets, racing in the third and eighth races. Lefty decided they'd better bet both the horse and the driver and went to book it with Johnny Sovereign.

That night Teo had a dream in which his cousin Alaina was riding him. She hadn't aged – the same bronze-skinned, virgin body he had spied on through the birdshit-splattered skylight on the roof in El Paso where his uncle, Jupo, kept a *palomar*. Uncle Jupo had taken him in when Teo was fourteen after his mother had run off with a cowboy. It became Teo's job to care for his uncle's pigeons. He was seventeen when Uncle Jupo caught him on the roof with his trousers open, spying on Alaina in her bath. His uncle knocked him down and smashed Teo's face into the pebbled roof as if trying to grind out his eyes, then sent him packing with eight dollars in his pocket. In the dream, Alaina still looked so young that Teo was ashamed to have dreamed it. The pain of her love bites woke him at dawn, and even after waking, his nipples ached from the fierce way her small teeth had pulled at his body, as if his flesh was taffy. Waiting under his door was an envelope with eight hundred dollars and a note: 'It was the driver. Thanks. Lefty.'

The third message arrived in a rainstorm. 'Lone Star.' Teo woke Lefty Antic out of a drunken stupor. They pored over the harness races, but the only possibility was a driver named T. North whose first name, Lefty thought, was Tex, and whose last name suggested the North Star. Then they checked the thoroughbreds at Arlington, and found a long shot named Bright Venus. 'The Evening Star!' Lefty said, smiling. Track conditions would be sloppy, and Bright Venus was a mudder. Lefty had the shakes so bad he could barely get dressed, but, convinced it was the score they'd been building to, he went off to lay their bets with Sovereign. Teo bet a thousand to win.

That night he had a nightmare that he was in El Paso, where he'd begun his career as a *luchador*, wrestling on the Lucha Libre circuit at fiestas and rodeos. In the dream he was wrestling the famous Ernesto 'La Culebra' Aguirre, the Snake, named for the plumed serpent Quetzalcoatl, the Aztec god of human sacrifice. Lucha Libre wrestlers often took the names of super-heroes and Aztec warriors, and Teo once really had wrestled the Snake, though not in El Paso. That match was in Amarillo, back in the days when Teo was making a name for himself as a masked *luchador* called the Hummingbird. He'd come upon his identity in an illustrated encyclopedia of the gods of Mexico. The Hummingbird was Huitzilopochtli, the Mayan sun god; the illustration showed a hawklike warrior bird rising from a thorny maguey plant. According to the caption, the thorns symbolized the Hummingbird's beak, and after Spain destroyed the Mayan empire, the thorns of the Hummingbird became the crown Jesus wore. Huitzilopochtli's sacred colors were sun white and sky blue, so those were the colors of the costume – mask, tank top, and tights – that Teo wore. When Teo put on the mask, he'd feel transformed by a surge of energy and strength. As the Hummingbird, he defied the limitations of his body and performed feats that marveled the crowds. He flew from ropes, survived punishing falls, lifted potbellied fighters twice his size high off their feet and slammed them into submission. To keep his identity secret, he would put on his mask miles from the ring, and afterward he wore it home. The nights before bouts he took to sleeping in his mask.

It was at a carnival in El Paso that he saw Alaina again, standing ringside with a group of high school friends, mostly boys. It had been three years since his uncle had thrown him out without giving him a chance to say goodbye to her. The boys must have come to see the *rudo* billed as El Huracán – the Hurricane – but known to fans as El Flatoso – Windy – for his flatulence in the ring. El Flatoso, with his patented move of applying a head scissors, then gassing his opponent into unconsciousness, was beloved by high school boys and drunks. Teo had been prepared to be part of the farce of fighting him until he saw Alaina in the crowd. He could feel her secretly watching him through her half-lowered eyelashes with the same intensity that he knew she'd watched him when he'd spied on her through the skylight. Suddenly, the vulgar spectacle he was about to enact was intolerable. The match was supposed to last for half an hour, but when El Flatoso came clownishly propelling himself with farts across the ring, the Hummingbird whirled up and delivered a spinning kick that knocked the *rudo* senseless. He didn't further humiliate El Flatoso by stripping off his mask, and the boys at ringside cursed, demanding their money back, before dejectedly dragging Alaina off with them. But he saw her look back and wave, and he bowed to her. Later that night, there was a light rap on the door of the trailer that served as his dressing room. Alaina stood holding an open bottle of mescal. 'Don't take it off,' she whispered as he began to remove his mask. Though they'd yet to touch, she stood unbuttoning her blouse. 'I don't believe this is happening,' he said, and she answered, 'Unbelievable things happen to people on the edge.' She spoke like a woman, not a girl, and when she unhooked her bra, her breasts were a woman's, full, tipped with nipples the shade of roses going brown, not the buds of the girl he'd spied on. He knelt before her and kissed her dusty feet. She raised her skirt, and he buried his face in her woman smell. He wanted the mask off so he could smear his cheeks with her. 'Leave it on,' she commanded, 'or I'll have to go.' He rose, kissing up her body, until his lips suckled her breasts and their warm, sweet-sour sweat coated his tongue, and suddenly her sighs turned to a cry. 'No, too sensitive,' she whispered, pushing him gently away, then she opened his shirt and kissed him back hard, fiercely biting and sucking his nipples as if he were a woman. 'My *guainambi*,' she said, using the Indian word for hummingbird.

It was months before he saw her again, this time at a rodeo in Amarillo – a long way from El Paso – where he stood in the outdoor ring waiting for his bout with the Snake. The loose white shirt she wore didn't conceal her pregnancy, and for a moment he wondered if the child could be his, then realized she'd already been with child when she'd knocked on his trailer door. La Culebra, in his plumed sombrero, rainbow-sequined cape, and feathered boa, was the star of the Lucha Libre circuit, and it had been agreed that the Hummingbird was to go down to his first defeat in a close match that would leave his honor intact so that a rivalry could be built. But when Teo saw Alaina there at ringside, he couldn't accept defeat. He and the Snake slammed each other about the ring, grappling for the better part of an hour under a scorching sun with Teo refusing to be pinned, and finally in a clinch the Snake told him, 'It's time, *pendejo*, stop fucking around,' and locked him in his signature move, the boa constrictor. But the Hummingbird slipped it, and when the Snake slingshotted at him off the ropes, the Hummingbird spun up into a helicopter kick. The collision dropped them both on their backs in the center of the ring. 'Cocksucker, this isn't El Flatoso you're fucking with,' the Snake told him as he rose spitting blood. The legend surrounding La Culebra was that he'd once been a heavyweight boxer. He'd become a *luchador* only after he'd killed another boxer in the ring, and now, when he realized they weren't following the script, he began using his fists. The first punch broke Teo's nose, and blood discolored his white-and-blue mask, swelling like a blood blister beneath the fabric. The usual theatrics disappeared, and the match became a street fight that had the fans on their feet cheering, a battle that ended with the Snake flinging the Hummingbird out of the ring. The fall fractured Teo's kneecap, his head bounced off the pavement, and as he lay stunned, unable to move for dizziness and pain, the Snake leaped down onto his chest from the height of the ring, stomping the breath from his body, and tore off the bloodied mask of the Hummingbird as if skinning him, then spit in his flattened face. Teo, his face a mask of blood, looked up into the jeering crowd, but he never saw Alaina again.

In Teo's nightmare, the Snake humiliated him not only by tearing off his Hummingbird mask and exposing his identity to the crowd but by derisively shouting '*Las tetas!*' and tearing off Teo's tank top, exposing a woman's breasts weeping milky tears. At dawn, when Teo groaned out of his dream, with his stomped, body-slammed chest aching and his heart a throbbing bruise, there was no envelope of winnings waiting. That morning Teo knocked repeatedly on Lefty Antic's door without an answer. The thought occurred to him that the saxophone player had taken off with their money, not out of crookedness but on a drunken binge. It was only in the afternoon, when Teo bought a newspaper and checked the racing scores at Arlington, that he learned Bright Venus had finished dead last. He checked the harness results at Sportsman's, and there was a story about a buggy overturning in the third race and its driver, Toby North, being critically injured when a trotting horse crushed his chest.

It seemed as if a vicious practical joke had been played on them all, but when the next message came, Teo knocked again on Lefty Antic's door. He hadn't seen the saxophone player since Lefty had staggered out to place their bets on Bright Venus. There still was no answer, and Teo, filled with a terrible sense of abandonment and foreboding, sure that Lefty Antic was dead inside, got the landlord to open the door, only to find the room empty and orderly. Alone, feeling too apprehensive simply to ignore the message, Teo studied the racing pages looking for clues as he'd seen Lefty Antic do. It seemed to him that the new rain-smudged message, 'delay plaza,' referred to the mayor, Richard Daley, and when he could find no connection whatsoever at any of the race tracks, he took the El train downtown. There wasn't a Daley Plaza in Chicago, but there was an open square near City Hall, and Teo walked there, not sure what he was looking for, yet hoping to recognize it when he saw it. But no sign presented itself, nothing was going on in the square but a rally for a young senator from Massachusetts, an Irish Catholic like the mayor, who was running for president in a country that Teo figured would never elect a Catholic.

The messages have continued to arrive, and Teo continues to save them, and the cigar box fills with scraps of paper his pigeons have brought home from God knows where. Teo can't shake the foreboding or the loneliness. His sleep is haunted by the recurrent dream of a funeral that extends the length of a country of ruined castles and burning ghettos. He's part of the procession following the casket, ascending a pyramid, its steps dark and slippery with the blood of what's gone before. He doesn't want to see what's at the summit. Unable to return to sleep, sometimes he spreads the messages on the table and tries to piece them together, to see if the torn edges fit like the pieces of a jigsaw puzzle or if the words can be arranged into a coherent sentence. He senses some story, some meaning, connecting them, but the words themselves baffle him: *knoll, motorcade, six seconds, bloodstone . . .*

And it's not dreams alone that disrupt his sleep. There's an increasing tenderness in his chest that waking doesn't dispel. In the darkness, his nipples ache as if they've been pinched with tongs; the palpitations of his heart resonate like spasms through soft tissue. His flesh feels foreign to his breastbone. He can feel his inflamed mounds of chest swelling beneath his undershirt, and he brushes his fingertips across his chest, afraid of what he'll find. He's put on weight, and his once sculpted chest has grown flabby, his weight lifter's pectorals drooping to fat. Come morning, he reassures himself that's all it is – fat, he's simply getting fat, and this strange pain will also pass.

Better to ignore it. He avoids studying the bathroom mirror when he shaves.

Sometimes, after midnight, he thinks he hears Lefty Antic playing his saxophone softly on the roof, but it's only wind vibrating the rusted chimney hood, streaming clouds rasping against a rusty moon, the hoot of pigeons. He hasn't seen the sax player since they lost their stake on 'Lone Star.'

Teo has written his own notes – 'Who are you? What do you want?' – and attached them to those pigeons of his who have brought the strange messages. Noah-like, he's sent them flying out over the wet rooftops to deliver his questions, but those pigeons haven't returned home, and it takes a lot to lose a homing pigeon. They fly in a dimension perilous with hawks and the ack-ack fire of boys armed with rocks, slingshots, and pellet guns. Fog and blizzards disorient them, storms blow them down, and yet instinct brings them home on a single wing, with flight feathers broken, missing a leg or the jewel of an eye.

Teo has decided that since his communiqués go unanswered and his birds don't return, he will refuse to accept further messages. All week he has kept his remaining pigeons cooped. And now this morning, attached to a strange pigeon, another message, the first in Spanish: *asesino*. 'Murder' or 'assassin,' Teo doesn't know which.

He'd like to ease the loneliness, if not the foreboding, and tell Zip about the messages. But until this afternoon, when he found Zip drinking alone and obviously needing someone to talk to, Teo has been reluctant to talk about anything more personal than Zip's favorite subject: fishing. True, Zip was obviously curious about Teo's wrestling career, but it didn't seem right to tell the insignificant story of the Hummingbird to a man who is so careful never to speak of war wounds.

'This feels like we're in some kind of joke,' Zip says, opening his palm and allowing the pigeon to step from Teo's hand to his.

'What do you mean?' Teo asks.

'You know,' Zip says, 'there's all these jokes that start: A man walks into a bar with a parrot, or a man walks into a bar with a dog, or a gorilla, or a cockroach. You know, all these guys walking into all these bars with every animal on the ark. So in this one, a man – no, a wrestler, a masked wrestler – walks into a bar with a pigeon.'

'So, what's the punch line?' Teo asks.

'You're asking me?' Zip says. 'It's *your* pigeon.'

'No, not one of mine.'

'Yeah, but you brought it in here.'

'But the joke is your idea.'

'Jesus, we got no punch line,' Zip says. 'You know what that means?'

'What?'

'We'll never get out of the joke.'

Whitey calls.

Joe, lying on the bare mattress, naked but for mismatched socks, doesn't answer. He knows it's Whitey on the phone. Joe can almost smell his cigar.

What day is it? Must be Thursday, because yesterday was Wednesday, a day's reprieve Johnny Sovereign never knew he had. Joe can have the conversation with Whitey without bothering to lift the receiver.

—Joe, what the fuck's going on with you?

—Hey, Whitey, you ball-buster, *vaffancul*!

Are these ball-busting calls some kind of psychological warfare? Maybe Whitey knows about Gloria Candido, and the whole thing with Johnny Sovereign is a setup. Maybe it's Whitey arranging for these women to distract Joe from doing his job, giving Whitey an excuse other than being a fucking *cornuto* to have Joe clipped. Could Whitey be that smart, that devious? Maybe Whitey has tipped off Sovereign to watch his back around Joe and Sovereign is waiting for Joe to make his move. Or maybe the women are good luck, guardian angels protecting him from some scheme of Whitey's.

Joe quietly lifts the receiver from the cradle. He listens for Whitey to begin blaring, *To, Joe, whatthefuck?* but whoever is on the line is listening, too. Joe can hear the pursy breathing. It could be Whitey's cigar-sucking, emphysemic huff. Joe slides the stiletto from his right sock, holds it to the mouthpiece, thumbs off the safety, touches the trigger button, and the blade hisses open: *Ssswap!* Then he gently sets down the receiver.

Joe dresses quickly. The shirt he's been wearing since Tuesday reeks, so he switches to the white shirt Marisol left behind even though it smells of perfume. She's left a trail of rusty footprints down the hall from the kitchen as if she stepped on broken glass, and Joe splashes them with Rémy and mops them with the dirty shirt he won't be wearing, then kills the bottle, washing down a mix of painkillers. There's a soft wheeze from his closet, as if an accordion is shuddering in its sleep. When he dials Johnny Sovereign's number, Vi answers on the third ring.

'Johnny home?'

'He'll be back around six or so,' Vi says. 'Can I take a message?'

'So where is he?'

'Can I take your number and have him call you back?'

'Do you even know?'

'Know what?' Vi asks. 'Who's calling?'

'An acquaintance.'

'You called yesterday and the day before.'

Joe hangs up.

The Bluebird is doing fifty down the cracked alleys, and when a bag lady steps from between two garbage cans, she has to drop her bag to get out of the way. Joe rolls over her shopping bag, bulging from a day's foraging, and in the rearview mirror sees her throwing hex signs in his wake. He pulls up behind Sovereign's, and there's that smell of trash, oil, and pigeons, compounded by a summer breeze. Joe can sense someone eyeing him from inside the empty garage, and he eases his right hand into the pocket of his sport coat and flicks the safety off the .22, uncomfortably aware of how useless the small-caliber pistol is at anything but point-blank range. A gray cat emerges from Sovereign's garage, carrying in its mouth a pigeon still waving a wing. The cat looks furtively at Joe, then slinks into the morning glories, and from the spot where the cat disappeared, Grace steps out. Morning glories are clipped to her tangled black curls. She's wearing a morning-glory-vine necklace, vine bracelets, and what looks like a bedraggled bridesmaid's gown, if bridesmaids wore black. Her bare feet are bloody, probably from walking on glass. 'Long time, no see, Joey,' she says. 'I been with the Carmelites.'

Joe recalls Sal asking if he was going to her closed-casket wake. 'You had a thing with her, didn't you?' Sal had asked.

'No way!' Joe told him. 'A little kissyface after a party once. I don't know why she made up all those stories.'

'That whole Fandetti family is bonkers,' Sal said.

Nelo, her father, a Sicilian from Taylor Street, operates an escort service, massage parlors, and a strip bar on South Wabash, but he brought his four daughters up in convent school. The official story was that Grace wasted away with leukemia, but rumor had it that it was a botched abortion. Now, Joe realizes old man Fandetti is even crazier than he thought, faking his daughter's death in order to avoid the humiliation of an illegitimate pregnancy. No surprise she's a nutcase. He wonders if they collected insurance on her while they were at it.

'If you stick your finger inside, you can feel the electric,' Grace says and demonstrates by poking her finger into a flower. 'That hum isn't bees. Electric's what gives them their blue. You should feel it. Come here and put your finger in.'

'Where's your shoes, Grace?'

'Under the bed, so they think I'm still there.'

'Still where? What are you doing here?'

'Come here, Joey, and put your finger in. You'll feel what the bee's born for. They're so drunk on flower juice!' She walks to the car and leans in through the window on the passenger side, and the straps of her black gown slip off her shoulders, and from its décolletage breasts dangle fuller than he remembers from that one night after a birthday party at Fabio's when he danced with her and they sneaked out to the parking lot and necked in his car. She'd looked pretty that night, made up like a doll, pearls in her hair, and wearing a silky dress with spaghetti straps. That was what she called them when he slipped them down and kissed her breasts. She wanted to go further, pleaded with him to take her virginity, but he didn't have a rubber and it wasn't worth messing with her connected old man.

'Know what was on the radio?'

'When?' Joe asks. He's aware that he's staring, but apparently still stoned on that hash oil, he can't take his eyes off her breasts. His reactions feel sluggish; he has to will them. He realizes he's been in a fog . . . he's not sure how long, but it's getting worse.

She opens the door and sinks into the leather seat and humming tunelessly flicks on the car radio. 'I Only Have Eyes for You' is playing. 'Our song, Joey!'

'Grace, we don't have a song.'

'The night we became lovers.'

'Why'd you tell people that?'

'You got me in trouble, Joey, and in the Carmelites I had to confess it to the bishop. We weren't supposed to talk, but he made me show and tell.'

Joe flicks off the radio. It's like turning on the afternoon: birdsong, pigeons cooing, flies buzzing trash, the bass of bees from a thousand blue gramophones.

'All the sisters were jealous. They called me Walkie-Talkie behind my back. They thought I didn't understand the sacredness of silence, but that's not true. They think silence is golden, but real silence is terrifying. We're not made for it. I could tell you things, Joey, but they're secrets.'

'Like what, Grace? Things somebody told you not to tell me?'

'Things God whispers to me. Joey, you smell like a girl.'

'I think you can't tell 'cause you don't know. Tell me one secret God said just so I see if either of you knows anything.'

'I know words to an accordion. If you turn on your radio you'll hear stars singing the song of a thousand crackles. I know about you and girls. I know what's in your gym bag.'

'Yeah, what?'

'They're your way of being totally alone.'

'What's in the gym bag, Grace?'

'I know you can't stop staring at my tits. I don't mind, you can see. Oh, God! Windshields glorify the sun! Feel.'

'Not here, Grace.'

'Okay, at your place.'

'That's not a good idea,' Joe says, but he can't stay here with her either, so he eases the car into gear and drives slowly up the alley. The top of her dress is down, and against his better judgment – almost against his will – he turns onto

Twenty-fifth, crosses Rockwell, the boundary between two-flats and truck docks. He drives carefully, his eyes on a street potholed by semis, but aware of her beside him with her dirty feet bloody and her bare breasts in plain view. Rockwell is empty, not unusual for this time of day. They're approaching a railroad viaduct that floods during rainstorms. A block beyond the viaduct is Western Avenue, a busy street that in grade school he learned is the longest street in the world, just like the Amazon is the longest river, so they called it Amazon Avenue. Western won't be deserted, and across Western is the little Franciscan church of St Michael's and the old Italian parish where he lives.

'I'm a Sister of Silence, so you need to be nice to me like I always was to you.'

'I've always been nice to you, too, Grace.'

'I could have had men hurt you, Joey, but I didn't.'

They're halfway through the streaky tunnel of the railroad viaduct and he hits the brakes and juts his arm out to brace her from smacking the windshield. 'I don't like when people threaten me, Grace. It really makes me crazy.'

'Let's go to your place, Joey. Please drive. I hate when the trains go over. All those tons of steel on top of you, and the echoes don't stop in your head even after the train is gone.'

'There's no train.'

'It's coming. I can feel it in my heart. My heart is crying.' She squeezes a nipple and catches a milky tear on a fingertip and offers it to him, reaching up to brush it across his lips, but Joe turns his face away. When he does, she slaps him. He catches her arm before she can slap him again, and under the viaduct, minus the glare of sun in his eyes, he sees her morning-glory-vine bracelets are scars welted across her wrists. Whistle wailing, a freight hurtles over, vibrating the car. He releases her arm, and she clamps her hands over her ears. Her bare feet stamp a tantrum of bloody imprints on the floor mat.

'Get out!' Joe yells over the concussions of boxcars, and he reaches across her body to open the door. She looks at him in amazement, then mournfully steps out into the gutter, her breasts still exposed. Without looking back, he guns into the daylight on the other side, catches the green going yellow on Western, veers into traffic, rattles across the bridge wheeled by pigeons that spans the Sanitary Canal. He isn't going back to his place, he's not heading to pick up his laundry, and until he finishes this job he's not going to Fabio's or any of the hangouts where he might run into Whitey. It's Thursday, and Joe's been seeing Gloria Candido on the sly on Thursdays, when Julio goes to his grandmother's after school, but Joe isn't going to Gloria's either. He's in the flow of Amazon Avenue, popping painkillers, Grace's handprint still hot on his face. He heads south to see what's at the end of the longest street in the world. The radio is off as if he's broken contact, and he'd drive all night if not for hallucinations of headlights coming head-on. Finally he has to pull over and close his eyes. When he wakes, not sure he was ever really asleep, he's parked on a shoulder separated from a field by rusty barbed wire netted in spider silk suspending pink droplets of sun. The blank highway is webbed like that as far as he can see. He thinks, I could just keep going, and at the next gas station, on an impulse, Joe decides he will keep going if she doesn't answer the phone. But then he doesn't have enough change to make the call. 'Make it collect, for Vi Sovereign,' he tells the operator.

'Who should I say is calling?' the operator asks.

'Tell her a friend who's been calling, she'll know.' And when the operator does, Vi accepts the call. 'Where you calling from?' Vi asks. 'I hear cars.'

'A phone booth off Western Avenue. Johnny home?'

'You're calling early,' she says. 'He'll be home around noon or so for lunch.'

'You don't know where he is or what he's doing? I can hear it in your voice. Did he even come home last night?'

'What do you keep calling for? If you're trying to tell me something about Johnny, just say it. You somebody's husband? What's your name?'

'Maybe we'll meet sometime. I'd pay you back for the phone call, but then you'd know it was me.'

'I'll recognize your voice.'

'Better you don't,' Joe says, and hangs up.

Before noon, he pulls up behind Johnny Sovereign's. From the longest street in the world, he's back to idling in a block-length alley, and yet it's oddly peaceful there, private, a place that's come to feel familiar, and he's so tired and wired at the same time that he'd be content just to drowse awhile with the sun soothing his eyelids. He lights a smoke, chucks the crushed, empty pack out the window, checks the empty alley in the rearview mirror, and notices the handprint still visible on his face. He catches his own eyes glancing uncomfortably back, embarrassed by the intimacy of the moment, as if neither he nor his reflection wants anything to do with each other. He puts on a pair of sunglasses he keeps in the visor, and when he looks up through their green lenses, a tanned blonde with slender legs, in a halter top and short turquoise shorts, stands beside the morning glories. She's wearing sunglasses, too.

'Hi, Joe, they told me I'd find you here. I been waiting all morning, thinking how it would be when I saw you. I missed you so much, baby. I thought I could live without you, but I can't.'

'Capri,' he says.

She smiles at the sound of her name. 'My guy, my baby.'

'Oh fuck, fuck, not you, baby. I didn't care about the others, but not you, too.' He hasn't realized until now that he's been waiting for this moment ever since, without warning, her letters had stopped, leaving a silence that has grown increasingly ominous. Her last letter ended: 'Sometimes I read the weather in your city, so that I can imagine you waking up to it, living your life without me.' After a month with no word, he'd asked Sal if he'd heard anything about her, but he hadn't. In all likelihood she'd met someone, and Joe thought he'd be making a fool of himself getting in touch. Even so, he tried calling, but her number was disconnected.

'I'm back, baby. Aren't you glad to see me?' She steps toward the car and removes her sunglasses. He can't meet her eyes any more than he can meet his own in the mirror. If he could speak, the words he'd say – 'I'm crying in my heart' – wouldn't be his, and when she reaches her arms out, Joe slams the car into reverse, floors it, and halfway down the alley, skidding along garbage cans, hits a bag lady. He can hear her groan as the air goes out of her. He sees her sausage legs kicking spasmodically from where he's knocked her, pinned and thrashing between two garbage cans. Joe keeps going.

Nothing's more natural than sky.

From here railroad tracks look like stitching that binds the city together. If shadows can be trusted, the buildings are growing taller. From up here, gliding, it's clear there's a design: the gaps of streets and alleys are for the expansion of shadow the way lines in a sidewalk allow for the expansion of pavement in the heat.

With a message to carry, there isn't time to ride a thermal of blazing roses, to fade briefly from existence like a daylight moon. What vandal cracked its pane? The boy whose slingshot shoots cat's-eye marbles? The old man with a cane, who baits a tar roof with hard corn then waits with his pellet gun, camouflaged by a yellowed curtain of Bohemian lace?

Falcons that roost among gargoyles, feral cats, high-voltage wires, plate glass that mirrors sky – so many ways to fall from blue. When men fly they know by instinct they defy.

It's not angels the Angelus summons but iridescent mongrels with blue corkers in the history of their genes, and carriers, fantails, pouters, mondains – marbled, ring-necked, crested – tipplers, tumblers, rollers, homers homeless as prodigals, all circling counterclockwise around the tolling belfry of St Pius as flying against time. Home lost, but not the instinct to home. Message lost, but not the instinct to deliver.

From up here it's clear the saxophone emitting dusk on a rooftop doesn't know it plays in harmony with the violin breaking hearts on the platform of an El, or with the blind man's accordion on an empty corner, breaking no heart other than its own. Or with the chorus of a thousand blackbirds. Love can't keep silent, and this is its song.

'You need a fucken ark to get through that shit,' Johnny Sovereign says.

The flooded side street is a dare: sewers plugged, hydrants uncapped, scrap wood wedged against each gushing hydrant mouth to fashion makeshift fountains.

'Think of it as a free car wash,' Joe says.

'I don't see you driving your T-bird through.'

'I might if it was whitewashed with baked pigeon shit. Go, man!'

They crank up the windows and Sovereign guns the engine

and drops the canary-yellow Pancho into first. By second gear, water sheets from the tires like transparent wings, then the blast of the first hydrant cascades over the windshield, and Sovereign, driving blind, flicks the wipers on and leans on the horn. By the end of the block they're both laughing.

'You can turn your wipers off now,' Joe says. He can hear the tires leaving a trail of wet treads as they turn down Cermak. 'Where you going, man?' Joe asks.

'Expressway,' Sovereign says. 'I thought you wanted to see what this muther can do opened up. You sure you don't want to drive?'

'I'm too wiped.'

'You look wiped. Rough night?' Sovereign smirks. 'Come on, you drive. A ride like this'll get the blood pumping.'

'Yo, it ain't like I'm driving a fucken Rambler.'

'No, no, your T-bird's cool, but this is a fucking bomb.'

'I'll ride shotgun. But I want to see what it does from jump. I heard zero to sixty in eight-point-one. Go where the dragsters go.'

'By 3 V's?'

'Yeah, 3 V's is good,' Joe says. 'Private. We can talk a little business there, too.'

The 3 V's Birdseed Company, a five-story dark brick factory with grated windows, stands at the end of an otherwise deserted block. The east side of the street is a stretch of abandoned factories; the west side is rubble, mounds of bricks like collapsed pyramids where factories stood before they were condemned. Both sides of the street are lined with dumped cars too junky to be repoed or sold, some stripped, some burned. Summer nights kids drag-race here.

'Park a sec. We'll oil up,' Joe says. They've driven blocks, but he can still hear the wet treads of the tires as Sovereign pulls into a space among the junkers along the curb. Joe unzips the gym bag he's lugged with him into Sovereign's Bonneville and hoists out the Scotch bottle. There's not more than a couple swallows left. 'Haig pinch. Better than Chivas.'

Sovereign takes a swig. 'Chivas is smoother,' he says. He offers Joe a Marlboro. Joe nips off the filter, Sovereign lights them up and flicks on the radio to the Cubs' station. 'I just want to make sure it's Drabowsky pitching. I took bets.'

'Who'd bet on the fucken Cubs?'

'Die-hard fans, some loser who woke up from a dream with a hunch, the DP's around here bet on Drabowsky. Who else but the Cubs would have a pitcher from Poland? Suckers always find a way to figure the odds are in their favor.'

It's Moe Drabowsky against the Giants' Johnny Antonelli. Sovereign flashes an in-the-know smile, flicks the radio off, then takes a victorious belt of Scotch and passes it to Joe. 'Kill it,' Joe says, and when Sovereign does, Joe lobs the empty pinch bottle out the window and it cracks on a sidewalk already glittering with shards of muscatel pints and shattered fifths of rotgut whiskey. Sun cascades over the yellow Bonneville. 'Man, those mynahs scream,' Sovereign says. 'Sounds like goddamn Brookfield Zoo. Hear that one saying a name?'

In summer, the windows behind the grates on the fifth floor of 3 V's are open. The lower floors of the factory are offices and stockrooms. The top floor houses exotic birds – parakeets, Java birds, finches, canaries, mynahs. Sometimes there's an escape, and tropical birds, pecked by territorial sparrows, flit through the neighborhood trees while people chase beneath with fishing nets, hoping to snag a free canary.

'It's the sparrows,' Joe says. 'They come and torment the fancy-ass birds. "*Cheep-cheep*, asshole, you're jackin off on the mirror in a fucken cage while I'm out here singing and flying around." Drives the 3 V's birds crazy and they start screeching and plucking out their feathers. You ever felt that way?'

'What? In a cage?' Sovereign asks. 'No fucken way, and I don't intend to. So, what's the deal?' He actually checks his jeweled Bulova as if suddenly realizing it's time in his big-shot day for him to stop gabbing about birds and get down to business. 'Whitey say something about me getting a little more of the local action? Setting craps up on weekends?'

'Yeah, local action,' Joe says. 'That's what I want to talk to you about.'

'I'm in,' Johnny says. 'I'm up for whatever moves you guys have in mind, Joe.'

'There's just one minor problem to work out,' Joe says. 'Whitey thinks you're skimming.'

'Huh?' Sovereign says.

'You heard me,' Joe says. 'Look, I know your mind is going from fucken zero to sixty, but the best thing is to forget trying to come up with bullshit no one's going to believe anyway and to work this situation out.'

'Joe, what you talking about? I keep books. I always give an honest count. No way I would pull that.'

'See, that's pussy-ass bullshit. A waste of our precious time. Whitey checked your books. He had Vince, the guy who set the numbers up in the first place, check them. They double-checked. You fucked up, Johnny, so don't bullshit me.'

'I never took a nickel beyond my percentage. There gotta be a mistake.'

'You saying you may have made a miscalculation? That your arithmetic is bad?'

'Not that I know of.'

'Where'd you get the scratch for this car?'

'Hey, I'm doing all right. I mean, and I owe on it. The bank fucking owns it.'

'More bullshit, you paid cash. Whitey checked. You been making book here, gambling it Uptown and losing, drinking hard, cheating on Vi . . .'

'Vi? What you talking about? She's got nothing to do with nothing.'

'Why wouldn't you stay home with a primo lady like that? You're out of control, man. Your fucken Pancho's leaking oil. With your fear of cages, next you'll be talking to the wrong people. You're a punk-ass bullshitter and a bad risk.'

'Joe, I swear to you—'

'You swear?'

'On my mother's grave. Swear it on my children.'

'You cross your heart and hope to die, too?'

'Huh?'

'Like little kids say?'

'I know how kids talk, Joe. I got a baby girl and a little boy, Johnny Junior.'

'So, swear it like you mean it,' Joe says, exhaling smoke and flicking his cigarette out the window. 'I cross my heart . . .' Sovereign looks at Joe as if he can't be serious, and Joe stares him down.

'Cross my heart . . .' Sovereign says.

'No, you got to actually cross your heart,' Joe says, crossing his own heart, and when, to illustrate further, Joe reaches with his left hand to open Sovereign's sport coat, Sovereign flinches, then smiles, chagrined at being so jumpy. Instead of making a move to resist Joe touching him, Sovereign drags on his cigarette. 'Nice pricey sport coat, nice monogrammed shirt,' Joe says, holding Sovereign by the lapel. 'Sure there's a heart in here to cross, Johnny?' Joe brings his right hand up to check for a heartbeat. 'Relax, I'm just fucking with you.' Joe smiles, then touches the trigger on the stiletto he's palmed from his argyle sock, the blade darting out as he thrusts, slamming Sovereign back against the car door, the cigarette shooting from his mouth as he groans *uuuhhh*.

Sovereign's hands are pressed to where the blade is buried. He looks down at the bloodied pearl handle of the stiletto sticking from his chest, his eyes bulging, teeth gritted so that the muscles knot out from his jaw.

'Don't move, it's in clean,' Joe says. 'Just let it go.'

'Oh, my God, oh, oh,' Sovereign exhales, and an atomized spray of blood hangs in the sunlit air between them. The 3 V's birds raise a junglish chatter against the everyday chirp of sparrows. The hot car fills with Sovereign's gasping for breath and with the smell of garlic, of the mortadella sausage on the blade, and then an acrid smell, calling to Joe's mind a line of kindergartners. Sovereign has peed his pants. His right hand, smeared with the blood soaking through his monogrammed shirt, slips down his body, weakly feeling as if to brush away a burning cigarette. There's no cigarette, his cigarette has slipped between the seats. Joe guides Sovereign's hand back to his chest and Sovereign grits his teeth again and groans from the soul, then closes his eyes. Tears well out from under his red lashes. His skin has gone translucent white, making his liverish freckles stand out like beads of blood forced through his pores.

'Not Vi,' Sovereign says. 'Oh, please, not Vi. I got little kids.' Blood gurgles in his throat, he tries to clear it and begins to choke and Joe clamps a handkerchief over his mouth and Sovereign keeps swallowing, breathing hard, but otherwise not struggling, as if the pain of the knife has pinned him to the door.

'I told you not to talk. Just let it go. I tried to do you a favor, man. Whitey wants you turned into hamburger. I let you off easy,' Joe says, removing his bloodied handkerchief from Sovereign's mouth.

Sovereign is shaking his head no-no, trying to form words with his open mouth. A bubble of bloody spit breaks on his lips. All he can do is whisper. His body has slouched so that Joe looks into Sovereign's dilated nostrils, which are throwing cavernous shadows. Joe leans closer to hear what Sovereign's trying to say.

'Bullshit,' Johnny Sovereign manages. The word sends up a hanging, reddish spray. 'You just wanted to see if it worked.'

'Fuck you,' Joe says. 'You got a reprieve you didn't even know you had. What did you do with the time?' But even as he says it, Joe realizes Sovereign is right. He wanted to see what the knife could do, and how stupid was that, because now he's stuck talking with a dying mook. He should have just put a couple into Sovereign's brain and walked the fuck away instead of getting cute, sitting here listening to birds chatter, beside a guy with his jaw grinding and red eyelashes pasted shut by the tears leaking down his cheeks as his life hemorrhages away, the muscle that once pumped five quarts a minute, a hundred thousand heartbeats a day – how many in a life? – no longer keeping time. Joe's not sure how long they've been here. He wants the knife back but worries that if he pulls it out Sovereign will start to thrash and yell, and the wound will gush. Sovereign makes a sound as if he's gargling, syrupy blood dribbles from the corner of his mouth as his head rolls to the side, and then he's quiet. Tears dry on his cheeks.

'Sovereign,' Joe says. 'Johnny? You still here?' Joe can hardly speak for the dryness of his own mouth. He's aware of how terribly thirsty he is, and of how suddenly alone. Heat rays in as if the windshield of the Pancho is God's magnifying glass. Now

Joe can hear the name Sovereign was talking about – some 3 V's bird repeating *betty betty betty*. He can't sit any longer listening to the nonstop jabber of the last sounds Sovereign heard.

'Johnny.'

Joe digs the shotgun out of the gym bag. His handkerchief is bloody so he uses his jockstrap to wipe down the sawed-off shotgun he'll leave behind, jammed in Sovereign's piss-soaked crotch. He tries to ease out the stiletto. Blood wells up without gushing. Joe tugs harder but can't dislodge the knife, maybe because his hands have started to shake. He's drenched with sweat, and takes his jacket off. How did his white shirt get spattered with blood? He removes his shirt. The lapels of his powder-blue sport coat are speckled, too, but the splash pattern that's good for eating spaghetti makes it look as if the blood might be part of the coat. He wipes the car and knife handle down with the shirt. In the gym bag, there's a wrinkled gray tank top with the faded maroon lettering CHAMPS over an insignia of crossed boxing gloves. Joe pulls that on and slips his jacket over it, and then, for no reason, fits the jockstrap over Sovereign's face so that it looks as if he's wearing a mask or a blindfold. At the shotgun blast, flocks rise, detonated from the factory roofs, and Joe imagines how on the top floor of 3 V's the spooked birds batter their cages.

Friday afternoon, a red clothespin day at the Zip Inn. Ball game on the TV, Drabowsky against the Giants' Johnny Antonelli, top of the fifth and the Cubs down 2–0 on a Willie Mays homer. The jukebox, Zip apologizes, is on the fritz. No 'Ebb Tide,' no 'Sing, Sing, Sing,' no 'Cucurrucucu Paloma.'

Teo sits on a stool, balancing the quarters that he was going to feed to the jukebox on the wooden bar.

'One more, on the house,' Zip says. His white shirt looks slept in, his bow tie askew, his furrowed face stubbled, eyes bloodshot. It's clear he's continued the pace from yesterday. Teo turns his shot glass upside down. Zip turns it back up. 'To Friday,' Zip says.

'We already drank to Friday.' Teo turns his shot glass back down. 'We drank to Friday yesterday, and to Saturday, Sunday, Monday, Tuesday, and Wednesday.'

'We missed Thursday.'

'Yesterday was Thursday, we started out drinking to Thursday.'

'Yeah, but today's fucking special.'

'Every day's special. Isn't that the point of drinking to them?' Teo asks.

'There is no point,' Zip says. 'That's the point.'

Teo shrugs. 'So why's today special? An anniversary?'

'*Special*'s the wrong word,' Zip says. He looks as if the right word might be *doomed*.

Something is eating at Zip, but Teo doesn't know how to ask what. Yesterday, Teo stayed drinking with him until the after-work crowd started filtering in. By then, Teo was half loaded. He put the wounded Spanish pigeon back in his bowling bag and went home, tended to the coop, then fell into bed and, for the first night in weeks, slept undisturbed by dreams. 'Look, compadre, if there's something I can do . . .'

'Have a brew,' Zip says. He sets a Hamm's before Teo, and a bag of pretzels, and rings up one of the quarters that Teo has balanced on the bar. 'You bring your feathered friend with the bum wing?'

'No,' Teo says, 'but I got something you been asking about.' From the bowling bag on the barstool beside him, Teo lifts out a blue head mask and sets it face up, flat on the bar. The face has the design of a golden beak and iridescent white feathers

195

that fan into flames around flame-shaped eyes. The luminous colors are veined with brownish bloodstains. 'You wanted to see, so I brought it.'

'Goddamn.' Zip smiles, looking for a moment like his old self. 'This is what you wrestled in? Pretty wild. So, what was your ring name?'

'La Colibrí.'

'Like the vegetable?'

'It's a kind of bird,' Teo says.

'You got the rest of the outfit in there?'

Teo unfolds the matching blue tights, and Zip holds them up, smiling skeptically at Teo.

'They stretch,' Teo says.

'Not that much they don't.'

'Yeah, they do. I'm wearing the top. Same material.' Teo unbuttons his checked short-sleeved shirt. Underneath, he's wearing an iridescent blue tank top. Its bulgy front is spotted with faded blood, like the canvas of a ring.

'I wish I could of seen you in the ring, amigo, must have been something.' Zip picks up the mask. He looks as if he'd like to try it on if he had two hands to pull it over his head. 'Can you actually see to fight out of this?'

'Sure,' Teo says, 'it's got holes for the eyes.'

'Let's see.' Zip hands the mask to Teo, and when Teo hesitates, Zip says, 'Come on. What the hell?'

'What the hell,' Teo agrees, and pulls it over his head. It's the first time in years that he's worn it, and he's amazed to feel a reminiscent surge of energy, but maybe that's merely the whiskey kicking in on an empty stomach.

'You are one fierce-looking warrior,' Zip says. 'You should come in here wearing the whole outfit, just amble in and sit down, open up your book, and if somebody asks, "Who's that?"

I'll tell them: "Him? The new security. Guards the hard-boiled eggs – which are now a buck apiece in order to pay for security. Salt's still free.'"

On the TV, the Hamm's commercial, *'From the land of sky-blue waters,'* plays between innings.

'Can you drink beer through that?' Zip asks.

When Teo laughs, it's the mask itself that seems to be laughing, the mask that chugs down a bottle of Hamm's.

'Why's Goldblatt's got you disguised in a dress when they could have a goddamn superhero patrolling the aisles? You're wasting your talent. You could be a rent-a-wrestler, make up business cards. Headlocks for hire, Half nelsons fifty percent off. I need an autographed picture for the wall. Hey, I could sponsor you, advertise on your jersey.'

'Have a Nip at the Inn of Zip,' Teo says.

'You're a poet!' Zip sets them up with two more cold ones and rings up another of the quarters Teo has balanced on the bar. 'Can the Kohlrabi still kick ass?' Zip asks.

'Fight again?' Teo asks. Even wearing the blue tank top and the mask, even after the first good night's sleep in a long time, even with the sunlight streaming through the door and whiskey through his veins, on a Friday afternoon, and nowhere to be but here, drinking cold beer and joking with his new friend, Teo knows that's impossible.

'What if there was no choice?' Zip asks. 'If it was him or you? Say you catch somebody stealing and he pulls a knife? Could you do whatever it took? Is it worth it? Purely theoretical, what if somebody hired you to watch their back in a situation like that?'

The undisguised undercurrent of desperation in these questions makes Teo recall the message from the Spanish pigeon: *'Asesino.'* Murder. The slip of paper is still in Teo's pocket. There's an eerie feeling of premonition about it. He'd been thinking maybe of showing it to Zip to see what he made of it, but not now. 'Purely theoretical, you keep protection back there?' Teo asks.

'Funny you should ask, I was just looking through my purely theoretical ordnance last night,' Zip says. 'Swiss Army knife, USMC 45 missing the clip. Ever seen one of these?' Zip reaches beneath the bar and sets a short, gleaming sword in front of Teo.

Teo runs his finger along the Oriental lettering engraved on the blade.

'Careful, it's razor-sharp,' Zip says. 'Never found out what the letters mean, probably something about honor that gets young men killed. Guys said the Japs used to sharpen these with silk. I don't know if that's true, but all the dead Jap soldiers had silk flags their families gave them when they went to war. Made good souvenirs. GIs took everything you could imagine for souvenirs. Bloody flags, weapons, gold teeth, polished skulls until there was an order against those. Wonder what happened to all that shit? Probably stuffed away forgotten in boxes in basements and attics all over the country. Only thing I took was this. It's a samurai knife used for hari-kari. They'd sneak in at night and cut your throat, so we slept two in a foxhole, me and Domino Morales, one dozing, the other doing sentry. You'd close your eyes dead tired knowing your life depended on your buddy staying awake.' Zip weighs the sword in his hand, then sets it back under the bar and lifts a length of sawed-off hickory bat handle that dangles by a rawhide loop from a hook beside the cash register. 'This used to be enough,' he says, 'but the way things are these days you gotta get serious if you want to defend yourself. Whoa!' Zip exclaims, gesturing with the bat at the TV screen. 'Banks got all of that one.'

On the TV, Jack Brickhouse is into his home-run call: 'Back she goes . . . way back . . . back! . . . back! Hey! Hey!'

'Hey! Hey!' Joe Ditto says. He stands in the emblazoned doorway in his sunglasses and factory steel-toes, his powder-blue sport coat looking lopsided and pouchy where the gun weighs down his right pocket. He's wearing the sport coat over a wrinkled gym top, and in his left hand he holds a gym bag. He's sweating as if he's just come from a workout. 'Didn't mean to startle you, Mr Zip. I thought you were going to brain your customer here. This masked marauder didn't pay his bar tab? You want I should speak to him?'

Zip hangs the bat back on its hook, and Joe sets the gym bag down and straddles a stool beside Teo. No introductions are made. On the right side of Joe's face, beneath a four-day growth of beard, there's a hot-looking handprint. 'What's so interesting?' Joe asks, when he catches Zip staring. 'You don't like the new look from the other side of Western?' He tucks in his Champs tank top as if it's his gym shirt-sport coat combination that Zip was staring at. 'Fucken hot out there,' Joe says. 'I need a cold one. You need an air conditioner in here, Mr Zip.'

'They're too noisy,' Zip says. 'You can't hear the ball game.'

'Hey, I'm not trying to sell you one,' Joe says. He drains his beer in three gulps and slams down the bottle. Teo's remaining two quarters teeter onto their sides. 'Hit me again, Mr Zip. And a shot of whatever you're drinking. What's score?'

'Cubs down two to one. Banks just hit one.'

'Drabowsky still pitching? You know where he's from?'

'Ozanna, Poland,' Zip says like it's a stupid question. 'He's throwing good.'

'You bet on him?' Joe asks. When he raises the shot glass, his hand is so shaky that he has to bring his mouth to the glass.

'I don't bet on baseball,' Zip says.

'Hit me again, Mr Zip. And one for yourself.' From a roll of bills, Joe peels a twenty onto the bar. 'What are you drinking, Masked Marvel? Zip, give Zorro here a Hamm's-the-beer-refreshing.'

Zip sets them up, and the three men sit in silence, looking from their drinks to the ball game as if waiting for some signal to down their whiskeys. Their dark reflections in the long mirror behind the bar wait, too. Teo glances at the mirror, where a man in a blue Hummingbird mask glances back. He knows the guy in the sunglasses beside him is mob, and can't help noticing that Zip has gone tensely quiet, unfriendlier than he's ever seen him. It makes him aware of how Zip set the samurai sword within reach, and of the message from the Spanish pigeon.

On the TV, Jack Brickhouse says, 'Oh, brother, looks like a fan fell out of the bleachers,' and his fellow sportscaster, Vince Lloyd, adds, 'Or jumped down, Jack.' Brickhouse, as if doing play-by-play, announces, 'Now, folks, he's running around the outfield!' and Vince Lloyd adds, 'Jack, I think he's trying to hand Willie Mays a beer!'

'That's Lefty!' Teo exclaims.

'Lefty? Lefty Antic?' Zip asks. 'You sure?'

'The sax player. He's my neighbor.'

'Here come the Andy Frain ushers out on the field,' Brickhouse announces. 'They'll get things back under control.'

'Look at him run!' Teo says.

'Go, Lefty!' Zip yells. 'He ain't going down easy.'

Without warning, the TV blinks into a commercial: '*From the land of sky-blue waters . . .*'

'Shit!' Joe says. 'That was better than the fucking game. Guy had some moves.'

'You know Lefty, the sax player?' Teo asks Zip.

'Hell, I got him on the wall,' Zip says, and from among the photo gallery of softball teams with *Zipln* lettered on their jerseys he lifts down a picture of a young boxer with eight-ounce gloves cocked. The boxer doesn't have a mustache, but it's easy to recognize the sax player. 'He made it to the Golden Glove Nationals,' Zip says. 'Got robbed on a decision.'

'That southpaw welterweight from Gonzo's Gym. I remember him from when I was growing up,' Joe Ditto says. 'Kid had fast hands.' He raises his shot glass, and they all drink as if to something.

'Well, back to baseball, thank goodness,' Jack Brickhouse says. 'Vince, it's unfortunate, but a few bad apples just don't belong with the wonderful fans in the friendly confines of beautiful Wrigley field.'

'Best fans in the game, Jack,' Vince says.

'They didn't want to show him beating the piss out of the Andy Frains,' Joe says.

'Lefty's good people. Hasn't put Korea behind him yet, that's all,' Zip says.

Until yesterday, Teo couldn't gimp on his bum knee into the Zip Inn without wondering how Zip could put behind him the war that took his arm. Now he knows. Zip hasn't.

'Hit me again, Mr Zip,' Joe says. 'A double. And get yourself and Masked Man, here.' Joe turns Teo's shot glass up.

Teo turns it back down.

Joe turns it back up. 'Hey, mystery challenger, we're having a toast.' Joe props Lefty's photo up against a bottle of Hamm's. 'To a man who knows how to really enjoy a Cubs game.' This time, his hand steadier, Joe clinks each of their glasses.

'Gimme a pack of Pall Malls, Mr Zip. So, what's with the mask?' Joe asks Teo. 'Off to rob a savings and loan? A nylon's not good enough? Goddamn, you got the whole outfit here,' he says, examining the tights that Teo hasn't stuffed back into his bowling bag. 'You one of those street wrestlers on Cinco de Mayo or something?'

'Used to be,' Teo says.

With his long-neck beer bottle, Joe parts Teo's open shirt to get a look at his tank top. 'Who'd you fight as, the Blue Titman? Jesus, Mr Zip, check the boobs out on this guy. That's some beery-looking bosom you're sporting, hombre. They squirt Hamm's? This might be the best tit in Little Village.' Joe lights a smoke, offers one to Teo, who refuses. 'Mr Zip, hit me again, and Knockers here, too,' Joe says. He's holding Teo's glass so that Teo can't turn it over. Zip pours and Joe takes a sip of beer. Then his hand snakes along the bar and into Teo's bag of pretzels. Joe munches down a pretzel, and his hand snakes back for another, except this time it snakes inside Teo's shirt for a quick feel before Teo pulls away.

Zip appears to be busy rinsing out a glass.

'Ever go home after a hard day's wrestling and just spend a quiet evening getting some off yourself, or does there have to be a commitment first?' Joe asks. 'I'm just fucking with you, friend. I used to love to watch wrestling when I was a kid. I didn't know it was a fake. You know, I didn't mind finding out Santa Claus was bullshit, but Gorgeous George and Zuma the Man from Mars – he wrestled in a mask, too – that hurt.'

'It's not always fake,' Teo says.

'What fucken planet are you from? How do you think Gorgeous George could have done against Marciano? Would you consider a little private contest that wasn't fixed?'

'I don't wrestle anymore,' Teo says.

'See, but this may be my only chance to say I wrestled a pro. I'm just talking arm wrestling here,' Joe says, and assumes the position, with his elbow on the bar. 'We'll wrestle for a drink, or a twenty, or the world championship of the Zip Inn, whatever you want.'

'I'm retired,' Teo says.

'Come on,' Joe says, 'beside experience you got forty pounds on me. If your friend Lefty can jump out of the bleachers and take on the Andy Frain ushers, you and me can have a friendly little match. Mr Zip has winner. Left-handed, of course. You can referee, Mr Zip, and hey, that little matter of business for today, let's forget it. Another time, maybe. Who you betting on, or do you not bet on arm wrestling, either?'

'Twenty on El Kohlrabi,' Zip says.

Teo looks at Zip, surprised.

'Purely theoretical,' Zip says, 'but you can take him.'

'Purely,' Teo says, and smiles, then leans his arm on the bar and he and Joe Ditto clench hands.

'*Una momento*,' Joe says. He removes his sport coat and folds it over his gym bag, takes a puff of Pall Mall, then drops to the floor and does ten quick push ups with a hand clap after each. 'Needed to warm up.'

Teo removes his shirt to free up his shoulder. Both men, now in tank tops, clench hands again. Joe is still wearing his sunglasses, and his half-smoked cigarette dangles from his lip. Zip counts one, two, wrestle! and they strain against each other, muscle and tendon surfacing along their forearms. Joe gives slightly, then struggles back to even, seems to gain leverage, and gradually forces Teo's arm downward.

The crowd at Wrigley is cheering, and Jack Brickhouse breaks into his home-run call: 'Back she goes, back, back, way back . . .'

'Goddamn, come on, *luchador*,' Zip urges; his left hand slaps the bar with a force that sends the red clothespin flying off the sleeve folded over the stump of his right arm.

Gripping the edge of the bar with his left hand and grunting,

Teo heaves his right arm up until it's back even, but his surge of momentum stalls. He and Joe Ditto lean into each other. They've both begun to sweat, their locked hands are turning white, arms straining, faces close together, separated by the smoke of Joe's dangling Pall Mall. 'My friend,' Joe says from the side of his mouth, 'you smell like pigeons.'

Out on the street, sirens wail as if every cop, ambulance, and fire truck in Little Village is rushing past. The lengthening ash of Joe's cigarette tumbles to the bar. Joe spits out the butt, and it rolls across the bar top onto the floor, where Zip grinds it out. Their arms have begun trembling in time to each other, but neither budges. Teo turns his face from Joe and finds himself looking into the mirror. A man in a blue mask looks back reproachfully; he won't allow another defeat. Teo closes his eyes and concentrates on breathing, resolved to ignore the pain, to welcome it, and to endure until Joe tires and he makes one last, desperate move. Teo knows that final assault will be a sign of weakness; if he can hold it off, he'll win.

'*From the land of sky-blue waters*' tom-toms from the TV, and Joe's left hand slowly snakes across the bar to Teo's tank top. At its touch, Teo pushes back harder, but Joe won't give. His right arm resists Teo's concentrated force while his left hand gently brushes, then fondles Teo's chest.

'Got you where I want you now,' Joe says. 'Cootchie-cootchie-coo, motherfucker.'

Our father figured that we'd want to see the sewer rat he'd captured, and he was right about that, so he waited to kill it until Mick and I came home. It was a Saturday in summer, and I'd taken Mick to the icy swimming pool at Harrison High. Our hair, towels, and the wet swimsuits we wore beneath our jeans still smelled of chlorine as we walked down the gangway into the sunny back yard where Sir had an enormous rat imprisoned in a glass canister. It had a wide-angled mouth and metal lid, the kind of rounded jar that's often used for storing flour or sugar. The rat filled it up and behind the thick convex glass appeared distorted and even larger, with magnified beady eyes, buck teeth, handlike rodent feet, and a scaly bald tail. I looked for rabies foam around its whiskers. Sir had used the canister to store dago bombs. Every few weeks, he'd lift the sewer cover over the pipe in the basement, light a dago bomb, and drop it down the sewer. The echoey sewer amplified the explosion. Sir said the noise chased off rats. The fireworks from the canister were gone; I'd been planning to pilfer a few for Fourth of July, but I never saw them again. I don't know what Sir did with them, or how he managed to catch the rat in the jar. I didn't ask at the time, maybe because we were too involved with preparations for its execution.

My father had me take the garden hose and fill the large galvanized metal washtub that he always referred to in Polish as the *balja*. We used the *balja* for mixing cement and, sometimes, for rinsing the mud out of crayfish we caught with string and chicken livers at the Douglas Park lagoon. When the *balja* was brim full, Sir brought over the rat-in-a-jar, as we'd begun to call it. I stood on one side of the tub and Mick on the other. Mick had stripped down to his bathing suit and cowboy boots as if he planned a dip in the *balja* himself. He'd put on his cowboy hat and was holding his favorite toy, a cork-shooting shotgun. Mick's toy box was an arsenal: matched six-shooters that shot caps, a Davy Crockett musket to go with a coonskin cap, squirt guns of various calibers, pirate swords and flintlock pistols, a Buck Rogers ray gun. They were mostly made of plastic, but not the shotgun. It had a blued metal barrel and a wooden stock, and broke at the center like a real shotgun. Breaking it was how one pumped it up enough to shoot the corks that came with it. If you jammed the muzzle into the dirt after a rain, it would shoot clots of mud. Holding the rat-in-a-jar with one hand on the bottom and the other on the lid, Sir lowered it into the *balja*. The rat looked worried. When the glass canister was entirely immersed, Sir slowly raised the metal lid so that water could seep in. Mick and I moved in closer on either side of him, trying to see. Sir lifted the lid a little more, and the rat shot straight up out of the tub and splashed back down into the water. Mick and I jumped back, but Sir grabbed the shotgun by the barrel out of Mick's hand, and as the wet rat scrambled over the side of the washtub, Sir knocked it back into the water. 'Da-dammit!' Sir yelled. He was thwacking at the *balja*, sending up swooshes of water, and the rat squirted out between blows and ran for the homemade board fence separating our yard from the woodpiles and uncooped chickens in Kashka's yard next door. We scrambled after it, and Sir managed to hack the rat one more time as it squeezed through the fence and crawled off into a woodpile.

We stood peering through the fence.

'Da-damn,' Sir muttered.

'My gun!' Mick said. Sir handed it back to him. 'You ruined my gun.' A piece of the wooden stock had splintered off, and the connection between the barrel and stock was noticeably loose. One more good whack would have snapped it in two.

'Is that rat blood?' I said. There was a red, sticky smear along the side of the stock.

'I nailed it a couple good ones,' Sir said.

Mick dropped the shotgun as if it might be carrying rabies and walked away, fighting back tears.

For a week or so the shotgun lay in the back yard where Mick dropped it, rusting in rain, bleaching in sun. Finally, Mick forgave our father enough to pick up the gun again. The blood-stain was now a permanent feature of the splintered stock, and though the gun was the worse for wear, it had acquired a mystique it hadn't had before its baptism in rat blood. It became Mick's favorite toy all over again, the weapon he'd always take with him when he went down the alley to play guns with his best friend, JJ – short for Johnny Junior.

Johnny Senior was Johnny Sovereign.

When Johnny Sovereign was found dead in his own car, with a jockstrap on his face and his balls blown off, it was big news in the neighborhood, but Mick knew nothing about the specifics. My parents and I never discussed the murder openly at home. Mick had simply been told that it wasn't a good time to go play at his friend JJ's house, that he should wait until JJ called him. But Mick got bored waiting, so after a few days he decided to sneak over to JJ's for a visit. He pulled on his cowboy boots, armed himself with the rat-blood shotgun, and snuck off down the alley. Alleys were secret thoroughfares for kids, and as long as Mick was sneaking away from our house, he decided he'd also sneak up on JJ. Surprise attack was one of their favorite games. He went past the garage where JJ's father parked the yellow car, but the garage was empty. As always, pigeons hooted from inside. At the Sovereigns' back fence, overgrown with morning glories and sizzling with bees, Mick paused, as he and JJ often did, to poke a finger inside a morning glory. He and JJ would pretend the flower was a socket, but unlike an electric socket, a morning glory was safe to stick your finger into. If you held it there long enough, you'd feel connected to the power coming through the tangled green wires of the vines.

Recharged with morning-glory power, Mick snuck past the back fence into the small patch of grassless back yard that led into a shadowy gangway. Instead of going to the back door, he sidled along the house, crouching under the back windows. He'd approached this way several times before to ambush JJ. He liked to catch JJ when he was least expecting it – still in his pajamas, eating Sugar Pops at the breakfast table.

The curtained kitchen window was partially opened, and Mick slowly rose and slid the barrel of the shotgun through the slit between the drawn curtains. He was into the make-believe of the game, and his heart pounded with a combination of tension and repressed laughter. When he heard the scream, he froze.

'Oh, God, no, please, please, I beg you,' a woman's voice cried. 'I don't know anything about what Johnny did. Please, I won't say anything. I have two little kids.' It was JJ's mother, Vi, who'd always been nice to Mick. She was weeping hysterically, repeating, 'Please, please, I wouldn't recognize your voice, you never called, I don't know who you are, it was all Johnny, for the love of Jesus, I'm begging you don't, please, I'm still young.'

Mick will drop the shotgun and, crying hysterically himself, race through the alleys back home, but not before peering through a crack in the curtains and seeing JJ's mother on her knees on the kitchen linoleum, tears streaming down her face as she pleads for her life, unaware perhaps that the straps of her yellow slip have slid down her shoulders, spilling forth my brother's first glimpse of a woman's naked breasts.

A Minor Mood

The concertina sleeping beside Lefty has started to wheeze. It's the middle of the night, even the streetlights have their misty blinders on, and the concertina can't seem to catch her breath. In the dark Lefty listens to her ragged sighs. He can't sleep to the concertina's labored breathing. He's worried. He can't help thinking about what happened with the glockenspiel, how he would wake to find her place beside him on the bed empty, and then, from the other side of the locked bathroom door, he'd hear her heart hammering arrhythmically and flat, a dissonant rise and fall of scales. Once it began, it went on like that night after night. The neighbors complained; finally, he lost his lease. And one day at dusk, he found himself standing on a street of pawnshops and tattoo parlors, with nowhere to go and only a pawn ticket to show for what had been his life. He'd wandered out with a tattoo – not a rose or an anchor or a snake or a heart, but a single note of indelible blue, a nameless note without a staff, only an eighth note, really – stung onto his shoulder.

Afterward, he spent a long and, in retrospect, mournful time alone before becoming entangled with the tuba. He met her at a tuba fest, and for a while it seemed as if they were destined for each other, until the dreams started. Disturbing dreams in which he ran lost and breathless through twisting corridors, dreams he'd wake from in the dark to a borborygmus of gurgled moans, blats, grunts, drones, which seemed drawn out longer each night, like the vowels of whales – melancholy whales. At first, he tried to tell himself that it was only gas. But the signs and symptoms were undeniably clear, and this time he didn't wait for landlords or court orders to tell him it was over. He'd already been evicted from sleep. One afternoon, while the tuba was away for a valve job, Lefty, groggy with insomnia, packed what he could fit into a suitcase that once cushioned a saxophone and left the rest behind.

In the years that followed, home was wherever he set that suitcase down – a sad succession of flophouses and transient hotels, dumps that seemed tenanted by fugitives from the collective unconscious: Depression Deco lobbies; ill-lit corridors lined with doors emitting smells like whispers and whispers like smells; restless, rheumatic rooms that creaked and groaned under their own dingy weight, rooms that came furnished with desperation, and wallpapered with worn, fitful dreams. He carried a sax case but was past his time for saxophones and their slinky, sultry, seductive ways; their nocturnal predilections and swanky pretensions were for breaking the hearts of younger men. On his deathbed, his father had gestured him closer and before dying whispered in his ear, 'The wallflowers, son, go for the wallflowers. They'll appreciate it.' But his father was wrong about that as he was about everything else. The wallflowers were a vain, angry, neurotic, and anything but appreciative lot. Sometimes, in a fog, down by the docks, he'd hear sounds echoing the warning that lights could not convey – buoys dinging their bells, the moody moans of foghorns – and he'd think about the glockenspiel, recalling the sensitive touch of her mallets, and the patterns her glittering vertebrae left along his skin. He'd feel the blue tattoo ache like a bruise from bite marks on his shoulder. He'd think about the tuba until he could feel again a ghostly impression of her hard, cool mouthpiece and taste the brass against his lips (a taste not unlike that of his own blood after a fistfight), and then he'd recall the way his breath flowed into her, as if there was no filling her up, as if she was sucking it from the deepest pocket of his body, leaving him hollow. He had carried that hollowness within him for years; he didn't want to feel hollow any longer. Whatever came after the tuba would have to arrive on a breath of its own.

Now, he listens to the concertina wheeze, and perhaps to find a little respite from his worries, Lefty remembers nights as a child when his lungs sounded like wind blowing past a tattered shade, and his bronchial tubes gave recitals of the croup. While his father was God knows where, and his mother was at work, his grandmother would come to nurse him. It was a large family on his father's side, and his grandmother managed to love them all and yet showed such special affection toward Lefty – maybe because his father was always God knows where – that everyone called her Lefty's Gran, even if she was their grandmother, too.

Lefty's Gran would show up whenever he was sick, carrying her green mesh shopping bag. She always carried that bag in case she suddenly had to do some shopping, or on the chance she stumbled upon something valuable lying in the street. Even if it served no other purpose, it was good for carrying her purse in. When she came to see Lefty, the shopping bag would also contain the chartreuse protrusions of a half-dozen lemons and the blue-green bulge of an economy-size jar of Vicks VapoRub, against which other, lesser bottles clinked.

The sight of her would set Lefty coughing.

'So, Louis,' his gran would say – oddly Lefty's Gran refused to call her grandson Lefty – 'So, Louis, I hear you got the Krupa again.'

The lemons and Vicks were part of her cure for the Krupa. But before unloading the shopping bag, before doing anything else, Lefty's Gran would fill the apartment with steam. She'd go from room to room, balancing pie pans and cookie trays on the tops of radiators, and as she set them up they'd bang like cymbals punctuating her stream of muttering: 'Kid's got the Krupa (*Bang!*), the Gene (*Bam!*), the drummer man (*Boom!*), Krupa (*Crash!*).

'Hey, Louis (*Wham!*), whatayou got?'

'The Gene Krupa.'

'You can say that again (*Blam!*).'

'The Gene Krupa.'

'Ha!' Lefty's Gran would expel a laugh resounding like a cymbal clap, as if he'd just said something surprisingly hilarious even though she had taught him the you-can-say-that-again routine. 'You can bet your *dupa* (*Bing!*) you got the Krupa (*Bong!*).'

She'd fill the pie pans and cookie trays to the brim with water; she'd set kettles and pots on every burner of the stove and let them boil; she'd turn the shower on hot in the bathroom and let it pour down clouds of steam; she'd hook the vaporizer up beside Lefty's bed, fuel it with a glob of Vicks, and aim its snorky exhalations in his direction. The entire flat began to heave with breath.

While the steam rose like genies rushing out of bottles, Lefty's Gran would rub camphor oil on his chest and on his neck, where his glands were swollen; she'd dab a streak of Vicks along his upper lip as if she was drawing a mustache. Then, she'd undo the babushka that she wore whether she was outside or in. She'd whisk it off with the flourish of a magician doing a trick, and years would disappear. When he saw her blurred in steam, minus her babushka, Lefty could imagine his grand-mother as a girl. He wondered if she kept her head covered because her hair looked younger than she did. It was a lustrous ash blond, so springy with curls that it looked fake, as if she might be wearing a wig. This girlishness that she kept hidden was like a secret between them.

She'd twine her satiny babushka around his throat, and over the babushka she would wrap a rough woolen scarf that was reserved for these occasions and known as the croup scarf. The scarf, a clashing maroon-and-pea-green plaid anchored at one end by a big safety pin, retained past smells of camphor and Vicks. Its scratchy wool chapped his chin where his skin wasn't protected by the babushka.

By then, the flat was expanding with steam. Mirrors disap-peared in the mist they reflected. Through the mist, the wallpaper, a pattern of vines and flowers, opened into three dimensions and came alive like flora in a rain forest. The back-ground noise of outside traffic transformed into screeches of monkeys and tropical birds. Steam smoldered along the insides of windows and made them sweat; it condensed on the ceiling into beads that hung like rain above Lefty's bed. He was sweating, too, sweating out the fever; germs were fleeing his body through the portholes of his pores.

In the kitchen, lost in steam, Lefty's Gran was squeezing lemons. He could hear the vigorous, musical rattle of her spoon as she stirred honey and a splash of boiling water into syrup, then added lemon juice, and last, but not least, a dash of whiskey – Jim Beam – which was the brand of choice for all his relatives, by tradition referred to simply as Beam. *Beam* as in a ray of light.

Even stuffed up, Lefty could smell its fiery perfume.

The apartment was filling with aromas: pie tins and cookie trays baking on top of merrily knocking radiators; menthol, eucalyptus, camphor, lemon; and through the steam, like a searchlight glancing through fog: Beam. Lefty's Gran stirred the lemon and honey concoction together in a coffee mug but served it in jigger-size portions, although they referred to a jigger as a shot glass – another family tradition. It seemed an apt name, as far as Lefty was concerned, for a glass that had the shape, density, and sometimes the wallop of a slug.

He'd sip his medicinal drink until it was cool enough, then belt it down as if drinking a toast: *Na zdrowie*, germs, take this! When the shot glass was empty, his gran would bring a refill on the theory that he needed fluids. She'd have a couple belts herself on the theory that she needed fluids, too.

'*Na zdrowie*,' she'd say – bottoms up!

'*Na zdrowie*,' he'd answer – down the hatch! On such white winter mornings – white steam on one side of the pane, white snow on the other – propped on a throne of pillows with the babushka like a raja's turban wound around his swollen glands; with menthol, eucalyptus, camphor, lemon, and through the steam, his gran materializing with a mug in one hand and a bottle of Beam in the other – on white mornings like that, how could a boy not conclude that being sick might almost be worth the joy of getting well? Those were mornings to be tucked away at the heart of life, so that later, whenever one needed to draw upon a recollection of joy in order to get through troubled times, it would be there, an assurance that once one was happy and one could be happy again.

Sometimes, on those mornings, Lefty would wonder how his room, its window clouded as if the atmosphere of Venus was pressed against the pane, must have looked from the street. He wondered how it sounded to strangers passing by. Could they hear the vaporizer hissing like a reed instrument missing a reed? Could they hear his gran, who was now sipping Beam straight from the bottle, singing 'You Are My Sunshine' in her Polish patois? She loved that song. 'Not to be morbid,' she'd say, 'but sing "Sunshine" at my funeral.'

Not to be morbid, but when that time came, Lefty played it on the sax, his breath Beamy, played it to heaven, his back braced against the steeple of St Pius.

She taught Lefty to play the measuring spoons like castanets in accompaniment to her gypsylike singing. She was playing the radiators with a ladle as if they were marimbas. Lefty was up, out of bed, flushed, but feeling great, and in steam that was fading to wisps, he was dancing with his gran. Her girlish curls tossed as around and around the room they whirled, both of them singing, and one or the other dizzily breaking off the dance in order to beat or plunk or blow some instrument they'd just invented: Lefty strumming the egg slicer; Lefty's Gran oompahing an empty half-gallon of Dad's Old Fashioned Root Beer; Lefty bugling 'Sunshine' through the cardboard clarion at the center of a toilet-paper roll; Lefty's Gran chiming a closet of empty coat hangers; Lefty shake-rattle-and-rolling the silverware drawer; Lefty's Gran Spike Jonesing the vacuum cleaner; Lefty, surrounded by pots and lids, drum-soloing with wooden spoons, while Lefty's Gran, conducting with a potato masher, yelled, 'Go, Krupa, go!'

How would it look to some stranger who had crept to the window and seen a boy and his gran carrying on as if they'd *both* been miraculously cured of the croup, doing the hokey-pokey face-to-face with the babushka between their teeth?

It would have looked the way it appears to him now, peering in at the memory, like a stranger through a blurred window, straining to hear the beat of pots and the faint, off-key rendition of a vaguely familiar song.

And how would it look to the boy and his gran if they were peering in on him now, watching at the window while an unshaven stranger with a blue note on his shoulder worriedly paces in his dirty underwear, in the dead of night, to the sickly wheeze of a concertina? For a moment, Lefty almost expects to see their faces at the window, though the window is four stories up. He almost feels more like the boy staring in than the unshaven man who is pacing the floor. The boy and his gran seem more real to him than his room in the present. Suddenly, it's clear to him that memory is the channel by which the past conducts its powerful energy; it's how the past continues to love.

He moves directly to the suitcase buried in the back of the closet and rummages through it until he finds a scarf. It's not the old scarf of maroon-and-pea-green plaid anchored with a safety pin; this scarf is navy blue. Nor is it redolent of camphor and Vicks; this scarf smells of mothballs. But it's woolly and warm and will have to do. He gently wraps the scarf about the concertina, and immediately her labored wheezing softens and is muffled.

He doesn't own enough pots to constitute a drum set, or to occupy all four burners, but he fills the single pot he has and, with the fanfare of a cymbal crash, he sets it to boil.

He doesn't know about the concertina, but as the water rumbles into steam, *he's* feeling a little better already – less anxious. He's been worried about the concertina, and his worries have made him feel helpless. He should at least have recognized that something was wrong before it came to this. The concertina has been in a minor mood lately, one that Lefty's found contagious – wistful, pensive, melancholy, heartsick by turns – a mood that, for lack of perfect pitch, words can't exactly convey. Even music can only approximate – a G minor from a Chopin nocturne, perhaps; or the D minor of a Schubert quartet, the one called 'Death and the Maiden'; or, at times, an airy, disorganized noodling in no discernible key at all, like an orchestra tuning up; or a squeal like a bagpipe with a stomachache; or a drone as if the concertina were dreaming in a scale that only a sitar would find familiar. She's been in a minor mood that turns a polka into the blues, a jig into a dirge, a tarantella into a requiem. And a tango – how long has it been since he's heard her slink into the stylized passion of a tango?

Polka, jig, tarantella, tango . . . wistful, pensive, melancholy, heartsick . . . *menthol, eucalyptus, camphor, lemon.* He's found a mantra on which to meditate, a talismanic spell to chant.

He rifles through the cupboard, but he's out of honey. Not out, exactly; the fact is that he's never owned a jar of honey in his life. He opens the arctically austere cell of his refrigerator: a bottle of catsup, a jar of pickles, a couple containers of Chinese takeout that need to be pitched, but no lemon, not even a plastic citrus fruit ripening in there.

Fortunately, he does possess a shot glass and a bottle of whiskey – not Beam – but memory is, at best, approximate, and he bets Old Guckenheimer will do the trick. In honor and imitation of his gran, he belts down a couple quick doses to test its efficacy, and a couple more for the sake of fluids.

There's that fiery perfume!

Now it's the concertina's turn. Even distressed, the concertina looks lovely in the navy-blue scarf. It heightens her complexion of mother-of-pearl. Oh, he thinks, little beauty, sweet companion, the one I didn't realize I was searching for, who almost came to me too late; little squeeze box who taught my fingers to sing, who taught me how to close my eyes and let the music flow.

He loves her pliant fit between his palms, and the way her body stretches as she yawns rhapsodically. He loves to feel the pumping of her breath. It's like a summer breeze warmed by the bellows of her heart – although *bellows* has never seemed to him a word suited to her. There's nothing bellowy about her, no puffed-up sentiments, no martial clamor that might accompany the lockstep or goose step of a march, no anthems for football halftimes, or for saluting flags while windbags swell with their own rhetoric; and though, a few times in her company, he's heard angelic whispers – an echo of some great medieval organ – no hymns. Hers has always been a song of earth, of olive trees, vineyards, blossoming orchards melodic with bees.

Na zdrowie, little squeeze box.

He watches as, delicately, she inhales the fumes of whiskey – tiny sips starting at *do* and slowly ascending through *re, mi, fa, sol*, to a tremulous *la-ti*. And after the shot glass has been drained repeatedly, he lifts her gently from the bed and they begin to dance to a tune they play together, a tune whose seesaw rhythm is like the panting of lovers. Not a polka, jig, tarantella, or even a tango. They dance to a dance they've just invented, an ancient dance they've just recalled.

If there are strangers on the street at this late hour, they've stopped to listen as if, like dogs, they can cock their ears. They listen, inhaling the cool air, with their heads thrown back against the night. Their breaths plume; their eyes are locked on the faint wisps of dissolving constellations. And though it's a dark, American city street on which they've stopped, they know there isn't the need to feel afraid because, instead of danger, tonight the air carries music.

Na zdrowie, strangers.

Na zdrowie, music.

Then, in the long diminuendo of a sigh, the concertina folds up quietly, peacefully, exhaling a sweet, whiskey breath, and Lefty lies down on the pillow beside her, covers them both with a bedspread, and closes his eyes.

Sleep, like a barcarole, carries him away.

We Didn't

We did it in front of the mirror
and in the light. We did it in darkness,
in the water and the high grass.

—Yehuda Amichai, 'We Did It'

We didn't in the light; we didn't in darkness. We didn't in the fresh-cut summer grass or in the mounds of autumn leaves or on the snow where moonlight threw down our shadows. We didn't in your room on the canopy bed you slept in, the bed you'd slept in as a child, or in the backseat of my father's rusted Rambler, which smelled of the smoked chubs and kielbasa he delivered on weekends from my uncle Vincent's meat market. We didn't in your mother's Buick Eight, where a rosary twined the rearview mirror like a beaded, black snake with silver, cruciform fangs.

At the dead end of our lovers' lane – a side street of abandoned factories – where I perfected the pinch that springs open a bra; behind the lilac bushes in Marquette Park, where you first touched me through my jeans and your nipples, swollen against transparent cotton, seemed the shade of lilacs; in the balcony of the now defunct Clark Theater, where I wiped popcorn salt from my palms and slid them up your thighs and you whispered, 'I feel like Doris Day is watching us,' we didn't.

221

How adept we were at fumbling, how perfectly mistimed our timing, how utterly we confused energy with ecstasy.

Remember that night becalmed by heat, and the two of us, fused by sweat, trembling as if a wind from outer space that only we could feel was gusting across Oak Street Beach? Entwined in your faded Navajo blanket, we lay soul-kissing until you wept with wanting.

We'd been kissing all day – all summer – kisses tasting of different shades of lip gloss and too many Cokes. The lake had turned hot pink, rose rapture, pearl amethyst with dusk, then washed in night black with a ruff of silver foam. Beyond a momentary horizon, silent bolts of heat lightning throbbed, perhaps setting barns on fire somewhere in Indiana. The beach that had been so crowded was deserted as if there was a curfew. Only the bodies of lovers remained, visible in lightning flashes, scattered like the fallen on a battlefield, a few of them moaning, waiting for the gulls to pick them clean.

On my fingers your slick scent mixed with the coconut musk of the suntan lotion we'd repeatedly smeared over each other's bodies. When your bikini top fell away, my hands caught your breasts, memorizing their delicate weight, my palms cupped as if bringing water to parched lips.

Along the Gold Coast, high-rises began to glow, window added to window, against the dark. In every lighted bedroom, couples home from work were stripping off their business suits, falling to the bed, and doing it. They did it before mirrors and pressed against the glass in streaming shower stalls; they did it against walls and on the furniture in ways that required previously unimagined gymnastics, which they invented on the spot. They did it in honor of man and woman, in honor of beast, in honor of God. They did it because they'd been released, because they were home free, alive, and private, because they couldn't wait any longer, couldn't wait for the appointed hour, for the right time or temperature, couldn't wait for the future, for Messiahs, for peace on earth and justice for all. They did it because of the Bomb, because of pollution, because of the Four Horsemen of the Apocalypse, because extinction might be just a blink away. They did it because it was Friday night. It was Friday night and somewhere delirious music was playing – flutter-tongued flutes, muted trumpets meowing like cats in heat, feverish plucking and twanging, tom-toms, congas, and gongs all pounding the same pulsebeat.

I stripped your bikini bottom down the skinny rails of your legs, and you tugged my swimsuit past my tan. Swimsuits at our ankles, we kicked like swimmers to free our legs, almost expecting a tide to wash over us the way the tide rushes in on Burt Lancaster and Deborah Kerr in *From Here to Eternity* – a love scene so famous that although neither of us had seen the movie, our bodies assumed the exact position of movie stars on the sand and you whispered to me softly, 'I'm afraid of getting pregnant,' and I whispered back, 'Don't worry, I have protection,' then, still kissing you, felt for my discarded cutoffs and the wallet in which for the last several months I had carried a Trojan as if it was a talisman. Still kissing, I tore its flattened, dried-out wrapper, and it sprang through my fingers like a spring from a clock and dropped to the sand between our legs. My hands were shaking. In a panic, I groped for it, found it, tried to dust it off, tried as Burt Lancaster never had to, to slip it on without breaking the mood, felt the grains of sand inside it, a throb of lightning, and the Great Lake behind us became, for all practical purposes, the Pacific, and your skin tasted of salt and to the insistent question that my hips were asking your body answered yes, your thighs opened like wings from my waist as we surfaced panting from a kiss that left you pleading

Oh, Christ yes, a yes gasped sharply as a cry of pain so that for a moment I thought that we *were* already doing it and that somehow I had missed the instant when I entered you, entered you in the bloodless way in which a young man discards his own virginity, entered you as if passing through a gateway into the rest of my life, into a life as I wanted it to be lived *yes* but Oh then I realized that we were still floundering unconnected in the slick between us and there was sand in the Trojan as we slammed together still feeling for that perfect fit, still in the *Here* groping for an *Eternity* that was only a fine adjustment away, just a millimeter to the left or a fraction of an inch farther south though with all the adjusting the sandy Trojan was slipping off and then it was gone but *yes* you kept repeating although your head was shaking *no-not-quite-almost* and our hearts were going like mad and you said, *Yes. Yes, wait . . . Stop!*

'What?' I asked, still futilely thrusting as if I hadn't quite heard you.

'Oh, God!' you gasped, pushing yourself up. 'What's coming?'

'Gin, what's the matter?' I asked, confused, and then the beam of a spotlight swept over us and I glanced into its blinding eye.

All around us lights were coming, speeding across the sand. Blinking blindness away, I rolled from your body to my knees, feeling utterly defenseless in the way that only nakedness can leave one feeling. Headlights bounded toward us, spotlights crisscrossing, blue dome lights revolving as squad cars converged. I could see other lovers, caught in the beams, fleeing bare-assed through the litter of garbage that daytime hordes had left behind and that night had deceptively concealed. You were crying, clutching the Navajo blanket to your breasts with one hand and clawing for your bikini with the other, and I was trying to calm your terror with reassuring phrases such as 'Holy shit! I don't fucking believe this!'

Swerving and fishtailing in the sand, police calls pouring from their radios, the squad cars were on us, and then they were by us while we struggled to pull on our clothes.

They braked at the water's edge, and cops slammed out, brandishing huge flashlights, their beams deflecting over the dark water. Beyond the darting of those beams, the far-off throbs of lightning seemed faint by comparison.

'Over there, goddamn it!' one of them hollered, and two cops sloshed out into the shallow water without even pausing to kick off their shoes, huffing aloud for breath, their leather cartridge belts creaking against their bellies.

'Grab the sonofabitch! It ain't gonna bite!' one of them yelled, then they came sloshing back to shore with a body slung between them.

It was a woman – young, naked, her body limp and bluish beneath the play of flashlight beams. They set her on the sand just past the ring of drying, washed-up alewives. Her face was almost totally concealed by her hair. Her hair was brown and tangled in a way that even wind or sleep can't tangle hair, tangled as if it had absorbed the ripples of water – thick strands, slimy-looking like dead seaweed.

'She's been in there awhile, that's for sure,' a cop with a beer belly said to a younger, crew-cut cop, who had knelt beside the body and removed his hat as if he might be considering the kiss of life.

The crew-cut officer brushed the hair away from her face, and the flashlight beams settled there. Her eyes were closed. A bruise or a birthmark stained the side of one eye. Her features appeared swollen, her lower lip protruding as if she was pouting.

An ambulance siren echoed across the sand, its revolving red light rapidly approaching.

'Might as well take their sweet-ass time,' the beer-bellied cop said.

We had joined the circle of police surrounding the drowned woman almost without realizing that we had. You were back in your bikini, robed in the Navajo blanket, and I had slipped on my cutoffs, my underwear dangling out of a back pocket.

Their flashlight beams explored her body, causing its whiteness to gleam. Her breasts were floppy; her nipples looked shriveled. Her belly appeared inflated by gallons of water. For a moment, a beam focused on her mound of pubic hair, which was over-lapped by the swell of her belly, and then moved almost shyly away down her legs, and the cops all glanced at us – at you, especially – above their lights, and you hugged your blanket closer as if they might confiscate it as evidence or to use as a shroud.

When the ambulance pulled up, one of the black attendants immediately put a stethoscope to the drowned woman's swollen belly and announced, 'Drowned the baby, too.'

Without saying anything, we turned from the group, as unconsciously as we'd joined them, and walked off across the sand, stopping only long enough at the spot where we had lain together like lovers, in order to stuff the rest of our gear into a beach bag, to gather our shoes, and for me to find my wallet and kick sand over the forlorn, deflated Trojan that you pretended not to notice. I was grateful for that.

Behind us, the police were snapping photos, flashbulbs throbbing like lightning flashes, and the lightning itself, still distant but moving in closer, rumbling audibly now, driving a lake wind before it so that gusts of sand tingled against the metal sides of the ambulance.

Squinting, we walked toward the lighted windows of the Gold Coast, while the shadows of gapers attracted by the whirling emergency lights hurried past us toward the shore.

'What happened? What's going on?' they asked without waiting for an answer, and we didn't offer one, just continued walking silently in the dark.

It was only later that we talked about it, and once we began talking about the drowned woman it seemed we couldn't stop.

'She was pregnant,' you said. 'I mean, I don't want to sound morbid, but I can't help thinking how the whole time we were, we almost – you know – there was this poor, dead woman and her unborn child washing in and out behind us.'

'It's not like we could have done anything for her even if we had known she was there.'

'But what if we *had* found her? What if after we had – you know,' you said, your eyes glancing away from mine and your voice tailing into a whisper, 'what if after we did it, we went for a night swim and found her in the water?'

'But, Gin, we didn't,' I tried to reason, though it was no more a matter of reason than anything else between us had ever been.

It began to seem as if each time we went somewhere to make out – on the back porch of your half-deaf, whiskery Italian grandmother, who sat in the front of the apartment cackling at *I Love Lucy* reruns; or in your girlfriend Tina's basement rec room when her parents were away on bowling league nights and Tina was upstairs with her current crush, Brad; or way off in the burbs, at the Giant Twin Drive-In during the weekend they called Elvis Fest – the drowned woman was with us.

We would kiss, your mouth would open, and when your tongue flicked repeatedly after mine, I would unbutton the first button of your blouse, revealing the beauty spot at the base of your throat, which matched a smaller spot I loved above a corner of your lips, and then the second button, which opened

227

on a delicate gold cross – which I had always tried to regard as merely a fashion statement – dangling above the cleft of your breasts. The third button exposed the lacy swell of your bra, and I would slide my hand over the patterned mesh, feeling for the firmness of your nipple rising to my fingertip, but you would pull slightly away, and behind your rapid breath your kiss would grow distant, and I would kiss harder, trying to lure you back from wherever you had gone, and finally, holding you as if only consoling a friend, I'd ask, 'What are you thinking?' although of course I knew.

'I don't want to think about her but I can't help it. I mean, it seems like some kind of weird omen or something, you know?'

'No, I don't know,' I said. 'It was just a coincidence.'

'Maybe if she'd been farther away down the beach, but she was so close to us. A good wave could have washed her up right beside us.'

'Great, then we could have had a *ménage à trois*.'

'Gross! I don't believe you just said that! Just because you said it in French doesn't make it less disgusting.'

'You're driving me to it. Come on, Gin, I'm sorry,' I said. 'I was just making a dumb joke to get a little different perspective on things.'

'What's so goddamn funny about a woman who drowned herself and her baby?'

'We don't even know for sure she did.'

'Yeah, right, it was just an accident. Like she just happened to be going for a walk pregnant and naked, and she fell in.'

'She could have been on a sailboat or something. Accidents happen; so do murders.'

'Oh, like murder makes it less horrible? Don't think that hasn't occurred to me. Maybe the bastard who knocked her up killed her, huh?'

'How should I know? You're the one who says you don't want to talk about it and then gets obsessed with all kinds of theories and scenarios. Why are we arguing about a woman we don't even know, who doesn't have the slightest thing to do with us?'

'I *do* know about her,' you said. 'I dream about her.'

'You dream about her?' I repeated, surprised. 'Dreams you remember?'

'Sometimes they wake me up. In one I'm at my *nonna*'s cottage in Michigan, swimming for a raft that keeps drifting farther away, until I'm too tired to turn back. Then I notice there's a naked person sunning on the raft and start yelling, "Help!" and she looks up and offers me a hand, but I'm too afraid to take it even though I'm drowning because it's her.'

'God! Gin, that's creepy.'

'I dreamed you and I are at the beach and you bring us a couple hot dogs but forget the mustard, so you have to go all the way back to the stand for it.'

'Hot dogs, no mustard – a little too Freudian, isn't it?'

'Honest to God, I dreamed it. You go back for mustard and I'm wondering why you're gone so long, then a woman screams that a kid has drowned and everyone stampedes for the water. I'm swept in by the mob and forced under, and I think, This is it, I'm going to drown, but I'm able to hold my breath longer than could ever be possible. It feels like a flying dream – flying underwater – and then I see this baby down there flying, too, and realize it's the kid everyone thinks has drowned, but he's no more drowned than I am. He looks like Cupid or one of those baby angels that cluster around the face of God.'

'Pretty weird. What do you think all the symbols mean? Hot dogs, water, drowning . . .'

'It means the baby who drowned inside her that night was

a love child – a boy – and his soul was released there to wander through the water.'

'You don't really believe that?'

We argued about the interpretation of dreams, about whether dreams are symbolic or psychic, prophetic or just plain nonsense, until you said, 'Look, Dr Freud, you can believe what you want about your dreams, but keep your nose out of mine, okay?'

We argued about the drowned woman, about whether her death was a suicide or a murder, about whether her appearance that night was an omen or a coincidence which, you argued, is what an omen is anyway: a coincidence that means something. By the end of summer, even if we were no longer arguing about the woman, we had acquired the habit of arguing about everything else. What was better: dogs or cats, rock or jazz, Cubs or Sox, tacos or egg rolls, right or left, night or day? – we could argue about anything.

It no longer required arguing or necking to summon the drowned woman; everywhere we went she surfaced by her own volition: at Rocky's Italian Beef, at Lindo Mexico, at the House of Dong, our favorite Chinese restaurant, a place we still frequented because when we'd first started seeing each other they had let us sit and talk until late over tiny cups of jasmine tea and broken fortune cookies. We would always kid about going there. 'Are you in the mood for Dong tonight?' I'd whisper conspiratorially. It was a dopey joke, meant for you to roll your eyes at its repeated dopiness. Back then, in winter, if one of us ordered the garlic shrimp we would both be sure to eat them so that later our mouths tasted the same when we kissed.

Even when she wasn't mentioned, she was there with her drowned body – so dumpy next to yours – and her sad breasts, with their wrinkled nipples and sour milk – so saggy beside yours, which were still budding – with her swollen belly and her pubic bush colorless in the glare of electric light, with her tangled, slimy hair and her pouting, placid face – so lifeless beside yours – and her skin a pallid white, lightning-flash white, flashbulb white, a whiteness that couldn't be duplicated in daylight – how I'd come to hate that pallor, so cold beside the flush of your skin.

There wasn't a particular night when we finally broke up, just as there wasn't a particular night when we began going together, but it was a night in fall when I guessed that it was over. We were parked in the Rambler at the dead end of the street of factories that had been our lovers' lane, listening to a drizzle of rain and dry leaves sprinkle the hood. As always, rain revitalized the smells of smoked fish and kielbasa in the uphol-stery. The radio was on too low to hear, the windshield wipers swished at intervals as if we were driving, and the windows were steamed as if we'd been making out. But we'd been arguing, as usual, this time about a woman poet who had committed suicide, whose work you were reading. We were sitting, no longer talking or touching, and I remember thinking that I didn't want to argue with you anymore. I didn't want to sit like this in hurt silence; I wanted to talk excitedly all night as we once had. I wanted to find some way that wasn't corny – sounding to tell you how much fun I'd had in your company, how much knowing you had meant to me, and how I had suddenly realized that I'd been so intent on becoming lovers that I'd overlooked how close we'd been as friends. I wanted you to know that. I wanted you to like me again.

'It's sad,' I started to say, meaning that I was sorry we had reached the point of silence, but before I could continue you challenged the statement.

'What makes you so sure it's sad?'

'What do you mean, what makes me so sure?' I asked, confused by your question.

You looked at me as if what was sad was that I would never understand. 'For all either one of us knows,' you said, 'death could have been her triumph!'

Maybe when it really ended was the night I felt we had just reached the beginning, that one time on the beach in the summer when our bodies rammed so desperately together that for a moment I thought we did it, and maybe in our hearts we did, although for me, then, doing it in one's heart didn't quite count. If it did, I supposed we'd all be Casanovas.

We rode home together on the L train that night, and I felt sick and defeated in a way I was embarrassed to mention. Our mute reflections emerged like negative exposures on the dark, greasy window of the train. Lightning branched over the city, and when the train entered the subway tunnel, the lights inside flickered as if the power was disrupted, though the train continued rocketing beneath the Loop.

When the train emerged again we were on the South Side of the city and it was pouring, a deluge as if the sky had opened to drown the innocent and guilty alike. We hurried from the L station to your house, holding the Navajo blanket over our heads until, soaked, it collapsed. In the dripping doorway of your apartment building, we said good night. You were shivering. Your bikini top showed through the thin blouse plastered to your skin. I swept the wet hair away from your face and kissed you lightly on the lips, then you turned and went inside. I stepped into the rain, and you came back out, calling after me.

'What?' I asked, feeling a surge of gladness to be summoned back into the doorway with you.

'Want an umbrella?'

I didn't. The downpour was letting up. It felt better to walk back to the station feeling the rain rinse the sand out of my hair, off my legs, until the only places where I could still feel its grit were in the crotch of my cutoffs and each squish of my shoes. A block down the street, I passed a pair of jockey shorts lying in a puddle and realized they were mine, dropped from my back pocket as we ran to your house. I left them behind, wondering if you'd see them and recognize them the next day.

By the time I had climbed the stairs back to the L platform, the rain had stopped. Your scent still hadn't washed from my fingers. The station – the entire city it seemed – dripped and steamed. The summer sound of crickets and nighthawks echoed from the drenched neighborhood. Alone, I could admit how sick I felt. For you, it was a night that would haunt your dreams. For me, it was another night when I waited, swollen and aching, for what I had secretly nicknamed the Blue Ball Express.

Literally lovesick, groaning inwardly with each lurch of the train and worried that I was damaged for good, I peered out at the passing yellow-lit stations, where lonely men stood posted before giant advertisements, pictures of glamorous models defaced by graffiti – the same old scrawled insults and pleas: FUCK YOU, EAT ME. At this late hour the world seemed given over to men without women, men waiting in abject patience for something indeterminate, the way I waited for our next times. I avoided their eyes so that they wouldn't see the pity in mine, pity for them because I'd just been with you, your scent was still on my hands, and there seemed to be so much future ahead.

For me it was another night like that, and by the time I reached my stop I knew I would be feeling better, recovered enough to walk the dark street home making up poems of longing that I never wrote down. I was the D. H. Lawrence of not doing it, the voice of all the would-be lovers who ached and squirmed. From our contortions in doorways, on stairwells, and in the bucket seats of cars we could have composed a Kama Sutra of interrupted bliss. It must have been that night when I recalled all the other times of walking home after seeing you, so that it seemed as if I was falling into step behind a parade of my former selves – myself walking home on the night we first kissed, myself on the night when I unbuttoned your blouse and kissed your breasts, myself on the night when I lifted your skirt above your thighs and dropped to my knees – each succeeding self another step closer to that irrevocable moment for which our lives seemed poised.

But we didn't, not in the moonlight, or by the phosphorescent lanterns of lightning bugs in your back yard, not beneath the constellations we couldn't see, let alone decipher, or in the dark glow that replaced the real darkness of night, a darkness already stolen from us, not with the skyline rising behind us while a city gradually decayed, not in the heat of summer while a Cold War raged, despite the freedom of youth and the license of first love – because of fate, karma, luck, what does it matter? – we made not doing it a wonder, and yet we didn't, we didn't, we never did.

The Coast of Chicago

Chopin in Winter

The winter Dzia-Dzia came to live with us in Mrs Kubiac's building on Eighteenth Street was the winter that Mrs Kubiac's daughter, Marcy, came home pregnant from college in New York. Marcy had gone there on a music scholarship, the first person in Mrs Kubiac's family to go to high school, let alone college.

Since she had come home I had seen her only once. I was playing on the landing before our door, and as she came up the stairs we both nodded hi. She didn't look pregnant. She was thin, dressed in a black coat, its silvery fur collar pulled up around her face, her long blond hair tucked into the collar. I could see the snowflakes on the fur turning to beads of water under the hall light bulb. Her face was pale and her eyes the same startled blue as Mrs Kubiac's.

She passed me almost without noticing and continued up the next flight of stairs, then paused and, leaning over the banister, asked, 'Are you the same little boy I used to hear crying at night?'

Her voice was gentle, yet kidding.

'I don't know,' I said.

'If your name is Michael and if your bedroom window is on the fourth floor right below mine, then you are,' she said. 'When you were little sometimes I'd hear you crying your heart out

237

at night. I guess I heard what your mother couldn't. The sound traveled up.'

'I really woke you up?'

'Don't worry about that. I'm a very light sleeper. Snow falling wakes me up. I used to wish I could help you as long as we were both up together in the middle of the night with everyone else snoring.'

'I don't remember crying,' I said.

'Most people don't once they're happy again. It looks like you're happy enough now. Stay that way, kiddo.' She smiled. It was a lovely smile. Her eyes seemed surprised by it. 'Too-da-loo.' She waved her fingers.

'Too-da-loo.' I waved after her. A minute after she was gone I began to miss her.

Our landlady, Mrs Kubiac, would come downstairs for tea in the afternoons and cry while telling my mother about Marcy. Marcy, Mrs Kubiac said, wouldn't tell her who the child's father was. She wouldn't tell the priest. She wouldn't go to church. She wouldn't go anywhere. Even the doctor had to come to the house, and the only doctor that Marcy would allow was Dr Shtulek, her childhood doctor.

'I tell her, "Marcy, darling, you have to do something,"' Mrs Kubiac said. '"What about all the sacrifices, the practice, the lessons, teachers, awards? Look at rich people – they don't let anything interfere with what they want."'

Mrs Kubiac told my mother these things in strictest confidence, her voice at first a secretive whisper, but growing louder as she recited her litany of troubles. The louder she talked the more broken her English became, as if her worry and suffering were straining the language past its limits. Finally, her feelings overpowered her; she began to weep and lapsed into Bohemian, which I couldn't understand.

I would sit out of sight beneath the dining-room table, my plastic cowboys galloping through a forest of chair legs, while I listened to Mrs Kubiac talk about Marcy. I wanted to hear everything about her, and the more I heard the more precious the smile she had given me on the stairs became. It was like a secret bond between us. Once I became convinced of that, listening to Mrs Kubiac seemed like spying. I was Marcy's friend and conspirator. She had spoken to me as if I was someone apart from the world she was shunning. Whatever her reasons for the way she was acting, whatever her secrets, I was on her side. In daydreams I proved my loyalty over and over.

At night we could hear her playing the piano – a muffled rumbling of scales that sounded vaguely familiar. Perhaps I actually remembered hearing Marcy practicing years earlier, before she had gone on to New York. The notes resonated through the kitchen ceiling while I wiped the supper dishes and Dzia-Dzia sat soaking his feet. Dzia-Dzia soaked his feet every night in a bucket of steaming water into which he dropped a tablet that fizzed, immediately turning the water bright pink. Between the steaming water and pink dye, his feet and legs, up to the knees where his trousers were rolled, looked permanently scalded.

Dzia-Dzia's feet seemed to be turning into hooves. His heels and soles were swollen nearly shapeless and cased in scaly calluses. Nails, yellow as a horse's teeth, grew gnarled from knobbed toes. Dzia-Dzia's feet had been frozen when as a young man he walked most of the way from Krakow to Gdansk in the dead of winter escaping service in the Prussian army. And later he had frozen them again mining for gold in Alaska. Most of what I knew of Dzia-Dzia's past had mainly to do with the history of his feet.

Sometimes my uncles would say something about him. It sounded as if he had spent his whole life on the move – selling dogs to the Igorot in the Philippines after the Spanish-American War; mining coal in Johnstown, Pennsylvania; working barges on the Great Lakes; riding the rails out West. No one in the family wanted much to do with him. He had deserted them so often, my uncle Roman said, that it was worse than growing up without a father.

My grandma had referred to him as *Pan Djabel*, 'Mr Devil,' though the way she said it sounded as if he amused her. He called her a *gorel*, a hillbilly, and claimed that he came from a wealthy, educated family that had been stripped of their land by the Prussians.

'Landowners, all right!' Uncle Roman once said to my mother. 'Besides acting like a bastard, according to Ma, he actually *was* one in the literal sense.'

'Romey, shhh, what good's bitter?' my mother said.

'Who's bitter, Ev? It's just that he couldn't even show up to bury her. I'll never forgive that.'

Dzia-Dzia hadn't been at Grandma's funeral. He had disappeared again, and no one had known where to find him. For years Dzia-Dzia would simply vanish without telling anyone, then suddenly show up out of nowhere to hang around for a while, ragged and smelling of liquor, wearing his two suits one over the other, only to disappear yet again.

'Want to find him? Go ask the bums on skid row,' Uncle Roman would say.

My uncles said he lived in boxcars, basements, and abandoned buildings. And when, from the window of a bus, I'd see old men standing around trash fires behind billboards, I'd wonder if he was among them.

Now that he was very old and failing he sat in our kitchen,

his feet aching and numb as if he had been out walking down Eighteenth Street barefoot in the snow.

It was my aunts and uncles who talked about Dzia-Dzia 'failing.' The word always made me nervous. I was failing, too – failing spelling, English, history, geography, almost everything except arithmetic, and that only because it used numbers instead of letters. Mainly, I was failing penmanship. The nuns complained that my writing was totally illegible, that I spelled like a DP, and threatened that if I didn't improve they might have to hold me back.

Mother kept my failures confidential. It was Dzia-Dzia's they discussed during Sunday visits in voices pitched just below the level of an old man's hearing. Dzia-Dzia stared fiercely but didn't deny what they were saying about him. He hadn't spoken since he had reappeared, and no one knew whether his muteness was caused by senility or stubbornness, or if he'd gone deaf. His ears had been frozen as well as his feet. Wiry white tufts of hair that matched his horned eyebrows sprouted from his ears. I wondered if he would hear better if they were trimmed.

Though Dzia-Dzia and I spent the evenings alone together in the kitchen, he didn't talk any more than he did on Sundays. Mother stayed in the parlor, immersed in her correspondence courses in bookkeeping. The piano rumbled above us through the ceiling. I could feel it more than hear it, especially the bass notes. Sometimes a chord would be struck that made the silverware clash in the drawer and the glasses hum.

Marcy had looked very thin climbing the stairs, delicate, incapable of such force. But her piano was massive and powerful-looking. I remembered going upstairs once with my mother to visit Mrs Kubiac. Marcy was away at school then. The piano stood unused – top lowered, lid down over the keys – dominating the apartment. In the afternoon light it gleamed deeply, as if its dark wood were a kind of glass. Its pedals were polished bronze and looked to me more like pedals I imagined motormen stamping to operate streetcars.

'Isn't it beautiful, Michael?' my mother asked.

I nodded hard, hoping that Mrs Kubiac would offer to let me play it, but she didn't.

'How did it get up here?' I asked. It seemed impossible that it could fit through a doorway.

'Wasn't easy,' Mrs Kubiac said, surprised. 'Gave Mr Kubiac a rupture. It come all the way on the boat from Europe. Some old German, a great musician, brang it over to give concerts, then got sick and left it. Went back to Germany. God knows what happened to him – I think he was a Jew. They auctioned it off to pay his hotel bill. That's life, huh? Otherwise who could afford it? We're not rich people.'

'It must have been very expensive anyway,' my mother said.

'Only cost me a marriage,' Mrs Kubiac said, then laughed, but it was forced. 'That's life too, huh?' she asked. 'Maybe a woman's better off without a husband?' And then, for just an instant, I saw her glance at my mother, then look away. It was a glance I had come to recognize from people when they caught themselves saying something that might remind my mother or me that my father had been killed in the war.

The silverware would clash and the glasses hum. I could feel it in my teeth and bones as the deep notes rumbled through the ceiling and walls like distant thunder. It wasn't like listening to music, yet more and more often I would notice Dzia-Dzia close his eyes, a look of concentration pinching his face as his body swayed slightly. I wondered what he was hearing. Mother had said once that he'd played the fiddle when she was a little girl, but the only music I'd even seen him show any interest in before was the 'Frankie Yankovitch Polka Hour,' which he turned up loud and listened to with his ear almost pressed to the radio. Whatever Marcy was playing, it didn't sound like Frankie Yankovitch.

Then one evening, after weeks of silence between us, punctuated only by grunts, Dzia-Dzia said, 'That's boogie-woogie music.'

'What, Dzia-Dzia?' I asked, startled.

'Music the boogies play.'

'You mean from upstairs? That's Marcy.'

'She's in love with a colored man.'

'What are you telling him, Pa?' Mother demanded. She had just happened to enter the kitchen while Dzia-Dzia was speaking.

'About boogie-woogie.' Dzia-Dzia's legs jiggled in the bucket so that the pink water sloshed over onto the linoleum.

'We don't need that kind of talk in the house.'

'What talk, Evusha?'

'He doesn't have to hear that prejudice in the house,' Mom said. 'He'll pick up enough on the street.'

'I just told him boogie-woogie.'

'I think you better soak your feet in the parlor by the heater,' Mom said. 'We can spread newspaper.'

Dzia-Dzia sat, squinting as if he didn't hear.

'You heard me, Pa. I said soak your feet in the parlor,' Mom repeated on the verge of shouting.

'What, Evusha?'

'I'll yell as loud as I have to, Pa.'

'Boogie-woogie, boogie-woogie, boogie-woogie,' the old man

muttered as he left the kitchen, slopping barefoot across the linoleum.

'Go soak your head while you're at it,' Mom muttered behind him, too quietly for him to hear.

Mom had always insisted on polite language in the house. Someone who failed to say 'please' or 'thank you' was as offensive to her ears as someone who cursed.

'The word is "yes," not "yeah,"' she would correct. Or 'If you want "hey," go to a stable.' She considered 'ain't' a form of laziness, like not picking up your dirty socks.

Even when they got a little drunk at the family parties that took place at our flat on Sundays, my uncles tried not to swear – and they had all been in the army and the marines. Nor were they allowed to refer to the Germans as Krauts, or the Japanese as Nips. As far as Mom was concerned, of all the misuses of language, racial slurs were the most ignorant, and so the most foul.

My uncles didn't discuss the war much anyway, though whenever they got together there was a certain feeling in the room as if beneath the loud talk and joking they shared a deeper, sadder mood. Mom had replaced the photo of my father in his uniform with an earlier photo of him sitting on the running board of the car they'd owned before the war. He was grinning and petting the neighbor's Scottie. That one and their wedding picture were the only photos that Mom kept out. She knew I didn't remember my father, and she seldom talked about him. But there were a few times when she would read aloud parts of his letters. There was one passage in particular that she read at least once a year. It had been written while he was under bombardment, shortly before he was killed.

244

When it continues like this without letup you learn what it is to really hate. You begin to hate them as a people and want to punish them all – civilians, women, children, old people – it makes no difference, they're all the same, none of them innocent, and for a while your hate and anger keep you from going crazy with fear. But if you let yourself hate and believe in hate, then no matter what else happens, you've lost. Eve, I love our life together and want to come home to you and Michael, as much as I can, the same man who left.

I wanted to hear more but didn't ask. Perhaps because everyone seemed to be trying to forget. Perhaps because I was afraid. When the tears would start in Mom's eyes I caught myself wanting to glance away as Mrs Kubiac had.

There was something more besides Mom's usual standards for the kind of language allowed in the house that caused her to lose her temper and kick Dzia-Dzia out of his spot in the kitchen. She had become even more sensitive, especially where Dzia-Dzia was concerned, because of what had happened with Shirley Popel's mother.

Shirley's mother had died recently. Mom and Shirley had been best friends since grade school, and after the funeral, Shirley came back to our house and poured out the story.

Her mother had broken a hip falling off a curb while sweeping the sidewalk in front of her house. She was a constantly smiling woman without any teeth who, everyone said, looked like a peasant. After forty years in America she could barely speak English, and even in the hospital refused to remove her babushka.

245

Everyone called her Babushka, Babush for short, which meant 'granny', even the nuns at the hospital. On top of her broken hip, Babush caught pneumonia, and one night Shirley got a call from the doctor saying Babush had taken a sudden turn for the worse. Shirley rushed right over, taking her thirteen-year-old son, Rudy. Rudy was Babushka's favorite, and Shirley hoped that seeing him would instill the will to live in her mother. It was Saturday night and Rudy was dressed to play at his first dance. He wanted to be a musician and was wearing clothes he had bought with money saved from his paper route. He'd bought them at Smoky Joe's on Maxwell Street – blue suede loafers, electric-blue socks, a lemon-yellow one-button roll-lapel suit with padded shoulders and pegged trousers, and a parrot-green satin shirt. Shirley thought he looked cute.

When they got to the hospital they found Babush connected to tubes and breathing oxygen.

'Ma,' Shirley said, 'Rudy's here.'

Babush raised her head, took one look at Rudy, and smacked her gray tongue.

'Rudish,' Babush said, 'you dress like nigger.' Then suddenly her eyes rolled; she fell back, gasped, and died.

'And those were her last words to any of us, Ev,' Shirley wept, 'words we'll carry the rest of our lives, but especially poor little Rudy – *you dress like nigger.*'

For weeks after Shirley's visit, no matter who called, Mom would tell them Shirley's story over the phone.

'Those aren't the kind of famous last words we're going to hear in this family if I can help it,' she promised more than once, as if it were a real possibility. 'Of course,' she'd sometimes add, 'Shirley always has let Rudy get away with too much. I don't see anything cute about a boy going to visit his grand-mother at the hospital dressed like a hood.'

246

Any last words Dzia-Dzia had he kept to himself. His silence, however, had already been broken. Perhaps in his own mind that was a defeat that carried him from failing to totally failed. He returned to the kitchen like a ghost haunting his old chair, one that appeared when I sat alone working on penmanship.

No one else seemed to notice a change, but it was clear from the way he no longer soaked his feet. He still kept up the pretense of sitting there with them in the bucket. The bucket went with him the way ghosts drag chains. But he no longer went through the ritual of boiling water: boiling it until the kettle screeched for mercy, pouring so the linoleum puddled and steam clouded around him, and finally dropping in the tablet that fizzed furiously pink, releasing a faintly metallic smell like a broken thermometer.

Without his bucket steaming, the fogged windows cleared. Mrs Kubiac's building towered a story higher than any other on the block. From our fourth-story window I could look out at an even level with the roofs and see the snow gathering on them before it reached the street.

I sat at one end of the kitchen table copying down the words that would be on the spelling test the next day. Dzia-Dzia sat at the other, mumbling incessantly, as if finally free to talk about the jumble of the past he'd never mentioned – wars, revolutions, strikes, journeys to strange places, all run together, and music, especially Chopin. 'Chopin,' he'd whisper hoarsely, pointing to the ceiling with the reverence of nuns pointing to heaven. Then he'd close his eyes and his nostrils would widen as if he were inhaling the fragrance of sound.

It sounded no different to me, the same muffled thumping and rumbling we'd been hearing ever since Marcy had returned home. I could hear the intensity in the crescendos that made the silverware clash, but it never occurred to me to care what she was playing. What mattered was that I could hear her play each night, could feel her playing just a floor above, almost as if she were in our apartment. She seemed that close.

'Each night Chopin – it's all she thinks about, isn't it?'

I shrugged.

'You don't know?' Dzia-Dzia whispered, as if I were lying and he was humoring me.

'How should I know?'

'And I suppose how should you know the "Grande Valse brillante" when you hear it either? How should you know Chopin was twenty-one when he composed it? – about the same age as the girl upstairs. He composed it in Vienna, before he went to Paris. Don't they teach you that in school? What are you studying?'

'Spelling.'

'Can you spell *dummkopf*?'

The waves of the keyboard would pulse through the warm kitchen and I would become immersed in my spelling words, and after that in penmanship. I was in remedial penmanship. Nightly penmanship was like undergoing physical therapy. While I concentrated on the proper slant of my letters my left hand smeared graphite across the loose-leaf paper.

Dzia-Dzia, now that he was talking, no longer seemed content to sit and listen in silence. He would continually interrupt.

'Hey, Lefty, stop writing with your nose. Listen how she plays.'

'Don't shake the table, Dzia-Dzia.'

'You know this one? No? "Valse brillante."'

'I thought that was the other one.'

'What other one? The E-flat? That's "Grande Valse brillante." This one's A-flat. Then there's another A-flat – Opus 42 – called "Grande Valse." Understand?'

He rambled on like that about A- and E-flat and sharps and

opuses and I went back to compressing my capital *M*s. My homework was to write five hundred of them. I was failing penmanship yet again, my left hand, as usual, taking the blame it didn't deserve. The problem with *M* wasn't my hand. It was that I had never been convinced that the letters could all be the same widths. When I wrote, *M* automatically came out twice as broad as *N, H*, double the width of *I*.

'This was Paderewski's favorite waltz. She plays it like an angel.'

I nodded, staring in despair at my homework. I had made the mistake of interconnecting the *M*s into long strands. They hummed in my head, drowning out the music, and I wondered if I had been humming aloud. 'Who's Paderewski?' I asked, thinking it might be one of Dzia-Dzia's old friends, maybe from Alaska.

'Do you know who's George Washington, who's Joe DiMaggio, who's Walt Disney?'

'Sure.'

'I thought so. Paderewski was like them, except he played Chopin. Understand? See, deep down inside, Lefty, you know more than you think.'

Instead of going into the parlor to read comics or play with my cowboys while Mom pored over her correspondence courses, I began spending more time at the kitchen table, lingering over my homework as an excuse. My spelling began to improve, then took a turn toward perfection; the slant of my handwriting reversed toward the right; I began to hear melodies in what had sounded like muffled scales.

Each night Dzia-Dzia would tell me more about Chopin, describing the preludes or ballades or mazurkas, so that even if I hadn't heard them I could imagine them, especially Dzia-Dzia's favorites, the nocturnes, shimmering like black pools.

'She's playing her way through the waltzes,' Dzia-Dzia told me, speaking as usual in his low, raspy voice as if we were having a confidential discussion. 'She's young but already knows Chopin's secret – a waltz can tell more about the soul than a hymn.'

By my bedtime the kitchen table would be shaking so much that it was impossible to practice penmanship any longer. Across from me, Dzia-Dzia, his hair, eyebrows, and ear tufts wild and white, swayed in his chair, with his eyes squeezed closed and a look of rapture on his face as his fingers pummeled the tabletop. He played the entire width of the table, his body leaning and twisting as his fingers swept the keyboard, left hand pounding at those chords that jangled silverware, while his right raced through runs across tacky oilcloth. His feet pumped the empty bucket. If I watched him, then closed my eyes, it sounded as if two pianos were playing.

One night Dzia-Dzia and Marcy played so that I expected at any moment the table would break and the ceiling collapse. The bulbs began to flicker in the overhead fixture, then went out. The entire flat went dark.

'Are the lights out in there, too?' Mom yelled from the parlor. 'Don't worry, it must be a fuse.'

The kitchen windows glowed with the light of snow. I looked out. All the buildings down Eighteenth Street were dark and the streetlights were out. Spraying wings of snow, a snow-removal machine, its yellow lights revolving, disappeared down Eighteenth like the last blinks of electricity. There wasn't any traffic. The block looked deserted, as if the entire city was deserted. Snow was filling the emptiness, big flakes floating steadily and softly between the darkened buildings, coating the fire escapes, while on the roofs a blizzard swirled up into the clouds.

Marcy and Dzia-Dzia never stopped playing.

'Michael, come in here by the heater, or if you're going to stay in there put the burners on,' Mom called.

I lit the burners on the stove. They hovered in the dark like blue crowns of flame, flickering Dzia-Dzia's shadow across the walls. His head pitched, his arms flew up as he struck the notes. The walls and windowpanes shook with gusts of wind and music. I imagined plaster dust wafting down, coating the kitchen, a fine network of cracks spreading through the dishes.

'Michael?' Mother called.

'I'm sharpening my pencil.' I stood by the sharpener grinding it as hard as I could, then sat back down and went on writing. The table rocked under my point, but the letters formed perfectly. I spelled new words, words I'd never heard before, yet as soon as I wrote them their meanings were clear, as if they were in another language, one in which words were understood by their sounds, like music. After the lights came back on I couldn't remember what they meant and threw them away.

Dzia-Dzia slumped back in his chair. He was flushed and mopped his forehead with a paper napkin.

'So, you liked that one,' he said. 'Which one was it?' he asked. He always asked me that, and little by little I had begun recognizing their melodies.

'The polonaise,' I guessed. 'In A-flat major.'

'Ahhh.' He shook his head in disappointment. 'You think everything with a little spirit is the polonaise.'

'The "Revolutionary" étude!'

'It was a waltz,' Dzia-Dzia said.

'How could that be a waltz?'

'A posthumous waltz. You know what "posthumous" means?'

'What?'

'It means music from after a person's dead. The kind of waltz that has to carry back from the other side. Chopin wrote it to a young woman he loved. He kept his feelings for her secret but never forgot her. Sooner or later feelings come bursting out. The dead are as sentimental as anyone else. You know what happened when Chopin died?'

'No.'

'They rang the bells all over Europe. It was winter. The Prussians heard them. They jumped on their horses. They had cavalry then, no tanks, just horses. They rode until they came to the house where Chopin lay on a bed next to a grand piano. His arms were crossed over his chest, and there was plaster drying on his hands and face. The Prussians rode right up the stairs and barged into the room, slashing with their sabers, their horses stamping and kicking up their front hooves. They hacked the piano and stabbed the music, then wadded up the music into the piano, spilled on kerosene from the lamps, and set it on fire. Then they rolled Chopin's piano to the window – it was those French windows, the kind that open out and there's a tiny balcony. The piano wouldn't fit, so they rammed it through, taking out part of the wall. It crashed three stories into the street, and when it hit it made a sound that shook the city. The piano lay there smoking, and the Prussians galloped over it and left. Later, some of Chopin's friends snuck back and removed his heart and sent it in a little jeweled box to be buried in Warsaw.'

Dzia-Dzia stopped and listened. Marcy had begun to play again very faintly. If he had asked me to guess what she was playing I would have said a prelude, the one called 'The Raindrop.'

*

I heard the preludes on Saturday nights, sunk up to my ears in bathwater. The music traveled from upstairs through the plumbing, and resonated as clearly underwater as if I had been wearing earphones.

There were other places I discovered where Marcy's playing carried. Polonaises sometimes reverberated down an old trash chute that had been papered over in the dining room. Even in the parlor, provided no one else was listening to the radio or flipping pages of a newspaper, it was possible to hear the faintest hint of mazurkas around the sealed wall where the stovepipe from the space heater disappeared into what had once been a fireplace. And when I went out to play on the landing, bundled up as if I was going out to climb on the drifts piled along Eighteenth Street, I could hear the piano echoing down the hallways. I began to creep higher up the stairs to the top floor, until finally I was listening at Mrs Kubiac's door, ready to jump away if it should suddenly open, hoping I would be able to think of some excuse for being there, and at the same time almost wishing they would catch me.

I didn't mention climbing the stairs in the hallway, nor any of the other places I'd discovered, to Dzia-Dzia. He never seemed interested in anyplace other than the kitchen table. It was as if he were attached to the chair, rooted in his bucket.

'Going so early? Where you rushing off to?' he'd ask at the end of each evening, no matter how late, when I'd put my pencil down and begun buckling my books into my satchel.

I'd leave him sitting there, with his feet in his empty bucket, and his fingers, tufted with the same white hair as his ears, still tracing arpeggios across the tabletop, though Marcy had already stopped playing. I didn't tell him how from my room, a few times lately after everyone was asleep, I could hear her playing as clearly as if I were sitting at her feet.

Marcy played less and less, especially in the evenings after supper, which had been her regular time.

Dzia-Dzia continued to shake the table nightly, eyes closed, hair flying, fingers thumping, but the thump of his fingers against the oilcloth was the only sound other than his breathing – rhythmic and labored as if he were having a dream or climbing a flight of stairs.

I didn't notice at first, but Dzia-Dzia's solos were the start of his return to silence.

'What's she playing, Lefty?' he demanded more insistently than ever, as if still testing whether I knew.

Usually now, I did. But after a while I realized he was no longer testing me. He was asking because the sounds were becoming increasingly muddled to him. He seemed able to feel the pulse of the music but could no longer distinguish the melodies. By asking me, he hoped perhaps that if he knew what Marcy was playing he would hear it clearly himself.

Then he began to ask what she was playing when she wasn't playing at all.

I would make up answers. 'The polonaise . . . in A-flat major.'

'The polonaise! You always say that. Listen harder. Are you sure it's not a waltz?'

'You're right, Dzia-Dzia. It's the "Grande Valse."'

'The "Grande Valse" . . . which one is that?'

'A-flat, Opus 42. Paderewski's favorite, remember? Chopin wrote it when he was twenty-one, in Vienna.'

'In Vienna?' Dzia-Dzia asked, then pounded the table with his fist. 'Don't tell me numbers and letters! A-flat, Z-sharp, Opus 0, Opus 1,000! Who cares? You make it sound like a bingo game instead of Chopin.'

I was never sure if he couldn't hear because he couldn't

remember, or couldn't remember because he couldn't hear. His hearing itself still seemed sharp enough.

'Stop scratching with that pencil all the time, Lefty, and I wouldn't have to ask you what she's playing,' he'd complain.

'You'd hear better, Dzia-Dzia, if you'd take the kettle off the stove.'

He was slipping back into his ritual of boiling water. The kettle screeched like a siren. The windows fogged. Roofs and weather vanished behind a slick of steam. Vapor ringed the overhead light bulbs. The vaguely metallic smell of the fizzing pink tablets hung at the end of every breath.

Marcy played hardly at all by then. What little she played was muffled, far off as if filtering through the same fog. Sometimes, staring at the steamed windows, I imagined Eighteenth Street looked that way, with rings of vapor around the streetlights and headlights, clouds billowing from exhaust pipes and manhole covers, breaths hanging, snow swirling like white smoke.

Each night water hissed from the kettle's spout as from a blown valve, rumbling as it filled the bucket, brimming until it slopped over onto the warped linoleum. Dzia-Dzia sat, bony calves half submerged, trousers rolled to his knees. He was wearing two suits again, one over the other, always a sure sign he was getting ready to travel, to disappear without saying goodbye. The fingers of his left hand still drummed unconsciously along the tabletop as his feet soaked. Steam curled up the arteries of his scalded legs, hovered over his lap, smoldered up the buttons of his two vests, traced his mustache and white tufts of hair until it enveloped him. He sat in a cloud, eyes glazed, fading.

*

I began to go to bed early. I would leave my homework unfinished, kiss Mother good night, and go to my room.

My room was small, hardly space for more than the bed and
bureau. Not so small, though, that Dzia-Dzia couldn't have fit.
Perhaps, had I told him that Marcy played almost every night
now after everyone was sleeping, he wouldn't have gone back
to filling the kitchen with steam. I felt guilty, but it was too late,
and I shut the door quickly before steam could enter and fog
my window.

It was a single window. I could touch it from the foot of the
bed. It opened onto a recessed, three-sided air shaft and faced
the roof of the building next door. Years ago a kid my age named
Freddy had lived next door and we still called it Freddy's roof.

Marcy's window was above mine. The music traveled down
as clearly as Marcy said my crying had traveled up. When I
closed my eyes I could imagine sitting on the Oriental carpet
beside her huge piano. The air shaft actually amplified the music
just as it had once amplified the arguments between Mr and
Mrs Kubiac, especially the shouting on those nights after Mr
Kubiac had moved out, when he would return drunk and try
to move back in. They'd argued mostly in Bohemian, but when
Mr Kubiac started beating her, Mrs Kubiac would yell out in
English, 'Help me, police, somebody, he's killing me!' After a
while the police would usually come and haul Mr Kubiac away.
I think sometimes Mom called them. One night Mr Kubiac
tried to fight off the police, and they gave him a terrible beating.
'You're killing him in front of my eyes!' Mrs Kubiac began to
scream. Mr Kubiac broke away and, with the police chasing
him, ran down the hallways pounding on doors, pleading for
people to open up. He pounded on our door. Nobody in the
building let him in. That was their last argument.

The room was always cold. I'd slip, still wearing my clothes, under the goose-feather-stuffed *piersyna* to change into my pajamas. It would have been warmer with the door open even a crack, but I kept it closed because of the steam. A steamed bedroom window reminded me too much of the winter I'd had pneumonia. It was one of the earliest things I could remember: the gurgling hiss of the vaporizer and smell of benzoin while I lay sunk in my pillows watching steam condense to frost on the pane until daylight blurred. I could remember trying to scratch through the frost with the key to a wind-up mouse so that I could see how much snow had fallen, and Mother catching me. She was furious that I had climbed out from under the warmth of my covers and asked me if I wanted to get well or to get sicker and die. Later, when I asked Dr Shtulek if I was dying, he put his stethoscope to my nose and listened. 'Not yet.' He smiled. Dr Shtulek visited often to check my breathing. His stethoscope was cold like all the instruments in his bag, but I liked him, especially for unplugging the vaporizer. 'We don't need this anymore,' he confided. Night seemed very still without its steady exhaling. The jingle of snow chains and the scraping of shovels carried from Eighteenth Street. Maybe that was when I first heard Marcy practicing scales. By then I had grown used to napping during the day and lying awake at night. I began to tunnel under my *piersyna* to the window and scrape at the layered frost. I scraped for nights, always afraid I would get sick again for disobeying. Finally, I was able to see the snow on Freddy's roof. Something had changed while I'd been sick – they had put a wind hood on the tall chimney that sometimes blew smoke into our flat. In the dark it looked as if someone was standing on the roof in an old-fashioned helmet. I imagined it was a German soldier. I'd heard Freddy's landlord was German. The soldier stood at attention, but his head slowly turned back and forth and hooted with each gust of wind. Snow drove sideways across the roof, and he stood banked by drifts, smoking a cigar. Sparks flew from its tip. When he turned completely around to stare in my direction with his faceless face, I'd duck and tunnel back under my *piersyna* to my pillows and pretend to sleep. I believed a person asleep would be shown more mercy than a person awake. I'd lie still, afraid he was marching across the roof to peer in at me through the holes I'd scraped. It was a night like that when I heard Mother crying. She was walking from room to room crying like I'd never heard anyone cry before. I must have called out because she came into my room and tucked the covers around me. 'Everything will be all right,' she whispered; 'go back to sleep.' She sat on my bed, toward the foot where she could look out the window, crying softly until her shoulders began to shake. I lay pretending to sleep. She cried like that for nights after my father was killed. It was my mother, not I, whom Marcy had heard.

It was only after Marcy began playing late at night that I remembered my mother crying. In my room, with the door shut against the steam, it seemed she was playing for me alone. I would wake already listening and gradually realize that the music had been going on while I slept, and that I had been shaping my dreams to it. She played only nocturnes those last weeks of winter. Sometimes they seemed to carry over the roofs, but mostly she played so softly that only the air shaft made it possible to hear. I would sit huddled in my covers beside the window listening, looking out at the white dunes on Freddy's roof. The soldier was long gone, his helmet rusted off. Smoke blew unhooded; black flakes with sparking edges wafted out like burning snow. Soot and music and white gusts off the crests buffeted the pane. Even when the icicles began to leak and the streets to turn to brown rivers of slush, the blizzard in the air shaft continued.

Marcy disappeared during the first break in the weather. She left a note that read: 'Ma, don't worry.'

'That's all,' Mrs Kubiac said, unfolding it for my mother to see. 'Not even "love," not even her name signed. The whole time I kept telling her "do something," she sits playing the piano, and now she does something, when it's too late, unless she goes to some butcher. Ev, what should I do?'

My mother helped Mrs Kubiac call the hospitals. Each day they called the morgue. After a week, Mrs Kubiac called the police, and when they couldn't find Marcy, any more than they had been able to find Dzia-Dzia, Mrs Kubiac began to call people in New York – teachers, old roommates, landlords. She used our phone. 'Take it off the rent,' she said. Finally, Mrs Kubiac went to New York herself to search.

When she came back from New York she seemed changed, as if she'd grown too tired to be frantic. Her hair was a different shade of gray so that now you'd never know it had once been blond. There was a stoop to her shoulders as she descended the stairs on the way to novenas. She no longer came downstairs for tea and long talks. She spent much of her time in church, indistinguishable among the other women from the old country, regulars at the morning requiem mass, wearing babushkas and dressed in black like a sodality of widows, droning endless mournful litanies before the side altar of the Black Virgin of Czestochowa.

By the time a letter from Marcy finally came, explaining that the entire time she had been living on the South Side in a Negro neighborhood near the university, and that she had a son whom she'd named Tatum Kubiac – 'Tatum' after a famous jazz pianist – it seemed to make little difference. Mrs Kubiac visited once but didn't go back. People had already learned to glance away from her when certain subjects were mentioned – daughters, grandchildren, music. She had learned to glance away from herself. After she visited Marcy she tried to sell the piano, but the movers couldn't figure how to get it downstairs, nor how anyone had ever managed to move it in.

It took time for the music to fade. I kept catching wisps of it in the air shaft, behind walls and ceilings, under bathwater. Echoes traveled the pipes and wallpapered chutes, the bricked-up flues and dark hallways. Mrs Kubiac's building seemed riddled with its secret passageways. And, when the music finally disappeared, its channels remained, conveying silence. Not an ordinary silence of absence and emptiness, but a pure silence beyond daydream and memory, as intense as the music it replaced, which, like music, had the power to change whoever listened. It hushed the close-quartered racket of the old building. It had always been there behind the creaks and drafts and slamming doors, behind the staticky radios, and the flushings and footsteps and crackling fat, behind the wails of vacuums and kettles and babies, and the voices with their scraps of conversation and arguments and laughter floating out of flats where people locked themselves in with all that was private. Even after I no longer missed her, I could still hear the silence left behind.

Blight

During those years between Korea and Vietnam, when rock and roll was being perfected, our neighborhood was proclaimed an Official Blight Area.

Richard J. Daley was mayor then. It seemed as if he had always been, and would always be, the mayor. Ziggy Zilinsky claimed to have seen the mayor himself riding down Twenty-third Place in a black limousine flying one of those little purple pennants from funerals, except his said WHITE SOX on it. The mayor sat in the backseat sorrowfully shaking his head as if to say 'Jeez!' as he stared out the bulletproof window at the winos drinking on the corner by the boarded-up grocery.

Of course, nobody believed that Zig had actually seen the mayor. Ziggy had been unreliable even before Pepper Rosado had accidentally beaned him during a game of 'it' with the bat. People still remembered as far back as third grade when Ziggy had jumped up in the middle of mass yelling, 'Didja see her? She nodded! I asked the Blessed Virgin would my cat come home and she nodded yes!'

All through grade school the statues of saints winked at Ziggy. He was in constant communication with angels and the dead. And Ziggy sleepwalked. The cops had picked him up once in the middle of the night for running around the bases in Washtenaw Playground while still asleep.

When he'd wake up, Ziggy would recount his dreams as if they were prophecies. He had a terrible recurring nightmare in which atomic bombs dropped on the city the night the White Sox won the pennant. He could see the mushroom cloud rising out of Comiskey Park. But Zig had wonderful dreams, too. My favorite was the one in which he and I and Little Richard were in a band playing in the center of St Sabina's roller rink.

After Pepper brained him out on the boulevard with a bat – a fungo bat that Pepper whipped like a tomahawk across a twenty-yard width of tulip garden that Ziggy was trying to hide behind – Zig stopped seeing visions of the saints. Instead, he began catching glimpses of famous people, not movie stars so much as big shots in the news. Every once in a while Zig would spot somebody like Bo Diddley going by on a bus. Mainly, though, it would be some guy in a homburg who looked an awful lot like Eisenhower, or he'd notice a re-appearing little gray-haired fat guy who could turn out to be either Nikita Khrushchev or Mayor Daley. It didn't surprise us. Zig was the kind of kid who read newspapers. We'd all go to Potok's to buy comics and Zig would walk out with the *Daily News*. Zig had always worried about things no one else cared about, like the population explosion, people starving in India, the world blowing up. We'd be walking along down Twenty-second and pass an alley and Ziggy would say, 'See that?'

'See what?'

'Mayor Daley scrounging through garbage.'

We'd all turn back and look but only see a bag lady picking through cans.

Still, in a way, I could see it from Ziggy's point of view. Mayor Daley *was* everywhere. The city was tearing down buildings for urban renewal and tearing up streets for a new expressway, and everywhere one looked there were signs in front of the rubble reading:

SORRY FOR THE INCONVENIENCE
ANOTHER IMPROVEMENT
FOR A GREATER CHICAGO
RICHARD J. DALEY, MAYOR

Not only were there signs everywhere, but a few blocks away a steady stream of fat, older, bossy-looking guys emanated from the courthouse on Twenty-sixth. They looked like a corps of Mayor Daley doubles, and sometimes, especially on election days, they'd march into the neighborhood chewing cigars and position themselves in front of the flag-draped barbershops that served as polling places.

But back to blight.

That was an expression we used a lot. We'd say it after going downtown, or after spending the day at the Oak Street Beach, which we regarded as the beach of choice for sophisticates. We'd pack our towels and, wearing our swimsuits under our jeans, take the subway north.

'North to freedom,' one of us would always say.

Those were days of longing without cares, of nothing to do but lie out on the sand inspecting the world from behind our sunglasses. At the Oak Street Beach the city seemed to realize our dreams of it. We gazed out nonchalantly at the white-sailed yachts on the watercolor-blue horizon, or back across the Outer Drive at the lake-reflecting glass walls of high-rises as if we took such splendor for granted. The blue, absorbing shadow would deepen to azure, and a fiery orange sun would dip behind the glittering buildings. The crowded beach would gradually empty, and a pitted moon would hover over sand scalloped with a million footprints. It would be time to go.

'Back to blight,' one of us would always joke.

I remember a day shortly after blight first became official. We were walking down Rockwell, cutting through the truck docks, Zig, Pepper, and I, on our way to the viaduct near Douglas Park. Pepper was doing his Fats Domino impression, complete with opening piano riff: *Bum-pah-da bum-pa-da dummmmm . . .*

> *Ah foun' mah thrill*
> *Ahn Blueberry Hill . . .*

It was the route we usually walked to the viaduct, but since blight had been declared we were trying to see our surroundings from a new perspective, to determine if anything had been changed, or at least appeared different. Blight sounded serious, biblical in a way, like something locusts might be responsible for.

'Or a plague of gigantic, radioactive cockroaches,' Zig said, 'climbing out of the sewers.'

'Blight, my kabotch,' Pepper said, grabbing his kabotch and shaking it at the world. 'They call this blight? Hey, man, there's weeds and trees and everything, man. You shoulda seen it on Eighteenth Street.'

We passed a Buick somebody had dumped near the railroad tracks. It had been sitting there for months and was still crusted with salt-streaked winter grime. Someone had scraped WASH ME across its dirty trunk, and someone else had scrawled WHIP ME across its hood. Pepper snapped off the aerial and whipped it back and forth so that the air whined, then slammed it down on a fender and began rapping out a Latin beat. We watched him smacking the hell out of it, then Zig and I picked up sticks and broken hunks of bricks and started clanking the headlights and bumpers as if they were bongos and congas, all of us chanting out the melody to 'Tequila.' Each time we grunted out the word *tequila*, Pepper, who was dancing on the hood, stomped out more windshield.

We were revving up for the viaduct, a natural echo chamber where we'd been going for blues-shout contests ever since we'd become infatuated with Screamin' Jay Hawkins's 'I Put a Spell on You.' In fact, it was practicing blues shouts together that led to the formation of our band, the No Names. We practiced in the basement of the apartment building I lived in: Zig on bass, me on sax, Pepper on drums, and a guy named Deejo who played accordion, though he promised us he was saving up to buy an electric guitar.

Pepper could play. He was a natural.

'I go crazy,' was how he described it.

His real name was Stanley Rosado. His mother sometimes called him Stashu, which he hated. She was Polish and his father was Mexican – the two main nationalities in the neighborhood together in one house. It wasn't always an easy alliance, especially inside Pepper. When he got pissed he was a wild man. Things suffered, sometimes people, but always things. Smashing stuff seemed to fill him with peace. Sometimes he didn't even realize he was doing it, like the time he took flowers to Linda Molina, a girl he'd been nuts about since grade school. Linda lived in one of the well-kept two-flats along Marshall Boulevard, right across from the Assumption Church. Maybe it was just that proximity to the church, but there had always been a special aura about her. Pepper referred to her as 'the Unadulterated One.' He finally worked up the nerve to call her, and when she actually invited him over, he walked down the boulevard to her house in a trance. It was late spring, almost summer, and the green boulevard stretched like an enormous lawn before Linda Molina's house. At its center was a blazing garden of tulips. The city had planted them. Their stalks sprouted tall, more like corn than flowers, and their colors seemed to vibrate in the air. The tulips were the most beautiful thing in the neighborhood. Mothers wheeled babies by them; old folks hobbled for blocks and stood before the flowers as if they were sacred.

Linda answered the door and Pepper stood there holding a huge bouquet. Clumps of dirt still dangled from the roots.

'For you,' Pepper said.

Linda, smiling with astonishment, accepted the flowers; then her eyes suddenly widened in horror. 'You didn't—?' she asked.

Pepper shrugged.

'*Lechón!*' the Unadulterated One screamed, pitching a shower of tulips into his face and slamming the door.

That had happened a year before and Linda still refused to talk to him. It had given Pepper's blues shouts a particularly soulful quality, especially since he continued to preface them, in the style of Screamin' Jay Hawking with the words 'I love you.' *I love you! Aiiyyaaaaaa!!!*

Pepper even had Screamin' Jay's blues snork down.

We'd stand at the shadowy mouth of the viaduct, peering at the greenish gleam of light at the other end of the tunnel. The green was the grass and trees of Douglas Park. Pepper would begin slamming an aerial or board or chain off the girders, making the echoes collide and ring, while Ziggy and I clonked empty bottles and beer cans, and all three of us would be shouting and screaming like Screamin' Jay or Howlin' Wolf, like those choirs of unleashed voices we'd hear on *Jam with Sam*'s late-night blues show. Sometimes a train streamed by, booming overhead like part of the song, and we'd shout louder yet, and I'd remember my father telling me how he could have been an opera singer if he hadn't ruined his voice as a kid imitating trains. Once, a gang of black kids appeared on the Douglas Park end of the viaduct and stood harmonizing from bass through falsetto just like the Coasters, so sweetly that though at first we tried outshouting them, we finally shut up and listened, except for Pepper keeping the beat.

We applauded from our side but stayed where we were, and they stayed on theirs. Douglas Park had become the new boundary after the riots the summer before.

'How can a place with such good viaducts have blight, man?' Pepper asked, still rapping his aerial as we walked back.

'Frankly, man,' Ziggy said, 'I always suspected it was a little fucked up around here.'

'Well, that's different,' Pepper said. 'Then let them call it an Official Fucked-Up Neighborhood.'

Nobody pointed out that you'd never hear a term like that from a public official, at least not in public, and especially not from the office of the mayor who had once promised, 'We shall reach new platitudes of success.'

Nor did anyone need to explain that Official Blight was the language of revenue, forms in quintuplicate, grants, and federal aid channeled through the Machine and processed with the help of grafters, skimmers, wheeler-dealers, an army of aldermen, precinct captains, patronage workers, their relatives and friends. No one said it, but instinctively we knew we'd never see a nickel.

Not that we cared. They couldn't touch us if we didn't. Besides, we weren't blamers. Blight was just something that happened, like acne or old age. Maybe declaring it official mattered in that mystical world of property values, but it wasn't a radical step, like condemning buildings or labeling a place a slum. Slums were on the other side of the viaduct.

Blight, in fact, could be considered a kind of official recognition, a grudging admission that among blocks of factories, railroad tracks, truck docks, industrial dumps, scrapyards, expressways, and the drainage canal, people had managed to wedge in their everyday lives.

Deep down we believed what Pepper had been getting at: blight had nothing to do with ecstasy. They could send in the building inspectors and social workers, the mayor could drive through in his black limo, but they'd never know about the music of viaducts, or churches where saints winked and nodded, or how right next door to me our guitar player, Joey 'Deejo' DeCampo, had finally found his title, and inspired by it had begun the Great American Novel, *Blight*, which opened: 'The dawn rises like sick old men playing on the rooftops in their underwear.'

We had him read that to us again and again.

Ecstatic, Deejo rushed home and wrote all night. I could always tell when he was writing. It wasn't just the wild, dreamy look that overcame him. Deejo wrote to music, usually the 1812 Overture, and since only a narrow gangway between buildings separated his window from mine, when I heard bells and cannon blasts at two in the morning I knew he was creating.

Next morning, bleary-eyed, sucking a pinched Lucky, Deejo read us the second sentence. It ran twenty ballpoint-scribbled loose-leaf pages and had nothing to do with the old men on the rooftops in their underwear. It seemed as though Deejo had launched into a digression before the novel had even begun. His second sentence described an epic battle between a spider and a caterpillar. The battle took place in the gangway between our apartment buildings, and that's where Deej insisted on reading it to us. The gangway lent his voice an echoey ring. He read with his eyes glued to the page, his free hand gesticulating wildly, pouncing spiderlike, fingers jabbing like a beak tearing into green caterpillar guts, fist opening like a jaw emitting shrieks. His voice rose as the caterpillar reared, howling like a damned soul, its poisonous hairs bristling. Pepper, Ziggy, and I listened, occasionally exchanging looks.

It wasn't Deejo's digressing that bothered us. That was how we all told stories. But we could see that Deejo's inordinate fascination with bugs was surfacing again. Not that he was alone in that, either. Of all our indigenous wildlife – sparrows, pigeons, mice, rats, dogs, cats – it was only bugs that suggested the grotesque richness of nature. A lot of kids had, at one time or another, expressed their wonder by torturing them a little. But Deejo had been obsessed. He'd become diabolically adept as a destroyer, the kind of kid who would observe an ant hole for hours, even bait it with a Holloway bar, before blowing it up with a cherry bomb. Then one day his grandpa Tony said, 'Hey, Joey, pretty soon they're gonna invent little microphones and you'll be able to hear them screaming.'

He was kidding, but the remark altered Deejo's entire way of looking at things. The world suddenly became one of an infinite number of infinitesimal voices, and Deejo equated voices with souls. If one only listened, it was possible to hear tiny choirs that hummed at all hours as on a summer night, voices speaking a language of terror and beauty that, for the first time, Deejo understood.

It was that vision that turned him into a poet, and it was really for his poetry, more than his guitar playing, that we'd recruited him for the No Names. None of us could write lyrics, though I'd tried a few takeoffs, like the one on Jerry Lee Lewis's 'Great Balls of Fire':

> *My BVDs were made of thatch,*
> *You came along and lit the match,*
> *I screamed in pain, my screams grew higher,*
> *Goodness gracious! My balls were on fire!*

We were looking for a little more soul, words that would suggest Pepper's rages, Ziggy's prophetic dreams. And we might have had that if Deejo could have written a bridge. He'd get in a groove like 'Lonely Is the Falling Rain':

> *Lonely is the falling rain,*
> > *Every drop*
> > *Tastes the same,*
> *Lonely is the willow tree,*
> > *Green dress draped*
> > *Across her knee,*
> *Lonely is the boat at sea . . .*

Deejo could go on listing lonely things for pages, but he'd never arrive at a bridge. His songs refused to circle back on themselves. They'd just go on and were impossible to memorize.

He couldn't spell, either, which never bothered us but created a real problem when Pepper asked him to write something that Pepper could send to Linda Molina. Deejo came up with 'I Dream,' which, after several pages, ended with the lines:

> *I dream of my arms*
> *Around your waste.*

Linda mailed it back to Pepper with those lines circled and in angry slashes of eyebrow pencil the exclamations: *Lechón! Estúpido!! Pervert!*

Pepper kept it folded in his wallet like a love letter.

But back to *Blight*.

We stood in the gangway listening to Deejo read. His seemingly nonstop sentence was reaching a climax. Just when the spider and caterpillar realized their battle was futile, that neither could win, a sparrow swooped down and gobbled them both up.

It was a parable. Who knows how many insect lives had been sacrificed in order for Deejo to have finally arrived at that moral?

We hung our heads and muttered, 'Yeah, great stuff, Deej, that was good, man, no shit, keep it up, be a bestseller.'

He folded his loose-leaf papers, stuffed them into his back pocket, and walked away without saying anything.

Later, whenever someone would bring up his novel, *Blight*, and its great opening line, Deejo would always say, 'Yeah, and it's been all downhill from there.'

As long as it didn't look as if Deejo would be using his title in the near future, we decided to appropriate it for the band. We considered several variations – Boys from Blight, Blights Out, the Blight Brigade. We wanted to call ourselves Pepper and the Blighters, but Pepper said no way, so we settled on just plain Blighters. That had a lot better ring to it than calling ourselves the No Names. We had liked being the No Names at first, but it had started to seem like an advertisement for an identity crisis. The No Names sounded too much like one of the tavern-sponsored softball teams the guys back from Korea had formed. Those guys had been our heroes when we were little kids. They had seemed like legends to us as they gunned around the block on Indians and Harleys while we walked home from grade school. Now they hung out at corner taverns, working on beer bellies, and played softball a couple of nights a week on teams that lacked both uniforms and names. Some of their teams had jerseys with the name of the bar that sponsored them across the back, but the bars themselves were mainly named after beers – the Fox Head 400 on Twenty-fifth Street, or the Edelweiss Tap on Twenty-sixth, or down from that the Carta Blanca. Sometimes, in the evenings, we'd walk over to Lawndale Park and watch one of the tavern teams play softball under the lights. Invariably some team calling itself the Damon Demons or the Latin Cobras, decked out in gold-and-black uniforms, would beat their butts.

There seemed to be some unspoken relationship between being nameless and being a loser. Watching the guys from Korea after their ball games as they hung around under the buzzing neon signs of their taverns, guzzling beers and flipping the softball, I got the strange feeling that they had actually chosen anonymity and the loserhood that went with it. It was something they looked for in one another, that held them together. It was as if Korea had confirmed the choice in them, but it had been there before they'd been drafted. I could still remember how they once organized a motorcycle club. They called it the Motorcycle Club. Actually, nobody even called it that. It was the only nameless motorcycle gang I'd ever heard of.

A lot of those guys had grown up in the housing project that Pepper and Ziggy lived in, sprawling blocks of row houses known simply as 'the projects,' rather than something ominous sounding like Cabrini-Green. Generations of nameless gangs had roamed the projects, then disappeared, leaving behind odd, anonymous graffiti – unsigned warnings, threats, and imprecations without the authority of a gang name behind them.

It wasn't until we became Blighters that we began to recognize the obscurity that surrounded us. Other neighborhoods at least had identities, like Back of the Yards, Marquette Park, Logan Square, Greektown. There were places named after famous intersections, like Halsted and Taylor. Everyone knew the mayor still lived where he'd been born, in Bridgeport, the neighborhood around Sox Park. We heard our area referred to sometimes as Zone 8, after its postal code, but that never caught on. Nobody said, 'Back to Zone 8.' For a while Deejo had considered *Zone 8* as a possible title for his novel, but he finally rejected it as sounding too much like science fiction.

As Blighters, just walking the streets we became suddenly aware of familiar things we didn't have names for, like the trees we'd grown up walking past, or the flowers we'd always admired that bloomed around the blue plastic shrine of the Virgin in the front yard of the Old Widow. Even the street names were mainly numbers, something I'd never have noticed if Debbie Weiss, a girl I'd met downtown, hadn't pointed it out.

Debbie played sax, too, in the band at her all-girls high school. I met her in the sheet-music department of Lyon & Healy's music store. We were both flipping through the same Little Richard songbooks. His songs had great sax breaks, the kind where you roll onto your back and kick your feet in the air while playing.

'Tenor or alto?' she asked without looking up from the music.

I glanced around to make sure she was talking to me. She was humming 'Tutti Frutti' under her breath.

'Tenor,' I answered, amazed we were talking.

'That's what I want for my birthday. I've got an alto, an old Martin. It was my uncle Seymour's. He played with Chick Webb.'

'Oh, yeah,' I said, impressed, though I didn't know exactly who Chick Webb was. 'How'd you know I played sax?' I asked her, secretly pleased that I obviously looked like someone who did.

'It was either that or you've got weird taste in ties. You always walk around wearing your neck strap?'

'No, I just forgot to take it off after practicing,' I explained, effortlessly slipping into my first lie to her. Actually, I had taken to wearing the neck strap for my saxophone sort of in the same way that the Mexican guys in the neighborhood wore gold chains dangling outside their T-shirts, except that instead of a cross at the end of my strap I had a little hook, which looked like a mysterious Greek letter, from which the horn was meant to hang.

We went to a juice bar Debbie knew around the corner from the music store. I had a Coco-Nana and she had something with mango, papaya, and passion fruit.

'So how'd you think I knew you played sax? By your thumb callus?' She laughed.

We compared the thumb calluses we had from holding our horns. She was funny. I'd never met a girl so easy to talk to. We talked about music and saxophone reeds and school. The only thing wrong was that I kept telling her lies. I told her I played in a band in Cicero in a club that was run by the Mafia. She said she'd never been to Cicero, but it sounded like really the pits. 'Really the pits' was one of her favorite phrases. She lived on the North Side and invited me to visit. When she wrote her address down on a napkin and asked if I knew how to get there I said, 'Sure, I know where that is.'

North to Freedom, I kept thinking on my way to her house the first time, trying to remember all the bull I'd told her. It took over an hour and two transfers to get there. I ended up totally lost. I was used to streets that were numbered, streets that told you exactly where you were and what was coming up next. 'Like knowing the latitude,' I told her.

She argued that the North Side had more class because the streets had names.

'A number lacks character, David. How can you have a feeling for a street called Twenty-second?' she asked.

She'd never been on the South Side except for a trip to the museum.

I'd ride the Douglas Park B train home from her house and pretend she was sitting next to me, and as my stop approached I'd look down at the tarpaper roofs, back porches, alleys, and back yards crammed between factories and try to imagine how it would look to someone seeing it for the first time.

At night, Twenty-second was a streak of colored lights, electric winks of neon glancing off plate glass and sidewalks as headlights surged by. The air smelled of restaurants – frying burgers, pizza parlors, the cornmeal and hot-oil blast of *taquerías*. Music collided out of open bars. And when it rained and the lights on the oily street shimmered, Deejo would start whistling 'Harlem Nocturne' in the backseat.

I'd inherited a '53 Chevy from my father. He hadn't died, but he figured the car had. It was a real Blightmobile, a kind of mustardy, baby-shit yellow where it wasn't rusting out, but built like a tank, and rumbling like one, too. That car would not lay rubber, not even when I'd floor it in neutral, then throw it into drive.

Some nights there would be drag races on Twenty-fifth Place, a dead-end street lined with abandoned factories and junkers that winos dumped along the curb. It was suggested to me more than once that my Chevy should take its rightful place along the curb with the junkers. The dragsters would line up, their machines gleaming, customized, bull-nosed, raked, and chopped, oversize engines revving through chrome pipes; then someone would wave a shirt and they'd explode off, burning rubber down an aisle of wrecks. We'd hang around watching till the cops showed up, then scrape together some gas money and go riding ourselves, me behind the wheel and Ziggy fiddling with the radio, tuning in on the White Sox while everyone else shouted for music.

The Chevy had one customized feature: a wooden bumper. It was something I was forced to add after I almost ruined my life forever on Canal Street. When I first inherited the car all I had was my driver's permit, so Ziggy, who already had his license, rode with me to take the driving test. On the way there, wheeling a corner for practice, I jumped the curb on Canal Street and rumbled down the sidewalk until I hit a NO PARKING sign and sent it flying over the bridge. Shattered headlights showered the windshield and Ziggy was choking on a scream caught in his throat. I swung a U and fled back to the neighborhood. It took blocks before Ziggy was able to breathe again. I felt shaky too and started to laugh with relief. Zig stared at me as if I were crazy and had purposely driven down the sidewalk in order to knock off a NO PARKING sign.

'Holy Christ! Dave, you could have ruined your life back there forever,' Zig told me. It sounded like something my father would have said. Worries were making Ziggy more nervous that summer than ever before. The Sox had come from nowhere to lead the league, triggering Zig's old nightmare about atom bombs falling on the night the White Sox won the pennant.

Besides the busted headlights, the sign pole had left a perfect indentation in my bumper. It was Pepper's idea to wind chains around the bumper at the point of indentation, attach the chains to the bars of a basement window, and floor the car in reverse to pull out the dent. When we tried it the bumper tore off. So Pepper, who saw himself as mechanically inclined, wired on a massive wooden bumper. He'd developed a weird affection for the Chevy. I'd let him drive and he'd tool down alleys clipping garbage cans with the wooden front end in a kind of steady bass-drum beat: *boom boom boom.*

Pepper reached the point where he wanted to drive all the time. I understood why. There's a certain feeling of freedom you can get only with a beater, that comes from being able to wreck it without remorse. In a way it's like being indestructible, impervious to pain. We'd cruise the neighborhood on Saturdays, and everywhere we looked guys would be waxing their cars or tinkering under the hoods.

I'd honk at them out the window on my sax and yell, 'You're wasting a beautiful day on that hunk of scrap.'

They'd glance up from their swirls of simonize and flip me the finger.

'Poor, foolish assholes,' Pepper would scoff.

He'd drive with one hand on the wheel and the other smacking the roof in time to whatever was blaring on the radio. The Chevy was like a drum-set accessory to him. He'd jump out at lights and start bopping on the hood. Since he was driving, I started toting along my sax. We'd pull up to a bus stop where people stood waiting in a trance and Pepper would beat on a fender while I wailed a chorus of 'Hand Jive'; then we'd jump back in the Chevy and grind off, as if making our getaway. Once the cops pulled us over and frisked us down. They examined my sax as if it were a weapon.

'There some law against playing a little music?' Pepper kept demanding.

'That's right, jack-off,' one of the cops told him, 'It's called disturbing the peace.'

Finally, I sold Pepper the Chevy for twenty-five dollars. He said he wanted to fix it up. Instead, he used it as a battering ram. He drove it at night around construction sites for the new expressway, mowing down the blinking yellow barricades and signs that read: SORRY FOR THE INCONVENIENCE . . .

Ziggy, who had developed an eye twitch and had started to stutter, refused to ride with him anymore.

The Sox kept winning.

One night, as Pepper gunned the engine at a red light on Thirty-ninth, the entire transmission dropped out into the street. He, Deejo, and I pushed the car for blocks and never saw a cop. There was a slight decline to the street and once we got it moving, the Chevy rolled along on its own momentum. Pepper sat inside steering. With the key in the ignition the radio still played.

'Anybody have any idea where we're rolling to?' Deejo wanted to know.

'To the end of the line,' Pepper said.

We rattled across a bridge that spanned the drainage canal, and just beyond it Pepper cut the wheel and we turned off onto an oiled, unlighted cinder road that ran past a foundry and continued along the river. The road angled downhill, but it was potholed and rutted and it took all three of us grunting and struggling to keep the car moving.

'It would have been a lot easier to just dump it on Twenty-fifth Place,' Deejo panted.

'No way, man,' Pepper said. 'We ain't winos.'

'We got class,' I said.

The road was intersected by railroad tracks. After half an hour of rocking and heaving we got the Chevy onto the tracks and from there it was downhill again to the railroad bridge. We stopped halfway across the bridge. Pepper climbed onto the roof of the car and looked out over the black river. The moon shined on the oily surface like a single, intense spotlight. Frankie Avalon was singing on the radio.

'Turn that simp off. I hate him,' Pepper yelled. He was peeing down onto the hood in a final benediction.

I switched the radio dial over to the late-night mush-music station – Sinatra singing 'These Foolish Things' – and turned the volume up full blast. Pepper jumped down, flicked the headlights on, and we shoved the car over the bridge.

The splash shook the girders. Pigeons crashed out from under the bridge and swept around confusedly in the dark. We stared over the side half expecting to see the Chevy bob back up through the heavy grease of the river and float off in the moonlight. But except for the bubbles on the surface, it was gone. Then I remembered that my sax had been in the trunk.

A week later, Pepper had a new car, a red Fury convertible. His older cousin Carmen had co-signed. Pepper had made the first payment, the only one he figured on making, by selling his massive red-sparkle drum set – bass, snare, tom-tom, cymbals, high hat, bongos, conga, cowbell, woodblock, tambourine, gong – pieces he'd been accumulating on birthdays, Christmases, confirmation, graduation, since fourth grade, the way girls add pearls to a necklace. When he climbed behind those drums, he looked like a mad king beating his throne, and at first we refused to believe he had sold it all, or that he was dropping out of school to join the marines.

He drove the Fury as gently as a chauffeur. It was as if some of the craziness had drained out of him when the Chevy went over the bridge. Ziggy even started riding with us again, though every time he'd see a car pass with a GO GO SOX sign he'd get twitchy and depressed.

Pennant fever was in the air. The city long accustomed to losers was poised for a celebration. Driving with the top down brought the excitement of the streets closer. We were part of it. From Pepper's Fury the pace of life around us seemed different, slower than it had from the Chevy. It was as if we were in a speedboat gliding through.

Pepper would glide repeatedly past Linda Molina's house, but she was never out as she'd been the summer before, sunning on a towel on the boulevard grass. There was a rumor that she'd gotten knocked up and had gone to stay with relatives in Texas. Pepper refused to believe it, but the rest of us got the feeling that he had joined the marines for the same reason Frenchmen supposedly joined the Foreign Legion.

'Dave, man, you wanna go by that broad you know's house on the North Side, man?' he would always offer.

'Nah,' I'd say, as if that would be boring.

We'd just drive, usually farther south, sometimes almost to Indiana, where the air smelled singed and towering foundry smokestacks erupted shooting sparks, like gigantic Roman candles. Then, skirting the worst slums, we'd head back through dark neighborhoods broken by strips of neon, the shops grated and padlocked, but bands of kids still out splashing in the water of open hydrants, and guys standing in the light of bar signs, staring hard as we passed.

We toured places we'd always heard about – the Fulton produce mart with its tailgate-high sidewalks, Midway Airport, skid row – stopped for carryout ribs, or at shrimp houses along the river, and always ended up speeding down the Outer Drive, along the skyline-glazed lake, as if some force had spun us to the inner rim of the city. That was the summer Deejo let his

hair get long. He was growing a beard, too, a Vandyke, he called
it, though Pepper insisted it was really trimmings from other
parts of Deejo's body pasted on with Elmer's glue.

Wind raking his shaggy hair, Deejo would shout passages from
his dog-eared copy of *On the Road*, which he walked around
reading like a breviary ever since seeing Jack Kerouac on *The
Steve Allen Show*. I retaliated in a spooky Vincent Price voice,
reciting poems off an album called *Word Jazz* that Deej and I
had nearly memorized. My favorite was 'The Junkman,' which
began:

> *In a dream I dreamt that was no dream,*
> *In a sleep I slept that was no sleep,*
> *I saw the junkman in his scattered yard . . .*

Ziggy dug that one, too.

By the time we hit downtown and passed Buckingham
Fountain with its spraying, multicolored plumes of light, Deejo
would be rhapsodic. One night, standing up in the backseat
and extending his arms toward the skyscraper we called God's
House because of its glowing blue dome – a blue the romantic,
lonely shade of runway lights – Deejo blurted out, 'I dig beauty!'

Even at the time, it sounded a little extreme. All we'd had
were a couple of six-packs. Pepper started swerving, he was
laughing so hard, and beating the side of the car with his fist,
and for a while it was as if he was back behind the wheel of
the Chevy. It even brought Ziggy out of his despair. We rode
around the rest of the night gaping and pointing and yelling,
'Beauty ahead! Dig it!'

'Beauty to the starboard!'

'Coming up on it fast!'

'Can you dig it?'

'Oh, wow! I am digging it! I'm digging beauty!'

Deejo got pimped pretty bad about it in the neighborhood. A long time after that night, guys would still be asking him, 'Digging any beauty lately?' Or introducing him: 'This is Deejo. He digs beauty.' Or he'd be walking down the street and from a passing car someone would wave, and yell, 'Hey, Beauty-Digger!'

The last week before the Fury was repoed, when Pepper would come by to pick us up, he'd always say, 'Hey, man, let's go dig some beauty.'

A couple of weeks later, on a warm Wednesday night in Cleveland, Gerry Staley came on in relief with the bases loaded in the bottom of the ninth, threw one pitch, a double-play ball, Aparicio to Kluszewski, and the White Sox clinched their first pennant in forty years. Pepper had already left on the bus for Parris Island. He would have liked the celebration. Around eleven p.m. the air-raid sirens all over the city began to howl. People ran out into the streets in their bathrobes crying and praying, staring up past the roofs as if trying to catch a glimpse of the mushroom cloud before it blew the neighborhood to smithereens. It turned out that Mayor Daley, a lifelong Sox fan, had ordered the sirens as part of the festivities.

Ziggy wasn't the same after that. He could hardly get a word out without stammering. He said he didn't feel reprieved but as if he had died. When the sirens started to wail, he had climbed into bed clutching his rosary which he still had from grade-school days, when the Blessed Mother used to smile at him. He'd wet the bed that night and had continued having accidents every night since. Deej and I tried to cheer him up, but what kept him going was a book by Thomas Merton called *The Seven*

Storey Mountain, which one of the priests at the parish church had given him. It meant more to Zig than *On the Road* did to Deejo. Finally, Ziggy decided that since he could hardly talk anyway, he might be better off in the Trappists like Thomas Merton. He figured if he just showed up with the book at the monastery in Gethsemane, Kentucky, they'd have to take him in.

'I'll be taking the vow of silence,' he stammered, 'so don't worry if you don't hear much from me.'

'Silence isn't the vow I'd be worrying about,' I said, still trying to joke him out of it, but he was past laughing and I was sorry I'd kidded him.

He, Deejo, and I walked past the truck docks and railroad tracks, over to the river. We stopped on the California Avenue Bridge, from which we could see a succession of bridges spanning the river, including the black railroad bridge we had pushed the Chevy over. We'd been walking most of the night, past churches, under viaducts, along the boulevard, as if visiting the landmarks of our childhood. Without a car to ride around in, I felt like a little kid again. It was Zig's last night, and he wanted to walk. In the morning he intended to leave home and hitchhike to Kentucky. I had an image of him standing along the shoulder holding up a sign that read GETHSEMANE to the oncoming traffic. I didn't want him to go. I kept remembering things as we walked along and then not mentioning them, like that dream he'd had about him and me and Little Richard. Little Richard had found religion and been ordained a preacher, I'd read, but I didn't think he had taken the vow of silence. I had a fantasy of all the monks with their hoods up, meditating in total silence, and suddenly Ziggy letting go with an ear-splitting, wild, howling banshee blues shout.

The next morning he really was gone.

Deejo and I waited for a letter, but neither of us heard anything.

'He must have taken the vow of silence as far as writing, too,' Deejo figured.

I did get a postcard from Pepper sometime during the winter, a scene of a tropical sunset over the ocean, and scrawled on the back the message 'Not diggin' much beauty lately.' There was no return address, and since Pepper's parents had divorced and moved out of the projects I couldn't track him down.

There was a lot of moving going on. Deejo moved out after a huge fight with his old man. Deej's father had lined up a production-line job for Deejo at the factory where he'd worked for twenty-three years. When Deej didn't show up for work the first day his father came home in a rage and tried to tear Deejo's beard off. So Deej moved in with his older brother, Sal, who'd just gotten out of the navy and had a bachelor pad near Old Town. The only trouble for Deejo was that he had to move back home on weekends, when Sal needed more privacy.

Deejo was the last of the Blighters still playing. He actually bought a guitar, though not an electric one. He spent a lot of time listening to scratchy old 78s of black singers whose first names all seemed to begin with either Blind or Sonny. Deejo even cut his own record, a paper-thin 45 smelling of acetate, with one side blank. He took copies of it around to all the bars that the guys from Korea used to rule and talked the bartenders into putting his record on the jukebox. Those bars had quieted down. There weren't enough guys from the Korean days still drinking to field the corner softball teams anymore. The guys who had become regulars were in pretty sad shape. They sat around, endlessly discussing baseball and throwing dice for drinks. The jukeboxes that had once blasted the Platters and

Buddy Holly had filled up with polkas again and with Mexican songs that sounded suspiciously like polkas. Deejo's record was usually stuck between Frank Sinatra and Ray Charles. Deej would insert a little card handprinted in ballpoint pen: HARD-HEARTED WOMAN BY JOEY DECAMPO.

It was a song he'd written. Deejo's hair was longer than ever, his Vandyke had filled in, and he'd taken to wearing sunglasses and huaraches. Sometimes he would show up with one of the girls from Loop Junior College, which was where he was going to school. He'd bring her into the Edelweiss or the Carta Blanca, usually a wispy blond with scared eyes, and order a couple of drafts. The bartender or one of us at the bar would pick up Deejo's cue and say, 'Hey, how about playing that R5?' and feed the jukebox. 'Hard-hearted Woman' would come thumping out as loud as the 'She's-Too-Fat Polka,' scratchy as an old 78, Deejo whining through his nose, strumming his three chords.

> Hard-hearted woman,
> Oh yeah, Lord,
> She's a hard-hearted woman,
> Uuuhhh . . .

Suddenly, despite the Delta accent, it would dawn on the girl that it was Deejo's voice. He'd kind of grin, shyly admitting that it was, his fingers on the bar tapping along in time with the song, and I wondered what she would think if she could have heard the one I wished he had recorded, the one that opened:

> The dawn rises,
> Uuuhhh,
> Like sick old men,

Oh, Lord,
Playing on the rooftops in their underwear,
Yeah . . .

Back to blight.

It was a saying that faded from my vocabulary, especially after my parents moved to Berwyn. Then, some years later, after I quit my job at UPS in order to hide out from the draft in college, the word resurfaced in an English-lit survey class. Maybe I was just more attuned to it than most people ordinarily would be. There seemed to be blight all through Dickens and Blake. The class was taught by a professor nicknamed 'the Spitter.' He loved to read aloud, and after the first time, nobody sat in the front rows. He had acquired an Oxford accent, but the more excitedly he read and spit, the more I could detect the South Side of Chicago underneath the veneer, as if his *th*s had been worked over with a drill press. When he read us Shelley's 'To a Skylark,' which began 'Hail to thee, blithe spirit,' I thought he was talking about blight again until I looked it up.

One afternoon in spring I cut class and rode the Douglas Park B back. It wasn't anything I planned. I just wanted to go somewhere and think. The draft board was getting ready to reclassify me and I needed to figure out why I felt like telling them to get rammed rather than just saying the hell with it and doing what they told me to do. But instead of thinking, I ended up remembering my early trips back from the North Side, when I used to pretend that Debbie Weiss was riding with me, and when I came to my stop on Twenty-second Street this time it was easier to imagine how it would have looked to her – small, surprisingly small in the way one is surprised returning to an old grade-school classroom.

I hadn't been back for a couple of years. The neighborhood

was mostly Mexican now, with many of the signs over the stores in Spanish, but the bars were still called the Edelweiss Tap and the Budweiser Lounge. Deejo and I had lost touch, but I heard that he'd been drafted. I made the rounds of some of the bars looking for his song on the jukeboxes, but when I couldn't find it even in the Carta Blanca, where nothing else had changed, I gave up. I was sitting in the Carta Blanca having a last, cold *cerveza* before heading back, listening to 'CuCuRuCuCu Paloma' on the jukebox and watching the sunlight streak in through the dusty wooden blinds. Then the jukebox stopped playing, and through the open door I could hear the bells from three different churches tolling the hour. They didn't quite agree on the precise moment. Their rings overlapped and echoed one another. The streets were empty, no one home from work or school yet, and something about the overlapping of those bells made me remember how many times I'd had dreams, not prophetic ones like Ziggy's, but terrifying all the same, in which I was back in my neighborhood, but lost, everything at once familiar and strange, and I knew if I tried to run, my feet would be like lead, and if I stepped off a curb, I'd drop through space, and then in the dream I would come to a corner that would feel so timeless and peaceful, like the Carta Blanca with the bells fading and the sunlight streaking through, that for a moment it would feel as if I'd wandered into an Official Blithe Area.

Bijou

The film that rumor has made the *dernier cri* of this year's festival is finally screened.

It begins without credits, challenging the audience from its opening frame. Not only has it been shot in black and white, but the black and white do not occur in usual relationships to one another. There is little gray. Ordinary light has become exotic as zebras.

Perhaps in the film's native country they are not familiar with abstract reductions such as black and white. There, even vanilla ice cream is robin's-egg blue, and licorice almost amethyst when held to the sun. No matter what oppressive regime, each day vibrates with the anima of primitive paintings – continual fiesta! As ambulances siren, they flash through color changes with the rapidity of chameleons. In the modern hospital, set like a glass mural against the sea, ceiling fans oscillate like impaled wings of flamingos above the crisp rhythm of nurses.

Black and white are not native to these latitudes. And gray requires the opaque atmosphere of Antwerp or Newcastle, Pittsburgh or Vladivostok, requires the Industrial Revolution, laissez-faire, imperialism, Seven Year Plan, Great Leap Forward, pollution, Cold War, fallout, PCB, alienation . . .

Nor does the film appear to be alluding to the classic black-and-white films of Fritz Lang, King Vidor, Orson Welles. Nor to the social realism of the forties or neo-realism of the fifties. In fact, the only acknowledged influence is an indirect one, that of an obscure poem by Victor Guzman, the late surrealist dentist of Chilpancingo.

Trees, for example, are blinding white, rather than the darknesses so often etched against a dying sky.

Shade is white.

Fruit is white.

Asphalt roads are white.

It is the windowpanes through which one sees them that are black. Smoked with kerosene or smeared with shoe polish for secrecy or air-raid blackouts, who can determine?

It is true that at times the film closely resembles a negative – the moon a sooty zero in a silver nitrate night. But the gimmick of shooting in negative is used with restraint. It's obvious that the filmmakers are after something beyond the simple reversal of the values of light.

Take the clouds – plumed, milky black in an albino, noon sky. But are they clouds? Or the smoke from a burning village, bombs, an erupting volcano?

In another sequence, an execution, there is a close-up of bullets being x'd to make the heads dumdum. The lead is white. And later, when the flour-sack hoods are removed from the prisoners, the wounds are white. The camera pans along the riddled convent wall. In the distance, mountains rise tipped with anthracite. To put it another way, black is not meant to define white, nor vice versa.

The first color goes almost unnoticed.

The pink washrag of a cat's tongue as it grooms in the bleached shadow of the jail.

Almost unnoticed – but a subconscious shock registers through the theater.

Gradually, it becomes apparent that tongues, only tongues, are assuming color: dogs panting in the dust of traffic, snakes and geckos flicking from drainpipes, color licking and poking from a thousand tiny caves.

Even tongues ordinarily colorless take on brilliance: the black lash of the butterfly uncoils azure at the flower; the cow masticating its cud lolls a tongue suddenly crimson as black jeeps siren past down the alabaster highway to the interior.

There, the guerrillas have been ambushed, surrounded, betrayed. A chopper flattens palms as it drops in CIA advisers. The camera pans the faces of the rebels in macro-lens close-ups as if a boil or a louse swelling among beads of sweat might reveal a man's character; or as if white hairs sprouting from a mole, or a childhood scar beneath a stubble beard might tell his past.

And it is here that the tongues begin to obsess the camera, that the realistic soundtrack of bird caws, gunshots, shouting, machinery, is intercut with the whispered litany of Guzman's lines from 'Laughing Gas': *gold-dust tongues, ocher tongues eating earth, walking tongue, candy tongue, milky tongue, sleeper's tongue, passion's tongues, cankered tongues, tongues tinctured yellow, flaming tongue, hovering tongues of epiphany* . . .

The screen is nearly technicolor with tongues.

Canisters of nerve gas explode.

Then, in a sequence more excruciating than any since *The Battle of Algiers*, the guerrillas are captured. Scene follows scene documenting torture in the modern military state. Cattle prods are used for confessions, electrodes taped to eyelids, tongues, genitals.

At night, out by the black fire, the guards have begun to drink. Soon they cannot tolerate the refined torments of electricity. Fists, truncheons, empty bottles, boots pummel bone.

The prisoners refuse to talk.

Near dawn, in a drunken rage, the guards take them one by one and mock their silence by tearing out their tongues with wire snips. They are forced to kneel, mouths wedged open with a wooden stake, and tongues forceped out in a scream and dark gush of blood – blue, green, yellow, orange, violet, red tongues. The tongues are collected in a coffee can the way ears are sometimes collected, and stored on the colonel's desk. Each new victim stares at the can as he is questioned for the final time. The tongues brim over and flop to the floor and the guards pass out from drunkenness, their own tongues gaping from snoring jaws.

'Raspberry tongues,' Guzman wrote, 'the entrails of a clown.'

The audience stares in silence. Some have turned away; there have been gasps. But, on the whole, they have been conditioned to accept, almost to expect, this violence on screen. They have watched blood spurt and limbs dismembered in Peckinpah's choreographed slow motion, brains sprayed across a wall, bodies explode, monks topple in flaming gasoline, eyes gouged, chain saws buzzing through bone, decapitations in 3-D. They are not at the festival to censor but to discern: where is violence statement and where merely further exploitation? When does Art become carnography? Is this perhaps the Cinema of Cruelty?

They watch as the next morning a young private is assigned to clean up the night's excesses. He takes the coffee can to bury in the old graveyard behind the cathedral while bells chime through an intermittent hiss of wind and mewing of gulls. His shovel bites dirt and he breathes louder with every scoopful he flings over his shoulder into the blurred eye of climbing sun. He sweats, his breath becomes panting, then gagging, and suddenly he's doubled over retching into the hole, mumbling the Lord's Prayer in between spasms. Still heaving, he rises, kicks the can in, frantically raking over loose dirt, smacking it down with the flat of the shovel, raining down blows as if he were killing a snake.

The sound track cuts off.

The whump of the shovel is the last sound, though on screen the soldier continues to beat the earth.

Now the screen seems even more unrelievedly black and white – no more background strumming of guitars, no mountain flutes, birdcalls, wind, distant thunder of gunfire. Not even the unavoidable drone of a jet overhead on its way to another country. A world of action suddenly mute as Griffith's galloping Klan, as Méliès blasting off for the moon, as Chaplin twirling a cane. There is only the faint, nearly subliminal metronome of ticking sprockets audible from the projection booth in the now-silent theater. But as the silence continues, the steady clack seems increasingly obtrusive, and the suspicion begins to arise that the racket of sprockets *is* the sound track. There's something too rickety about its clatter – a sound that evokes, perhaps by design, evenings long ago, when after the supper dishes were cleared, a father, who served as director, would set up a projector with tinny spools while children removed pictures from a wall to transform it into a screen, and then the lights would be extinguished and home movies would beam into unsteady focus – silent, unedited, the mugging face of each family member plainer than memory, appearing as they once were, startlingly young, innocent of time.

Subtitles begin to appear. Too fast to read. Partially telegraphed messages. Single words or parts of words flashed on screen: AWE DIS KER.

Static as the words, a progression of freeze-frames, the bled tones of tabloid photos dissolve one into another: peasants on their way to market, slum children, children with rickets, a beggar with yaws, fruit loaders sweating at an outdoor market of gutted fish, piled monkey skulls, tourists.

In churches and universities, on corners beneath bug-clouded lights, people are opening their mouths to speak, but everywhere it appears the mouths are black, gaping holes. There is only continual silence, intercut dissolves, subtitles flashing on and off, sometimes like fading neon signs, sometimes like a collage, commenting on the action (WHERE THERE IS NO FREEDOM WORDS FILL THE MOUTH WITH BLOOD).

The footage continues running faster, almost blurred, as if a documentary were being filmed from a speeding train – assassinations, bombed motorcades, bombed restaurants, bombed schools, strikes, soldiers firing into a crowd, smoldering bodies, mothers in mourning, black coffins, black flags, the revolt of students, the revolt of the army, newspaper offices ransacked by blackshirts, presses smashed, mobs, fires, men hauled out into the street and lynched from lampposts before the shattered windows of the capitol, streets littered with books from the gutted library, and all the while a sound rising from underground as if the clatter of sprockets has become a subway train roaring down a tunnel, its brake shoe scraping metal from track, metal on metal whining into a siren-pitched screech (EVEN THE HANGED HAVE NO TONGUES TO PROTRUDE!).

The house lights flick on. The audience, many of them North Americans, is stunned. Some talk as if making sure they still can. Some weep. Others leave the theater cursing – what? The film? The oppressors? It isn't clear. Someone in the balcony shouts, 'Bravo!' And another in front, 'Long live the revolution!' People are up from their seats and applauding as if it were a live presentation.

'The ultimate praise for a film,' one critic is heard to remark on his way to the lobby, 'is to treat it as if it were a play deserving curtain calls, to confuse celluloid images with flesh and blood, to transcend the isolated private dream state of the movie theater by merging with the mass in simple applause.'

Tomorrow the Arts sections will carry rave reviews: 'a new and daring fusion of avant-garde technique with documentary sensibility . . .'

A journalist for the *Voice* will write: 'Uncompromisingly powerful, it demands to be seen, though a film like this might be better kept secret, protected from the corrupting influence of the Hollywood glamour and promotion machine, the invidious American penchant for reducing substance to marketable style.'

While another reviewer, writing for a more conservative publication will comment: 'This looks like the year for Terrorist Cinema. Another fad pretending to usher in a change of consciousness but lacking the moral imperative of the civil rights movement and peace marches that launched the 60s.'

The audience files out through the mirrored lobby, backs turned on the posters of stars, out under the winking marquee, squinting at the pink smolder of dusk. Behind them, on the silver screen in the houselit theater, a final frame hovers like the ghost-image phenomena sometimes haunting TV screens, a blown-up image that could only have been shot by a camera implanted in a mouth, of an indigo tongue working at a husk of popcorn stuck in a gold-capped molar.

And across this image a delayed rolling of credits begins: the names of actors, writers, cameramen, assistant director, director, producer, editors, sound, music, makeup, gaffers, soldiers, officers, generals, politicians – a cast of thousands – workers, students, peasants, the audience, the victims, the maimed, the maddened, the myriad names of the dead.

Pet Milk

Today I've been drinking instant coffee and Pet milk, and watching it snow. It's not that I enjoy the taste especially, but I like the way Pet milk swirls in the coffee. Actually, my favorite thing about Pet milk is what the can opener does to the top of the can. The can is unmistakable – compact, seamless looking, its very shape suggesting that it could condense milk without any trouble. The can opener bites in neatly, and the thick liquid spills from the triangular gouge with a different look and viscosity than milk. Pet milk isn't *real* milk. The color's off, to start with. There's almost something of the past about it, like old ivory. My grandmother always drank it in her coffee. When friends dropped over and sat around the kitchen table, my grandma would ask, 'Do you take cream and sugar?' Pet milk was the cream.

There was a yellow plastic radio on her kitchen table, usually tuned to the polka station, though sometimes she'd miss it by half a notch and get the Greek station instead, or the Spanish, or the Ukrainian. In Chicago, where we lived, all the incompatible states of Europe were pressed together down at the staticky right end of the dial. She didn't seem to notice, as long as she wasn't hearing English. The radio, turned low, played constantly. Its top was warped and turning amber on the side where the tubes were. I remember the sound of it on winter afternoons after school, as I sat by her table watching the Pet milk swirl and cloud in the steaming coffee, and noticing, outside her window, the sky doing the same thing above the railroad yard across the street.

And I remember, much later, seeing the same swirling sky in tiny liqueur glasses containing a drink called a King Alphonse: the crème de cacao rising like smoke in repeated explosions, blooming in kaleidoscopic clouds through the layer of heavy cream. This was in the Pilsen, a little Czech restaurant where my girlfriend, Kate, and I would go sometimes in the evening. It was the first year out of college for both of us, and we had astonished ourselves by finding real jobs – no more waitressing or pumping gas, the way we'd done in school. I was investigating credit references at a bank, and she was doing something slightly above the rank of typist for Hornblower & Weeks, the investment firm. My bank showed training films that emphasized the importance of suitable dress, good grooming, and personal neatness, even for employees like me, who worked at the switchboard in the basement. Her firm issued directives on appropriate attire – skirts, for instance, should cover the knees. She had lovely knees.

Kate and I would sometimes meet after work at the Pilsen, dressed in our proper business clothes and still feeling both a little self-conscious and glamorous, as if we were impostors wearing disguises. The place had small, round oak tables, and we'd sit in a corner under a painting called 'The Street Musicians of Prague' and trade future plans as if they were escape routes. She talked of going to grad school in Europe; I wanted to apply to the Peace Corps. Our plans for the future made us laugh and feel close, but those same plans somehow made anything more than temporary between us seem impossible. It was the first time I'd ever had the feeling of missing someone I was still with.

The waiters in the Pilsen wore short black jackets over long white aprons. They were old men from the old country. We went there often enough to have our own special waiter, Rudi, a name he pronounced with a rolled *R*. Rudi boned our trout and seasoned our salads, and at the end of the meal he'd bring the bottle of crème de cacao from the bar, along with two little glasses and a small pitcher of heavy cream, and make us each a King Alphonse right at our table. We'd watch as he'd fill the glasses halfway up with the syrupy brown liqueur, then carefully attempt to float a layer of cream on top. If he failed to float the cream, we'd get that one free.

'Who was King Alphonse anyway, Rudi?' I sometimes asked, trying to break his concentration, and if that didn't work I nudged the table with my foot so the glass would jiggle imperceptibly just as he was floating the cream. We'd usually get one on the house. Rudi knew what I was doing. In fact, serving the King Alphonses had been his idea, and he had also suggested the trick of jarring the table. I think it pleased him, though he seemed concerned about the way I'd stare into the liqueur glass, watching the patterns.

'It's not a microscope,' he'd say. 'Drink.'

He liked us, and we tipped extra. It felt good to be there and to be able to pay for a meal.

Kate and I met at the Pilsen for supper on my twenty-second birthday. It was May, and unseasonably hot. I'd opened my tie. Even before looking at the dinner menu, we ordered a bottle of Mumm's and a dozen oysters apiece. Rudi made a sly remark when he brought the oysters on platters of ice. They were freshly opened and smelled of the sea. I'd heard people joke about oysters being aphrodisiac but never considered it anything but a myth – the kind of idea they still had in the old country.

We squeezed on lemon, added dabs of horseradish, slid the oysters into our mouths, and then rinsed the shells with champagne and drank the salty, cold juice. There was a beefy-looking couple eating schnitzel at the next table, and they stared at us with the repugnance that public oyster-eaters in the Midwest often encounter. We laughed and grandly sipped it all down. I was already half tipsy from drinking too fast, and starting to feel filled with a euphoric, aching energy. Kate raised a brimming oyster shell to me in a toast: 'To the Peace Corps!'

'To Europe!' I replied, and we clunked shells.

She touched her wineglass to mine and whispered, 'Happy birthday,' and then suddenly leaned across the table and kissed me.

When she sat down again, she was flushed. I caught the reflection of her face in the glass-covered 'The Street Musicians of Prague' above our table. I always loved seeing her in mirrors and windows. The reflections of her beauty startled me. I had told her that once, and she seemed to fend off the compliment, saying, 'That's because you've learned what to look for,' as if it were a secret I'd stumbled upon. But, this time, seeing her reflection hovering ghostlike upon an imaginary Prague was like seeing a future from which she had vanished. I knew I'd never meet anyone more beautiful to me.

We killed the champagne and sat twining fingers across the table. I was sweating. I could feel the warmth of her through her skirt under the table and I touched her leg. We still hadn't ordered dinner. I left money on the table and we steered each other out a little unsteadily.

'Rudi will understand,' I said.

The street was blindingly bright. A reddish sun angled just

above the rims of the tallest buildings. I took my suit coat off and flipped it over my shoulder. We stopped in the doorway of a shoe store to kiss.

'Let's go somewhere,' she said.

My roommate would already be home at my place, which was closer. Kate lived up north, in Evanston. It seemed a long way away.

We cut down a side street, past a fire station, to a small park, but its gate was locked. I pressed close to her against the tall iron fence. We could smell the lilacs from a bush just inside the fence, and when I jumped for an overhanging branch my shirt sleeve hooked on a fence spike and tore, and petals rained down on us as the sprig sprang from my hand.

We walked to the subway. The evening rush was winding down; we must have caught the last express heading toward Evanston. Once the train climbed from the tunnel to the elevated tracks, it wouldn't stop until the end of the line, on Howard. There weren't any seats together, so we stood swaying at the front of the car, beside the empty conductor's compartment. We wedged inside, and I clicked the door shut.

The train rocked and jounced, clattering north. We were kissing, trying to catch the rhythm of the ride with our bodies. The sun bronzed the windows on our side of the train. I lifted her skirt over her knees, hiked it higher so the sun shone off her thighs, and bunched it around her waist. She wouldn't stop kissing. She was moving her hips to pin us to each jolt of the train.

We were speeding past scorched brick walls, gray windows, back porches outlined in sun, roofs, and treetops – the landscape of the El I'd memorized from subway windows over a lifetime of rides: the podiatrist's foot sign past Fullerton; the bright pennants of Wrigley Field, at Addison; ancient hotels with

TRANSIENTS WELCOME signs on their flaking back walls; peeling and graffiti-smudged billboards; the old cemetery just before Wilson Avenue. Even without looking, I knew almost exactly where we were. Within the compartment, the sound of our quick breathing was louder than the clatter of tracks. I was trying to slow down, to make it all last, and when she covered my mouth with her hand I turned my face to the window and looked out.

The train was braking a little from express speed, as it did each time it passed a local station. I could see blurred faces on the long wooden platform watching us pass – businessmen glancing up from folded newspapers, women clutching purses and shopping bags. I could see the expression on each face, momentarily arrested, as we flashed by. A high school kid in shirt sleeves, maybe sixteen, with books tucked under one arm and a cigarette in his mouth, caught sight of us, and in the instant before he disappeared he grinned and started to wave. Then he was gone, and I turned from the window, back to Kate, forgetting everything – the passing stations, the glowing late sky, even the sense of missing her – but that arrested wave stayed with me. It was as if I were standing on that platform, with my schoolbooks and a smoke, on one of those endlessly accumulated afternoons after school when I stood almost outside of time simply waiting for a train, and I thought how much I'd have loved seeing someone like us streaming by.

Childhood and Other Neighborhoods

The Palatski Man

He reappeared in spring, some Sunday morning, perhaps Easter, when the twigs of the catalpa trees budded and lawns smelled of mud and breaking seeds. Or Palm Sunday, returning from mass with handfuls of blessed, bending palms to be cut into crosses and pinned on your Sunday dress and the year-old palms removed by her brother, John, from behind the pictures of Jesus with his burning heart and the Virgin with her sad eyes, to be placed dusty and crumbling in an old coffee can and burned in the back yard. And once, walking back from church, Leon Sisca said these are what they lashed Jesus with. And she said no they aren't, they used whips. They used these, he insisted. What do you know? she said. And he told her she was a dumb girl and lashed her across her bare legs with his blessed palms. They stung her; she started to cry, that anyone could do such a thing, and he caught her running down Twenty-fifth Street with her skirt flying and got her against a fence, and grabbing her by the hair, he stuck his scratchy palms in her face, and suddenly he was lifted off the ground and flung to the sidewalk, and she saw John standing over him very red in the face; and when Leon Sisca tried to run away, John blocked him, and Leon tried to dodge around him as if they were playing football; and as he cut past, John slapped him across the face; Leon's head snapped back and his nose started to bleed. John didn't chase him and he ran halfway down the block, turned around and yelled through his tears with blood dripping on his white shirt: I hate you goddamn you I hate you! All the dressed-up people coming back from church saw it happen and shook their heads. John said, c'mon, Mary, let's go home.

No, it wasn't that day, but it was in that season on a Sunday that he reappeared, and then every Sunday after that through the summer and into the fall, when school would resume and the green catalpa leaves fall like withered fans into the birdbaths, turning the water brown, the Palatski Man would come.

He was an old man who pushed a white cart through the neighborhood streets ringing a little golden bell. He would stop at each corner, and the children would come with their money to inspect the taffy apples sprinkled with chopped nuts, or the red candy apples on pointed sticks, or the *palatski* displayed under the glass of the white cart. She had seen taffy apples in the candy stores and even the red apples sold by clowns at circuses, but she had never seen *palatski* sold anywhere else. It was two crisp wafers stuck together with honey. The taste might have reminded you of an ice-cream cone spread with honey, but it reminded Mary of Holy Communion. It felt like the Eucharist in her mouth, the way it tasted walking back from the communion rail after waiting for Father Mike to stand before her wearing his rustling silk vestments with the organ playing and him saying the Latin prayer over and over faster than she could ever hope to pray and making a sign of the cross with the host just before placing it on someone's tongue. She knelt at the communion rail close enough to the altar to see the silk curtains drawn inside the open tabernacle and the beeswax candles flickering and to smell the flowers. Father Mike was moving down the line of communicants, holding the chalice, with the altar boy, an eighth-grader, sometimes even John, standing beside him in a lace surplice, holding the paten under each chin; and she would close her eyes and open her mouth, sticking her tongue out, and hear the prayer and feel the host placed gently on her tongue. Sometimes Father's hand brushed her bottom lip, and she would feel a spark from his finger, which Sister said was static electricity, not the Holy Spirit.

Then she would walk down the aisle between the lines of communicants, searching through half-shut eyes for her pew, her mind praying, Jesus, help me find it. And when she found her pew, she would kneel down and shut her eyes and bury her face in her hands praying over and over, thank you, Jesus, for coming to me, feeling the host stuck to the roof of her mouth, melting against her tongue like a warm, wheaty snowflake; and she would turn the tip of her tongue inward and lick the host off the ridges of her mouth till it was loosened by saliva and swallowed into her soul.

Who was the Palatski Man? No one knew or even seemed to care. He was an old man with an unremembered face, perhaps a never-seen face, a head hidden by a cloth-visored cap, and eyes concealed behind dark glasses with green, smoked lenses. His smile revealed only a gold crown and a missing tooth. His only voice was the ringing bell, and his hands were rough and red as if scrubbed with sandpaper and their skin very hard when you opened your hand for your change and his fingers brushed yours. His clothes were always the same – white – not starched and dazzling, but the soft white of many washings and wringings.

No one cared and he was left alone. The boys didn't torment him as they did the peddlers during the week. There was constant war between the boys and the peddlers, the umbrella menders, the knife sharpeners, anyone whose business carried him down the side streets or through the alleys. The peddlers came every day, spring, summer, and autumn, through the alleys behind the back-yard fences crying, 'Rags ol irn, rags ol irn!' Riding their ancient, rickety wagons with huge wooden-spoked wheels, heaped high with scraps of metal, frames of furniture, coal-black cobwebbed lumber, bundles of rags and filthy newspapers. The boys called them the Ragmen. They were all old, hunched men, bearded and bald, who bargained in a stammered foreign English and dressed in clothes extracted from the bundles of rags in their weather-beaten wagons.

Their horses seemed even more ancient than their masters, and Mary was always sorry for them as she watched their slow, arthritic gait up and down the alleys. Most of them were white horses, a dirty white as if their original colors had turned white with age, like the hair on an old man's head. They had enormous hooves with iron shoes that clacked down the alleys over the broken glass, which squealed against the concrete when the rusty, metal-rimmed wheels of the wagon ground over it. Their muzzles were pink without hair, and their tongues lolled out gray; their teeth were huge and yellow. Over their eyes were black blinders, around their shoulders a heavy black harness that looked always ready to slip off, leather straps hung all about their bodies. They ate from black, worn leather sacks tied over their faces, and as they ate, the flies flew up from their droppings and climbed all over their thick bodies and the horses swished at them with stringy tails.

The Ragmen drove down the crooked, interconnecting alleys crying, 'Rags ol irn, rags ol irn,' and the boys waited for a wagon to pass, hiding behind fences or garbage cans; and as soon as it passed they would follow, running half bent over so that they couldn't be seen if the Ragman turned around over the piles heaped on his wagon. They would run to the tailgate and grab onto it, swinging up, the taller ones, like John, stretching their legs onto the rear axle, the shorter ones just hanging as the wagon rolled along. Sometimes one of the bolder boys would try to climb up on the wagon itself and throw off some of the junk. The Ragman would see him and pull the reins, stopping the wagon. He would begin gesturing and yelling at the boys, who jumped from the wagon and stood back laughing and hollering, 'Rags ol irn, rags ol irn!' Sometimes he'd grab a makeshift whip, a piece of clothesline tied to a stick, and stagger after them as they scattered laughing before him, disappearing over fences and down gangways only to reappear again around the corner of some other alley; or, lying flattened on a garage roof, they'd suddenly jump up and shower the wagon with garbage as it passed beneath.

Mary could never fully understand why her brother participated. He wasn't a bully like Leon Sisca and certainly not cruel like Denny Zmiga, who tortured cats. She sensed the boys vaguely condemned the Ragmen for the sad condition of their horses. But that was only a small part of it, for often the horses as well as their masters were harassed. She thought it was a venial sin and wondered if John confessed it the Thursday before each First Friday, when they would go together to confession in the afternoon: Bless me, Father, for I have sinned, I threw garbage on a Ragman five times this month. For your penance say five Our Fathers and five Hail Marys, go in peace. She never mentioned this to him, feeling that whatever made him do it was a part of what made him generally unafraid, a part of what the boys felt when they elected him captain of the St Roman Grammar School baseball team. She couldn't bear it if he thought she was a dumb girl. She never snitched on him. If she approached him when he was surrounded by his friends, he would loudly announce, 'All right, nobody swear while Mary's here.'

At home he often took her into his confidence. This was what she liked the most, when, after supper, while her parents watched TV in the parlor, he would come into her room, where she was doing her homework, and lie down on her bed and start talking, telling her who among his friends was a good first sacker, or which one of the girls in his class tried to get him to dance with her at the school party, just talking and sometimes even asking her opinion on something like if she thought he should let his hair grow long like that idiot Peter Noskin, who couldn't even make the team as a right fielder. What did she think of guys like that? She tried to tell him things back. How Sister Mary Valentine had caught Leon Sisca in the girls' washroom yesterday. And then one night he told her about Raymond Cruz, which she knew was a secret because their father had warned John not to hang around with him even if he was the best pitcher on the team. He told her how after school he and Raymond Cruz had followed a Ragman to Hobotown, which was far away, past Western Avenue, on the other side of the river, down by the river and the railroad tracks, and that they had a regular town there without any streets. They lived among huge heaps of junk, rubbled lots tangled with smashed, rusting cars and bathtubs, rotting mounds of rags and paper, woodpiles infested with river rats. Their wagons were all lined up and the horses kept in a deserted factory with broken windows. They lived in shacks that were falling apart, some of them made out of old boxcars, and there was a blacksmith with a burning forge working in a ruined shed made of bricks and timbers with a roof of canvas.

He told her how they had snuck around down the riverbank in the high weeds and watched the Ragmen come in from all parts of the city, pulled by their tired horses, hundreds of Ragmen arriving in silence, and how they assembled in front of a great fire burning in the middle of all the shacks, where something was cooking in a huge, charred pot.

Their scroungy dogs scratched and circled around the fire while the Ragmen stood about and seemed to be trading among one another: bales of worn clothing for baskets of tomatoes, bushels of fruit for twisted metals, cases of dust-filled bottles for scorched couches and lamps with frazzled wires. They knelt, peering out of the weeds and watching them, and then Ray whispered let's sneak around to the building where the horses are kept and look at them.

So they crouched through the weeds and ran from shack to shack until they came to the back of the old factory. They could smell the horses and hay inside and hear the horses sneezing. They snuck in through a busted window. The factory was dark and full of spiderwebs, and they felt their way through a passage that entered into a high-ceilinged hall where the horses were stabled. It was dim; rays of sun sifted down through the dust from the broken roof. The horses didn't look the same in the dimness without their harnesses. They looked huge and beautiful, and when you reached to pat them, their muscles quivered so that you flinched with fright.

'Wait'll the guys hear about this,' John said.

And Ray whispered, 'Let's steal one! We can take him to the river and ride him.'

John didn't know what to say. Ray was fourteen. His parents were divorced. He had failed a year in school and often hung around with high school guys. Everybody knew that he had been caught in a stolen car but that the police let him go because he was so much younger than the other guys. He was part Mexican and knew a lot about horses. John didn't like the idea of stealing.

'We couldn't get one out of here,' he said.

'Sure we could,' Ray said. 'We could get on one and gallop out with him before they knew what was going on.'

'Suppose we get caught,' John said.

'Who'd believe the Ragmen anyway?' Ray asked him. 'They can't even speak English. You chicken?'

So they picked out a huge white horse to ride, who stood still and uninterested when John boosted Ray up on his back and then Ray reached down and pulled him up. Ray held his mane and John held onto Ray's waist. Ray nudged his heels into the horse's flanks and he began to move, slowly swaying toward the light of the doorway.

'As soon as we get outside,' Ray whispered, 'hold on. I'm gonna goose him.'

John's palms were sweating by this time because being on this horse felt like straddling a blimp as it rose over the roofs. When they got to the door, Ray hollered, 'Heya!' and kicked his heels hard, and the horse bolted out, and before he knew what had happened, John felt himself sliding, dropping a long way, and then felt the sudden hard smack of the hay-strewn floor. He looked up and realized he had never made it out of the barn, and then he heard the shouting and barking of the dogs and, looking out, saw Ray half riding, half hanging from the horse, which reared again and again, surrounded by the shouting Ragmen, and he saw the look on Ray's face as he was bucked from the horse into their arms. There was a paralyzed second when they all glanced toward him standing in the doorway of the barn, and then he whirled around and stumbled past the now-pitching bulks of horses whinnying all about him and found the passage, struggling through it, bumping into walls, spiderwebs sticking to his face, with the shouts and barks gaining on him, and then he was out the window and running up a hill of weeds, crushed coal slipping under his feet, skidding up and down two more hills, down railroad tracks, not turning around, just running until he could no longer breathe, and above him he saw a bridge and clawed up the grassy embankment till he reached it.

It was rush hour and the bridge was crowded with people going home, factory workers carrying lunch pails and businessmen with attaché cases. The street was packed with traffic, and he didn't know where he was or what he should do about Ray. He decided to go home and see what would happen. He'd call Ray that night, and if he wasn't home, then he'd tell them about the Ragmen. But he couldn't find his way back. Finally he had to ask a cop where he was, and the cop put him on a trolley car that got him home.

He called Ray about eight o'clock, and his mother answered the phone and told him Ray had just got in and went right to bed, and John asked her if he could speak to him, and she said she'd go see, and he heard her set down the receiver and her footsteps walk away. He realized his own heartbeat was no longer deafening and felt the knots in his stomach loosen. Then he heard Ray's mother say that she was sorry but that Ray didn't want to talk to him.

The next day, at school, he saw Ray and asked him what happened, if he was angry that he had run out on him, and Ray said, no, nothing happened, to forget it. He kept asking Ray how he got away, but Ray wouldn't say anything until John mentioned telling the other guys about it. Ray said if he told anybody he'd deny it ever happened, that there was such a place. John thought he was just kidding, but when he told the guys, Ray told them John made the whole thing up, and they almost got into a fight, pushing each other back and forth, nobody taking the first swing, until the guys stepped between them and broke it up. John lost his temper and said he'd take any of the guys who wanted to go next Saturday to see for themselves. They could go on their bikes and hide them in the weeds by the river and sneak up on the Ragmen. Ray said go on.

So on Saturday John and six guys met at his place and pedaled toward the river and railroad tracks, down the busy trucking streets, where the semis passed you so fast your bike seemed about to be sucked away by the draft. They got to Western Avenue and the river, and it looked the same and didn't look the same. They left the street and pumped their bikes down a dirt road left through the weeds by bulldozers, passing rusty barges moored to the banks, seemingly abandoned in the oily river. They passed a shack or two, but they were empty. John kept looking for the three mounds of black cinders as a landmark but couldn't find them. They rode their bikes down the railroad tracks, and it wasn't like being in the center of the city at all, with the smell of milkweeds and the noise of birds and crickets all about them and the spring sun glinting down the railroad tracks. No one was around. It was like being far out in the country. They rode until they could see the skyline of downtown, skyscrapers rising up through the smoke of chimneys like a horizon of jagged mountains in the mist. By now everyone was kidding him about the Ragmen, and finally he had to admit he couldn't find them, and they gave up. They all pedaled back, kidding him, and he bought everybody Cokes, and they admitted they had had a pretty good time anyway, even though he sure as hell was some storyteller.

And he figured something must have happened to Ray. It hit him Sunday night, lying in bed trying to sleep, and he knew he'd have to talk to him about it Monday when he saw him at school, but on Monday Ray was absent and was absent on Tuesday, and on Wednesday they found out that Ray had run away from home and no one could find him.

No one ever found him, and he wasn't there in June when John and his classmates filed down the aisle, their maroon robes flowing and white tassels swinging almost in time to the organ, to receive their diplomas and shake hands with Father Mike. And the next week it was summer, and she was permitted to go to the beach with her girlfriends. Her girlfriends came over and giggled whenever John came into the room.

On Sundays they went to late mass. She wore her flowered-print dress and a white mantilla in church when she sat beside John among the adults. After mass they'd stop at the corner of Twenty-fifth Street on their way home and buy *palatski* and walk home eating it with its crispness melting and the sweet honey crust becoming chewy. She remembered how she used to pretend it was manna they'd been rewarded with for keeping the Sabbath. It tasted extra good because she had skipped break-fast. She fasted before receiving communion.

Then it began to darken earlier, and the kids played tag and rolivio in the dusk and hid from each other behind trees and in doorways, and the girls laughed and blushed when the boys chased and tagged them. She had her own secret hiding place down the block, in a garden under a lilac bush, where no one could find her; and she would lie there listening to her name called in the darkness, Mary Mary free free free, by so many voices.

She shopped downtown with her mother at night for new school clothes, skirts, not dresses, green ribbons for her dark hair, and shoes without buckles, like slippers a ballerina wears. And that night she tried them on for John, dancing in her nightgown, and he said you're growing up. And later her mother came into her room – only the little bed lamp was burning – and explained to her what growing up was like. And after her mother left, she picked up a little rag doll that was kept as an ornament on her dresser and tried to imagine having a child, really having a child, it coming out of her body, and she looked at herself in the mirror and stood close to it and looked at the colors of her eyes: brown around the edges and then turning a milky gray that seemed to be smoking behind crystal and toward the center the gray turning green, getting greener till it was almost violet near her pupils. And in the black mirror of her pupils she saw herself looking at herself.

The next day, school started again and she was a sixth-grader. John was in high school, and Leon Sisca, who had grown much bigger over the summer and smoked, sneered at her and said, 'Who'll protect you now?' She made a visit to the church at lunchtime and dropped a dime in the metal box by the ruby vigil lights and lit a candle high up on the rack with a long wax wick and said a prayer to the Blessed Virgin.

And it was late in October, and leaves wafted from the catalpa trees on their way to church on Sunday and fell like withered fans into the birdbaths, turning the water brown. They were walking back from mass, and she was thinking how little she saw John anymore, how he no longer came to her room to talk, and she said, 'Let's do something together.'

'What?' he asked.

'Let's follow the Palatski Man.'

'Why would you want to do that?'

'I don't know,' she said. 'We could find out where he lives, where he makes his stuff. He won't come around pretty soon. Maybe we could go to his house in the winter and buy things from him.'

John looked at her. Her hair, like his, was blowing about in the wind. 'All right,' he said.

So they waited at a corner where a man was raking leaves into a pile to burn, but each time he built the pile and turned to scrape a few more leaves from his small lawn, the wind blew and the leaves whirled off from the pile and sprayed out as if alive over their heads, and then the wind suddenly died, and they floated back about the raking man into the grass softly, looking like wrinkled snow. And in a rush of leaves they closed their eyes against, the Palatski Man pushed by.

They let him go down the block. He wasn't hard to follow, he went so slow, stopping at corners for customers. They didn't have to sneak behind him because he never turned around. They followed him down the streets, and one street became another until they were out of their neighborhood, and the clothes the people wore became poorer and brighter. They went through the next parish, and there was less stopping because it was a poorer parish where more Mexicans lived, and the children yelled in Spanish, and they felt odd in their new Sunday clothes.

'Let's go back,' John said.

But Mary thought there was something in his voice that wasn't sure, and she took his arm and mock-pleaded, 'No-o-o-o, this is fun, let's see where he goes.'

The Palatski Man went up the streets, past the trucking lots full of semis without cabs, where the wind blew more grit and dirty papers than leaves, where he stopped hardly at all. Then past blocks of mesh-windowed factories shut down for Sunday and the streets empty and the pavements powdered with brown

317

glass from broken beer bottles. They walked hand in hand a block behind the white, bent figure of the Palatski Man pushing his cart over the fissured sidewalk. When he crossed streets and looked from side to side for traffic, they jumped into doorways, afraid he might turn around.

He crossed Western Avenue, which was a big street and so looked emptier than any of the others without traffic on it. They followed him down Western Avenue and over the rivet-studded, aluminum-girdered bridge that spanned the river, watching the pigeons flitting through the cables. Just past the bridge he turned into a pitted asphalt road that trucks used for hauling their cargoes to freight trains. It wound into the acres of endless lots and railroad yards behind the factories along the river.

John stopped. 'We can't go any further,' he said.

'Why?' she asked. 'It's getting interesting.'

'I've been here before,' he said.

'When?'

'I don't remember, but I feel like I've been here before.'

'C'mon, silly,' she said, and tugged his arm with all her might and opened her eyes very wide, and John let himself be tugged along, and they both started laughing. But by now the Palatski Man had disappeared around a curve in the road, and they had to run to catch up. When they turned the bend, they just caught sight of him going over a hill, and the asphalt road they had to run up had turned to cinder. At the top of the hill Mary cried, 'Look!' and pointed off to the left, along the river. They saw a wheat field in the center of the city, with the wheat blowing and waving, and the Palatski Man, half man and half willowy grain, was pushing his cart through the field past a scarecrow with straw arms outstretched and huge black crows perched on them.

'It looks like he's hanging on a cross,' Mary said.

'Let's go,' John said, and she thought he meant turn back home and was ready to agree because his voice sounded so determined, but he moved forward instead to follow the Palatski Man.

'Where can he be going?' Mary said.

But John just looked at her and put his finger to his lips. They followed single file down a trail trod smooth and twisting through the wheat field. When they passed the scarecrow, the crows flapped off in great iridescent flutters, cawing at them while the scarecrow hung as if guarding a field of wings. Then, at the edge of the field, the cinder path resumed sloping down-hill toward the river.

John pointed and said, 'The mounds of coal.'

And she saw three black mounds rising up in the distance and sparkling in the sun.

'C'mon,' John said, 'we have to get off the path.'

He led her down the slope and into the weeds that blended with the river grasses, rushes, and cattails. They sneaked through the weeds, which pulled at her dress and scratched her legs. John led the way; he seemed to know where he was going. He got down on his hands and knees and motioned for her to do the same, and they crawled forward without making a sound. Then John lay flat on his stomach, and she crawled beside him and flattened out. He parted the weeds, and she looked out and saw a group of men standing around a kettle on a fire and dressed in a strange assortment of ill-fitting suits, either too small or too large and baggy. None of the suit pieces matched, trousers blue and the suitcoat brown, striped pants and checked coats, countless combinations of colors. They wore crushed hats of all varieties: bowlers, straws, stetsons, derbies, homburgs. Their ties were the strangest of all, misshapen and dangling to their knees in wild designs of flowers, swirls, and polka dots.

'Who are they?' she whispered.

'The Ragmen. They must be dressed for Sunday,' John hissed.

And then she noticed the shacks behind the men, with the empty wagons parked in front and the stacks of junk from uprooted basements and strewn attics, even the gutted factory just the way John had described it. She saw the dogs suddenly jump up barking and whining, and all the men by the fire turn around as the Palatski Man wheeled his cart into their midst.

He gestured to them, and they all parted as he walked to the fire, where he stood staring into the huge black pot. He turned and said something to one of them, and the man began to stir whatever was in the pot, and then the Palatski Man dipped a small ladle into it and raised it up, letting its contents pour back into the pot, and Mary felt herself get dizzy and gasp as she saw the bright red fluid in the sun and heard John exclaim, 'Blood!' And she didn't want to see anymore, how the men came to the pot and dipped their fingers in it and licked them off, nodding and smiling. She saw the horses filing out of their barn, looking ponderous and naked without their harnesses. She hid her face in her arms and wouldn't look, and then she heard the slow, sorrowful chanting and off-key wheezing behind it. And she looked up and realized all the Ragmen, like a choir of bums, had removed their crushed hats and stood bareheaded in the wind, singing. Among them someone worked a dilapidated accordion, squeezing out a mournful, foreign melody. In the center stood the Palatski Man, leading them with his arms like a conductor and sometimes intoning a word that all would echo in a chant. Their songs rose and fell but always rose again, sometimes nasal, then

320

shifting into a rich baritone, building always louder and louder, more sorrowful, until the Palatski Man rang his bell and suddenly everything was silent. Not men or dogs or accordion or birds or crickets or wind made a sound. Only her breathing and a far-off throb that she seemed to feel more than hear, as if all the church bells in the city were tolling an hour. The sun was in the center of the sky. Directly below it stood the Palatski Man raising a *palatski*.

The Ragmen had all knelt. They rose and started a procession leading to where she and John hid in the grass. Then John was up and yelling, 'Run!' and she scrambled to her feet, John dragging her by the arm. She tried to run but her legs wouldn't obey her. They felt so rubbery pumping through the weeds and John pulling her faster than she could go with the weeds tripping her and the vines clutching like fingers around her ankles.

Ragmen rose up in front of them and they stopped and ran the other way but Ragmen were there too. Ragmen were everywhere in an embracing circle, so they stopped and stood still, holding hands.

'Don't be afraid,' John told her.

And she wasn't. Her legs wouldn't move and she didn't care. She just didn't want to run anymore, choking at the acrid smell of the polluted river. Through her numbness she heard John's small voice lost over and over in the open daylight repeating, 'We weren't doin' anything.'

The Ragmen took them back to where the Palatski Man stood before the fire and the bubbling pot. John started to say something but stopped when the Palatski Man raised his finger to his lips. One of the Ragmen brought a bushel of shiny apples and another a handful of pointed little sticks. The Palatski Man took an apple and inserted the stick and dipped it into the pot

321

and took it out coated with red. The red crystallized and turned hard, and suddenly she realized it was a red candy apple that he was handing her. She took it from his hand and held it dumbly while he made another for John and a third for himself. He bit into his and motioned for them to do the same. She looked up at John standing beside her, flushed and sweaty, and she bit into her apple. It was sweeter than anything she'd ever tasted, with the red candy crunching in her mouth, melting, mingling with apple juice.

And then from his cart he took a giant *palatski*, ten times bigger than any she had ever seen, and broke it again and again, handing the tiny bits to the circle of Ragmen, where they were passed from mouth to mouth. When there was only a small piece left, he broke it three ways and offered one to John. She saw it disappear in John's hand and watched him raise his hand to his mouth and at the same time felt him squeeze her hand very hard. The Palatski Man handed her a part. Honey stretched into threads from its torn edges. She put it in her mouth, expecting the crisp wafer and honey taste, but it was so bitter it brought tears to her eyes. She fought them back and swallowed, trying not to screw up her face, not knowing whether he had tricked her or given her a gift she didn't understand. He spoke quietly to one of the Ragmen in a language she couldn't follow and pointed to an enormous pile of rags beside a nearby shack. The man trudged to the pile and began sorting through it and returned with a white ribbon of immaculate, shining silk. The Palatski Man gave it to her, then turned and walked away, disappearing into the shack. As soon as he was gone, the circle of Ragmen broke and they trudged away, leaving the children standing dazed before the fire.

'Let's get out of here,' John said. They turned and began walking slowly, afraid the Ragmen would regroup at any second, but no one paid any attention to them. They walked away. Back through the wheat field, past silently perched crows, over the hill, down the cinder path that curved and became the pitted asphalt road. They walked over the Western Avenue bridge, which shook as a green trolley, empty with Sunday, clattered across it. They stopped in the middle of the bridge, and John opened his hand, and she saw the piece of *palatski* crushed into a little sour ball, dirty and pasty with sweat.

'Did you eat yours?' he asked.

'Yes,' she said.

'I tried to stop you,' he said. 'Didn't you feel me squeezing your hand? It might have been poisoned.'

'No,' she lied, so he wouldn't worry, 'it tasted fine.'

'Nobody believed me,' John said.

'I believed you.'

'They'll see now.'

And then he gently took the ribbon that she still unconsciously held in her hand – she had an impulse to clench her fist but didn't – and before she could say anything, he threw it over the railing into the river. They watched it, caught in the drafts of wind under the bridge, dipping and gliding among the wheeling pigeons, finally touching the green water and floating away.

'You don't want the folks to see that,' John said. 'They'd get all excited and nothing happened. I mean nothing really happened, we're both all right.'

'Yes,' she said. They looked at each other. Sunlight flashing through latticed girders made them squint; it reflected from the slits of eyes and off the river when their gaze dropped. Wind swooped over the railing and tangled their hair.

'You're the best girl I ever knew,' John told her.

They both began to laugh, so hard they almost cried, and

John stammered out, 'We're late for dinner – I bet we're gonna really get it,' and they hurried home.

They were sent to bed early that night without being permitted to watch TV. She undressed and put on her nightgown and climbed under her covers, feeling the sad, hollow Sunday-night feeling when the next morning will be Monday and the weekend is dying. The feeling always reminded her of all the past Sunday nights she'd had it, and she thought of all the future Sunday nights when it would come again. She wished John could come into her room so they could talk. She lay in bed tossing and seeking the cool places under her pillow with her arms and in the nooks of her blanket with her toes. She listened to the whole house go to sleep: the TV shut off after the late news, the voices of her parents discussing whether the doors had been locked for the night. She felt herself drifting to sleep and tried to think her nightly prayer, the Hail Mary before she slept, but it turned into a half dream that she woke out of with a faint recollection of Gabriel's wings, and she lay staring at the familiar shapes of furniture in her dark room. She heard the wind outside like a low whinny answered by cats. At last she climbed out of her bed and looked out the lace-curtained window. Across her back yard, over the catalpa tree, the moon hung low in the cold sky. It looked like a giant *palatski* snagged in the twigs. And then she heard the faint tinkle of the bell.

He stood below, staring up, the moon, like silver eyeballs, shining in the centers of his dark glasses. His horse, a windy white stallion, stamped and snorted behind him, and a gust of leaves funneled along the ground and swirled through the street-light, and some of them stuck in the horse's tangled mane while its hooves kicked sparks in the dark alley. He offered her a *palatski*.

She ran from the window to the mirror and looked at herself in the dark, feeling her teeth growing and hair pushing through her skin in the tender parts of her body that had been bare and her breasts swelling like apples from her flat chest and her blood burning, and then in a lapse of wind, when the leaves fell back to earth, she heard his gold bell jangle again as if silver and knew that it was time to go.

The Cat Woman

There was an old *buzka* on Luther Street known as the Cat Woman, not because she kept cats but because she disposed of the neighborhood's excess kittens. Fathers would bring them in cardboard boxes at night after the children were asleep and she would drown them in her wash machine. The wash machine was in the basement, an ancient model with a galvanized-metal tub that stood on legs and had a wringer. A thick cord connected it to a socket that hung from the ceiling and when she turned it on the light bulb in the basement would flicker and water begin to pour.

She lived with her crazy grandson, Swantek. His first name was George, but everyone, including the nuns at school, called him Swantek. It could be spit out like a swear word. Even his *buzka* called him that, after his father, Big Swantek, a brawling drunk who'd beat her daughter regularly, then disappeared after she died. It was rumored Swantek's mother had committed suicide and that's why her funeral was held in a Russian Orthodox parish across the city.

One day Swantek took clothespins and hung the bodies of the drowned kittens by their tails from the clothesline in the back yard – like a line of wet socks covered with lint. When the Cat Woman saw it, she chased him around the yard and out the alley gate, beating his legs with a broomstick. Mrs Panova,

327

the old lady in the house next door, went inside as if nothing unusual were happening. But the people in the big apartment building across the alley hung out of their windows cheering and laughing like an audience in a gallery.

Despite the black-and-blue marks that appeared again and again on his body, it seemed that as the Cat Woman got older, Swantek got crazier. He sneaked around the railroad tracks instead of going to school. He took to sleeping nights in the abandoned cars along the dead-end side streets behind Spiegel's warehouse. When winter came the cops chased him out. The next night, every junk car down the block went up in flames.

That winter he was seen crouching naked by the chimney on the peak of his roof, beckoning to ten-year-old stick-legged Bonnie Buford as she trudged down the alley to school. Finally, his grandma seemed to give up on him and the bodies began to accumulate on the clothesline. People believed that Swantek had even run a few through the wringer and after a while nobody brought boxes of litters anymore.

Within a year the neighborhood was full of stray cats. Toms sprayed fences, sides of houses, inside hallways and sheds, so that after a rain it seemed the entire world reeked of cat sexuality.

When summer came with its sweltering nights, insomnia spread like a plague. Windows were raised in the huge apartment buildings, and after dark the long alleyways amplified screeching operas of cats. Curses and garbage rained down from the fire escapes. One night in August someone opened up with a .22.

By then irritability had become a habit. In the dime store, under slowly revolving ceiling fans, women argued over places in line and babies bawled. Gangs of older boys carrying baseball bats and knives patrolled heat-vapored streets. Behind sun-beaten shades bodies in sweat-stained underwear tossed in fitful naps.

Taverns filled. Nights grew frenzied with boozy shouting and jukebox music. News of those nights spread and people swarmed from other parts of the city to release their own madness where it couldn't threaten their everyday lives. Men drank and tried to sleep with other men's wives. Windows shook as sirens shrieked by. Even the soundest sleepers, who'd slept through the cats, were kept awake, pacing their rooms. At dawn strangers stumbled about sidewalks spattered with vomit and blood, trying to remember where they'd parked their cars.

Neighborhood men lost their jobs and stood on corners watching traffic, sipping wine from twisted paper bags. Buildings turned shabby. People rolled their car windows up when they had to ride through, staring out at dirty sidewalks, at shivering bums, faded women, ragged kids, cats blinking from doorways.

No one brought laundry anymore to the old woman who had supported herself and her grandson by taking in wash. Her basement and yard still smelled of powdered soap, but everywhere the clothes were gray. She'd long ago stopped flinging bread crusts onto the garage roof for sparrows. Every other day, the Russian lady next door invited her in for cabbage soup. She'd take a bowl back to her grandson, carefully wash the dish, bring it back two days later saying, '*Spaceeba*, missus, for the soup and your bowl.'

And Mrs Panova would tell her, 'Come in and have another. I always have a pot on the stove.'

The two ladies sat at the table, spoons clacking against the sides of the bowl, blowing on each spoonful with nothing more to say, radio on the polka station. And later, at home, the Cat Woman fit her cardboard-soled house slippers over her bandaged, swollen feet and crept through her house, fingering the rosary.

But Swantek needed more than soup and prayers. He'd moved

into the basement, never coming out, sleeping on a pile of old drapes beside the empty furnace, vomiting up cabbage in the corners and covering it with newspapers, touching himself in the dark and smelling an aching smell like bleach, hearing cats yowl on the other side of the snowdrifted black-paned windows, the floorboards creaking continually overhead, where his *buzka*, the Cat Woman, padded.

The Long Thoughts

All the while he and his mother argued, the Vulcan continued to page through a beautiful leather-bound volume of Goya's etchings he'd borrowed from the Art Institute library. The dim, dirty-shaded lamplight yellowed the pages. It yellowed their whole cramped living room, turning it brown in the corners. Between the peeling wallpaper chrysanthemums and worn florals of the carpet it was one of the most depressing rooms I knew. The blinds were always drawn.

'Christ!' Vulk said. 'I'd give anything to draw like that.' The etching showed a bunch of human parts hacked off and hanging from a tree.

'Quit dreaming,' his mother said. 'Why don't you face the fact that you ain't even got the talent to pass half your regular subjects instead of trying to make your friends think you're some kind of genius? You think they believe that bullshit? They're laughing at you behind your back and getting ahead while you make a big, damn fool out of yourself.'

Vulk's head fell to the side, looking too big for his short body. He opened his mouth, let his jaw gape and his tongue loll out, shaking his hair down into his face and rolling his eyes. 'I am destroyed by your profundity,' he said.

'I'd start to worry if I could look so convincingly retarded,' his mother told him.

Vulk just sat there flipping pages and making lip farts. 'You musta done something irregular when I was in the womb,' he said.

'You didn't get your low IQ from me!'

'Low, my ass,' he said. 'It's one-forty.'

'How the hell would you know what it is?'

'Because I snuck in the office and looked up my file after you scared the shit out of me with that IQ bullshit. And I don't have a distended anus either, by the way.' He turned to me. 'You know she used to tell me my anus was distended from sitting on the toilet so much. You must be some fuckin' nurse,' he said to her.

'Your son just said *fuck* in here again,' she yelled into the darkened dining room. 'He's playing the big shot in front of his friends – as usual.'

'Yaaah!' Vulk yelled at her. 'Watch it! The Specter's looking up your dress.'

His mother shot a glance over to where I sat on the floor, catching me hastily looking away as if I really had been looking up her dress. She glared at Vulk, her eyes magnified behind her white cat-framed glasses like an attacking owl's. I rolled over on my side under the coffee table trying not to laugh, remembering how their fighting used to embarrass me – now it seemed so funny it ached.

'Shit-ass,' she hissed at him. 'Lew, are you deaf?' she hollered. 'I said Thomas is going too far in here again.'

Through the legs of furniture I could see Vulk's father outlined against the space heater in the darkened dining room, watching the portable TV. The set spread its pale glow over the dirty supper dishes that surrounded it on the table. The blue flames of the space heater were reflected on the screen.

'Tom, how many times do I have to ask you not to talk to

your mother like that?' His voice sounded even wearier than usual. 'Take it easy on my ulcer, will you?'

Screams filtered through the hoofbeats and gunshots in the dining room. They weren't coming from the TV set. 'Philip and Rosemary are fighting in the kitchen again,' Vulk's father groaned. 'Oh, Jesus Christ!'

'Goddammit!' his mother said, and stormed out of the room in the direction of the screaming. It got worse. We could hear Vulk's father going ooh, oooohh in the dark.

'Come in here – you gotta hear this,' Vulk said. We went into his room. It was right off the front door. It must have been an entrance closet at one time but Vulk had squeezed a mattress into it. It filled the entire room and curled up at the corners. One side of it was heaped with paperbacks that almost reached the ceiling. Most of them were on psychology but there was a lot of science fiction too. On the other side a row of shelves looked ready to pull out of the plaster and bury what remained of the mattress in an avalanche of flattened paint tubes, tempera bottles, brushes, crayons, an infinite variety of stuff. The walls looked like a palette splotched and smeared with swirling rainbows, half-obscured slogans, unfinished sketches. On the ceiling he'd painted a hawklike creature wearing long underwear and a cape with a huge V for Vulcan on his chest. We sat down on each side of the record player in the sunken middle of the mattress. 'Listen to this,' he said. 'I got it out of the library today. Shit, I didn't even know they let you take out records.'

'What've they got?'

'Mostly classical.'

I gave him the finger. He was on this big classical-music kick and I didn't like a lot of it.

'No, listen to this,' he said. 'You'll dig it.'

'What is it?'

'Debussy. Piano music.'

'As long as it isn't that fuckin' opera. At least turn it up.'

About one a.m. his father came to the door in his underwear and asked us to turn it down. Vulk insisted that it had to be played loud or we'd miss the dynamics, so his father told us if we didn't like it to get the hell out of the house, which we did.

It was early in January and the street and trees were pale with snow. The cold seemed to intensify the quiet. Now and then a car would grind by, its snow chains jangling. We walked along past the button factory and then down the dark block past the church and grammar school we had both attended. The spire of the church threw a shadow over the street. The neighborhood didn't look so bad at night under the snow.

'Let's go see if Harry is still up,' Vulk said.

We turned the corner, walking down the street I lived on. Harry lived about fifteen blocks away. He had a car that sometimes worked. It was a long walk and my ears were already beginning to feel brittle.

'Did you tell them about what happened?' I asked.

'Not yet,' Vulk said, 'I figure O'Donnel will call them up.'

It was snowing lightly again, almost like snow being blown off the roofs and trees as we walked underneath. It didn't seem as cold when it snowed.

'What are you gonna do?'

'Shit, I don't know,' he said. 'Keep going to the Institute at night. Just quit, I guess. What the hell do I need a diploma for?'

We passed the apartment house I lived in. The lights were all out.

'I could probably get back into Harrison and graduate from there,' Vulk said. 'They never *really* kicked me out of there. I just kinda stopped going, you know ... shit, O'Donnel still might call the cops.'

'I don't think so,' I said.

'You can't tell. Nobody thought they'd expel seniors either. He's crazy! When they had their inquisition this afternoon he shows the other priests all the shit he got out of my locker. First he holds up this book of nudes, so I mention I'm taking night classes at the Art Institute, then he shows them the pills, so I say they're for my old man's ulcers and must have got in there by mistake, then he starts reading passages out of some of the paperbacks in this weird tone of voice, like he's breathing real hard – it was unbelievable – I thought he was going to start beating off right there. Then he shows them this Coke bottle with a Tampax in it for a wick and I try and tell them it's an art object and Schmidt, who's supposed to be defending me, starts yelling he doesn't want it on his conscience that he defended such scum and they all agree I'm too warped to graduate from a Catholic school.'

'Too warped! Jesus Christ!' I was laughing so hard I lurched over a snowbank. 'Too fuckin' warped!' Our laughter came echoing back down the corridor of buildings. We cut across a block of lots where they'd knocked the buildings down, crunching over ice and rubble, stamping through dead weeds behind billboards.

I was thinking about that morning with Vulk and I as usual starting the day by kneeling on the floor in detention. We'd been there so long that I'd come to accept the fact that school would always start at seven-thirty for me. The room was full of guys slumped down sleeping, copying homework, passing around comic books, or matching for dimes. The group of us who were never able to get out of it had to kneel on the floor in front of O'Donnel's desk. We had an *esprit de corps* – everybody had a special name. Tom's was the Vulcan; mine was the Specter.

O'Donnel came in and sat behind his desk for a while staring at us. We all hung our heads, smirking into our collars and not looking him in the eye, which pissed him off. He got up from his desk and walked over to the edge of the platform it was set on, standing right before us. Then he kicked Vulk right in the stomach, his leg tossing up his cassock, his black shoe buried for a moment in Vulk's leather jacket. Vulk doubled over, then looked up and called him a sonofabitch.

'You bum! I'm going to have your ass thrown out of here today, Vukovich,' O'Donnel shouted at him. 'We just searched your locker and found *drugs*.' Spit flew out of his lips when he talked. He looked all around the silent room, then back at Vulk. 'There's a meeting in the rector's office at one regarding your expulsion. You have the right to bring a member of the faculty to defend you. Now get out.'

After Vulk left, O'Donnel glared at the rest of us. 'I hope you losers learn something from this,' he said. 'You think it's all a big joke, huh, that you're tough guys? That's how easy it is to eliminate the rotten apples. He ain't gonna find a decent job the rest of his life. He's got drugs on his record now and it'll follow him wherever he goes.' He was so worked up his bald head had turned almost purple and the veins jutted out of his bulldog neck above his collar. 'Some guys only learn the hard way!'

'I notice they didn't return the nudes they stole from me,' Vulk said. 'Maybe they're redecorating the bathroom in the monastery.'

We turned down Twenty-sixth Street, walking past the boulevard, the stoplights looking pink behind the blowing snow. It was a business street and there were occasional cars passing slowly with fuzzy headlights. We passed the county jail with its dilapidated wall and blue-lit watchtowers.

'Listen to that,' I said. We stopped under a streetlight, snow floating down, and faced the jail. The voice came again from one of the barred buildings beyond the wall – 'Hey, you guys' – then something else we couldn't make out.

'Whataya waaaannnt?' we shouted together.

'Hey, you guys,' the voice came back, but we still couldn't catch the rest of it.

We gave up and walked on. 'It sounded like "mushrooms and sausage with anchovies" to me,' I said.

'No, I think it was "Hey, you guys, how about a little?"'

'It was goddamn spooky.'

'Makes you feel really free just walkin' the streets,' Vulk said. He scooped a handful of snow off the windshield of a car. 'Hey, it's good packin'.'

We walked the rest of the way to Harry's throwing snowballs at the streetlights.

There was nobody home. We lobbed snowballs at Harry's window for about five minutes and then climbed the rickety back stairs and shook the door. Nobody answered. We looked around outside to see if his car was there but it wasn't.

'He must have gone somewhere,' Vulk said.

'No doubt about it.' My gloves were soaked and my fingers frozen from throwing snowballs. My feet felt like concrete. We walked back to Twenty-sixth. The stores were gated and dimmed for the night. An occasional neon sign blinked across the sidewalk snow.

'I'm hungry,' Vulk said. 'Let's go sit in a restaurant.'

'You got any money?'

'No. How about you?'

'Fifteen cents.'

'Fifteen cents! Petit bourgeois.'

'Your mama, hose nose.'

He didn't say anything. I could see he was trying to think of a comeback. He was staring at the ground, his large eyes reminding me as always of a beagle's, brown and sad even when he laughed. His big nose and stocking cap made him look like one of the dwarfs. I knew he was sensitive about his nose and felt a little guilty pimping him about it when there were just the two of us. I guess he'd gone through life never being able to find the right retort.

'Just remember Cyrano,' he said.

'It's probably distended from too much picking.'

'Here's something distended,' he said, grabbing his crotch.

'There's a meal for a working-class artist.' I pointed to a gray crust of bread lying along the curb by a fire hydrant. It was surrounded by a suspicious yellow stain melted into the snow.

'You know I say disgusting things sometimes,' Vulk said, 'but *everything* you say is disgusting.'

'You're just too warped to realize my profundity.'

'No doubt about it.'

We passed an all-night Laundromat, cleanly lit in white neon and empty.

'Let's sit in there awhile before I die,' I said.

We went in. There was a red-lettered sign by the door that warned NO LOITERING. Vulk shook his fist at it.

'Suppose the cops come?' he said.

'We'll say we were doing our laundry. I got a dirty snot-rag. How about you?'

'I use my sleeve. Maybe I can wash my sleeve.'

I was testing the money changers. Nothing came out. I went over to the pay phone and opened the coin-return slot. There was a dime in it.

'Eureka! Eureka!' I yelled, showing it to Vulk. He came over and examined it carefully, biting it a few times.

'Hmmm, you can always depend on the lumpenproletariat to sniff out the crumbs. Probably some blind old lady lost it.'

'Maybe we can give it back.' I dropped it in the phone. 'Hello, hello, operator? I'd like to report finding a dime in one of your phones down here on Twenty-sixth Street. I'd like to return it to the proper party.'

'You want to return a dime?'

'No doubt about it.'

'Just a minute,' she said. 'I'll connect you with the supervisor.' There was a giggle in her voice and it gave me a warm flush. I stood there holding the receiver for about a minute.

'Maybe they're tracing the call,' Vulk said.

'Hello,' the supervisor said.

'Yes, hello, are you there?'

'Sorry to keep you waiting – you're trying to return a dime?'

'That's right, but I don't want the phone company keeping it. It says *e pluribus unum* on it if that's any aid in identification.'

'All right, just hang up and we'll put it in our lost-and-found.'

'Thank you.' The connection was broken; the phone belched. I opened the return slot and there was the dime.

We sat down in the shining plastic contour chairs along the wall. It was a few minutes before two by the Coca-Cola clock. The Laundromat smelled of soap and bleach like a chlorinated swimming pool. The lines of washing machines gleamed. The dryers, set in the opposite wall, looked like a row of looted safes. It was nice and warm, my feet thawed and began to burn, I unzipped my jacket.

'Boy, this is the life.'

'No doubt about it,' Vulk said. He got up and wrung his gloves out on the floor. 'Loan me your dime.' He walked over to one of the dryers, stuck his gloves in, and turned it on. 'A little entertainment on a frosty night.'

We both sat there watching the dryer spinning around and around. I lit a cigarette. It was quiet enough to hear the wind outside through the dryer's hum, and the tiny creaks that rooms make. I put my head on my arm and closed my eyes. The heat was making me groggy. I started thinking about the homework I hadn't done. It seemed I had spent my whole life worrying about assignments I hadn't done. Suddenly more than anything I just wanted to be in bed. To get there we'd have to walk out again through the cold. It seemed stupid just sitting here; why had I let Vulk talk me into going to Harry's? Then I thought of the two of us walking down the street and him telling me that everything I said was disgusting in his most affected voice. I started laughing.

'What's so funny?' he kept asking.

I tried to tell him but every time I began, the image of the dirty crust in the snow rose up and made me laugh harder. It really was disgusting. Finally I managed to get it all out.

'What the hell's funny about that?' he coughed out. We were both holding our stomachs and crying, we were laughing so hard. 'We need a fix,' he said. He took out a little box of Nodoz and offered it to me. 'First one's free, kid.'

'If you hadn't squandered my dime we could get a couple cups of coffee.'

I inserted my last dime in the coffee machine, which we kicked and beat, but still got only one cup out of it. The coffee was almost tasteless and hot. We sat there passing the steaming paper cup back and forth and popping Nodoz. I lit another cigarette. The first one was decomposing in the smeary puddles by our feet.

'Did you ever read anything by Shelley?' I asked. We'd read *Adonais* the day before in lit. class.

'I read something about his life,' Vulk said. 'He was pretty

340

cool for his time, really into screwing, didn't give a shit about what the bourgeois thought.'

'Like Ginsberg,' I said. 'No shit, when I read that poem it made me think of *Howl*.'

'Yeah, but I don't think he was queer. Ginsberg's all around crazier. You ever read anything about van Gogh's life?'

'"I saw the best minds of my generation destroyed by madness,"' I recited to the hum of the drier. 'Van Gogh's life *was* one long howl, man.' We looked at one another and howled together, our voices amplified by the Laundromat.

'Maybe you got to go crazy to paint stars like that,' the Vulcan said.

'You know reading about artists is almost as depressing as reading *The Lives of the Saints*. They all end up starving or shooting themselves or cutting their ears off. Half of them couldn't even screw without catching the syph and their dicks rotting off.' I started thinking about it, totaling them up: Poe drunk in the gutter, De Quincey hooked on opium, Keats with TB, Charlie Parker, van Gogh. The Vulcan. And me showing him my poems.

'Here we go,' he said. A cop walked in, his car's blue light glancing across the plate-glass window in the front. 'What are you guys doing here?'

'Just sittin'.'

'Can't you read?' he said, gesturing toward the NO LOITERING sign. 'Get your asses out of here.'

We stood up to leave, trying to act superior. I looked at the flattened coffee cup and smashed cigarette butts lying in the puddle on the floor.

'Wait a minute,' he demanded. 'How old are you guys?'

'Eighteen.'

'Let's see some IDs.'

341

There was a curfew for people younger than eighteen and we both stood there searching through all our pockets like we'd lost our cards. Finally we handed them over. He stood there squinting at them, trying to compute our ages.

'Hey, you're seventeen. And you're still sixteen,' he said to me. 'You guys wanta wait at the station for your parents to come pick you up?'

We stood there looking belligerent, not saying anything.

'I could arrest you for loitering. What the hell are you doing here at quarter past two anyway?'

'Sitting.'

'Oh, yeah?' He was still studying our names and convictlike photographs on our student-rate bus cards. 'If anything's wrong we'll know where to come looking for you. Now, get home fast.'

We trudged outside.

'We showed him a thing or two,' Vulk said.

'Yeah.'

'Why didn't you tell him your old man was Mayor Daley?'

'The prick is following us,' I said. The squad car was cruising slowly behind us, its headlights dimmed. 'Let's turn down the next street.'

Vulk had his Chap Stick out and was smearing it on his lips.

'Oh, no,' I said.

He was filling his mouth up with lighter fluid. The squad car came up even with us, the cop glaring through a half-opened window. We could hear the police calls. We stepped off the curb into the intersection. Vulk had his Zippo lighter out. He stopped in the middle of the street, turned to the squad car, and lit his lighter, spitting out an enormous yellow flame.

We took off down the side street, both yelling '*Fuck you*' at the top of our voices. I looked over my shoulder to see if the cop had turned yet. He wasn't there.

'He might be coming around the block,' Vulk said. 'We better turn in.'

We cut down an alley, jogging through the ruts the garbage trucks had made in the snow, our breath panting out before us. The snow was piled high against the garbage cans.

'It was funnier when I did it in Martin's class,' Vulk said.

'You're really an asshole. I could see my old man getting a call at work to come get me out of jail.'

The alley kept going, broken by streets. It looked like a crooked blue tunnel under the streetlights. We plodded for a while without saying anything.

'The Specter and the Vulcan floating through the night,' he said.

'I'm freezing my ass off.'

'Offer it up.'

He stopped and I kept walking. 'Wait up,' he called. He was tugging a Christmas tree out of a hill of old snow, cardboard boxes full of frozen trash, and garbage bags filmed with new-fallen snow. It was a scraggly tree. Shreds of tinsel still dangled from its broken branches. We continued down the alley, Vulk dragging the tree by its tip, sweeping it behind him in the snow.

'We can warm up here,' he said, 'make a campfire to keep the wolves off.' He lifted the tree into a trash can. We dug around and found some newspapers and garbage bags and brushed the snow off. Vulk squirted lighter fluid over everything. But even the fluid couldn't get it going. It would flare up and then be flattened by a gust of wind. The inside pages of the newspaper burned for a minute or so, but the tree wouldn't catch. We watched the paper cinders waft glowing orange out of the garbage can, black flakes with sparks at their edges flying away into the snow and dying out. Vulk was spreading his hands over the top of the can.

'Ah, nothing like a roaring hearth. Want to set a garage on fire?'

'Not tonight,' I said.

After the paper burned away we gave up. The alleys seemed very dark after our staring at the flames.

'I forgot my gloves at the Laundromat,' Vulk said.

'You wanta go back?'

'Hell with 'em.'

We turned off down a side street. A dog barked at us from between the slats of a fence, his mouth steaming, making the silence ring. It had never seemed as quiet – no traffic, or stalled cars groaning, or snow shovels scraping for blocks around. We came out on the boulevard and left two rows of footprints across it. Our shadows passed through the shadows of trees etched in the snow by the moonlight.

'It doesn't look too bad,' I said.

'I wish I was good enough to paint it the way it is.'

We came to the turnoff for my street; Vulk lived farther down.

'You going home?' he asked.

'Yeah, I guess so. You get the long thoughts tonight.'

'You planned this,' he said. We always calculated who'd have the longer walk home, alone with his thoughts.

'I'm really going to be beat tomorrow. I think I'll sleep during Pig's class.' I didn't remember till I said it that Vulk had been expelled. 'Well, I guess you get to sleep late tomorrow.'

'Yeah, I guess so. I don't know. Maybe I might go down with you and just hang around, sit in Walgreens or something.'

'Okay, meet you at the bus stop.'

'Yeah, so long.' He turned and walked away into his thoughts.

I had the short thoughts. It was only a two-block walk past Luther Street and Washtenaw; time to wonder if Vulk was having his daydream of walking down a street in Paris and to worry again about the homework I hadn't done. Then I was before the apartment building where I lived with its dark hallway I'd been afraid of ever since I was a kid, feeling the wind blow through me, sifting up little funnels of snow off the ridges of drifts, flakes twirling in the streetlight. The street looked gentle, its soft brown slush matted white. I could feel the Nodoz making my heart pound. I could feel the spray of snow hit my face and hair, every particle, every second. I lit a cigarette, remembering the Debussy spinning over and over in Vulk's room and the two of us sitting there like madmen hunched above the record player, our eyes squeezed shut. I recalled it so clearly that for a moment I started to shake, then it slipped away, leaving me with a chill and the cigarette tasting like burned newspaper in the raw air, so I went in. My father was still working the double holiday shift at the PO and I had to clear the supper dishes from the table and wash them before going to sleep.

penguin.co.uk/vintage